Neville Sherriff completed high school in Hermanus, the Cape. He displayed an early interest in writing, winning his first award at the age of eight. He won the South African Writers' Circle award in 1990 for New Professional Writer of the Year for his first book, *Wings of Gold*. He lives in South Africa with his wife and cat.

NEVILLE SHERRIFF

THE
BRANNIGANS

PAN BOOKS
LONDON, SYDNEY AND AUCKLAND
in association with
MACMILLAN LONDON LIMITED

First published 1991 by Macmillan London Limited

This edition published 1992 by
PAN BOOKS LIMITED
a division of Pan Macmillan Publishers Limited
Cavaye Place London SW10 9PG
and Basingstoke
in association with Macmillan London Limited

Associated companies throughout the world

ISBN 0–330–31621–4

1 3 5 7 9 8 6 4 2

A CIP catalogue record for this book is available from
the British Library

Typeset by Macmillan Production Limited
Printed in England by Clays Limited, St Ives plc

To Alet

Part One

1912–1919

1912

July

The killing storm took the village by surprise. Moving in from
the north-west, it surfaced as a warning finger of cloud behind
the mountains curling into the Atlantic Ocean, wrapping itself
hungrily round the coastline, pushing aggressively up the
mountain slopes to spill down its sides as it rushed towards
the village and the open waters of the bay. The boats from the
fishing hamlet of Brannigan Bay were little more than white
dots on the ocean, far from the harbour and safety. Those on
shore who sensed the threat looked anxiously to sea and were
relieved to see the dots in motion, for it meant their crews had
seen the danger too.

The rain struck just as the first villagers reached the harbour.
It was a tiny enclave, tucked into the shelter of towering cliffs
on one side, protected by the rugged, curving coastline on the
other. The little jetty angled out towards the cliffs, narrowing
the entrance yet helping to keep out the breakers surging in
across the broad bay.

Those fishermen who had not gone out to sea that day
waited on the harbour shelf. They prepared the slipway,
readying the logs to carry each boat from the water to safety
up the slope, a pole struck through each of the iron rungs
secured to the bow and stern, four or five men on either side
to lift it. Speed was crucial when the boats rushed through
the narrow harbour entrance.

Two men stood on the side of the cliff to study the pattern
of water against the rocks and shout instructions to the boats
when they finally rounded the cliff base to wait for the right
swell on which to ride to safety.

Darkness moved in, the wind driving the dense rain
before it. The fishermen in the harbour worked fast and

3

silently, determined to be ready when the first boat arrived, for they knew what it was like to run from the storm, how weary their comrades would be.

One of the men shouted from the cliff top, the wind whipping away his cry. The tense group gathered below looked up and heard the muffled shout again. This time they understood. Mist. They saw it pushing through the rain, spreading across the breadth of the bay – the elements joining forces against frightened men.

The first of the women and children arrived in the harbour now, their faces drawn. A mother knelt and drew a crying child to her. Someone had lit fires on top of the cliffs, using the stacks of wood always kept in readiness there.

On the harbour shelf, Jay Brannigan, whose grandfather had founded the hamlet and given it his name, stared blankly at the heaving sea. Somewhere out there on the waters, in *Farer*, his boat, was his father, Fraser.

Jay had turned seventeen just the day before, a tall, powerfully built boy with thick, wavy brown hair that matched his dark complexion. He was not handsome but there was something about him that attracted people. It was the eyes, they said, a startling blue that seemed to change shade with his emotions.

He turned to the petite girl standing behind him and understood the fear on her face: her father was out there, too. Almost everyone had fathers or brothers on the boats.

'It'll be all right,' he tried to reassure her, rain trickling down his neck when he ran his hand across his wet hair. His khaki shirt was already soaked.

The wind plucked at the girl's auburn hair hanging in heavy tresses to her slender shoulders. She brushed it back when it spilled across her face, its thickness made denser by the rain. Magda de Vries was a year younger than Jay, the daughter of his father's closest friend, the giant Bull de Vries, a girl of unusual beauty, loved by all.

Jay loved her more than most. Perhaps one day, when he was a man and skipper of his own boat, he and Magda . . . No, they were both too young to think of such things.

Thrusting thoughts of Magda from him, he scanned the

4

mist again. Panic rose within him as the storm pushed at his shoulders. He had been far from the harbour when he had spotted it coming and run there at full speed. It was where he wanted to be and the wait would be long and agonising. The harbour was where everything began and ended, the heart of Brannigan Bay.

Whenever Jay studied the inlet, he marvelled at how his grandfather, Grant Brannigan, had noticed the tiny enclave along the bay's lengthy coastline, nestling between the sea and a gentle mountain range. The fisherman had been running from a storm, so the story went, and had already been at sea out of Cape Town for two days. He took shelter there for three days while he walked the land where no man had yet settled. He made it his bay and his town. Even now, fifty-three years later, although other men tended the affairs of the village Grant Brannigan's descendants were treated with respect.

Jay noticed his mother in the growing crowd on the harbour shelf and nodded to her reassuringly.

Frances Brannigan was a tall, severe-looking woman. She hated the sea: she had lost her first husband to it after only six months of marriage. Knowing this, Jay often wondered why she had married his father, another fisherman. The previous night, Jay's birthday, Fraser Brannigan had said, 'You're a man now. Soon you'll be ready to take over the boat.' Jay had beamed but Frances Brannigan had other ideas for her son.

He'll be finishing his schooling before he does anything of the sort,' she had said firmly, her tone conveying her old argument about a better life for Jay. 'We should go farming,' she often told his father. 'Get a small place in the Overberg, grow some wheat. When the debts are paid we could buy more land. It'd be a better life for Jay than going out on that sea day after day, with his wife and children never knowing whether he'd return.'

'A man can die on a farm as well,' Fraser Brannigan replied evenly. 'Jay will make his own choice some day.'

Now Jay caught his mother's glance again, noticed her chewing anxiously at her knuckles. He wanted to go to her but Magda moved closer to him, her body lightly touching his. He instinctively placed his arm about her shoulders.

She wore oilskins several sizes too large for her, which made her seem even more fragile and vulnerable. 'It's getting so dark,' she said. 'I'm scared, Jay. Will they see the fires?'

'I'm sure they will. They'll be here soon.' Water streamed across his face when he lowered his head to hers. 'Our dads are the best skippers, don't forget. They'll come in together – they always do!' He hoped his voice concealed the fear pulsing in his gut.

Magda clung tightly to him, unashamed of the embrace. Those of their peers who saw them would tease them the next day, but Jay could silence them with a warning snarl – or his fists. He had done so before.

Just as Jay said, 'I must go to my mother,' there came a cry from the cliff top. 'They're coming! They're coming!'

'There!' cried Jay a moment later as the first boat appeared through the mist. 'They risked staying close inshore,' he added, seeing how near the craft was to the base of the cliffs.

The two men clinging to the cliff face were shouting instructions to the crew. 'Aim for the jetty! Watch the swells – they're breaking far out! Hold the oars ready! Row now! Row!'

The boat lingered on the swells, its sails furled, waiting for the right wave on which to surf towards the harbour. The crew had their oars raised, but at the shouted commands from the cliff they lowered them and rowed with all their remaining strength when a mighty swell drove in on the harbour. The skipper hauled on the helm, steering for the jetty wall.

It appeared as if the boat would crash onto the jetty but then the current caught it, sweeping it through the narrow harbour entrance. For a moment it seemed the vessel would be pushed onto the rocks, then the skipper pulled frantically on the helm and it sped to safety. Jay saw it was the Norwegian, Org Nielsen, and his crew of eight. Org would have news of his father.

Rushing forward as the boat surged closer, Jay jumped into the icy water with the other helpers.

'*Farer*?' shouted Jay at the Norwegian skipper. 'What news of *Farer*?'

He felt a stab of alarm when Nielsen glanced quickly at him before looking away, but managed to restrain himself till the boat was secure. Only then did he rush to the skipper, grabbing hold of his arm before the Norwegian's wife could embrace him. 'What is it, Org?' he demanded. 'Tell me.'

Nielsen's face was grim as he gripped Jay's wrists. 'All I know is that her anchor got stuck and she got away late. The mist . . . I could not see more.' His voice trailed off as he pushed past Jay with a pat on his shoulder.

One of the crew said, 'Bull de Vries was waiting for him, Jay. They'll be fine.'

He scanned the crowd, searching for Frances, relieved to see her with Magda's mother Sarah.

The boats came in one after the other until seven lay on the slipway. There were only two to come: Farer and Bull de Vries's Urchin. Jay glanced at Magda and saw how pale she had gone.

'I think I saw them as I cleared Blake's Point,' a fisherman was saying. 'Can't be sure, though, it's a bloody mess out there.' He smiled at Jay but could not hide the concern in his eyes.

'Jay?' Magda was beside him again. 'Jay, I don't want him to die . . . I want my pa!'

'Be strong, Magda.' His words sounded empty, so corrosive was his own terror, now risen beyond his control. His father couldn't die – not yet! Jay wasn't ready to take over from him. Setting his jaw he stared, eyes aching, into the mist. Was there something? Yes – almost against the cliffs.

The shouts from the men on their rocky perch confirmed it. A boat – no, two – fought the swirling water at the foot of the rocks. Frantic voices rang down from the cliff face. 'Swing! Go! Row now!'

Magda clung tightly to him. 'They're safe, Jay! Oh, they're safe!' She was crying tears of relief.

Jay pulled free and raced for the water, eager to help. Bull de Vries stood in the stern of the lead boat, his oilskin cap washed off his head, his mop of unruly hair plastered wetly across his broad forehead.

Jay waved at him and swung his gaze towards Farer, now

tucked in behind *Urchin*. As he turned, he glimpsed the slow shake of Bull's head. Fear exploded icy cold within him. He could not take his eyes from those of his father's friend.

Farer was there, wasn't she? But he knew the answer: *Farer* had come in without her skipper.

The boats passed by on either side of him. Bull's gaze was fixed on Jay but he was watching his father's boat.

Jay remained in the icy water when the boats ground to a halt and the men jumped out. Fraser Brannigan and one other man were both missing. Jay's brain was too numb to conclude the identity of the second man; all he had seen was the wrong person at the helm and only six men at the oars.

He felt the weight of a hand on his shoulder turning him. Bull stood there, anguish in his eyes, his massive shoulders slumped. 'I'm sorry, my boy. Just the other side of Blake's Point – it was a huge wave, Jay. It swept back from the rocks and caught *Farer* as she turned from the shore.'

'She didn't go over, though?' The boat showed no sign of damage.

'No, but Moses was standing hauling in a loose line. He was washed overboard.'

Moses. The coloured fisherman who had served his father the longest. Were his wife and children at the harbour, too? Jay was unable to lift his gaze to where he could hear his mother wailing. All his attention was focused on Bull. The man had been there when it happened; he was the last link.

'Fraser went in after him.' Bull's voice cracked and Jay saw he was crying. 'He had to try, though he must have known there was no chance for either of them.'

'I know, Uncle Bull. The crew was his responsibility. That's what he always said.'

'I tried . . . both boats did, but . . . '

Jay studied the big man, his huge frame now slumped in defeat. The great Bull de Vries cried like a baby for the friend he had loved and now lost. Jay shivered and said, 'I know you tried, Uncle Bull. So does Dad, I'm sure.'

He let his hand fall from the skipper's shoulder. 'I have to go to my ma,' he said softly.

Frances Brannigan lay in a crumpled heap on the wet

ground. A crowd of women, their brief moment of selfish relief over, tried to comfort her. At first Jay thought she had fainted, then he heard her wail pitifully. He stood a few paces away, not knowing what to do or say, and decided he would talk to her later when she was over the worst of the shock.

Magda was there too, helping her mother lift Frances to her feet. Her eyes said everything when she turned to him; there was no need for words. Their roles could so easily have been reversed.

Jay stared numbly at the mist-shrouded sea, at the angry waves that over the years had taken so many of the town's sons.

Today they had taken Brannigan Bay's finest.

The storm continued into the next day, preventing the citizens of Brannigan Bay from paying their respects to Fraser Brannigan. Instead of an armada of fishing boats rowing to the spot where Fraser and one of his crew had fallen into the sea, the townspeople gathered at the water's edge, said prayers and tossed flowers onto the rolling waters. The roses, carnations, freshly picked daffodils and bluebells – Fraser Brannigan's favourite – were swept out on the tide and scattered across the waters of the bay.

Jay remained in the harbour long after the last of the mourners had returned to the warmth of their homes. Unable to share his rawness with others, he needed to be alone. The rain slanted in, beating against him where he sat shivering at the foot of the cliffs. His clothes, already soaked by the sea spray sweeping off the crashing waves, clung to him. Pulling his knees up to his chest, he clasped his arms about his legs.

Not far from where he sat, a lone fisherman checked that all was secure in the harbour. The boats had been pulled up as high as possible but, as Jay watched, waves rolled up the slipway to surge round their keels. Water crashed against the embankment protecting the steep path leading to the market square above the harbour. It was a fitting storm in which to have died and, somehow, it made the loss of his father more bearable.

He stood up slowly, flexing his legs. The rain continued to sear down as he left the protection of the cliffs and he had to wait a few moments for the surf to subside before he could dash from the rocks to the slipway.

The fisherman tending the boats frowned when he saw him. 'I was wondering what fool was sitting up there without oilskins,' he said. 'Why aren't you home with your ma, lad? She'll be needing you with her in this difficult time.'

Jay nodded. 'I'm going now.' He turned towards *Farer*, which lay at an angle on its keel.

The fisherman caught the glance and said, 'She's yours now, lad. Will you be taking her out?'

Jay stared at his father's boat, at the red gunwale worn smooth in places by hands working at oars, scarred in others by the marks of fishing lines. He had thought he was not ready – but perhaps it was not his decision to make. Like his grandfather and father he was a child of the sea; now it was his turn to be called. Yet he did not answer the fisherman, starting instead for the pathway leading to the top of the harbour.

Along the way he passed the row of stone huts where the fish were cleaned and displayed for sale. Gravel, washed loose by the rain, slid down the slope and rippled over his brown boots when he stopped beside the furthermost hut. It was the one his father used. *Had* used.

He slipped and fell once before he reached the top of the path, so that mud now caked the legs of his sodden trousers. Leaning his hands on the rock wall spanning the cliff face, he gazed down at the harbour.

He did not know how long he stood there, remembering the past and pondering the future, before he became aware of someone beside him. 'Magda! You shouldn't be out in this weather!' She wore her oversized oilskins, and her hat slipped across her face when he pulled her towards him. He pushed it back and wiped the water gently from her face.

'I was looking for you,' she replied. 'We're at your house and your ma's worried about you, Jay. I knew I'd find you here.'

He smiled at her. She was tiny with large brown eyes and

though her hair was tucked inside the hat, stray curls plastered wetly to the pale skin of her cheeks. Pulling the collar of her jacket higher, he said, 'Come. I was on my way home.'

It was only as they crossed the empty market square and approached the first row of whitewashed cottages that Jay said, 'I'm taking *Farer*. As skipper.'

Magda stopped and pulled away from him. 'But – your ma? What about school?'

He placed his hands on her shoulders, drawing her face close to his. Rain spilled from his hair and streaked across his cheeks; he blew it off before he spoke. 'How else can she survive, Magda? With *Farer* I can make enough money to keep us alive.'

'You could sell the boat, Jay. You know your ma wants you to farm.'

His laugh was bitter. 'Would it please you, Magda, if I were to farm? Somewhere in the Overberg where we might see each other once a year?'

She shook her head briskly, causing the rainwater to cascade from her hat onto her jacket. 'You must do what *you* want, Jay.'

'I want the sea.' And you, he almost added. He slipped his arm round her and began to walk again. 'I want to be a fisherman, like my dad and Grandpa Brannigan. We belong out there on those waves.'

'My pa said you'd take her out. He knew.'

Jay smiled. Yes, Bull would understand and could be depended on for help. But how would the crew feel about serving under one so young?

It was as if Magda read his mind for she said, 'If you decide to take *Farer*, Pa said he'd call the men together when the storm has passed. He said your dad's crew would have you – he's sure of it.'

Jay squeezed her shoulder. It was right that he took over his father's role. Magda believed in him, as did Bull de Vries. But he could not quell his nervousness at how his mother would respond. There had always been a distance between him and Frances, an emotional chasm neither of them had attempted to bridge. All that bound them together had been Jay's father.

He realised there would be no sense in delaying his announcement to take over *Farer*; he would not know how to break the news any less gently at another time.

1913

Monday, 14 December

The swell was gentle where the boat rocked on the ocean surface only a mile from the rugged Cape coastline; its skipper and crew could hear the breakers pound the rocks and rush into the many bays with their small, white beaches. A few yards away, sea gulls cackled over the feast of fish entrails drifting on the clear blue water. There were three other boats beside *Farer* in the area where the men had spotted the run of fish earlier that day and the craft rose and fell in sequence.

Jay Brannigan squinted into the sun to watch the tree-studded coast. He reached forward when one of the crew drew in another wriggling fish, jerked it off the hook and threw it onto the boat's floorboard. By the time Jay had his long-bladed knife inside the fish, the hook had been baited again and the line flung into the sparkling water.

Jay was just eighteen, four years younger than the youngest of his crew, but fully accepted by them all, both as a man and as their skipper. As physically strong as any of them, he had already proved he had inherited his father's ability to sense the places where fish would be found. Since he had been skipper, *Farer* constantly returned to the harbour with the richest catch of the fleet.

It had still been raining that morning seventeen months ago when Bull de Vries accompanied him to the harbour where all the skippers and crews were gathered to judge the weather. Four days had elapsed since the storm and the men were in need of their regular catch.

They all walked with Jay to *Farer*. His crew went into their practised routine of readying the boat for the water; lines and bait were loaded with many willing hands to help ease *Farer* into the cold sea. Then everyone stepped back and watched

13

the new skipper launch his vessel through the harbour entrance. Only when it was past the cliffs and had mounted the first swell did the next boat follow.

Jay remembered, too, the absence of his mother on that day. If anything, his announcement that he was becoming a fisherman had widened the gulf between them. 'The sea!' she had shrieked when he broke the news. 'The damn, damn sea! What is it with you men?' Jay had been glad of the presence of Magda and her parents. Bull's quiet expression of approval had helped him stand firm in the face of his mother's wrath.

'Skipper!'

Jay jerked from his reverie. 'What?'

The man who had called out pointed across Jay's shoulder. 'Whale,' he said.

The rest of the men had seen it too. Jay cursed silently because he, as skipper, should have been the first to spot the danger.

'Three of them,' someone said.

'Is there a calf with them?' asked Jay.

The man shook his head. 'Don't think so,' he replied, studying the huge grey bodies drifting a hundred yards from the group of boats.

Jay turned to the other boats, cupped his hands over his mouth, and called out. His voice carried clearly across the water. He pointed at the mammals, feeling somewhat redeemed when he realised none of the other crews had been aware of their presence.

'They're pulling in their lines,' a fisherman said. 'Skipper, they're pulling in their lines!' he repeated when Jay did not respond. A note of alarm rang in his voice and Jay recalled his father's tales of harrowing experiences with Southern Right whales that came too close to a boat. The potential danger was not new to him – but the physical exposure was.

'Don't panic,' he responded curtly. 'Let's see which way they're going.' He was reluctant to give up on the solid bank of fish running beneath his boat. A good few hours remained before they would have to return to the harbour and he doubted that *Farer* had yet taken a bigger catch than the other boats.

'Skipper,' the man tried again, 'those things are dangerous. You should see what they do to a boat with one lash of a tail!'

'I know! I know!' retorted Jay, angry with the man for highlighting the danger yet more annoyed with himself for delaying his decision. The fish – or the safety of his men? He didn't want to be the first boat to flee but neither did he want to be seen as waiting to follow their lead.

The whales were closer now, moving in with alarming speed. If they carried on in their present direction, they would pass between *Farer* and the other boats.

The other skippers were giving the order to leave. Oars flashed in the sun and plucked at the water.

'Skipper!'

'Shut up, damn you!' Jay spun round and glared at the man. The rest of the crew were watching the whales anxiously now. 'They're well away from us,' Jay told them, 'so let's get on with our job.'

One of his men, a German named Gottlieb Kessler, rose to his feet. 'You're being a hard-headed bastard, Jay,' he said in his broken English. 'It's all right if they move between us and shore but—'

Even as he spoke the whales veered suddenly, seeming to move directly at *Farer*. Someone screamed, 'Jesus!' and jerked his line from the water. He paid no heed to the fish squirming at the end of it.

There was no need for Jay to give any orders. The crew scrambled for their oars – no time to raise the sail. Frantically hauling up the anchor, Jay glanced over his shoulder at the whales, which were now frighteningly close.

The men's panic slowed their progress and *Farer* milled indecisively on the swell. 'Calm down!' yelled Jay, though his heart beat loudly in his chest and the helm felt slow and cumbersome in his hand. 'Find your rhythm!'

Ahead, at what seemed a long, lonely distance, the other two boats were racing away. Jay could see the men watching *Farer*. 'Row, damn you!' he shouted.

The three whales lay close to each other. They drifted on the tide, carried along almost lazily by the water pushing

15

towards the shore. The threat inherent in their size made it seem as though they were moving determinedly and rapidly towards the boat. The water swirled when they dived beneath the surface, then exploded in a burst of spray and foam as they rose from its grasp and fell back with a resounding crash, sending adrenaline rushing through Farer's crew.

'Row for the shore,' Jay ordered when he saw they could not outrun the whales. If Farer continued on its course, following the other boats, it would sail between the first and second whales. Just one careless flick of a tail could end its flight.

Jay jerked the helm and Farer responded sluggishly, turning on the rise of a swell to point its nose at the shore. Ahead lay a stretch of calm water, but Jay knew that a solid bank of bamboo awaited them only a few hundred yards from where the surf broke far out from the coastline. It would be all right, though, if only they could outdistance the whales then steer away from the shore.

Fear stabbed at him when he glanced back and saw how close they were. As he watched, one burst from the sea and seemed to hang motionless for an instant before plunging with a crash into the water again.

Turning away, Jay saw terror on the faces of his men and hoped his own was well concealed. Their bodies strained back and forth as they pulled at their oars, but Farer was making little headway. 'Row!' he shouted and heard the panic in his voice.

When he looked back, he knew it was too late for rowing or shouting. They were hemmed into a small space separating the giant bodies so completely in control in their environment.

'Skipper! Skipper!'

When Jay swung back, he saw the first whale disappear beneath the sea's surface.

The crew were ashen-faced, frozen into position on the hard wood thwarts, oars still, waiting. On the other boats, the men were all on their feet, watching Farer's fate.

Another whale blew out a fountain of water. The noise was frightening. The sound of the distant breakers seemed close and threatening.

'God . . . *there!*'

It was the last sound Jay heard before he was flung from *Farer* into the air. He plunged into the cold water. A powerful force spun him round, threatening to rip him apart.

A sudden calm followed, seemed false, and he did not move towards the surface which he could see as a shiny film of light beckoning to him. He felt pressure on his ears and lungs but, realising that his body was broken, he let himself drift slowly upwards.

The worst pain was the harsh light that jabbed at his eyes – that, and the raw burning in his throat. He knew he was alive and his legs and arms moved of their own accord while his numbed brain tried to grasp his situation.

'Jay! There he is! Jesus God, there he is!' Jay recognised Henry's voice and remembered how often he had rebuked him for blasphemy. Now his 'Jesus God' were such welcome, reassuring words.

He saw that *Farer* was still afloat but taking in water where the stern had been ripped away, and realised that the whale's tail had struck almost exactly where he had been sitting. The other boats were racing closer, and the men calling out reassurances.

When Jay reached *Farer*'s side, hands reached for him, pulling him from the water and causing the damaged boat to lurch dangerously. 'Leave me,' he called out. 'You'll capsize her! I can cling to the side till the others get here.' He glanced at the stern, his mind in command again. *Farer* was holding up well. She would stay afloat if they could transfer the crew to the other boats and tow her to harbour. Only then did he search for the whales and saw that they were nearer the shore and had veered off to the north.

The other boats moved in. Someone threw a line and *Farer* was pulled slowly closer. Jay refused to be taken aboard the other boats. 'We can keep two men on her,' he told them, hauling himself carefully aboard the stricken vessel once most of his men had been transferred. 'Gottlieb, will you join me?'

The German seated himself beside Jay. 'There's the helm,' he said, pointing at the piece of wreckage floating a few yards away.

17

Jay nodded and fastened the tow rope to *Farer*'s bow. He gave the signal and the men in the two overcrowded boats strained at the oars. It would be a long journey back to the safety of Brannigan Bay.

After a while, Gottlieb smirked and said, 'You make dumb mistake, huh? Too damn proud to run first.' His heavy frame jerked with laughter.

Jay felt a flash of anger that quickly disappeared when he glanced at his sodden clothes. 'Enjoy yourself, Kraut! It won't happen again.' His own laughter mingled with the German's.

'*Ja*, at least the Kraut is dry!' Gottlieb put his arm round Jay, adding, 'Not to worry, skipper, we all make mistakes when still children. That's how we learn!'

The exhilaration of the encounter with the whales was still upon Jay as he made his way from the harbour to the white-washed cottage he now shared with his mother, the place his grandfather had built and in which Jay had been born. It lay at the end of a cluster of houses, almost at the start of the few shops comprising the village centre.

The cottage overlooked the ocean but shielded its occupants from the worst of the sea wind that howled in over the top of the cliffs. It was a simple home, yet warm and secure and Jay loved it. From his room he could hear the sound of the surf pounding the rocks below, could feel and smell the wind on his face when he opened the front door in the mornings.

'You could have been killed, Jay Brannigan.' Magda was waiting for him at the front gate, for news of the episode had travelled fast.

'It would have served me right,' he muttered, then laughed as he recalled Gottlieb's lecture. 'I was bloody stupid.'

'You talk like a real fisherman these days,' Magda repri-manded him, but smiled when he clasped her to him and then led her into the kitchen. 'It's bloody this and bloody that all the time.'

'And you're bloody beautiful,' he said, squeezing her

tightly. She was just seventeen, but her figure had filled out and ripened, driving Jay mad with desire.

'Jay! Stop it! Your ma . . .'

'She's out visiting,' he replied, nipping the smooth skin of her neck with his teeth. He felt her shiver. 'Oh, Magda, you're so soft and nice and—'

'Jay! Stop it, please – Jay!' She pulled his hand from her breast and swung away from him. Her hair hung across her face, giving it a slightly wanton air as she stood there, chest heaving. 'We've got to stop this, Jay. We'll go too far one day.'

'We'll get married one day,' he replied, his face flushed with his need of her. 'Come here.'

'No!'

'Magda, it'll only be another year or so.'

'Then we'll wait.'

'I can't! Magda, I can't!' Sometimes he became erect from just watching her when he saw the way her hips swayed as she walked, how her dress strained under the weight of her full breasts. Oh, God, he was going to explode!

Magda had moved against the wall, her hands clutched defensively across her breasts. 'We must wait, Jay,' she whispered.

'It's as bad for you, too, isn't it? Do you ache as well down here?' He touched the bulge in his trousers.

She shut her eyes and nodded. 'You know I do.'

'Then come to me.'

She shook her head and seemed to squeeze more tightly against the wall. 'I must go,' she whispered, starting for the door.

Jay barred the way, gripping her shoulders roughly. Forcing her face to his, he crushed his lips to hers, ignoring her whimpered struggles as he pushed her against the wall. His hands fell to her buttocks and gripped them hard, raising her to him, pushing at her as if he could enter her body through the material of her dress.

Her cry of pain and fright made him realise what he was doing and he let her down gently to her feet and stepped back.

19

Her lips were bloody from the fierceness of his caress, and her eyes held a mixture of fear and anger. But the retort he expected did not come; instead, she stared at him in silent outrage.

All he said was, 'I'm sorry,' for he could not find the words to explain the enormity of his desire for her. It so often ended like this, with his lust overcoming the tender protectiveness he felt towards her. Every time it happened he told himself he was a fool for treating her like some of the village girls who were prepared to go with almost any of the younger men. Magda was not like that; there would be no other man for her – but only when she was ready . . . when they were married. Oh, the agony of having to wait!

He watched her wipe the trace of blood from her lips with the back of her hand before starting for the door. 'Magda . . . don't go. Not like this, not when—'

She turned at the touch of his hand on her arm. The flash of anger he had seen in her eyes was gone now but the disillusionment that showed in its place made him feel even more ashamed.

'It's all right, Jay.' Her voice sounded shaky. 'It's my fault for letting you touch me like that. I shouldn't come here when you're alone.'

'No, I'm to blame. It's just that I want you so much. I can't control myself.'

Though she watched him intently, he could not decipher what he saw in her eyes. 'You'll be leaving tomorrow,' he said lamely, resting his back against the wall.

'Yes.' The word was spoken quietly, without emotion. Magda and her mother were bound for Cape Town to visit Nick, Magda's brother, who had broken his leg badly when a boat slipped from its keel, forcing him into hospital to have the limb set. With the two days it took for the journey either way, Magda would be away for a week – a long time, Jay realised, for a couple to be parted when things were not right between them.

'I'll come to your place tonight, then. To say goodbye.'

'Yes.' This time he did not move into her path when she went out of the door.

Jay remained against the wall, finding the cool of the surface blending with the damp of his shirt a relief from the heat that had earlier conquered him. Then he turned and stared through the open doorway.

Magda was closing the garden gate behind her before she stepped into the quiet street. He watched her walk the short distance to her home, the natural swing of her hips a taunting reminder of the stimulus that had created the strain between them.

When she disappeared inside, he sighed and went to his bedroom. Did Magda suspect there were others from time to time? Girls he went with because he could not have her, girls who writhed and cried and thrust hard against him?

He forced thoughts of her body from his mind and concentrated instead on how they would both react to their week apart.

Sarah de Vries looked up when Magda entered the kitchen. Her resemblance to her daughter was strong although Sarah had lost the slimness of youth. Her hair, once dark auburn like Magda's, was streaked with grey. Her eyes and jaw, though, spelled out the strength instilled by years of being a fisherman's wife. Sarah had lived through hard times, and they had left their indelible mark upon her.

Magda smiled at her mother, but the older woman glared disapprovingly at her and pushed back a wayward lock of hair that had fallen across her forehead.

'You were at Jay's?' she asked as she busied herself with her baking again. With her and Magda being away for a week, there was much to be done to ensure Bull's comfort during their absence.

'Yes, Ma. His boat was smashed by a whale.'

'I know, child. Your pa already told me. You two shouldn't be alone in the house. People will talk.'

'It was only for a few minutes.'

'That's all it takes to get tongues wagging.'

Magda sighed resignedly; although both her parents approved of her relationship with Jay, Sarah seemed to think that young men and women had only one thing on their minds. At least, thought Magda miserably, she was right this time. 'Need any help, Ma?' she asked, shaking off the memory of Jay's behaviour.

Sarah sniffed. 'Most of it's done. You should have offered this morning, instead of . . . ' She sniffed again, self-pityingly. Sarah had no need to complete the sentence; her daughter knew how she resented her regular excursions from the house to draw when she should have been helping with the housework. Drawing was something for the idle rich, not for a young woman who would one day be a housewife. Magda whispered an apology as habitual as Sarah's reproach and started for her bedroom at the end of the dark passage.

The quiet of the room was a welcome relief, both from her mother's stifling disapproval and her encounter with Jay. What did she feel for him? she wondered. She had loved him from an early age, in some ways more than she loved Nick. To Magda, Jay had always been a hero, a symbol of the kind of man Brannigan Bay depended on. He had been her protector, her friend, but they were different now. Or were they? Had Jay really changed that much? The ruggedness of youth, which she had found so attractive, was still there but now it was displayed in more adult ways – like that afternoon. She wanted tenderness, needed gentle romance, not the harsh sexual demands that seemed to have become Jay's way.

There were still many things about him that she loved, but was he *right* for her? She had asked herself that question repeatedly, yet still lacked an answer. The best she had done was to admit that in some ways he was.

Within Magda lay a restlessness that intensified as she grew older. Though she realised maturity would make it easier to control, she knew, too, that until she had identified its source it would continue to plague her. So she watched her friends and tried to determine how she was different.

Most of the girls her age performed the traditional role of helping their mothers, to acquire the skills needed for the day they would start their own families. And it would be families here in Brannigan Bay, the husband a fisherman, their children marked at birth for the continuation of that tradition. Though Magda helped her mother about the house, she escaped regularly to draw. She had done well over the past year, with three of her sketches sold to visitors from Cape Town. At times she thought it might be the urge to draw that made her different. Perhaps she needed other places, scenes and people to broaden her scope. Perhaps it was that which raised doubts about Jay's suitability.

She sighed, knowing that now she had finished her schooling Jay would soon ask her to marry him. The only period of grace she would have was his determination first to ensure financial security for himself and his mother. Another year at the most, and then she would have to give her answer.

Friday

It was a bright, cloudless day when Preston Whitehead left Cape Town. Despite the summer heat he kept on his heavy white dust coat and the motoring veil that stretched down across his face. The small stretch of flesh left unprotected between the veil and his driving goggles was smeared with grime and a coating of dust clung to the fine blond hair sticking out below the rim of his cap. The car he drove was only a year old, a 1912 Ford his father had given him for his nineteenth birthday. It was the first time Preston had ever taken the noisy vehicle so far beyond the borders of the city.

When he motored through Sir Lowry's Village, nestling at the foot of the pass of the same name, coloured children ran alongside the car, laughing and shouting. Preston slowed to throw a handful of coins towards them. One of the rascals jumped on to the back of the Ford, holding on for dear life as the car bucked and bounced over the rutted track. Reaching for the handbrake, Preston brought it to a stop.

'Get off!' he shouted, but the street urchin had already made his getaway, not without relief. The boy stood a few yards away, enjoying the admiration his bravado had earned him in the eyes of his friends.

Preston smiled and pulled down the veil. He did not mind

the children's attention but was concerned that one of them might fall under the car's wheels. A dirty youngster in ragged clothing pointed at him and said something to his friends. They laughed, making Preston realise he was an amusing sight in his bulky clothing, cap and goggles. Few cars were around, and the sight of one added to the unusual garb of the motorists caused a stir of excitement in smaller villages.

The children ran after the Ford as it lurched down the dirt road, following Preston until he was well out of the village and had started up the first gradient of the pass winding its way up the Hottentots Holland Mountains.

Preston glanced uneasily at the mountain lying ahead. Would the Ford make it up the steep Sir Lowry's Pass? The ascent was seldom achieved without some mishap. Overheating was the main problem, and the first cars to cross the pass were forced to do so in reverse gear as the fuel supply – a gravity-feed system from the tank beneath the front seat – was often cut off when the vehicle was in a nose-up position.

Though the Ford behaved itself, Preston made regular stops to let the engine cool while he smoked a cigarette and enjoyed the view over False Bay. A brisk wind swept up from the sea and brushed the mountain so he unbuttoned the dust coat.

Finally he arrived at the top of the pass, stopping one last time before starting the more gradual descent on the other side. He wondered what it was like to undertake the journey by wagon. With the luxury of motorised vehicles available only to the wealthy, most people took the train to Sir Lowry's Village, then boarded wagons drawn by mules.

He hauled out his pocket watch. Four o'clock already; he must soon find a suitable spot to spend the night.

A little over an hour later Preston drove into the small town of Grabouw, nestling in the shoulders of the Houw Hoek Mountains. He quickly found the garage he had been told about before leaving Cape Town.

'Good afternoon,' he called out to the figure in dark blue overalls who appeared from inside at the sound of the car.

The garage proprietor, a burly man in his late forties,

gave a curt nod, implying disapproval of someone as young as Preston having charge of such expensive machinery. 'You come over the pass?' he growled.

'Yes. I took my time about it, though.' Preston stepped down and stripped off his dust coat, pushing back his cap and raising his goggles. He gave the bonnet of the Ford an affectionate pat. 'She behaved herself well – no signs of overheating.'

The man did not seem impressed. He spat into the dust and said, 'Where'd you get it?'

'The car? It's—' Preston stopped, knowing it would make matters worse if he explained the Ford was a present from Kevin Whitehead. 'It's my father's,' he said instead.

He turned away, pretending to fiddle with the leather straps securing the spare wheel, angry with himself for feeling ill at ease because he was rich. It was always like this when he came into contact with those less privileged than himself. He had earned the car for he was already active in Whitehead Enterprises, his father's fishing concern operating from Cape Town. Apart from the Ford, Kevin Whitehead had also granted his only son a 10 per cent share in the business.

Preston told himself it would be easier when he owned it all one day; then no one could accuse him of being a spoilt brat. He would take what his father had started and build it into a huge fishing empire. Preston Whitehead was determined not to be known as someone who lived off his inheritance; he would make it live for him.

'The tank needs filling,' he said, irritation in his voice making him sound sharp and cool.

The garage proprietor narrowed his eyes but went about the laborious task of filling the Ford's fuel tank from his supply of four-gallon tins. When he was done, he walked slowly round the car, kicking each tyre in turn. The impact sent up little clouds of dust. 'Only one spare?' he asked when he stepped back, as if satisfied with his inspection.

'Yes. What's so strange about that?'

'I'll tell you what's strange,' the other man replied with a snort. 'What's strange is that someone coming over the pass should carry only one spare wheel. This your first trip?'

'Yes. The road wasn't that bad.'

'Your journey isn't over yet. Going fishing?'

Preston followed the man's gaze to the rod and wicker basket stacked in the back of the car. 'Yes, at Brannigan Bay.'

'The easy part of your journey is over. The rest is little more than a dirt track, with rocky streams to cross along the way. I'd be carrying another spare if I were you.'

'And I suppose you just happen to have one in stock?' replied Preston, stripping off his leather driving gloves.

'Might have,' came the unruffled reply.

'I'll take it.'

The man disappeared into the back of the garage, sauntered out a few moments later with a tyre, and dropped it unceremoniously into the Ford, knocking the fishing rod aside. Preston bit back an angry response.

When he had paid for the tyre and petrol, he asked about a place to stay for the night. 'This isn't Cape Town,' was the retort. 'There's no fancy hotels here. The best you can do is join the mule wagon at the end of town. They always camp in a clearing there.'

Preston nodded curtly, climbed back into his driving gear, then heaved himself into the car. Reaching beneath the steering wheel he set the spark and throttle levers. He jumped out again, stepped quickly to the front of the car and pulled out the wire loop of the choke. The garage man watched with an amused smile as Preston ran back to switch on the ignition, then returned to crank the handle below the radiator. It took a few attempts before the engine spluttered into life.

He spotted the mule wagon heading for Brannigan Bay shortly after he left the garage, beneath a clump of trees a mile outside town. Beyond the trees was a large clearing sloping down to a swiftly flowing stream. The muleteer, who was busy with his animals when the Ford drew to a noisy halt beside the wagon, shook his head as Preston stepped down. 'That thing farts louder than my mules,' he said laconically.

Preston grinned. Once he had switched off the engine a group of male passengers strolled over from the wagon to inspect the vehicle. Turning to the muleteer, he asked, 'Mind if I set up camp with you for the night?'

'The land's open to all, son,' the older man replied. 'Can't offer you a meal, though – that's part of the fare.'

'I've got something, thanks.' He stepped back as the muleteer joined the passengers in their inspection of the Ford. Preston slipped out of his coat, removed his cap and brushed the worst dust from his hair with his hand. He glanced longingly at the stream; a decent wash would be welcome.

Two of the passengers started talking about the car. 'If you're going to Brannigan Bay,' said one, 'you'd be well advised to cover up those brass headlamps.'

Preston gave him a quizzical look. 'Cover them?'

'Yes. With cloth or canvas, else the sea air will tarnish them in no time. I'm sure the wife will have something for you.' He returned a few moments later with two cotton bags he helped tie round the lamps.

'I never thought of that,' said Preston after thanking him. 'All I had in mind was the fishing,' he added with a laugh.

'Well,' the muleteer piped up, 'Brannigan Bay's the best for that. You fish a lot?'

'Almost every weekend. I work for a fishing concern,' he added. 'I was due for a holiday and thought I'd see what Brannigan Bay had to offer.'

'Well, you won't find much else but fish there.' The man's glance and unspoken words spelled out that he, like so many others, judged Preston to be someone who needed more than just Nature to keep him entertained.

Preston felt a twinge of sadness. Spoilt and bored – that was always the impression he gave others. He had often wondered about that, and had studied himself intently in his bedroom mirror, seeking some sign of what others seemed to find in him. He had thought it might be the slightly amused expression – or was it sardonic, arrogant even? – which reflected from the dark green eyes below the long blond fringe of his hair. Or the mouth – it could be the too-full lips that hinted at a desire for the sensual. Yet no one seemed aware that he enjoyed solitude, happy to sit on a lonely rock overlooking the sea, planning his future. No one seemed to understand the kinship he felt with the restless ocean, how he knew with complete certainty that it was intertwined with his destiny. The sea had made his father rich; it would make *him* wealthy and powerful.

' . . . just the occasional dance,' the muleteer, who had sparked off his reverie, was saying.

'I'm only interested in the fishing,' Preston muttered softly.

He listened, half concentrating, to the men while they discussed the merits of the car versus the horse. After a while he excused himself and made his way to the stream. Stripping down to the waist, he took a bar of soap from his toilet bag and stepped into the river.

The water was cold yet refreshing. He quickly built up a lather and proceeded to wash his hair and torso. Soap suds spilled into his eyes, making them burn, so that he cursed softly and dunked his head under the water. When he broke the surface again, Preston saw the girl.

She seemed unaware of him and was strolling slowly along the bank of the stream, stopping now and then to dangle her hand in the clear water. The sun setting over the hill cast a halo effect around the mass of her dark auburn hair. He wondered why he hadn't noticed her among the passengers. Or was she not one of them?

She suddenly saw him standing half naked in the middle of the stream and glanced quickly away, her face filled with confusion.

'I'm sorry,' he called out, ' I didn't mean to startle you.'

Her smile was timid, reinforcing the impression of daintiness she had conveyed as Preston had watched her progress. Slight build, yet womanly. She's not beautiful, he thought as he smiled back at her, but there was something about her that would grab any man's attention – a combination of girlish chastity and blossoming womanhood.

'Are you from the wagon?' he asked quickly when she lowered her gaze, turning to go back up the bank.

She did not reply at first, taking a quick look over her shoulder as if checking whether someone was watching. 'Yes,' she replied softly.

'Then, my dear lady, I was foolish to have undertaken the journey by car. I had only the scenery to observe when I could have enjoyed so much more.' The flattery sprang routinely to his lips, and he realised with bitterness how much he sounded just like the shallow person so many assumed him to be.

Her gaze rested on his bare chest, causing something to tug within his stomach. She jerked her head up as if suddenly aware of how she was staring, then smoothed down her dress as if she did not know what to do with her hands. The gesture made her figure more alluring.

'I must help my ma with supper,' she said quickly and glanced towards the wagon again. 'I have to go.'

'What's your name?'

She swung her gaze in his direction. Again Preston felt an urgent tug within him. Those eyes, so big and innocent, yet offering so much.

'Magda.' Her voice was so soft he barely heard her.

'Magda,' he repeated, trying her name on his tongue. 'Magda.' He smiled but before he could say more she scurried off, providing him a brief flash of slim brown calves.

The water swirling round his legs was icy cold now and the shadows following in the wake of the departing sun made him shiver. He forced himself back under the water and finished washing.

Later, as he sat close to the tiny fire he had built to cook his meal, he caught sight of Magda as she moved among the passengers, serving some of the children and older folk. He hoped someone would invite him to join them beside their much larger fire.

When they eventually did, it was to share a bottle of brandy. But the company Preston sought had already retired with her mother.

He saw Magda again the next morning before he left. It was still dark when he awoke for the sun was hidden behind a layer of low grey cloud and a light drizzle, unusual for December. It trickled almost noiselessly down the side of the small canvas lean-to Preston had erected alongside the Ford.

He heard the muleteer muttering at his team of eight as he prepared for the next stage of the journey and, in his mind, the soft echo of the name that had teased his thoughts all night long. Magda, Magda, Magda. It was gentler than the pitter-patter of the rain, warmer than the flames he could see beside the wagon where a fire heated coffee for the travellers.

He shook his head, his eyes already searching for her among the shadowy shapes moving about in the dim light. He told himself he was being silly; he did not usually bother with peasant girls unless it was for a short spell of fun. It did not help; the girl entered his mind before sleep came, had lingered all night long and now still haunted him.

He spotted her bending over a coffee pot, a thick cloth wrapped around her hand and covering her slim wrist. As she lifted it, her hair fell forward and she had to brush it back with her free hand. The sight brought Preston from his shelter.

'Magda,' he said and smiled. 'Good morning.'

The dim firelight cast a shadow across her eyes, but Preston saw her lips flicker into a smile as she replied, 'Good morning . . . '

He stepped round the fire, the smell of freshly boiled coffee filling the air with its rich aroma. 'You didn't give me a chance to introduce myself yesterday,' he said. 'My name's Preston Whitehead.'

Her sudden laugh took him by surprise. 'Whitehead? How very fitting!'

Preston frowned, then realised she was referring to the colour of his hair. 'I suppose it is,' he said, laughing with her and thinking how childlike an observation it had been. Her response reminded him that he was dealing with a simple country girl but the next moment he was taken aback when she raised her face and looked him steadily in the eyes. He thought, A girl one moment, a woman the next. Yet she was not acting the part of either, but slipping naturally from one role to the other.

'Would you like some coffee, Mr Whitehead?' she asked, then stepped away from him as someone approached the fire. An older woman moved into the firelight, glancing warily at him before joining Magda.

'Mr Whitehead,' said Magda, 'may I introduce you to my mother, Mrs de Vries?' When the woman nodded stiffly, Magda quickly added, 'I was just offering Mr Whitehead some coffee before he starts his journey.'

'Yes,' said Preston, sensing the protectiveness of the older woman. 'I really didn't prepare very well for the trip. No coffee at all, I'm afraid.'

Sarah de Vries studied him for a moment, then said, 'Give the gentleman his coffee, child . . . then come and help with the packing.'

Magda filled a mug and held it out to Preston. 'I'll collect it from you when you're finished,' she said when it became obvious that her mother was not going to leave her alone with him.

'He can leave it by the fire,' said Sarah firmly. 'I'm sure he'll be on his way before the wagon goes. His contraption is faster and it'll scare the mules when he passes.'

Preston held back a chuckle. 'You're probably right, Mrs de Vries. I'll drink up and be on my way.'

'Good day to you, sir.'

'And to you, madam,' he replied, but his gaze settled on Magda. Her smile was fleeting and apologetic before she started away from the fire with her mother a short, herding step behind her.

Preston watched them join the other passengers loading their bedding and utensils onto the wagon. The sun was making headway now although a light rain continued to fall. He turned at the sound of the muleteer's voice.

'You think you'll find the way?'

'Yes, I'm just about to leave. I'm told my car will scare your mules if I should come past them.'

The man laughed. 'Not likely,' he said. 'They're too arrogant to be scared by anything – even a mechanical horse. Still, it's best if you go first. That way, we can lend a hand if things go wrong.'

'Let's hope it doesn't come to that, but thanks anyway. And for the company.' He threw the remaining coffee grounds onto the fire and glanced once more towards the wagon, but Magda was not in sight. 'Tell Miss de Vries I said thanks for the coffee,' he asked the muleteer before heading for the Ford.

He was packed in a few minutes with plenty of willing hands to help him get the Ford started. 'Watch out for the drifts,' someone warned. 'They're deeper than they seem and pretty rocky.'

'Avoid the sand,' added another. 'It'll be pretty loose this time of year.'

Preston waved and eased the car forward. As it rolled slowly down the slope he looked back in the hope of seeing Magda. All he glimpsed were the women standing in a group beside the wagon. He could not tell which was her but he was unconcerned: he would see her again in Brannigan Bay.

The splutter of the Ford could still be heard when Sarah took her daughter to one side. 'Shame on you, child!' she said. 'To be so brazen with a strange man! What would your pa say if he knew?'

'But—'

'And Jay? He would lose all his respect for you.'

'Ma, I didn't—'

'You're no longer a young girl, Magda. Strange men are not to be trusted, do you hear? And that one, with his fancy machine and city ways, he's not the kind you should be talking to.

'Yes, Ma.' It was easier to agree.

'And don't walk alone in the village while he's there, you hear me?'

'Yes, Ma.'

Satisfied with the response to her lecture, Sarah returned to the wagon. 'Come, child,' she called over her shoulder.

Magda ignored her and stayed where she was a little longer, staring at the bend in the road where Preston Whitehead had disappeared from sight. Perhaps her mother was right: Preston Whitehead might not be a decent sort. Yet she felt drawn to him, to his worldliness and the confident manner in which he dealt with her. He was so different from the young men of Brannigan Bay . . . from Jay.

'Magda, come along.' At the sound of her mother's voice Magda turned towards the wagon. As she was helped aboard, she wondered again whether Preston might be no more than a fancy man with odd ways. It was the novelty that had attracted her, just as she sometimes daydreamed about what it would be like to be rich and sophisticated . . .

Monday

Jay stepped back from *Farer* to admire his handiwork where he had laboriously painted the boat's name in black letters on the newly constructed white stern. He had been relieved to learn that the damage inflicted by the whale was slight and local craftsmen had repaired it.

Seagulls screeched in a tight circle overhead.

'Leave your mess elsewhere,' he grumbled, casting round for something to lay across the gunwhale for protection against the gull droppings. He found a plank near the water's edge and balanced it carefully in place.

Glaring up at the birds he sat on the slipway, his hands placed palms down behind him on the concrete. While he studied the boat's name he thought of Magda. She should have painted it; she was very artistic. The walls of many homes in Brannigan Bay displayed her work. Flowers, the mountains, seascapes, even people – she sketched them all with skill. She had seemed hesitant when he had asked her to help with *Farer*'s name so Jay had undertaken the task himself.

Magda worried him. Ever since that afternoon when he had come close to forcing himself on her, she had been different. Aloof, almost. Things were awkward between them and Jay didn't know how to make amends.

Since she had returned from Cape Town, he had visited her home regularly, but had spent more time talking with Bull than Magda. She always seemed to find some excuse to help her ma in the kitchen.

Jay pushed himself to his feet and carefully tested the paint with his fingernail. Still wet. He didn't want to leave the harbour until it was dry.

He sighed and stared out to sea. The boats would be coming

in soon. Some of his crew had taken up temporary positions on them and that upset him. His men, his responsibility, had been forced to work with others to feed their families. It had taken a full week to repair *Farer*.

The movement on the rocks to his left caught his eye. So, the stranger was still trying his luck. Jay had seen him venture onto the rocks well before lunch, a fancy wicker basket in his hand. A city boy – no doubt about that. Over the past three years news of Brannigan Bay's healthy climate and good fishing had spread far and wide, attracting more and more visitors. They were mainly older men, seasoned rock anglers. This one was quite young though, only a year or two older than Jay.

Giving the circling seagulls a last warning glance he started to scramble across the rocks, thinking he could give the stranger a few tips to help him bag at least one fish.

When he reached the young man he was surprised to see a pile of fish stacked in the basket. He had been too preoccupied with painting to notice the other's success. 'See you've had some luck, then,' he said, studying the fisherman's slender build.

The stranger turned without moving the rod in his hand. 'A little,' he replied, 'though I'd like to think there was *some* skill involved,' he added.

Jay smiled and knelt beside him, glancing quickly at the bait stacked in a small compartment in the side of the basket. 'You're going about it the right way,' he said, nodding in approval, 'so I reckon you're entitled to think that.'

They gazed out to sea, as if trying to spot the fish around the end of the line. Then the stranger shifted the rod to his left hand, held out his right and said, 'I'm Preston Whitehead.'

'Jay Brannigan.'

'As in Brannigan Bay?'

'The original . . . or, rather, the grandson of the original. He founded the town.'

Preston seemed to have lost interest in his fishing. 'You must feel pretty proud,' he said. 'It's a beautiful place.'

Jay acknowledged the compliment with a nod. 'This your first visit?'

'Yes, but not the last. Not if the fishing holds up like it did today.'

'Did you come with Saturday's wagon? The one from Cape Town?'

'No, I came by . . . I came with my father's car.'

Jay's face filled with excitement. 'A car? You drove here in a car? Where is it?'

'In the market square.'

'Will you show it to me?'

'Yes, if you want.'

'A car,' whispered Jay in awe. 'Very few come here.'

'Yes. I'll take you for a ride, if you like.'

A smile spread across Jay's face. 'Mister,' he said, 'you take me out in your car and I'll take *you* in my boat. Out there in the bay where the fish run thick and fast. You'll catch more than you ever dreamed possible!'

Preston returned his smile. 'It's a deal,' he said. They shook hands again.

'You ever been to sea?' asked Jay.

'Yes, but not very far. I—'

'Do you fish often? In Cape Town? That *is* where you're from, isn't it?'

'Yes. My father owns a fishing enterprise,' Preston said slowly. 'I don't go out in the boats though,' he added, 'except at the odd weekend. And then it's not far from shore.'

Jay felt uneasy. 'A fishing company,' he said and shook his head. 'And here I was trading a ride in my boat for one in your car. Not much excitement in it for you, is there?'

'I told you I haven't been out far. I think we've agreed on a fair trade.'

Jay rubbed the side of his sunburned face. 'How many boats?'

'What?'

'Boats. How many does your dad run?'

'I . . . Quite a few. About twenty, I'd say.'

'Twenty? Small ones like that?' Jay pointed towards where *Farer* lay.

Preston spoke so softly that Jay had to lean forward to hear. 'They're mainly deep-sea boats,' he said, 'with engines. There are some smaller ones, though, for catching crayfish.'

35

'Twenty boats,' Jay repeated, almost to himself. 'With engines.' He stared at the bay as though the big boats were cruising in over the horizon. His voice was tinged with resentment when he said, 'Perhaps it's a good thing they fish in deep waters.'

'Why?'

'If boats like that came into Brannigan Bay there'd be precious few fish left for us ordinary fishermen to catch. And without fish there'd be no reason for this village to exist.

'My father's boats are manned by fishermen,' Preston responded softly. '*Ordinary* fisherman.'

'But they no longer work for themselves. Their boats are not their own, where and when they fish is no longer their choice. They work for other men, making them rich so they can buy more boats and fancy cars.'

'That bothers you? My car?'

'No, I traded a ride in it for one in my boat, didn't I?'

'It seems you regret it now.'

Jay's quick smile broke the tension. He placed a huge hand on Preston's shoulder and said, 'No, I've no regrets. The sea has touched us both with its power. It's made your family rich and mine content. That's not enough reason for regrets or ill feelings.' He laughed and added, 'Anyhow, what would I do with a car? Brannigan Bay's too small!'

Preston laughed with him. 'In that case, let's get on with our trade. I've caught enough fish for one day.'

An hour later, after they had driven from one side of the village to the other, Jay felt he had made a firm friend in Preston Whitehead. 'Just wait till I tell my girl,' the young fisherman said proudly when Preston dropped him off near the harbour. 'And speaking of girls, there's a dance Wednesday night, on Christmas Eve. Will you come?'

'I – I don't know.'

'You must! It's great fun, and,' he added with a wink, 'there'll be plenty of girls to spare!'

'All right,' replied Preston with a chuckle. 'I'll come.'

As Preston drove back to his hotel he hoped he wouldn't have to rely on the women Jay had referred to. There was only one girl in Brannigan Bay in whom he was interested and he was determined to find her before then.

The sudden tightness in Magda's chest was almost painful. She studied her hands, her fingers toying with a chipped nail as she listened to her father talk of seeing Jay drive off in a car.

'I called to him to help unload the boat,' Bull was saying, 'but he was so busy talking to the stranger he didn't even hear me.' The big fisherman shook his head. 'Next thing there's an almighty clatter, and Jay and this fellow are bouncing off in a Ford motor car.'

'A car?' asked Magda, feeling her heart thumping. 'Whose – I mean, what car?'

'Some rich boy from Cape Town,' replied Bull. 'He and Jay were in the harbour when we came in. Tall fellow. Rather pale.'

Sarah's lips tightened and she glanced warningly at Magda. 'An instrument of the devil,' she said quietly. They were seated round the kitchen table. There was still a faint glimmer of sun outside, though it was almost eight o'clock in the evening.

Magda concentrated on her fingernail again. So he *was* in the village! Twice she had offered to fetch items Sarah needed from the general dealer and felt sure her mother had viewed this with some suspicion. Each time, Magda had lingered among the little group of shops as long as she could, hoping Preston might pass in his car. She kept telling herself she was being silly, that one chance meeting with a charming, handsome stranger was no reason to keep thinking of him and hoping they would see each other again. Anyhow, he was too old for her, too self-assured and worldly.

Still, she had been unable to quell her disappointment when he did not appear in the main street, obliging her to head for home. Her second trip to the village centre had been the previous afternoon, and since then she had tried to force thoughts of him from her mind.

Jay arrived at the house an hour later, his face flushed with excitement as he related his thrilling experience. Magda tried to appear interested in what he was saying but Preston's face danced before her eyes. Sarah, who listened to Jay with an expression of disapproval on her face, glanced at her now and then.

'We went all the way to the start of the beach,' Jay was saying excitedly as Bull lit his pipe.

'On that rough track?' Bull shook his head and blew out a dense cloud of smoke. 'Amazed that clattering thing could do it. Did *you* drive?'

'No. He offered to let me try but I thought I'd better not. I held the steering wheel for a little way, though.'

'Bloody foul-smelling contraption as far as I'm concerned.'

'Bull de Vries!' Sarah glanced at her husband. 'The only foul thing here is your language. And your pipe.'

Bull grunted an apology before turning to Magda. 'What do you think of Jay's adventure?'

She looked up quickly. 'It must have been very exciting,' she replied softly, glad it was dark in the kitchen.

Sarah said, 'Jay, it's not my place to talk to you like a mother, but take care with these city people. They have different ways, devious ways, and they tempt decent people like you with what they've got and what they know. Take care.'

Jay smiled at her. 'I will, Aunt Sarah. But he seems like a decent fellow. Full of money but friendly enough.'

'The devil has many ways that appear charming.' She looked directly at Magda as she spoke.

Bull puffed at his pipe, turned to Jay and said, 'It's hot tonight. When I was your age, I'd be out walking along the sea. Nowadays you youngsters are content just to sit about with the old folk.'

'Come, Magda,' Jay responded. 'Let's show your pa it's not true.' He moved round the table, stood behind her and rested his hands lightly on her shoulders.

'Don't stay out late,' called Sarah as they started for the gate.

'We won't, Aunt Sarah,' said Jay, and Magda knew he was pleased that she had not refused to join him; it was their first opportunity to be alone since her return from Cape Town.

'Remember what I said about the devil and his ways,' added Sarah as they reached the street.

It was only when they were some distance from the

house that Jay said, 'Your ma seems very concerned about the visitor.'

Magda shrugged, wondering whether she should tell Jay about having already met Preston. Better not, she decided. If Preston happened to raise it with him, she would pretend to remember it as though the occasion had little meaning for her. She said instead, 'Ma clings to the old ways. All outsiders are a threat to her. She would like Brannigan Bay to stay the way it's always been.'

'It hasn't changed.'

'Yes, it has – even I've seen that. More shops, another hotel, more homes. Did you know there are over a hundred children in school now?'

'The town has grown, that's all.'

They walked in silence until they reached the edge of the market square overlooking the harbour. It was low tide, the sea lapping gently at the base of the cliffs. 'One day,' Magda said, 'they'll want a bigger, safer harbour. Have you thought of that?'

Jay shook his head. 'We won't allow that,' he said firmly. 'It would be an invitation to the big boats to come in and take all our fish. That would mean the end of Brannigan Bay.'

'Perhaps not,' she said gently, understanding his anxiety. 'Perhaps the town will have other reasons for surviving. It might not always be because of the fish.'

She was pleased to hear him chuckle; at least she hadn't upset him. His arm slipped around her and he pulled her close. 'No, Magda. Fishing is what gave the place its reason for being. It's what must keep it alive. Always.'

'A fisherman, body and soul,' she said and laughed. 'Yes, Jay Brannigan, if it's up to you Brannigan Bay will stay just as it is.'

'This Preston Whitehead, his pa owns a fishing company. At least twenty boats, Magda. Twenty! With engines.'

'What's he like?' she asked nervously, turning her head aside so that Jay could not see her eyes.

'He seems all right,' he replied. 'You'll meet him . . . I told him to come to the Christmas Eve dance.'

Magda's heart thumped so loud she was sure Jay must be

able to hear it. She moved a little away from him. 'Do you think that's a good idea? I mean, he doesn't know anyone. He may feel out of place.' The thought of seeing Preston again made her feel dizzy with excitement.

'He seemed keen to come and finding him a partner should be easy. He's charming and he has a car. Most of the girls in town would give anything to ride in it,' he added.

Anything? Yes, thought Magda. There were those who would.

'I thought I might arrange for him to meet Christine. She's been to Cape Town a few times.'

The thought of Christine brought forth a fresh set of emotions, erasing for a moment her feelings about Preston. Christine had a bad reputation when it came to men. Had Jay gone to her after their last argument? Damn Christine for her loose ways, for her voluptuousness, for her – damn her for being a mature woman with whom Magda could not compete! No, that was not right; she was simply unwilling to compete. When Magda married Jay she would be pure, his wife and his woman at the same time. *If* she married Jay. God, was this what one chance meeting with another man had done to her? She was no better than Christine.

'What's wrong?' Jay asked suddenly.

'Nothing! Why?'

'You were frowning. Do you feel the same way as your ma, that this stranger is the tool of the devil?' The tone of his voice was teasing.

'He's of no concern to me,' she said quickly.

'What made you so angry, then?'

'Nothing. When will *Farer* be ready to take out?' she asked, changing the subject.

'I'll give her a final check tomorrow morning. I want to take Preston out in her.'

'Where's he staying?' She wished Jay would stop referring to the visitor, yet was angry with herself for responding.

'At the Crystal Lodge.'

Of course. No other place but the new hotel would be suitable for a rich young man. She wondered what it was like inside. Perhaps Christine would get to see it when . . .

'You're frowning again,' said Jay, turning her towards him so that he could raise her face with his fingers. An evening breeze lifted from the sea and swept along the cliffs to ruffle his hair. 'Magda,' he whispered, 'things are not right between us. Is it because of . . . that afternoon?'

'*That* afternoon, Jay, was just a week ago.'

'Are you saying things changed *before* then?'

'Are you sure things *have* changed?'

'Yes. I feel it.' His grip on her eased a little. 'I can understand your being upset by how I behaved,' he started. 'It was wrong of me, but . . . ' He gave a quick shrug as if abandoning his search for words to explain himself.

She sighed. 'If things seem wrong, it's because *you've* changed, Jay.'

He paused. 'I'm a man now,' he said at last.

'Yes. And I'm not yet a woman. Not the kind you want me to be.'

'Magda! That's not true! You're everything I want.'

'Not everything, Jay. That's why you still have to go with the others . . . You do, don't you?'

'No! I—'

'Don't lie to me, Jay. In a way I even understand it.'

'You're the only one I want, Magda. I'll marry you tomorrow if you'll agree!'

She laughed despite herself. 'Oh, Jay, you can hardly support yourself and your ma right now, let alone a wife!'

An angry look flashed across his face. 'That'll change soon,' he said in a low voice. 'Just two more seasons and things will be better. I won't be rich or have a car but things will be better.'

'I know, Jay, I know.'

'Then let's get married.'

She shook her head. 'It's not the money, Jay, it's just . . . I don't feel ready yet. Perhaps we'll both feel differently by the end of the two seasons you spoke of.'

'No! I'll want you as much then as I do now. I'll prove it to you, Magda, just watch me!'

She stood on her toes and kissed his cheek. 'We'll wait and see.'

His face beamed when she kissed him again, on the mouth this time. 'Now,' he said, 'what about the dance? Are you going with me?'

Magda lowered her eyes and thought of the past, of how he always asked as if there was the remotest chance she might go with someone else. It was still the same, but this time Preston would be there. Now that she and Jay had talked, their relationship might stabilise again. Seeing Preston could change that.

'You're taking a long time making up your mind,' Jay whispered into her hair.

She gazed into his earnest eyes, smiled and said, 'A little uncertainty won't do you any harm.' She relented when she saw his worried expression, and added, 'Of course I'll go with you.' Her breath almost left her as he hugged her tightly and laughed.

As Jay rocked her gently back and forth in his strong arms, she thought ahead to the dance, to how she would feel when she saw Preston Whitehead again.

The favourite place for Brannigan Bay's dances was a warehouse where flowers, mainly everlastings, were pressed and packed for export. On the morning before the Christmas Eve dance, the floor was smeared with candle wax to provide a smooth, slippery surface for the night's event.

The village girls spent the afternoon making final adjustments to their best dresses, washing their hair and baking the bread and cakes that would provide much-needed refreshment as the night wore on.

Even the visitors, most of them farming families from neighbouring towns, displayed a keen anticipation of what was to come. Rock anglers left their favourite spots by lunchtime to head for home to get ready. Those fishermen who had ventured out to sea made sure they were back in harbour by early afternoon.

It was Christmas Eve, no ordinary day, and by nightfall the village was buzzing with excitement.

Preston took a final look at himself in the mirror of his hotel bedroom. 'Handsome devil,' he said aloud and straightened his tie. 'You're going to sweep the local girls off their feet.' Yet, despite his banter, the eyes staring back at him from the mirror were troubled.

Local girls – would Magda be there? Since he arrived in Brannigan Bay, he had been just about everywhere, into every shop, down every road. But he had not seen her. He was sure he had come across every citizen, each visitor, cat and dog of the village. Everyone except Magda. He should have asked Jay about her when they had gone out to fish that morning, but he had not wanted to risk being teased. Perhaps he would see her tonight at the dance. Anticipation plucked deliciously at him as he turned away from the mirror.

His room overlooked the bay and he could tell it was going to be a perfect summer's night. As he watched, the mountains turned gold in the setting sun. Towards the south-east section of the bay the sea shimmered lazily in the fading light.

It's a special town, he thought as he pulled the curtains aside for a better view. He understood why Jay felt protective towards it. Brannigan Bay had beauty, charm – and, above all, potential.

In the few days he had been there, he had driven as far along the coast as he could, then walked for miles along rugged stretches of rocks. He had inspected every inlet, each sheltered bay that could be transformed into a safe harbour and finally selected the spot at which he would favour building one.

It lay a few miles to the west of the village. At first glance it seemed little more than an outcrop of rock thrusting out from the curve of the shore, appearing to offer little protection from the wide sweep of water. But Preston had watched the flow of the currents and visualised the long jetty that would hold back the force of the Atlantic. On the rocks above was sufficient level ground to build factories. There was space, too, at the side of the inlet, for construction of an adequate slipway for boat repairs.

He had spent many hours at the spot, imagining the big boats the harbour would hold, the safe base it would provide for excursions into the rich waters of the south

Atlantic. When he went out with Jay in *Farer*, Preston had a view of his chosen spot from the bay and knew that his decision was a wise one.

He had said nothing to Jay about his thoughts. He would have been angry and Preston respected the rugged young man who was so passionate about his village. They regarded the bounty of the sea from different viewpoints and were destined to clash if their individual needs were expressed in action. And clash they would, for Preston knew without doubt he would return one day to Brannigan Bay to make his dreams a reality. One day, when his father's fishing enterprise became his, he would put his inheritance to work in Brannigan Bay. But, for the moment, he and Jay were just two young men with dreams and they could suppress their differences in mutual liking and respect.

Grabbing his jacket from the bed, he tugged at his tie one last time. It was too hot an outfit but Preston was not sure how formal such a small-town dance might be. The sleeves of his white shirt were rolled up to the elbows and he slung the jacket across his shoulder as he left the room.

No hint of wind disturbed the air as he started the Ford and made his way to the dance venue, enjoying the attention of the small crowd standing outside in the balmy evening air. Jay came running from the hall, a welcoming expression on his flushed face. 'You're late,' he admonished Preston before grabbing hold of his arm to tug him towards the entrance. 'You'll be meeting plenty of people as the night wears on,' he said, 'so I'll not confuse you with too many introductions right now. Do you know the barn dance?'

Preston nodded, allowing himself to be led towards the door. 'At least, I think so!' he replied with a laugh.

'And the bon ton?'

'Oh, yes!'

'The waltz? The Lancers?'

Preston laughed and slapped Jay's shoulder as they went through the door. An elderly man was squeezing an unknown tune from a concertina, while a younger fellow tried his best to keep pace with a guitar. The pianist had given up and was watching his two fellow band members with a smirk that suggested his turn to impress the crowd would come.

'A grand evening,' Jay was saying above the noise of the concertina.

'It sure looks that way.'

Then Preston saw her.

She stood on the far side of the hall, her back to him as she and another girl put some finishing touches to the flowers. He knew straight away that it was Magda; there was no need for her to turn towards him. His gaze took in the swirl of thick auburn hair and her figure, slim yet full, moving lightly beneath the caressing folds of a light blue summer dress.

'Jay,' he started, fighting the breathlessness that gripped his chest, but his voice was drowned by the music.

Then he was pulled onward again, across the hall. Jay leaned close and shouted in his ear. 'I said there wouldn't be any introductions, but . . . ' His voice was lost as the pianist suddenly found his chance and joined in the mêlée with heavy hands that pounded wildly at the keys.

'What?' Preston jerked his gaze from Magda to his friend. Jay was sweating slightly, his teeth white in his suntanned face.

' . . . the prettiest girl in the village,' he finished saying. He pointed at Magda.

Preston smiled and followed him across the room.

It was less noisy in the corner where Magda stood. Jay tapped her shoulder and she turned slowly, smiling, then saw Preston.

'I told you she was the prettiest girl in the village,' Jay was saying, 'but did I tell you she was *my* girl?'

Preston stared at her. He heard Jay's words as if they came from far away, saw him standing beside Magda, his arm proudly around her waist, pulled her tightly to him. *His* girl. Magda was Jay's girl.

He felt himself step back as if he wanted to run away. He studied them both, the slender young woman surrounded by the arm of the tall, handsome man. No, he wanted to say – she's mine. Your town, your woman: they will both be mine. But all he said was, 'It seems that Brannigan Bay has much more to offer than just good fishing.' He glanced at Jay as he spoke. 'You're a very lucky man,' he added softly before turning to Magda.

There was a strange expression in her eyes, one of . . . fear? He heard Jay say his name, introducing him to her. Preston reached for her hand and raised it to his lips. Her skin, soft and dry despite the heat, held a light fragrance that teased his nostrils.

'Watch out,' Jay said, oblivious to the reaction between the two, 'the man's a charmer!' He laughed, removed his arm from around Magda, and said, 'Take her onto the floor, Preston. Find out just what we locals can do!' He smiled again before making his way into the swirling crowd where he plucked a plump woman into his arms and spun her round on the dance floor.

Preston was suddenly aware he still held Magda's hand in his. He released it slowly, his eyes fixed on hers. 'So, Magda of the mule wagon, we meet again.'

'So we do, Mr Whitehead.'

He cleared his throat. 'Do we dance, as Jay suggested?'

She stepped forward and was in his arms. Her body felt light, almost weightless, as he moved a few steps back so that they could join the other dancers.

'Jay's woman,' he said, starting to move in rhythm with the music. 'He didn't talk about you. I would if you were mine. All the time. To everyone.' He saw her blush.

'You shouldn't say such things. It's not right.'

'Not right? Magda, *we* are right – you and me! Surely you feel it too?'

She stiffened in his arms and Preston cursed himself. He must take care – she was obviously not used to men speaking to her like that. 'I'm sorry,' he said, 'but it's the truth.'

'Is it?'

'It's what I feel, and I know you feel the same. I can see it in your eyes.'

'I think . . . I think you see what you want to see. You also think it'll make a simple village girl's head spin. Isn't *that* the truth, Mr Whitehead?' She smiled as she spoke, removing the

46

sting from the words. It made Preston feel ineffectual against her.

'Magda,' he said slowly, 'I have said many things to many women, and I've been guilty of using charm, shall we say, on many occasions. But not tonight, not with you. I meant what I said. Please believe me.'

She stared up at him and Preston was not sure what message lingered in her eyes. At last she said, 'It's Christmas Eve, so let's dance, then get back to our friends. It's what this night is for. Friends.'

Much later, as it drew close to midnight and the band slowed the pace of their music, Preston followed when a group of weary dancers, Jay and Magda among them, moved outside and walked to the cliffs above the harbour. The sea shifted idly under the glow of a bright, full moon.

He stood beside Christine, to whom Jay had introduced him earlier in the evening. He thought her very pretty, and she had made it obvious that her interest in him went beyond displaying homespun hospitality. For a while he had flirted with her, his words and smile mechanical, but now he had eyes only for Magda who stood in the circle of Jay's arms. 'It's midnight,' someone said as the music drifting from the warehouse faded into silence.

One of the men started singing the first bars of 'Silent Night'. The others joined in and Jay's powerful baritone could be clearly heard.

Preston felt his lips move, heard the familiar words flow softly from his mouth. But his thoughts lay with the girl who had affected him like no other before. He had wanted many, had lusted strongly for them, yet with Magda it was something else, some force against which he had no defence. She would become his, she must. No one else would satisfy him now. But not tonight. Tonight she still belonged to Jay.

He became aware of Christine whispering in his ear. 'It'll be easier if we go to my place,' she was saying.

He smiled sadly, thinking how deeply Magda's influence had touched him. 'Perhaps next time I visit Brannigan Bay,' he said gently, not wanting to hurt her yet knowing he would anyway.

Christine pulled away. 'What's wrong with you?' she asked, frowning. 'I thought . . . '

'I'm rather tired and I'm leaving early tomorrow.' When had he made that decision? It did not matter; it was the right thing to do. He could not spend another day in Brannigan Bay now that he had seen Magda again, not now that he knew she was Jay's. There was much to do in Cape Town before he could return, the first task being to convince his father that it made good business sense to build a harbour in Brannigan Bay to cater for their growing fishing fleet. He would offer to oversee the project himself, perhaps even live in Brannigan Bay while construction took place. The village would know who he was then, what he meant to their future. The village, Jay Brannigan – and Magda.

Beside him Christine said, 'You'll come back to visit sometime?' Her face still bore the sting of his rejection.

Preston smiled and patted her cheek gently. 'Yes,' he said, 'Yes, I have to.'

1915

Jay felt his mother's eyes on him as he entered the kitchen
with a bundle of freshly chopped wood in his arms, placing
his load beside the black Dover wood-burning stove. It was
a monstrous contraption – its handles polished daily with
Brasso – that took up most of the wall space on one side of
the kitchen.

Arranging the fresh pieces of wood beside the existing
bundle, he said, 'Perhaps this year we can afford a coal-fed
Aga, Ma.' The de Vries family had one and spoke highly of its
advantages, although the task of cleaning it was unpopular.
First it had to be thoroughly scrubbed, then coated with
blacklead dissolved in water and polished until it shone.

'Coal is messy,' muttered Frances Brannigan. 'Wood is
better.'

'Coal is more efficient, Ma. More expensive but better.'

Frances shook her head. 'Wood costs us nothing. Coal
gives the food a smell.'

Jay sighed and straightened up. 'Yes, Ma,' he said to
end the conversation. If it could be called that, he thought
morosely.

His mother used it to touch on another matter, one that
Jay knew lay close to her heart. 'I don't know where I'll get
wood once you go,' she said, rocking slightly on her feet, a
motion that had become familiar to him over recent months.
'Who'll chop it for me?'

'I've told you I'm not going to war, Ma.' He helped
himself to a cup of strong black coffee from the pot
simmering constantly on one of the stove's plates.

Frances made a clucking noise with her tongue. 'All
men go to war. It's what you all think you were born

for – fighting the sea, fighting other men. You'll go, I know it.'

'No, it's not my war.'

'With all the other young men volunteering? You're only saying you'll stay to please me. You'll go.'

Jay wanted to shout at her but all he did was stare silently into his coffee. The war – how it tore at him! Many villagers were enlisting, caught up in the hysteria affecting young men, the call to duty that all felt had to be heeded. They discussed it in tight little groups, spreading the excitement and romance of battle among them. 'We'll show those Huns,' they would say. 'They never come up against real fishermen! What chance do they have against men who've fought the south-wester and chased the yellowtail?'

'I can't leave *Farer*,' said Jay at last.

'Don't lie to your mother, child. Half the men in town have already gone – including some of your crew. I'm the only thing holding you back. So go, Jay. It'll cause me suffering but there'll be those who'll look after me.'

Jay shut his eyes. It was true; his mother was one of the reasons why he had not volunteered. Yet it was not solely that or her obvious self-pity that stopped him. *Farer* needed its skipper for there were still those who looked to the boat to provide their livelihood. But also, Jay felt he had no quarrel with the Germans, reasoning that they had to be ordinary people like Gottlieb Kessler and his wife. It distressed him when the couple were suddenly viewed with suspicion and something close to scorn by many townspeople.

Then, too, there was Magda.

It was as if Frances could read his mind, for she said, 'If you and Magda were married . . . if there was a child, there'd be no need for you to feel so guilty about not going.'

'I don't feel any guilt,' snapped Jay. 'Magda has nothing to do with my decision.'

'That's right – talk to your ma as if she were one of your oarsmen.' Frances sniffed. 'I'm nothing but a burden to you. But it won't be for ever, Jay Brannigan . . . I feel God is calling me. I shan't be your millstone much longer,' she added with another loud sniff.

Jay could stand no more. Draining the remainder of his coffee he got up, scraping his chair on the worn linoleum floor. He made no excuse to his mother as he went outside into the fading light.

His fingers clamped round the few loose coins jangling in his trouser pocket as he pushed open the garden gate and headed down Main Street. Enough money for a beer. God, he needed it!

His mother was right in saying she had become a burden to him yet it was not because he found it difficult to care for her or resented her. What racked his nerves was her constant self-pity. Perhaps he should use the excuse of war to escape it, he thought bitterly. Her needs would be met by others but in that lay the problem: Jay's pride would not allow generous people like Bull de Vries to go short because Jay felt he must get away from his mother. No, he would remain in Brannigan Bay – there were plenty of others to play at soldiers.

The lights were already on in the bar of the Grand. Dilapidated though the place was, it remained the fishermen's choice although once they had tried the much smaller facility at the newer Crystal Lodge. They had felt out of place there, no fighting was allowed, and returned to their former haunt.

Jay heard laughter as he approached the old building. There was much of that these days, as if war were a thing to raise the spirit. At times Jay felt as if he was the only young man of his age left in the village, which was reinforced by the strange, almost accusing glances of some older folk. He suddenly wondered how Magda felt about it and realised they had never discussed it.

He hesitated before going inside, but the laughter and beer fumes mingling with tobacco smoke drifting through the open door beckoned to him.

The men turned to look when he entered. It was a natural movement, the kind anyone would make when someone walked into a crowded room, yet tonight it seemed to Jay as if they had been waiting for him, wanted answers from him. Shaking off the impression, he called out a greeting.

The men turned back to their drinks and conversations Jacob Erasmus, a young man with whom Jay had been friendl$

for a long time, signalled him closer. 'Thought you weren't coming,' he said as Jay pulled up a chair. Nick de Vries limped closer, still not fully recovered from the accident in which he had broken his leg.

'This place is quiet tonight,' said Jay, ordering a beer.

Nick laughed. 'Shit, man, there's a war on!'

'Not for us,' retorted Jay. 'I'm beginning to think we're the only three left in town!'

The sudden silence was awkward, making Jay glance sharply at Jacob. 'You too?' he asked softly.

Jacob nodded slowly.

'When did you sign up?'

'This morning.'

Jay laughed uneasily. 'Don't look so apologetic about it.'

Before Jacob could reply, Nick said, 'I'm going too.'

Jay reached for his beer and drank in silence. After a while he asked, 'Does your pa know?' Limp and all, Nick was going to be a soldier.

'Yes . . . I think he'd join up too if he were younger.'

Jay's voice sounded harsher than he intended. 'Who'd care for your family then?'

It was Jacob who answered, saying, 'It's different for you, Jay – your mother, I mean. At least I have two younger brothers to keep things going.'

'Don't make excuses for me, Jacob. I want no part of this war, that's all.'

The two men held each other's gaze for a moment, then turned to their drinks. Jacob said, 'We've been friends for too long to pass judgement on each other, Jay. We're each of us doing what we think is right.'

'I'm not passing judgement on anyone. I just don't want my decision defended. There's no need. If people think I'm a coward, then so be it.'

'Come on, Jay, that's not—'

'Not you, perhaps. But some others . . . Jacob, I've seen the way they look at me.'

Jacob gave an understanding nod.

'When will you leave?' asked Jay.

'Next Monday.'

Nick had stayed out of their earlier confrontation, but now he said, 'I'm told that Brannigan Bay has one of the highest number of volunteers in the Empire. In relation to its population, of course.'

'That's noble of us,' growled Jay before downing his beer. He immediately ordered another.

Nick had missed the sarcasm. 'A few more volunteers,' he went on, 'and we could be the highest. How about it, Jay? One more man – a Brannigan, at that – could just do it.'

Jay wanted to shake him and shout that war was more than just setting records. He managed to curb his anger and said quietly, 'Brannigan Bay also needs volunteers of another kind, Nick, those who stay to care for the town. There'll be many who need support in time to come.'

'Jay's right,' agreed Jacob, 'and the war will still increase those numbers.'

Nick stared at them in turn. 'I hadn't thought of that.'

'Most people haven't,' said Jay. 'That's the pity of it.' He finished his beer and stood up, sickened by the spirit prevailing in the bar. Even old men, who should have known better, were expounding the virtues of war. Then, too, Jay was saddened at the thought of Jacob leaving. He would miss him.

'Walk with me,' he said. 'Nick will watch your beer.'

Once they were outside, Jay said, 'Take care wherever it is they send you. The town will need its young men when the war's over.'

Jacob smiled. 'I'll miss you, Jay.'

'I'll miss you, too.'

They shook hands, although they would be seeing each other again before Jacob's departure. 'You'll look in on the family from time to time?' asked Jacob.

'Of course. They must speak up if they need anything.'

'I'll tell them. Thank you, Jay.'

They shuffled from foot to foot, wanting to say more but not knowing how. Then Jacob said, 'Well, I'd better be getting back inside before Nick drinks my beer.'

'I must pay a visit to Gottlieb. I don't think they've had an easy time lately. He hasn't been to the bar for weeks, and he didn't even come to the harbour today.'

'It's a shame,' replied Jacob. 'Gottlieb is a good man.'

Jay made no reply as he slapped Jacob's shoulder before turning away.

The Kesslers' cottage was on the western fringe of town overlooking the bay. A single lamp glowed dully in the kitchen as Jay approached the tiny house. He went to the back and knocked on the kitchen door, which was closed, the curtains drawn across the windows.

The silence inside the house was broken by the sound of a chair scraping back, followed by the shuffle of feet. 'Who is it?' Gertrude's voice.

'It's me. Jay.'

Again there was silence but Jay was sure he heard muffled voices. Gertrude called out again, her English, like Gottlieb's, still heavily broken despite their years in South Africa. 'Gottlieb is not well,' she said. 'He not want to see anyone, Jay.'

'Tell him it's me, Gertrude. I want to talk to him.' There was no response so Jay called, 'Gertrude, I need to talk. Open the door.'

He was about to knock again when the upper half creaked open. 'What's up with the loafer?' asked Jay with an apologetic smile, regretting having shouted at the woman. Then he noticed her distraught face and grabbed hold of the door in case she shut it on him. 'What is it, Gertrude? What's wrong?'

Without waiting for an answer, he pushed inside. The lamp on the kitchen table was set low, its light reflecting dully off Gottlieb's swollen face.

'Jesus Christ,' muttered Jay. 'What the hell happened?' He moved closer to the table at which Gottlieb sat. Both of Gottlieb's eyes were swollen shut and the skin across his brows was split. His left cheekbone was puffed up. Jay thought it might be broken. 'Jesus,' he muttered again.

Gertrude stood behind her husband. Placing her hands on his shoulders she said, 'For years he live here, but they beat him because he German. Why, Jay, why?'

Gottlieb reached up and laid his hand on hers.

'Enough, *Liebchen*.' When he spoke, Jay saw his mouth

54

was badly broken. His lips were torn and some teeth were missing.

'Who did this, Gottlieb?' Jay's voice was tight with anger. 'What swine did this to you?'

The German shook his head slowly. 'No matter,' he said softly. 'Two . . . three men. No matter.'

'When?'

'Last night. I was out walking. They jumped me from the bush. "Damn Hun!" they shouted. They beat me with a pipe or something. "Hun! Hun! Hun!" they shout.'

Jay slumped into a chair. 'Who, Gottlieb? You must have seen something. Was it Svenson?' he asked, thinking of the Swedish fisherman who had publicly voiced his antagonism towards the Kesslers. Olaf Svenson was a tough, ruthless character with whom Jay had had more than one clash. The two men were evenly matched but, on the last occasion, the night after *Farer* had been smashed by the whale, Svenson came off second best after taunting Jay by referring to him as Jonah. It had prompted the most brutal fight yet seen in the bar of the Grand.

Gottlieb was shaking his head. 'Don't know who, Jay,' he murmured.

'I'm sure it's Svenson, the bastard!' The Swede was cruel enough to do something like this to Gottlieb, and ever since their fight Jay had felt he was biding his time to take revenge. Perhaps beating Gottlieb, one of his crew, was more than just a matter of hooliganism. 'I'll wring the truth out of him,' he whispered and stood up.

'Leave it, Jay,' pleaded Gottlieb.

'No, my friend, I *can't* leave it – I'm your skipper, remember?' Gottlieb tried to smile. 'No,' continued Jay, 'the town must know this cannot be allowed to happen. Never again.' He nodded at Gertrude and left the house with its sadness and dismay tucked behind closed curtains and locked doors.

He shook with rage as he walked down the rocky path leading to the village. The sea was like his mood, angry and restless, hurling its frustration against the jagged coast, the sound of its fury filling the night. If this was what war made of people then he was glad he had decided to have no part in it.

He had gone only twenty yards from the Kesslers' cottage when he heard someone call his name. He stopped, not sure where the sound had come from.

'Brannigan!'

There – down on the rocks. Jay moved from the path and stared down. Nothing.

'Hun lover!'

His body stiffened. Wild anger flooded through him, along with a sense of delicious anticipation. They were there, had been watching the cottage while he visited Gottlieb. He had them now! He strained his eyes to see into the dark but detected no sign of anyone.

'Now we know why Brannigan won't go to war,' the voice called. 'He loves Huns, that's why!' A loud, crude bellow of laughter followed.

It was not the Swede; he would have recognised the man's voice. This was someone who spoke with an Afrikaans accent.

'Show yourselves, you bastards!' he shouted, already slithering down to the rocks. Two or three of them, Gottlieb had said, with a pipe or some other weapon. Jay told himself not to be reckless though the need to inflict punishment coursed wildly through him.

He saw movement on the rocks below. Although the moon was hidden behind a layer of low cloud, he recognised Svenson's bulky figure. But who were the two men with him?

They were coming towards him. 'Are you ready to go to war, Brannigan? Right now?' Jay suddenly knew who the second man was: Lucas somebody or other, the son of a farmer from Caledon. He often came to Brannigan Bay for weeks at a time and Jay had seen him hanging about with the Swede. He was a cocky, sadistic little man.

Searching frantically for something with which to arm himself, Jay tore a thin branch from a nearby tree and stripped it of its leaves. It was not the weapon he wanted – far too flimsy – but he could wield it like a sword if necessary. He waited, hoping for a glimpse of the third man before they were on him.

'Svenson,' he called out at the approaching shapes, 'I

know it's you. Haven't you learned your lesson yet?'

An evil laugh floated up to him. 'Tonight's *my* turn, Brannigan.'

This was madness, Jay told himself, but he wanted the physical conflict, though he had little hope of escaping unhurt. 'Come!' he shouted. 'Come here!'

He glanced down and saw they had stopped. They were talking among themselves, arguing even. Then one of them, the third man, moved off, making his way along the rocks towards the village. There was something familiar about the way he moved, but Jay could not quite grab hold of it. It was someone who knew him, that was for sure, someone who wasn't prepared to hurt him. Who would beat Gottlieb Kessler but not him?

When Jay sensed the indecision of the remaining two men, he saw his chance and scrambled madly down the rough slope. He was almost at the bottom before they were aware of his charge.

He was off balance when his feet hit the rocks but he gave an angry yell as he righted himself and rushed at the Swede.

Svenson stepped back to meet the attack, expecting a flurry of blows. Jay stopped short and jabbed him with the stick. It was a sharp, vicious blow to the stomach that sent the big man to his knees with a gasp of pain. The stick was still in Jay's hands and he swung it in a mighty arc, crashing it down across Svenson's face, using it like a whip. The Swede cried out, rolled onto his side and lay curled in agony.

Satisfied that he was no longer a threat, at least for the moment, Jay turned his attention to the second man.

Lucas had stood there in awe, frozen by the swiftness of the violence. Now that he alone faced Jay and his anger, he turned and ran. Jay swung the stick and hit him hard across the buttocks before he managed to escape.

Svenson was on his knees, holding his face in his hands, and Jay was satisfied to see a steady flow of blood pumping from the cut inflicted by the stick. He laid into the Swede again.

Svenson tried in vain to protect his head from the blows.

Jay was suddenly glad that the tree branch was not sturdier; the stinging cuts it made were a more intense punishment than a solid blow.

Svenson scrambled away but Jay followed, striking at the man's neck, his back and his buttocks. He laughed suddenly, wildly, thinking of his youth when teachers had meted out punishment to him. The big Swede was whimpering as he stumbled to his feet and began to run. Jay moved with him, swinging the stick and stopping only when Svenson had fled into the night.

He had let them off lightly but somehow the humiliation he had caused the Swede was more gratifying than the physical damage. Glancing at the Kessler cottage, he saw that the light had been doused. He wondered about going to them to tell them it was done – but was it? There was still the third man, the one who had refused to fight. Though winded by his clash with Svenson and Lucas, Jay started to run along the path, hoping he could still catch Gottlieb's third aggressor.

He was almost in the village when he realised who his quarry was – knew with complete certainty what had been familiar. The recognition both repelled and alarmed him as he made his way to the bar of the Grand. He had to know for sure.

The bar was crowded now but Jay paid no attention to the heads turning to see who had come in. It was only when he was inside that he became aware of the blood on his shirt.

Ignoring the curious glances, he studied the faces in the bar. The spot where Jacob Erasmus had been sitting was occupied by someone else.

'Jay! Jay! Over here in the corner!'

Jay peered through the layer of tobacco smoke. It was Jacob; he sat at a table with an older man. Jay elbowed his way through the crowd and stood beside the table. Jacob glanced at the bloodstains. 'What the hell happened to you?'

'I stepped on two dung beetles, that's all. A third got away.'

Jacob frowned. 'What are you talking about? I thought you'd gone to the Kesslers.'

'I did. That's where—'

'Jay,' said Jacob, 'sit down, for Christ's sake. Talk sense!

First Nick slinks off with some lame excuse, now you come in covered in blood. What the hell is—'

'Where's Nick?'

'I just told you, he – Jay! Where the hell are you off to now?' But Jay had gone.

The de Vries house was in darkness when Jay hammered on the door.

He knocked again, less violently this time, and the glow of a lamp appeared in a room at the side of the house.

Bull appeared at the door a moment later, his eyes thick with sleep, nightshirt hanging over hastily donned grey flannel trousers. 'Jay! I was wondering who . . . What's happened, boy?' he finished as he saw the blood on Jay's shirt. 'You been in a fight?'

'I'm sorry to wake you, Uncle Bull, but I have to talk. Something bad has happened.'

Bull opened the door. 'Come inside.' He put down the lamp on the kitchen table and frowned. 'What is it?'

Jay started telling him what had happened to Gottlieb Kessler, and of the fight with Svenson and Lucas. He was half-way through when first Sarah, then Magda appeared in the kitchen. Magda's hand flew to her mouth when she saw the blood on his shirt. 'Jay!' she said. 'You're hurt!'

'No, the blood's not mine.' He started to rise, wanting to go to her, to explain why he had to do what was to follow, but Bull's voice made him remain in his seat.

'Start from the beginning, Jay,' the older man said gruffly, glaring at the women for interrupting.

Jay repeated his tale. 'This is a terrible thing to have happened,' said Sarah, clutching her nightgown to her throat. 'The Kesslers are such good, kind people. Both of them.'

'Yes,' agreed Bull, 'but Jay has taken care of the swines. It won't happen again.' The look he gave the young man was one of pride.

'Uncle Bull,' he began, 'there – there were three men. The third didn't take part in the fight.'

'You know who it was?'

Jay moved his gaze from the fisherman and stared at Magda, his heart beating wildly in his chest. He was about to hurt her but what else could he do? Even if he handled it on his own and never told Bull, Magda would still hear about it. Perhaps it was better to speak to Bull himself. He turned back to the older man. 'Uncle Bull,' he said, 'I'm sorry . . . It was Nick. I recognised his limp.'

The older man's eyes were cold and hard. 'You are sure of this, Jay?'

Jay nodded, his eyes on Magda. Her gaze was lowered, focused on something only she could see. 'I'm not saying he was with them during the attack on Gottlieb though there were three men then, too.'

The big fisherman stared intently at his calloused hands. 'He's been swept up by this damn war,' he whispered. 'And he's been keeping wrong company.'

'I'm sorry,' said Jay. 'I had to tell you.'

Bull nodded. He glanced at his wife, then back at Jay. 'Where will he be now? At the Swede's house?'

'I think so.'

'Then let's find out. Wait here while I dress.'

'Pa? Please don't.' Magda moved in front of Bull, her hands reaching up to him. 'Nick is young. He probably regrets what happened. Let me talk to him. Please!'

'Hush, child,' said Bull, taking her hands in his. 'Nick was man enough to do what he did. He must be man enough to take his punishment.'

Sarah also laid a hand on her husband's shoulder. 'Let Jay handle it, Bull,' she pleaded. 'You'll kill Nick. Let Jay do it.'

Bull stood surrounded by his women. 'Nick is no longer a child,' he said stormily, 'and he is no longer my son.'

'Pa, no!' cried Magda. Jay's guts twisted at the agony in her voice and he kept his gaze fixed on the floor.

Pushing free, Bull moved back to him. 'In one thing they are right,' he said softly. 'I would kill Nick. I'll go with you, Jay, for I must witness his punishment. But perhaps it's fitting that you, as Gottlieb's skipper, deliver it.' He turned and went down the dark passage.

Sarah said, 'Don't be too harsh, Jay. For my sake,' and followed her husband.

When Jay looked up, Magda's eyes were on him. 'I'm sorry,' he said. 'I had to tell them. They would have learned of it anyway.'

She gave a violent shake of her head. 'No – not if you'd come to me instead. I could've spoken to Nick about it. I'm sure he—'

'Magda, I couldn't just leave it – Gottlieb is one of my men!'

'Nick is my brother.'

'I – I wish there'd been some other way.'

'There was, Jay, but you chose to be "the skipper" instead. You saw it as just another responsibility towards your men. What about me, Jay? What about your responsibility towards me?' The calm manner in which she spoke unnerved him more than if she had shouted at him.

Jay sighed. 'I'm sorry, it's too late now.'

'Yes. Don't hurt him badly, Jay. Do whatever you men need to restore your honour, to claim revenge, but no more than that.'

He nodded and mumbled, 'I promise,' as Magda left the room.

Bill smashed open the door to Svenson's cottage with his fist. He stepped inside with Jay behind him.

Lucas lay on a filthy cot. He covered his face with his hands when he saw who it was.

The Swede was in a chair, Nick on his knees beside him, a bloodstained cloth in his hands. He was busy rubbing it gently across the cuts on Svenson's face when he turned and saw his father. His expression made Jay wish he had been wrong.

Nick lowered his eyes as tears of shame sprang into them. 'I'm sorry,' he whispered hoarsely.

His father towered over him. 'Were you there?' he growled, his hands shaking at his sides. 'Were you there?' he asked again, his voice sounding almost gentle this time. 'The night Gottlieb was beaten?'

Nick did not answer. His hand, still holding the cloth, was

poised in the air as though about to administer further aid to the Swede.

'Answer me, boy!' shouted Bull. He seemed ready to leap at his son. Jay stepped closer.

Nick nodded and moved to his feet. 'Yes, I was there,' he said, turning to face his father. 'And I am ashamed, even though I did not strike a single blow.'

'Just being there and not stopping it is guilt enough,' replied Bull.

The young man flinched.

'Do it, Jay,' said Bull. 'Do your duty as a skipper.'

Jay stared at Nick. He shook his head and said, 'I think he's been punished enough, Uncle Bull. Gottlieb wouldn't want more and neither do I.'

'Do it, Jay!' Jay heard the pain in his voice.

Bull stepped up to his son. He raised his hand and held it motionless above his shoulder. Both the Swede and Lucas watched him.

'Uncle Bull . . . ' Jay pleaded, but made no move to stop him.

His hand came down slowly yet deliberately, a controlled force that seemed almost a caress as it struck his son's face. The sob that cracked from Bull melted with the sound of the impact. It was a slap, nothing more and nothing less, yet all the men knew it as a gesture of rejection. Bull de Vries had turned away his son. Jay felt rather than saw him rush out into the night.

'Go to your war, Nick,' said Jay, 'but don't come back to Brannigan Bay when it's over.' He glanced at Lucas and the Swede in turn. 'The same goes for you two,' he added.

'Jay! Talk to him . . . please! I was wrong and—'

'There's nothing I can tell him. There's nothing he wants to hear.' Jay shut the door quietly behind him as he went out into the night.

1916

July

At twenty, Magda was one of the few of her peers left unmarried. She knew that if it was not for the war and the accompanying shortage of men, she might have been the only one. Those who were still single baked, made clothes or helped their families. A few, like Christine, the girl who had partnered Preston Whitehead at that Christmas Eve dance, were occupied by soldiers and sailors sent to Brannigan Bay to recuperate from their war wounds. The woman's services sometimes went beyond the medical.

Though Magda, too, occasionally helped at the Red Cross centre, most of her spare time was spent drawing. She had sold fourteen to visitors over the past year. Her principal success had been a picture of a soldier resting in the shade of a tree in the French countryside. Although she had only seen a few photographs of France and its battlefields, usually in newspapers brought to the village from Cape Town, she had captured every nuance of the mood of an exhausted soldier demoralised by war. The man in the sketch – his face, its faraway expression – was her brother.

She had received just two letters from Nick since he had left Brannigan Bay. Behind the words written in a childlike scrawl she could sense his pain, his loneliness and fear, and the disillusioning reality of war. It hurt her that the letters had to be addressed to one of her girlfriends instead of to his home, and that her mother, who knew of their correspondence, refused to read them out of respect for her husband's stand. She would betray Bull if she read Nick's letters, Sarah had said.

Remembering that, Magda curbed her frustration and walked back to the sand dune where she had left her paper and charcoal among the hardy scrubs.

It was a long trek from the village to the section of beach she had chosen and Magda had left her parents' cottage shortly after daybreak. The winter morning had been cool then but now the sun was stronger, making it comfortably warm on the beach. It was her second successive day there, and her picture was almost complete.

'There's something missing,' she said aloud, talking to herself as she often did when drawing. She studied what she had done. There were the sea, the sand, the surf curling gently onto the beach, forcing aside the early-morning mist clinging to the shore. The rugged grasses on the sand dunes had captured the movement of the morning breeze.

Staring at it she thought, It's empty. It reflected her emotions. She reminded herself that that was how it should be – that, years later, when one gazed at a picture it should hold the spontaneity of the moment of its creation. It should carry back the artist or observer to whatever emotion dominated its birth. Would she want to be reminded of that? she wondered.

Magda reached resolutely for her charcoal. Boats, she decided, visualising a set of white sails beneath the clouds on the horizon. 'Too obvious,' she muttered. She decided it needed people . . . at a picnic. A chequered cloth spread on the sand, a basket of food, children playing in the shallows with a ball, their mother keeping a wary eye on them, a light breeze ruffling the edge of her dress.

Lowering her charcoal, she stared intently at the sketch again. 'It won't work,' she sighed. 'What it needs is . . . ' She stopped, narrowing her eyes to focus on the lone figure strolling near the surf about three hundred yards away.

She saw it was a soldier – No, an airman, she decided as she noticed the blue uniform. He walked stiffly, and Magda guessed he had come to the village to recover from wounds. Perhaps it was someone she had met at the Red Cross station, though she couldn't recall seeing any airmen there.

He was too far away for her to identify, but she could see that he was staring out to sea. Perhaps, thought Magda, her romantic instincts aroused by the sight of the slim figure, he was thinking about his comrades engaged in battle while he rested. It was just what she wanted, she decided. 'Don't walk too fast,' she muttered, glancing back at the man.

Her charcoal moved rapidly as she tried to capture his exact position and stance before he moved on. 'Stay there, please stay there,' she pleaded as he moved closer.

Her gaze flicked from the paper to her subject. She already had him in position and she studied his uniform for detail. Not too much, though; she had to keep the intrigue, the air of mystery. And the face? Should she make one up or use the young man's? It wouldn't really matter; she had kept his original position in perspective, too far away for a clear view of his features.

He would soon be close enough for her to see. He had spotted her too and seemed to be coming straight for her. Magda lowered her charcoal – she had put down enough to finish later – and wondered how the young man would react when he saw it. Perhaps she should ask him what he had been thinking about while he contemplated the sea.

She glanced back as she started to put away her things. His air corps cap was perched at a jaunty angle on his head and he removed his hands from his pockets as he made his way awkwardly up the dune.

'Hello,' he called out.

Recognition was instant when she faced him. Her heart leaped, then pounded furiously – painfully almost. She no longer had any need to be concerned about his face; she could draw Preston Whitehead with absolute clarity even if she never saw him again.

He had stopped a few paces away, his expression a mixture of surprise and joy. 'Magda, it's really you!' A smile spread slowly across his face as he slipped the cap from his head into his hand. He took a step closer and stopped again. She could hear the exertion of the climb in his heavy breathing.

'The subject of an artist,' he said with a gay laugh. 'I'd had another relationship in mind with you.'

His words made her blush and she turned away from him and continued packing things away. She heard him move in behind her to study the sketch.

'It's beautiful,' he said after a moment. 'You have talent, Magda.'

'It – it's not finished. I've no real training . . . just some books and—'

'You don't need training,' he interrupted. 'This comes from the soul. One cannot train that.' His gaze had moved to her face and she could no longer avoid his eyes when she straightened.

'I've thought of you often,' he continued, his voice low, 'ever since that night I learned you were Jay's. Sometimes, when I'm frightened or tired of the fighting, I need to think of gentle, beautiful things. That's when—'

'Preston, please!'

'I can't help it, Magda. I can't help this feeling I've had for you ever since we met. I can't deny it – I don't want to.'

She stared back at him, trying to fight her confusion.

'Did you ever think of me?'

Had she? Yes, but she had suppressed such thoughts whenever they arose. 'I think of all those I know, all those who went to war.'

'But you didn't know I had. Or did you?'

She had not – not for sure. Yet she had visualised him in uniform. 'No,' she said now, shaking her head. 'One just supposes . . . '

His smile seemed smug and a triumphant note surfaced in his voice when he said, 'So, you thought of me anyway!'

He's so cocky, thought Magda. I shouldn't even like him, let alone . . . What was it she felt towards him? She had never allowed herself to dwell on him for long so had never analysed the response he triggered in her whenever an image of him pierced the protective wall she raised against him. It was there, though, a warm fluttering excitement that threatened and shamed her, for she knew its extent and power.

'You're an airman,' she said to change the subject, her voice suddenly nervous.

'Yes. A pilot in the Royal Flying Corps. In France.'

'France,' she echoed. To her the word was synonymous with war, with scared and dying young men. With Nick.

'I was wounded three months ago,' he was saying.

'Does that make you a hero?'

Preston threw back his head and laughed, momentarily lightening the tension between them.

'No, I'm no hero!' He laughed again before adding, 'In fact, I was trying to make it back to base, scared out of my wits, when this German came roaring out of the clouds and opened up on my Camel.'

'Your what?' She knew she was gaping at him like a little girl but she was caught up in a vision of Preston in his plane, trying to dodge a much larger, menacing machine, spurts of ugly orange flame flicking from its guns.

'My Sopwith Camel, the plane I fly.'

'What happened?'

He smiled, his eyes teasing her. 'You want all the gory details?'

'No! I just—'

'I was hit, here, here and here.' He pointed his finger at his ribs.

'Did you crash?'

His amusement still showed on his lips. 'No, I think the German ran out of ammunition because he scooted off and I was able to limp home. It was a bloody close thing, that I can tell you!

'What happened then? Did they rush you to hospital?'

'I went to hospital for a month.'

'Did it hurt?'

'Magda, it's starting to hurt right now from all these questions.' He lowered himself awkwardly to the sand.

'You'll ruin your tunic,' she said, sitting down opposite him. 'I'm curious – I've never met a shot-down airman before.' It was easier just to banter with him.

'It hurt,' he told her, twirling his cap in his hands. 'I wasn't fit to fly when I was released from hospital and I was given three months' leave of recovery back in South Africa. I rather think my father had a hand in that, though. He has connections with one of the ministries – can't say I'm not grateful. At least I've seen you again.'

His words made her lower her gaze. 'When did you get to Brannigan Bay?' she asked softly.

'Two days ago, with my father. We're staying at the Crystal Lodge.'

'When – till when are you staying?' He had been here two days already.

'We're leaving tomorrow. I'm catching a ship to England the next day. I'll be fit to fly when I get back.'

'You'll fly again? After what happened?' She failed to prevent a note of alarm from springing into her voice.

'Of course! I was one of the lucky ones, Magda. I've been feeling guilty about having a holiday while others carry on with the fight.'

'Was that what you were thinking about out there? While you were walking?'

'Yes.'

She felt a fleeting satisfaction at having been right. 'It's strange,' she said and smiled shyly, 'I had a feeling about that while I was sketching you.'

'That's because what's between us is special . . . We sense things about each other.'

'What do you sense about me?' She realised she had not denied what he had just said.

'I sense you're pleased to see me but you're determined to hide it. Because it worries you.'

She flicked back her long hair with her hand. 'You're very sure of yourself, aren't you?'

'Only about you . . . because we're special, remember?'

An awkward silence ensued between them for a few moments. Preston played with his cap while Magda strained sand through her fingers. She still did not look at him until his hand gripped hers and opened the palm so that the last grains of sand stuck to the sweat on her skin. 'Not married yet, I see,' he said, gently releasing her hand.

'No.'

'Is Jay away? In the army – no, it would be the navy for him, I'm sure.'

'Jay has stayed here. His mother, you see, there's no one else to care for her.'

'You needn't make excuses for him. Not everyone is dumb enough to want to go to war. I didn't go for any patriotic

68

reason, merely for the adventure and what I thought would be glamour. Jay is more level-headed than that.'

'I wasn't defending him! I just—'

'That's what it sounded like.'

She stood up and picked up her drawing equipment. Had she been defensive? She had never queried Jay's decision not to volunteer – in fact, she was bitterly opposed to the war as too many young men were being killed or wounded. Perhaps her response had been prompted by what happened to Preston. She was wrong to compare the two men.

She heard the rustle of his tunic. Suddenly he was standing close behind her, his hands resting lightly on her shoulders. 'What will you do with your drawing?' he asked. The warmth of his breath on the bare flesh of her neck where she had pushed aside her hair sent a shiver down her back.

'Sell it.' Her voice sounded thin.

'Don't,' he said. 'But if you have to, sell it to me. Not that I need a drawing to remind me of you.'

'Why should you want to remember a simple village girl?'

'I've already told you, I think of you when I'm frightened. No, that's not quite true . . . I think of you often, at the strangest moments.'

'And that's why you've been in Brannigan Bay for two days already, yet we meet by chance?'

'Aha! So you *do* care!'

'No! I'm just trying to—'

'Magda, oh, Magda! I don't know what it is about you.' He slipped his arms around her, moving them down across her breasts to encircle her waist, pulling her in to him.

'No!'

'Yes! Stop fighting it! Stop running away from me, Magda.' She tried to pull free but he held her to him tightly. His hand slid downwards and cupped her where it was hot. She felt him against her buttocks, hard and urgent.

'Preston, no!' It was a whisper this time, an appeal that melted in the rush of her breath.

He held her without force, not pushing her, his lips moist and warm against her neck. Yet she did not pull free. Her legs, so near collapse a few moments ago, gave way and she leaned into his caress. Her entire being seemed one rush of heat. She thought, I am melting, melting.

He turned her in the circle of his arms. When he kissed her, it was with passion yet without abandon. It was gentle, and when his hands gripped her buttocks and pulled her into him, she responded with her own pressure and smothered cry of want.

Thoughts flashed through her reeling mind, trying to control her surrender. She wouldn't do this with Jay. She would have stopped it.

She felt sand beneath her knees. They were facing each other, their mouths locked together. His hands were on her thighs now, caressing her smooth skin as they moved upwards.

'Oh, God, Magda, you're so beautiful.' His ragged breaths blended with her gasps. He began taking off his jacket.

'Preston, we—'

'I leave tomorrow, Magda. Don't let me go . . . don't let me face the fear without the memory of this.'

A blurred image flickered through her mind as he pushed her back onto the jacket. Was it Jay? Or the fear that someone might come along the deserted beach and walk across that sand dune? Oh, God, she had already accepted what was about to happen.

She felt the weight of her skirt move higher up her legs. Sun touched her thighs. She was being lifted, her pants sliding down her legs. Yet she could not stop him when he touched her. Whatever she had tried to say became a sharp intake of breath that changed into a broken sigh. Oh, yes!

She opened her eyes to stare at him, then reached out, touched him, held him, instinctively knowing just how to guide him into her.

She took him inside her with only a short-lived moment of pain. Then her cries were like the contented mew of a kitten that twisted and turned under his stroking.

Beside them, the breeze whistled its own melody as it rustled the long coarse grass concealing the place where they lay.

*

Sarah was irritable when Magda came in through the kitchen door, 'Where've you been all this time, child?'

'Out drawing. I told you I was going, Ma.' She busied herself with putting away her drawing things, certain that her mother could tell from the flush on her face what had happened. Her body seemed to glow through her clothes. Everything glowed and throbbed deliciously – her body, her heart, her soul. If only she could feel shame or regret! Had one man, one half-hour, really made her so wicked? And she *was* wicked to feel so good, to want to laugh and sing. It was shameful to have lain with a man she hardly knew and was not sure she loved, to want more of him and anticipate the delight of the next time. It was immoral of her to long for the moment when it would happen again and she could strip off her clothes and feel his flesh against hers.

'I know very well what you told me,' snapped her mother, 'but Pa walked down to the beach to search for you and you weren't there.'

Her father? They could have been discovered!

'I – I was resting on a dune,' she said. 'Why did Pa want me?'

'Jay needed you, that's why,' replied Sarah tartly.

'Jay? Is something wrong?'

'He's upset. He's had some bad news and he wanted to have you with him, that's all. I was ashamed to say we didn't know where you were. You young people don't think—'

'What news, Ma? What's happened?'

'Don't interrupt me, child!' Sarah sniffed before she continued, saying, 'Jacob Erasmus is dead. He was Jay's closest friend.'

'Jacob? Dead?'

'In the war. At some place called Dellville Wood.'

'I'll go to Jay now. Is he at home?'

'He's with the Erasmus family, comforting them. He's a good man – something you don't seem to appreciate.'

Though the Erasmus cottage was only a few hundred yards away, Magda walked slowly, sadness replacing her earlier ecstasy. Jacob . . . She had liked him. He was funny, yet gentle. She could imagine Jay's grief. While he had needed her, she had been fornicating – no, fucking, she had heard it

71

called – with a near-stranger on the dunes, like a cat on heat, thrashing and groaning on the sand, wet and hot and sticky, clawing at the source of her pleasure. She was no better than Christine.

Jay came out to meet her when she entered the small unkempt garden of the Erasmus place. His face was grave. 'You've heard?' he asked.

'Yes. Jay, I – I'm very sorry.'

As she spoke she wondered whether she was offering sympathy for what had happened to Jacob or apologising for the thing Jay did not know about.

In the lounge of the Crystal Lodge, Kevin Whitehead glanced up from the book he was reading to stare at the tall shape of his son. 'You don't want to be overdoing your exercise now,' he said at the sight of Preston's flushed face. 'There'll be time for that before you get back.'

'It was just a short walk,' he replied lamely, seating himself beside his father.

'Still, those wounds of yours are a long way from healed.' He studied his son's face while the young man fiddled nervously with his cap. The war had caused him to lose his boyish looks, thought Kevin, but it suited him. When it was over Preston would be ready to take up his true role within Whitehead Enterprises. Perhaps his new maturity would bring with it the necessary patience: Preston's restlessness had always concerned him.

Kevin Whitehead remembered vividly their last bitter argument, just a few months before the outbreak of war when his son had returned from visiting Brannigan Bay with some wild idea of building a harbour there. Preston had been unwilling to accept his excuse of lack of capital or the knowledge that war was inevitable with an unpredictable effect on fish prices. Neither had Kevin been prepared to tell him the truth, which was that he regarded the idea as impractical and unnecessary. The atmosphere between father and son, which had never been relaxed or close, had been even more strained than usual for some time afterwards.

The outbreak of hostilities and Preston's announcement that he wished to volunteer had brought them closer again. Though concerned for his son's welfare, Kevin had not stood in his way, and had immediately contacted long-standing influential friends in England.

'Father?'

'What? Sorry, I was daydreaming.'

Preston flung his cap onto a nearby table. 'You were staring at me as if you were seeing me for the first time.'

'Perhaps I was,' Kevin admitted. 'I was thinking, too, of what you plan to do once the war's over. You still interested in the business?'

Preston nodded. 'I've never wanted anything else,' he said softly. He seemed about to say more but grinned instead and patted his father's knee. 'Think I'll rest for a while.'

'Good idea. I'll call you at lunch-time.'

After watching Preston make his way awkwardly up the flight of stairs leading to his room, Kevin reached for his book again. But the words would not focus and his mind tried instead to gain a grasp on the future. How long did he have? The doctor had said if he took it slow, stopped smoking his beloved cigars and eased himself out of the business, there was no reason his heart should not last for many years. To hell with that, he thought with uncharacteristic anger; he would not give up the business. He had built it up himself and it was Preston's inheritance. Just a few more years, that was all, enough time to be sure Preston was ready.

He sighed and tried again to concentrate on his book, wishing that the war would end.

Preston sat on the bed in his room, the same one he had occupied on his first visit to Brannigan Bay. He slowly unbuttoned his tunic while he stared at the drawing Magda had given him.

The events of the past hour seemed branded on his senses. The way his body tingled, the smell of her lingering on his lips, the fragrance of their lovemaking – every touch, look, sound spun continuously through his mind, as vivid as if they were only now taking place. Had it really happened?

Yes it *had*. It was as real as the emptiness of the life that awaited him when he left Brannigan Bay next day. All he had to carry him through the long days and nights, the fear and the longing, was the memory of what they had had. That – and the promise of what they might become.

He had not spoken to Magda of the future. The time had not been right; he had sensed her confusion when their love-making was over and had known he would spoil it with words. So he had let her leave him, knowing that the only thing which separated them was distance and time.

As he took off the rest of his clothes he promised himself that he would overcome both.

September

From her room Magda could hear the sounds of her mother working in the kitchen. Never before had she identified the noises so clearly, each sound seeming to strike a visual chord in her mind: the echo of the pot's lid as it was closed; the light scrape as her mother shifted it onto the Aga.

It was as if she had been away from home for a long time and now recalled nostalgically those things taken for granted when life was secure.

It was not nostalgia that filled Magda's mind today and neither was it a moment for recall. It was the disquieting cold knot lying in her stomach that heightened her senses. Her security had been cut from under her like wheat falling beneath a sharp scythe.

She shuddered as she stood up and moved towards the open door. She stopped and turned, as she had done twice already. Sinking onto the bed with her head in her hands, Magda bit back the tears that threatened. There had been enough tears, she told herself, thinking of the many nights when she had pushed her face into her pillow, sobbing in silent, lonely despair. It was time for talking – but therein lay her biggest fear.

It was wrong for a girl to fear her mother. Yet was it fear she felt for Sarah or a hesitancy to face her scorn when what Magda needed was support and understanding? Since she had become a woman, Magda had realised that she and her mother were two very different people with little in common.

She contemplated talking to her father instead; Bull would at least listen and try to understand. But that would only worsen things between her and her mother.

At last she pushed herself from the bed, knowing she would have to approach Sarah first. She hesitated again as she went through the bedroom door, then firmed her resolve and walked slowly down the passage. The kitchen sounds seemed oppressive now.

Magda stood at the entrance and watched her mother for a few moments. 'Ma,' she said softly, but Sarah did not hear. She was bent over, poking at something in the oven.

'Ma,' she called again, louder this time. 'I need to talk to you.'

Her mother slowly raised her head. 'What have you been doing all morning? I've needed your help.' Sarah busied herself with the pots, her back to her daughter.

Magda fought down the urge to turn and run away. 'We must talk, Ma. It's important.' This time Sarah glanced at her before wiping her hands on a cloth hanging on a hook behind the door.

'What is it? You're very pale these days.' She reached out and laid her hand lightly against Magda's brow. 'Are you sick?'

'No, Ma,' she replied, sitting down. 'Not sick. Can we have coffee?'

Sarah frowned but she poured two cups of black coffee, placing them on the table and pulling out a chair for herself. Neither woman took sugar, yet both stirred vigorously at the strong brew. The rattle of teaspoons filled the tiny kitchen.

Magda took a sip, then wiped her lips and stared at her mother. How to start . . . how to explain . . .

'Ma, I'm expecting a baby,' she blurted out, heart hammering. She had an urge to laugh hysterically at the bluntness of the announcement and the memory of how she had rehearsed what she would say.

Her mother's mouth hardened a little before she said, 'Jay's?'

Magda shook her head slowly, the cup clattering in its saucer. She pulled back her hand and held it on her lap.

'Whose?' Her mother's voice sounded dispassionate. Magda had expected rage, shame, scorn, anything but the quiet response of the woman sitting across from her, as if this were something awkward and unwanted that unfortunately happened now and then.

'Ma, it doesn't matter who the father is. I can't marry him, that's all.'

Sarah was silent for a moment. Then she said, 'It's that young one from Cape Town. You've seen him again, haven't you? I knew he had the devil in him.'

'Ma, I am as much to blame for this.'

'Did he force you?'

Magda shook her head.

Her mother's sigh was long and heavy. 'We must all bear the blame,' she said, rubbing a hand across her face. 'One thinks one knows one's children but . . . ' She sighed again, said, 'First Nick, now you. How could you do this to Jay? He loves you, respects you – but now?'

'He doesn't know yet.'

'And the father – that rich boy?'

'No! He must *never* learn of it!'

'We can force him to marry you, Magda. At least it will save us all shame.'

'No, Ma. I can't. He's not even here, he's somewhere in France, a pilot.'

'Oh, this war,' said Sarah bitterly. 'It brings out the worst in people.'

'What will I do, Ma? Must I leave Brannigan Bay?' The fear in Magda's voice added to her sudden panic and a tear rolled down each cheek.

The unexpected grip on her hand was strong. She stared down at her mother's hand and curled her fingers round flesh hardened by a lifetime of washing and housework and returned the pressure. It was the first time in years that they had touched like that.

'We'll see,' said Sarah. 'We'll talk to your pa – he'll know what to do.'

Bull sucked his pipe and thought of his daughter waiting in her room.

He wished Jay was the father; it would have ended Magda's senseless dilly-dallying about marrying him. If she had done so when Jay had last asked her none of this would have happened. Tucking the pipe into his shirt pocket, he went into the cottage.

Bull was glad he had brought in his boat – piled high with a good catch – early that afternoon. Sarah glanced at him as he passed through the kitchen but made no comment.

The door to Magda's room was closed when he stopped outside. He knocked once. The voice that answered sounded small and childlike.

She sat on the edge of the bed gazing miserably out of the window but turned when he entered the room and shut the door softly behind him.

He smiled, touched her hair and said, 'So, your ma tells me you're determined to make grandparents of us.' He chuckled, but it did not sound right to his ears; it was more like a crackle of sadness.

'Oh, Pa, I'm sorry.' She moved into his arms.

They sat side by side, Bull staring out of the window, watching the last flush of Namaqualand daisies swaying in the September wind. He did not know what to say to comfort her so he let the strength of his arms do it for her.

At last she raised her head and said, 'Have I shamed you, Pa?'

Bull smiled at her again. 'No, my love, that you cannot do.' He hugged her to him.

After a while he said, 'What they call shame is a strange thing. Sometimes what we think of as shame is something else. Bruised pride, for instance, or hurt. When someone shows that, others might see it as shame or scorn. It's easy to confuse the two.'

Magda pulled away from him. 'What are you trying to say, Pa?'

'A young man, one who loves you, is bound to feel pain that will burst from him in rage. You might feel he's ashamed of you. It will hurt you, as you have hurt him, but you must try to understand.'

'Jay?'

'Yes. You're the one who must tell him.'

'How do I explain my betrayal?'

'Betrayal?' Bull gave her a sidelong glance. 'If you have betrayed anyone, Magda, then it's yourself. Don't feel guilt as well – you'll have enough of a burden in time to come.'

'The child – what must I do?'

Bull stood up and moved to the open window. The wind is wet, he thought as he sniffed the air. It will bring rain. Seating himself beside her again, he said, 'The father . . . '

Magda shook her head. 'Did Ma tell you he's at war?'

'Yes.'

'He must never know, Pa. Promise me that if he ever returns to Brannigan Bay you won't—'

'I won't lay a hand on him, Magda. I promise.'

She gazed at him with bewildered eyes. 'Must I go away, Pa?'

Bull stared at the daisies and thought deeply. He had already lost one child; he could not bear to lose Magda as well. 'No,' he said at last. 'You'll stay here with us – whatever you decide to do about the child.'

'Everyone in the village will know.'

'They'll know anyway – they always do when a girl leaves the village and returns a few months later. But together we can face that.'

Magda moved into his arms again.

'Do you want to keep the baby?' asked Bull.

'Would it be wrong to give it up?'

'I don't know, child. Let's think on it awhile.' He curled a lock of her hair between his fingers and said, 'Go to Jay now and tell him. And remember what I told you about hurt pride.' He saw the apprehension in her eyes and added, 'Yes, it won't be easy.'

She was wiping away her tears when he stood up and left the room.

Jay stared at his hands. A thumbnail had cracked. Where had that happened? Probably on the boat.

Magda's voice sounded as though she was speaking from behind a mask, as if her words were being muffled to soften the messages they contained.

He felt no pain when he squeezed the cracked nail. It was numb, just like the rest of him. Frighteningly numb. The calm before the storm, the false flat of the sea before the north-westerly came screaming in.

He heard her talking but could make no sense of what she was saying.

'Jay? Are you listening to me?'

His head jerked up, his eyes straining to focus on her red eyes, her tearstained face, the turmoil etched there. It was all on her face, the face he had loved, which another had kissed and caressed and . . . *no*!

He pushed himself from the harbour wall and moved a few paces away. The saltiness of the wind blowing up from the sea stung his eyes.

'Say something, Jay! Say you hate and despise me – anything! Just say *something*!'

The numbness was threatened now by a ball of rage moving rapidly through him. 'Go,' he said thickly. 'Go away from me.'

'Jay, I—'

'Go!' Sudden feeling coursed through him, torment and revulsion blending in a dangerous cradle of molten anger. 'Take your bastard child, you dune whore,' he spat out, his voice so thick with rage the words sounded slurred. 'Take it and go!'

She was a frail figure, shoulders slumped, a lost child with auburn hair moving in the wind. Jay had never seen her look so beautiful. He was caught between striking out at her, ruining the beauty that had trapped him and another man, and rushing to her to pull her tightly to him. He wanted to protect her, to keep her safe from the force to which she had succumbed.

'Go,' he said again. It sounded like a plea as he pushed past her, controlling the urge to run towards the harbour path.

The harbour was still busy, though it was more than an hour since the last boat had come in. People milled about, buying fish that had not been sold to the trucks heading for markets in Cape Town and surrounding villages. Fishermen packed their gear into the huts lining the restraining wall of the harbour, boys helped their fathers clean out boats. There was conversation and laughter, the everyday sounds of people going about their lives. Someone called out to him but he walked on.

Three small dinghies were lying in the corner of the harbour, community property for use by anyone who wanted to row out and fish close inshore. Jay grabbed the nearest and pulled it single-handedly into the water. The late afternoon wind had whipped up the swells, rolling them into the harbour so that the dinghy took in water before Jay had his oars in position. He steadied the small craft, planted his feet wide apart and leaned into his task.

Rowing furiously for the harbour entrance, he kept his head turned to watch the swells. Once, when he glanced back, he saw Magda standing at the wall high above the harbour, watching him.

He kept up his pace even when he was beyond the cliffs, rowing in a punishing rhythm that strained his back and arm muscles. It helped, counterbalancing the pain that throbbed in his heart.

It was only later, when he was some distance out into the bay and could look back at the harbour where people had turned into unidentifiable shapes, that he allowed the pain inside to escape. It burst from him in a roar of anguish, was plucked away and smothered by the wind. Dry sobs jerked him like the sea tossing the dinghy.

When the exorcism was over, Jay saw it for the self-pity it was. He took control of the dinghy, turned it, and began to row back to the harbour. To Magda.

He would go to her now, tell her how sorry he was that he had added to her pain. He would tell her that she could depend on him, that he would help in whatever way he could, expecting nothing in return.

Rain started to fall in a light drizzle from the north-west as he neared the cliffs. His muscles ached, for nothing remained inside him to counter the physical pain.

Only one person stood in the harbour as Jay steadied the dinghy across a swell, waiting for the right one to carry him in. Even then, concentrating on the run of the sea, he recognised Bull's bulky form. He stood at the bottom of the shelf near the water's edge.

Jay heard him yell, 'Now!' just as he saw the swell curving round the edge of the cliffs. He leaned forward, dipped his oars and rowed. The dinghy sped in on the surf.

He jumped out when the craft hit the shallows, knowing it had neither the weight nor the strength of build to stand being washed up onto the harbour shelf. Bull stood ready to help him.

The big man gripped the bow as Jay pushed at the stern, trying to lift it from the water. He remembered how easily he had handled the boat in the grip of his anger. Together they hauled the dinghy to its resting place. Jay was out of breath when he stepped back and said, 'Thanks, Uncle Bull.'

Magda's father grunted, pushed his hands deep inside the pockets of his corduroys, then strolled towards the drying racks on the rocks near the sea. Rain sparkled in his thick bush of hair.

Jay followed, knowing the older man wanted to talk to him. He stopped beside him and said, 'Magda has told me. I'm sorry, Uncle Bull, I feel I'm somehow partly to blame. If only I'd insisted she marry me the last time, this—'

'As much as I love you,' interjected Bull, his gaze glued on the sea, 'I'll kill you if you call my daughter a whore again. Never use that word on Magda. Don't even think it in your private thoughts.'

Jay lowered his eyes although the older man was not facing him. 'She told you,' he said lamely.

'Yes. I tried to warn her how you'd feel.'

'I wanted to kill myself for it a while ago when I was out there.' He pointed with his chin towards the sea. 'I'll make my peace with her and pray she can forgive me.'

They stood silent side by side. After a while Jay said, 'What can I do to help?'

Bull wiped the rain from his face. 'Do you still love her, Jay? Despite what has happened?'

'Yes,' came the soft reply.

'Then come with me.'

Bull and Sarah waited patiently in the kitchen. 'More coffee, please,' said Bull, eyeing the old clock ticking loudly on the oak sideboard. 'How long does it take for two people to apologise?' he muttered.

Sarah placed a full cup of coffee in front of him just as Jay and Magda entered the room. Both wore sheepish expressions.

'Sit,' grunted Bull.

He waited until everyone was seated, took a gulp of coffee, leaned his forearms on the table and said, 'There are a few options open to us. The first concerns the child. If Magda decides to keep it, she must face all the consequences that go with it. If she gives it up, she can start again. Our second choice,' he added and turned towards Jay, 'is that she marry you right away.'

He watched Jay and Magda glance at each other and then at him. Magda said, 'I can't expect Jay to marry me now.'

Bull jutted out his jaw. 'He's said he still loves you. Do you love him?'

Magda hesitated, glanced at Jay. 'In some ways, yes, but—'

'Then you will learn the rest with time.'

'Jay can't be expected to accept another man's child.'

Bull scratched his ear; the suggestion he had in mind was not an easy one to make. 'You'll go to Caledon or even Cape Town to have the child. You'll give it up for adoption and we'll say it died at birth.'

'Bull!' It was the first time Sarah spoke.

Bull nodded. 'Yes,' he said, 'it's not right, but it will just be a lie.'

It was Magda who broke the lengthy silence that followed Bull's proposal. 'If I give up the child, Pa, there must be a further condition – one of *my* making.'

'What?' Bull felt exhausted; he was unaccustomed to playing with the futures of others. 'What?' he asked again.

'The child must be given to someone here in Brannigan Bay.'

'Here? Where you'll watch it grow, where it'll be a constant reminder to you?'

'It'd mean so much to me, just knowing where the child is and how it's doing. If it's happy, then it will help me to be happy with Jay.'

Her words made Jay jerk in his chair. 'Everyone would know,' he argued. 'The whole village would point at the child and say, "There goes Magda's little bastard." Have you thought of that? Whoever took the child would have to know the truth.'

There was a determined gleam in Magda's eyes when she turned to him. 'Pa's already suggested I go away to have the baby and that we say it died. I can stay away for a few weeks, supposedly recuperating from the loss. And yes,' she added, 'the parents will know the truth. But the people I have in mind can be trusted to keep our secret.'

Bull leaned forward. 'Who?'

'Gottlieb and Gertrude Kessler.'

Jay looked up in surprise.

'They're desperate for a baby, and they're good people. The child will have a fine home with them.'

'Magda is right,' said Bull. 'The Kesslers are a wise choice.' He saw his chance to finalise the matter. 'And you, Jay,' he asked, 'will you be married to Magda and accept that?'

Jay tapped the table top with his finger. He looked at Magda and said, 'Yes.'

Bull leaned back, folding his arms across his chest in a satisfied gesture. 'I'll talk to Gottlieb,' he said. 'This thing is my responsibility.' He saw the expression on Jay's face, smiled and added, 'This goes beyond you and one of your crew, my boy.' He was relieved when Jay returned his smile.

'Right!' continued Bull, slapping his open palm gently on the table. 'There's much to be considered before I visit Gottlieb. Why don't the two of you go outside and talk? Come back when you've made a final decision.'

He waited until Magda and Jay had closed the kitchen door behind them before he turned to Sarah. 'Wife,' he said with a long sigh, 'another cup of coffee, please – and make it strong.'

He slumped across the table. 'Answer me truthfully, Sarah. Did I do right?'

Sarah smiled. 'I think you did well, Bull de Vries, but time will tell.'

1917

The child, a boy, was born on 28 April, the same day that three
more young men from Brannigan Bay died on the battlefield.
Magda heard about the deaths two hours after they had taken
away the baby and given it to the Kesslers. She cried – for the
dead and for her baby.

She spent nearly a month at the simple cottage of an
aunt in Hout Bay near Cape Town. She had not seen the
woman for years and disapproval showed constantly on her
stern face. Magda knew it had not been easy for her father to
ask the favour. She reminded herself, too, of the lie she would
have to live, for already her parents would have spread word
that her child had died.

She was relieved when Jay came to fetch her; she wanted
to get back to Brannigan Bay and had missed him. He is a
good man, she thought, watching his strong hands on the
reins of the buggy he had borrowed to collect her. She knew
he must love her deeply to have married her and swore she
would never again betray that love. Her silent oath reminded
her of their love-making before her pregnancy had become
too advanced for it. They had been nervous with each other,
tense, the spectre of the other man hovering between them.
Magda vowed that that, too, would improve. With time they
would make it so.

Jay was cheerful along the journey, purposely so, Magda
thought, yet she found herself laughing with him, enjoying
the rugged strength that would be her protection in future.
It helped to take her mind off Preston Whitehead. She was
determined she would somehow force him from her conscious-
ness. She would never forget him – that was too much to

expect – but she could not allow him again to come between her and Jay.

It was only when they approached the outskirts of Brannigan Bay, after spending the night at the Houw Hoek Inn, that Magda thought of the lie that would pervade her life from now. She could visualise the women in the village, the compassion in their eyes, the murmured sympathies.

'There will be other children,' she would answer them. That would be the best response and would, at least, be the truth. She and Jay would have children of their own. Soon.

Yet as they drove into the village she could not stop herself from asking, 'What have they named him?'

Jay glanced at her, then returned his gaze to the horses. 'Wilhelm,' he said softly.

'It's a lovely name,' she said.

'It's also a German name,' replied Jay with a laugh. 'You should see Gottlieb – he's a useless fisherman now – can't wait to get home in the afternoons!' He chuckled and the sound so pleased Magda that she joined in.

Shifting closer to him, she laid her head on his shoulder and said, 'It's good to be back, Jay. It's good to be back with you.'

He smiled, flicked the whip, and the buggy clattered down the rocky main street of Brannigan Bay.

1918

The news, when it came, flashed through the country as though it was something unexpected. The past few months of speculation were forgotten as relief exploded into enthusiastic jubilation in every city, town and village.

It was 12 November 1918: the armistice had been signed and the Great War was over.

In the cities, thousands upon thousands of people flooded into the streets, giving full vent to their joy as they greeted and hugged complete strangers. Fireworks exploded overhead, trams blew their whistles, people sang, waved hastily made banners and cluttered the streets with piles of streamers and assorted bunting. They were happy, thankful, content – yet many lamented its coming too late to spare loved ones.

In Brannigan Bay the postmaster, who had two sons fighting in Europe, was the first to receive the news. He was a short, slight man with feet out of proportion to the rest of his body. He came hurtling out into Main Street, his number eleven shoes slapping up dust as he ran first in one direction, skidded to a halt, spun round hysterically, then started off in another.

The first people who came to investigate the cause of the shouting saw only shoes and dust, yet they understood his screams of delight.

'It's over! It's over! It's over!' the little man shouted at the top of his high-pitched voice, tripped over his feet and lay sprawled on the gravel. He squirmed, kicked, yelled and laughed and a passer-by, thinking the poor man was suffering a fit, ran to summon Aunt Agnes, well known for her herbal remedies.

The postmaster had himself almost under control and was

weeping soundlessly by the time most of the town's population had gathered in the street. They milled about in delirious confusion, kissed, laughed and cried. One fisherman was not so overjoyed by the news to miss seeing another kiss his wife more than once, using the opportunity to grasp her firmly by the buttocks. A vicious brawl ensued but was quickly brought under control.

A boy was despatched to call the fishermen who had already returned to harbour. He tore down the street, building up a good sweat in the afternoon heat. It took a while before the men could get some sense out of him but when they did they abandoned their catches and headed for town.

Magda spotted Jay as she came out of their cottage to investigate the commotion. 'What's going on?' she asked. 'Why all the shouting?' Sarah, who had been visiting her, pushed past them, unable to contain her curiosity.

Jay gripped Magda's shoulders and glanced at her swollen abdomen. 'The war's over, Magda. Our child will be born in a time of peace. Peace, Magda, peace!' He pulled her into his arms and held her tight.

She was crying when he released her, soft, quiet tears that rolled down her cheeks. 'It's really over?' she asked incredulously. 'Oh, Jay!' Moving back against his chest, she flung her arms around his neck. 'Thank God,' she whispered. 'Nick will be safe now.'

'They should all be home in a few months' time. Come,' said Jay, putting his arm round her waist, 'let me help my fat woman make her way to the excitement.'

Magda was eight months' pregnant, yet the clumsiness she had recently felt lifted from her as her soul filled with euphoria. She walked fast, pulling away from Jay. 'Hold on there!' he shouted.

She laughed with him gaily, dizzily, tasting the salty tears on her lips. Oh, Nick, Nick! It had been six months since she had last received a letter from him.

They found Bull and Sarah clinging to each other at the fringe of the crowd. Someone began singing, with other voices rapidly joining in. Bull pulled away from his wife to embrace Jay and Magda. 'It's a glorious day,' he said, his voice shaky.

Magda saw the mistiness in his eyes as he turned away. She latched onto his shirt. 'Pa?' she started, forcing him to face her again. 'He'll be coming home soon . . . to Brannigan Bay. There's no other place for him. Can this other war not end today as well? Please?' she begged, using her words, hands, eyes and the fresh tears that fell freely now.

For a moment it seemed as if Bull would draw her to him, as if he was about to say the words she longed to hear. All he did was take her hands in his to kiss them, then went back to Sarah without replying.

Magda turned to Jay but he was talking to a man standing beside him. All the elation she had felt only moments ago drained from her and she stood at the edge of the excited crowd like an outsider observing the joy of others.

Clanging bells sounded from the nearby Anglican church, the joyful peal adding to the clamour and feverish babble in the street, growing dominant as excited voices slowly subsided. People, first in ones and twos, then groups, drifted closer in response to the call. Anglican, Dutch Reformed, Catholic – all poured through the church's open doors, past the clergyman standing with a wide smile of welcome on his face.

'Where's your ma?' asked Magda when Jay took her arm to lead her towards the church. 'She'll want to be here.'

He scanned the remaining crowd but was sure that Frances was not there. 'I'll fetch her,' he said, kissing Magda's cheek. 'You go ahead and join your folks.'

The impromptu thanksgiving service was simple and poignant. Men and women wept openly for the living and the dead, for what had been and the future to come.

Magda walked beside her mother when they left the church. Bull lagged behind, talking animatedly with a group of men. Magda glanced back over her shoulder and said, 'I think today was the first time I saw Pa cry.'

Sarah smiled and linked her arm through her daughter's. 'Don't pester him, child. I feel that today has turned his thoughts about Nick. Let him make up his mind . . . hopefully before Nick returns.'

'I'll leave him in peace,' she promised.

'I'll go with you to your house,' said Sarah when they

neared the side street where both cottages stood. She laughed and added, 'It's strange. Even after all this time I find it hard to think of Jay's house as yours too. To me your home will always be with me and your pa.'

'Then I'm lucky – I have two homes!' Unlike Nick, she thought suddenly: he had none.

'It's a pity Jay and Frances missed the service,' Sarah was saying. 'I wonder what kept them.'

Jay was sitting on the kitchen steps when they reached the cottage, staring at the garden as if unaware of their approach. 'Jay?' called Magda. 'Is something wrong?'

'She's dead,' he whispered.

'*What?*'

'She's dead,' he repeated as Sarah moved quickly into the house. 'My mother is dead. She's dead in her chair. That's where I found her.'

'Oh, Jay!' Magda knelt and took his face in her hands.

He placed his hands on top of hers and smiled. 'It sounds a terrible thing to say,' he began, 'but in a way I'm almost relieved for her. She was never happy and even less so since my pa died.'

'Jay.' She did not know what else to say.

'At least,' he said, moving to his feet and helping Magda up, 'today's peace has touched my mother as well.'

It had touched others besides Frances Brannigan: on that same day, on a faraway front of the dying war where confusion still reigned, men died in conflict. One was from Brannigan Bay.

When Jay laid his mother to rest in the town's cemetery, much expanded since the outbreak of war, news came of the death of Nick de Vries.

1919

Preston Whitehead returned to South Africa in February. Almost the first thing he did was to persuade his parents they should enjoy a brief holiday together in Brannigan Bay.

'She goes well, Father,' he called out, referring to Kevin's new Model T Ford, which was fitted with acetylene lamps. 'Makes mine seem like a real Tin Lizzie!'

Kevin smiled indulgently. 'Yours wouldn't be much more than a heap of rust if I hadn't told Joe to look after it while you were away.'

'I'm glad it was in good hands,' replied Preston, knowing that Joe, the mechanic who tended the engines on the boats, would have enjoyed working on the Ford.

Lisa Whitehead sat on the back seat, appearing uncomfortable and out of place. 'How far to go?' she asked across Preston's shoulder. 'We seem to have been on this road – if one can call it that – for days.'

Preston glanced at her reflection in the car's mirror. 'Not long now, Mother. Another hour or so and we'll be there.'

'Another hour?' She sighed and tapped her husband's shoulder. 'Really, Kevin, I can't understand why on earth you should even consider a holiday out here in the wilderness. It's beyond me, really it is,' she finished with a loud sigh, slumping dejectedly against the seat cushions.

Preston's father was not perturbed; he was accustomed to his wife's ways. 'It's a village that's becoming increasingly popular among tourists. The climate is healthy, there's excellent fishing and I'm convinced real estate will be a wise investment.'

'People can hardly get there!'

91

'That'll change. Now that the war's ended the whole country will embark on a period of development.'

'What will my friends think,' muttered Lisa Whitehead, 'when I tell them we're holidaying in some primitive fishing village?'

Preston smiled at the thought of his mother trying to apply her social standards in Brannigan Bay. She was used to the luxuries of their large, two-storey house set in spacious grounds up against the slopes of Table Mountain. Five servants catered to her every need and her engraved copperplate visiting cards indicated which afternoon she would be at home to receive guests. His mother would find holidaying in Brannigan Bay a traumatic change.

When they finally crested the last hill and saw the growing village spread out before them, Preston slowed the Ford and turned off the main street.

'Where are you going?' asked his father. 'The Crystal Lodge lies straight ahead.'

'I want to show you the site I have in mind for our harbour. It's only a few minutes away.'

'You're still clinging to that foolish idea, are you? I told you it makes no sense to invest in an expensive harbour right now.'

'Wait till you see it.'

'I don't care whether it's the ideal place or not. Our bigger boats can travel from Cape Town and fish here. Why waste money on a harbour?'

Preston's mouth tightened. 'With a base here,' he argued, 'we could save time getting to the fishing banks. The boats could head all the way along the south coast.'

Kevin snorted. 'A pipe dream, boy,' he said, shaking his head. 'We've no capital available for grandiose schemes.'

Preston remained silent after that but vowed he would have his harbour some day – even if he had to wait until his father was gone and the company his.

When they arrived at the spot Kevin Whitehead could not fail to be impressed by what Preston showed him, though he clung to his earlier arguments.

'Can we go now?' wailed Lisa from the back of the car. 'I'm

filthy and need a bath.' The two men glanced at each other, sighed and turned back to the Ford.

Preston slowed one more time on the road to the hotel when he neared the street where he knew Magda lived. He promised himself he would get away from his parents as soon as he could and try to see her.

How she continued to haunt him! Even when he had been with other women, there had always been fleeting moments when he had wished it was her. He could still recall that moment on the sand dune with stark clarity, could feel her heat wrapped around him, his body enmeshed with hers. He remembered his surprise at her passionate need, as if she was the taker and he the giver. Perhaps it was his inability to make her his that made her so attractive to him. She allowed one to see and claim only that which she was prepared to give.

It made him want her even more.

Jay did not go to sea with *Farer* that day for he had finally given in to Magda's entreaties to rid their garden of an old fig tree that took up too much valuable space. Gottlieb Kessler took control of the boat and her crew.

The morning was warm and lethargic as Jay worked in the garden, his son Vaughn propped up in a home-made perambulator some yards away. The child's head was protected by an over-large hat, although he was positioned in the shade provided by the overhang of the cottage's thatched roof. 'This is not work for a fisherman,' grumbled Jay aloud.

He finished his task shortly before eleven o'clock and decided it was time to escape the house. 'Where are you going?' asked Magda as he started for the door.

'Down to the harbour. I have to be near the sea on a day like this.'

'Yes,' she agreed, getting to her feet. 'I think I'll take Vaughn for a walk.'

Jay kissed the baby's head, pecked Magda on the cheek, then headed for the harbour.

*

Magda pushed Vaughn slowly down Main Street, stopping when friends wanted to chat or admire her baby.

She pointed out the sights as she walked, explaining them to Vaughn as if he could understand her. 'Your daddy used to go to school in the Anglican church over there,' she said, rearranging the light blanket covering him. Unlike Jay she had attended the Dutch school, though these days one government school served all. There were other changes in the village: more shops and more homes – many of them holiday houses for wealthier tourists. The permanent population of the village had increased too, for many wounded servicemen who had been sent to Brannigan Bay to recuperate had fallen in love with it and subsequently returned there to stay. Property prices were enjoying a boom.

As she crossed the street, her attention was riveted on the man standing beside a parked car opposite the general dealer. Her stomach clenched as she recognised Preston.

She moved back onto the pavement on her side of the street, feeling an instinctive urge to run away. When she turned again, he was standing before her. 'Hello, Magda,' he said softly.

'Preston!' she exclaimed, trying to seem surprised. 'You're the last person—'

'The baby?'

'It's mine. And Jay's.'

He nodded slowly, and she was not sure what she saw in his eyes. Anger? Hurt?

'I see,' he said at last. 'When?'

'The child? December. The marriage was more than two years ago. In October nineteen sixteen.'

'October. Hardly three months after . . . ' She wanted to cringe from the pain in his voice.

'Preston,' she started, 'what happened was—'

'I thought you'd wait for me.'

'Neither of us made promises,' she said slowly. 'There was nothing to wait for.'

'I thought of you,' he whispered. 'I thought of you when I went back . . . during the fighting, in the quiet moments. When the war was over and there was no more fear there was

94

only you. Just you, Magda – you and me. Now this . . . '

For one fleeting moment she wished she could tell him about their child, about the little boy she sometimes saw around town with his parents, the child she could never acknowledge as hers. All she said was, 'Preston, we were caught up in a moment of madness we both created. It was a mistake.'

'Is that really all it was to you, Magda?'

'Preston, please . . . People are staring.'

He pulled back from her as sharply as if she had slapped his face. She turned away from his torment but his hand on her shoulder forced her back to him.

'You're walking away from me again. Is that how it's always going to be, Magda?'

When she did not reply he leaned closer, his face almost touching hers. 'I wish,' he whispered, 'that I'd made you pregnant – I wish I'd forced you to remember me.' His hand fell to his side as his eyes filled with a sadness, acceptance of defeat, then he turned away and started back to his car.

'Preston?'

He stopped, his back still towards her, then his shoulders slumped and he came slowly back to her.

'I had your child.' Even as Magda spoke, she knew she was making a mistake. Yet she owed at least that to him. He had a right to know. 'It was a boy.'

His expression did not change at first, almost as if he had not heard her. Then he frowned and stepped closer. 'We had a child . . . and you did not tell me?'

'Tell you? Preston, you were somewhere in France – how could I?'

'You weren't going to, though, were you? Even if you could.'

Magda bit her lip. She wanted nothing more than to run away from this man and his pain – and from the explanation he would demand, the claim she knew he would make. She pushed back her hair and said, 'I couldn't then. Things are different now.'

'Are they? Does your getting married make it so?'

'Perhaps. That – and time. It makes it different for us both. What would you have done, Preston, if you'd known?'

'I would have married you – I would have come for you.'

She had not intended her short laugh to sound as bitter as it did. 'Oh, Preston, that's so easy to say.'

He stared at her for a long time, then said, 'Where's the boy now?'

'Adopted. Somewhere in Johannesburg. I don't know with whom.'

'You had no right.'

'I had every right.'

'Damn you, Magda, he's *my* son too!'

'He belongs to neither of us any more. He's part of a brief past we shared, Preston.'

'The past.' His voice was a whisper. 'A mistake, a moment of madness. It's over as easily as that?'

'Had anything ever really started?'

'For *me* it did! That child is ours, it belongs with us! We should be together now, not standing here on the side of the street discussing him. You belong with me – not with some rough fisherman with nothing to offer you!'

Her chin tilted upwards when she said, 'That fisherman you speak of gives me love and happiness.'

'Does he know about us?'

'Everything.'

'Do you love him?'

'Yes.'

She expected a harsh reply, but none came. All Preston said was, 'It's not over for me, Magda. Not yet.' He held her gaze, then walked in quick strides towards his car.

Magda too walked away, her hands trembling on Vaughn's perambulator as she pushed him furiously down the road. Moments later Preston's Ford came past, heading down Main Street, but he did not glance her way.

The day was perfect, the sea shimmering in the sun, rolling gently over rocks and up beaches. Children played truant and made their way stealthily to favourite fishing spots and swimming holes. Dogs lay in patches of shade, panting rhythmically, while the village cats licked half-heartedly at their fur, ignoring the swallows swooping and dipping low across the hot earth.

Jay stopped near the harbour wall and let his lungs fill with the smell of the sea. He felt content; since Vaughn's birth, he and Magda had started to live a full life. The first two years of their marriage had been difficult, but they gradually began to overcome the anguish surrounding their union. There were times, too, when Jay sensed in Magda something akin to guilt, as if she felt she had been unfair towards him by agreeing to Bull's suggestion that they marry. At such moments he would wonder about her and Preston, whether she still felt something for him, wished she could be with him. The thought always brought with it a surging, jealous anger.

Shrugging thoughts of the past from his mind, he started down the harbour path. There was no sign of the fishing boats when he stared out to sea and he hoped all was going well with Gottlieb and the men on *Farer*.

The harbour was deserted – except for one boat undergoing repairs, all the others were out. The owner had abandoned his task and Jay guessed he was at home enjoying a beer or two. It was that kind of day.

He moved down the concrete shelf, stopped to take off his shoes, hobbled carefully over the pebbles, and entered the cool water. It felt good. Moving in deeper, he scooped up water in his hands, splashing it onto his face and neck.

The salt water stung his eyes and made him blink so that when he looked up he could only vaguely discern the shape of a man standing on a boulder at the edge of the harbour shelf. Slowly the shape took form.

'Preston,' he said in a low voice, fighting the urge to charge at his adversary. He had promised Magda he would neither harm Preston nor ever reveal the truth.

'Yes, it's me.' The challenging tone of his voice caused Jay to tense even more. 'I've seen Magda.'

Jay made no reply, though his fists curled into tight balls at his sides.

'She told me about our child.'

Jay was too stunned to react. Magda had told him? But why? They'd agreed . . .

'She's been yours for just a while, Jay. Perhaps she was frightened, confused, needed someone like you for support. But she's mine – she's always been mine.'

Jay's voice was a low growl. 'Get out of here,' he said. 'Go back to Cape Town . . . to your fancy house and your cars and your way of life. Go home, Preston, and stay there.'

Preston did not move and his jaw had tightened aggressively. 'If you really love her, Jay, you'll let her go. She's loyal to you, but it's me she wants.' He stepped onto a lower rock so that he stood only feet from Jay. 'It's me she really wants to be with,' he repeated softly, though his voice had a confident, determined ring.

Leaping from the water with a roar, Jay's hands clamped around Preston's waist and lifted him bodily from the rock. He hurled the lighter man into the shallows.

Preston spluttered and tried to get up but Jay straddled him, slamming his head against the hard bed of pebbles while Preston choked and coughed as salt water flowed into his mouth and nose. He struck out desperately, ineffectually, unable to escape his adversary's superior strength and weight.

Jay saw only the fear-filled face beneath him while in his heart and mind pounded all the doubts, fears and jealousies caused by the man who was now, at last, in his power. He struck at Preston's face but the sea water stripped the blow of its force, so that his fist seemed almost to caress Preston's skin. Gripping the struggling man by his lapels, he jerked him up and hit him. Blood coloured the shallow water surging about them and Jay hit him again.

'Jay! Stop! You'll kill him! Please stop!'

Turning to strike out at the hands that pulled futilely at his shoulders, he found himself staring into Magda's frightened face. A measure of sanity returned at the sight of his wife standing beside him in the water and Jay released the stunned Preston and eased himself to his feet.

Magda let her hands slip from his shoulders with a relieved sob. 'Help him out, Jay,' she said softly, and he surprised himself by complying immediately, dragging Preston from the water to lie spluttering on the harbour shelf.

Preston curled on his side, coughing and retching up the salt water he had swallowed. His eyes were still glazed from the blows but they flickered when Jay said, 'Remember what I told you, Whitehead. Stay away from Brannigan Bay and from Magda. They belong to me.' Preston's gaze moved past him to rest briefly on Magda's face before his head sagged back onto the concrete.

Rushing past Jay, she moved to his side, thankful she had been in time to stop the one-sided brawl for she was sure that Jay would have killed him. Whatever it was that had made her sense that Preston would meet Jay had come not a moment too soon. She had risked leaving Vaughn unattended and raced from the house to the harbour.

Jay clutched her arm fiercely, pulling her back when she knelt and reached for Preston's face. 'Leave him!' he shouted.

She tried to jerk free but his grip was so strong that her effort served only to pull her off balance and she put out her free hand to stop herself falling over. 'Jay! Let go, damn you!'

He released her so fast that she almost fell again. 'If you touch him, you stay with him,' he snarled. 'He said that's what you want, that now he's back you'd go with him.' His voice, earlier so filled with rage, had rapidly dwindled into a childish whine.

Magda's head jerked up. 'Is that what this was all about? A fight about who has the right to possess me? Damn you both!' she shouted, glaring at each in turn. Though still dazed, Preston turned away from her outburst, as sheepish as Jay.

'Just who do you think you are?' she demanded, her face flushed with anger. 'And what do you think *I* am? A dog's bone to be fought over, with the victor gaining the spoils?'

'He said he'd come to take you away,' Jay responded lamely, glancing down at Preston. Though the latter's eyes rested on Magda, he made no move to raise himself to his feet.

'And that automatically makes it so, does it? God, you men!' With an irritable toss of her head she started for the path, then turned and added, 'Go ahead and kill each other! It makes no difference to me.'

Both men waited, expecting more, yet none was forthcoming.

It was only when Magda was gone from sight that Jay glanced at Preston. 'Just get the hell out of here,' he muttered, then went after his wife.

'I had to tell him about his son. He seemed so – so dejected, almost lost.' Magda paced the kitchen floor as she spoke, her composure regained to the extent that she felt ashamed of her earlier outburst. 'I didn't tell him Wilhelm's name or that he's in Brannigan Bay. I can't help Preston being in the village, Jay,' she added quickly. 'He approached *me* – it wasn't the other way round.

Jay grunted.

'Would you have killed him?'

He glanced at her, then lowered his eyes. 'Yes,' he whispered.

'Thank God you didn't.'

'You still care for him, is that it?'

'Oh, Jay, it makes no difference if it was Preston or anyone else! How could your killing someone not concern me? I don't want a husband who goes to gaol or gets hanged! Didn't you think about what that would do to me?'

'I wasn't capable of thinking,' he muttered, his hands moving restlessly on the table top. 'Maybe he's learned his lesson and will leave us alone from now on. I told him to stay away from us.'

'You can't stop him coming here. You can't stop anyone!'

The look he gave her was long and appraising. 'And you, Magda,' he asked, 'what will you do when he returns? When he comes for you?'

'I told you both. I'm not some piece of merchandise a man can lay claim to whenever it suits him. I meant it, Jay.' She stood up, turned her back to him and went to the door.

His voice carried softly to her. 'He thinks he has a claim,' he said. 'He thinks the child gives him that right.'

'He's wrong,' she replied, but when she saw there were still doubts on his face, she moved to him and added, 'Stop fearing him, Jay.'

His arms went about her yet his embrace could not quell the chill that settled on her.

Kevin Whitehead stared at the bedraggled shape of his son on the bed. 'Young men of breeding don't go about fighting. You've disgraced your mother and me. Everyone in the hotel saw you enter in your present state. You should be ashamed of yourself.'

'It wasn't by choice, I assure you,' came the mumbled reply. 'The maniac attacked me.'

'Then why are you associating with such ruffians? Stay away from the harbour, Preston.' Kevin took out his pocket watch and grumbled, 'What's keeping the doctor? He should have been here ages ago.'

'Probably busy treating some horse.'

'Don't be testy, son. Your nose is broken, by the looks of things.'

'It feels that way.'

'Did you do or say something to set off the assault? Was he drunk? What started it?'

'A woman.'

The older man was angry now. 'A woman,' he repeated softly. 'You mean to tell me you were fighting over some local wench, some fishing peasant's daughter? You're a disappointment to me, Preston. I'd hoped your mother and I had instilled some sensible breeding in you, some measure of dignity and worth.'

Preston turned to glare at his father. 'She's not just some peasant,' he said forcefully. 'She's the mother of my child.'

Kevin Whitehead was about to say more but Preston's words stopped him in his tracks. His mouth hung open, moving slightly as if he was gasping for air. Then his shoulders slumped and he sank onto the bed. 'She's *what*?' he managed at last.

'The mother of my child. More than two years ago, during

101

the war, when I came here with you to recuperate.'

'Spare me the details,' interrupted Kevin, then sighed and added, 'I suppose she expects you to marry her. You bloody young fool, can't you see what she's up to? She's after our money – it's her chance to escape the backwaters! Bloody young fool,' he repeated.

Preston shook his head and winced in pain. 'No,' he whispered, 'you're wrong. She's already married, and she's not interested in money.'

'Already married? You mean—'

'No, no! She married only after she was expecting our child.'

'*Your* child? How do you know it's yours? She was probably—'

'Don't say it! Magda is very special and she's mine. She belongs with me.'

Kevin wiped a hand across his eyes and moved to the window. 'You're out of your mind,' he said in a low voice.

'No, I'm perfectly sane, and I'm going to make her mine. There must be some legal action we can take.'

'*We*?' yelled Kevin, spinning round. '*We*? You expect me to help you in your foolishness?'

'Yes.'

'Listen to me, Preston,' he said, his voice gentler now, 'I can understand how . . . Well, I was once young, too. A pretty girl can turn a man's head, I know. But wanting to marry . . . Son, don't feel duty-bound to do anything that drastic – she's as much to blame for what happened. At least she's married now so there's no chance she'll ruin your life. Just avoid her – and that vicious maniac, who I presume is her husband.'

'You really don't understand, do you? You think she's beneath us and that I can't possibly talk about love! You don't understand and you don't want to!'

Kevin's face tightened. He moved to the door and turned back to stare at Preston. 'Perhaps I don't,' he said through gritted teeth, 'but *you* had better understand *this*. I'm not handing over *my* company to a young man who can't even see the ruin of his own future.'

Preston glared back at him. 'What are you saying?'

'Just this. You'd better decide which is the more precious

to you – a woman who has already given herself to another man or future ownership of Whitehead Enterprises. I won't allow you both.'

'You'd disinherit me?'

Kevin Whitehead hesitated as he opened the door. 'Think about it, son. Decide which you value more.'

When the door had closed, Preston stared out of the window. His father was wrong. He *could* have both – but not at the same time, that was all.

It would have to be Whitehead Enterprises first – for that would give him Brannigan Bay. With it he'd get Magda.

There would be nothing left for Jay Brannigan.

Kevin stood just outside the door and lifted a hand to his chest as if that would calm the rapid beating of his heart. He took deep gulps of air and tried to relax. He had not meant what he had said, of course; if he denied Preston the company he might as well sell out right away. Perhaps it would bring his son to his senses – there was no time for an irrational quest for another man's woman. First the business – Preston had to become adept at that. Then he might not want anything else.

Time, thought Kevin Whitehead as he walked in slow, deliberate strides down the passage to his room. It seemed to come down to little else these days.

Part Two

1920–1933

1920

Unlike most of the country, Brannigan Bay escaped the throes of post-war depression, experiencing instead a tourist boom. With it came a flurry of building activity as the more well-to-do visitors decided it was their kind of town and warranted the acquisition of permanent holiday homes.

There was other growth as well. The Cape Town businessman who established a hardware supply store was soon followed by a second general dealer and the town's first liquor merchant. More permanent homes were needed.

Jay, too, was caught up by the fashion for building but the object of his attention was a fishing boat. 'Only a few days more,' he said to Magda, in gleeful anticipation. They were sitting on a wooden bench in the cool evening air outside their cottage. 'Did I tell you she's going to be painted all white?'

'Yes, Jay,' she replied before turning her attention back to her knitting. She did not add that it was the tenth time that evening he had talked about his boat and the third occasion on which he had mentioned its colour. 'White will be nice,' was all she said. When she looked at him again she knew that his mind had wandered back to the Cape Town dockyard where skilled hands planed, fitted and caulked the timbers of his new vessel.

They had argued about the boat. 'With the price those fancy boat-builders in Cape Town want to charge,' she had said, 'we could make a down payment on a bigger house for ourselves.' Magda had known that he felt guilty at having insisted the boat be constructed from imported rather than local timber.

Jay had countered with, 'The craft those fancy boat-builders make me will bring in enough money for us to build a mansion some day.'

'How?'

'She's bigger and faster, Magda. That means bigger, better catches. I can go further out to sea.'

'Next thing you'll be spending the extra money you make on an engine for her.'

They had sulked for a while, until Jay said, '*Farer* is old, Magda. She'll fall to pieces in a storm some day.'

'Don't try to get me to agree by frightening me, Jay Brannigan!'

He had fallen silent then but eventually Magda took pity on him. 'You're right. The boat is important – it's our livelihood.'

'Are you sure?'

'Order the boat, Jay.'

Now Magda folded away her knitting, realising she must appear the very epitome of a contented housewife to anyone who might wander past the cottage and see them sitting there. Yet although it had been more than a year since she had last seen Preston Whitehead, there were times, especially when she was alone at home or drawing outdoors, when his face sprang into her mind as clearly as if he were standing before her. She knew she would always feel something for him and even the knowledge that Preston had married someone else within months of their last meeting did little to oust him from her thoughts.

The feelings troubled her. Jay deserved more. Her love? He had that – or most of it – yet one small piece – was it even love? – one corner of her soul belonged to Preston.

Jay's voice broke into her troubled thoughts. 'Why so serious?'

Magda smiled quickly and placed a hand on his arm. 'What will you name her?'

'What?'

'The boat. What will you call her?'

Jay studied the sea, then said, 'I haven't decided yet. I'd have liked *Guiding Star* – but Jan's boat is already called that.'

'*Sea Horse*,' she whispered.

'*Sea Horse*? What kind of name is that for a boat? Horses and sailing have nothing in common, Magda.'

'Then what do you call those?' she retorted, pointing at the white caps of the waves. 'They're white horses, aren't they?'

Jay stared at the white crests of the rolling swell. 'Yes, but . . . '

'Your boat is going to be white like the horses riding the waves. I can stand here at the cottage wall and see her out in the bay like a white horse of the sea. It's a good name.'

He nibbled a fingernail and continued to stare at the sea. Then, after a lengthy silence, he said, 'You're right, it's a good name. *Sea Horse* it'll be – I'll even let you launch her!'

Magda smiled and took out her knitting again.

'I've never seen you knit so much. What is it?' he asked.

She held up the results of her efforts. Jay grinned and said, 'Booties. For Vaughn?'

Magda snorted. 'This small? Haven't you noticed how your son has grown?'

'Who, then? Oh . . . '

'Yes.'

'But they're pink!'

A gurgle of laughter burst from Magda. 'Oh, Jay. I knew our first child was going to be a boy. This time, it's a girl – I'm sure of it!'

Jay leaned back in his chair, his brow creased in thought. 'A girl,' he said softly.

'You're supposed to be happy, whatever the child is.'

'I am, I am! But a girl . . . '

'Did you have hopes of producing a brood of eight boys to work as your crew?'

He laughed with her, reached out and laid his hand over hers. 'I'm happy, Magda. Truly I am! She'll be beautiful – as beautiful as her mother. And,' he added softly, leaning closer to kiss her lips, 'I'll love her just as much.'

Grace Whitehead, *née* Connoley, took a careful sip of tea, finding the taste pronounced but interesting. It was like the country that had become her home – strong, rough, yet full of promise. She stared across the table at her husband but Preston was engrossed in the yellowed pages of an old book he had discovered in the office of the Crystal Lodge hotel.

Studying him she enjoyed as always the finely sculpted lines of his face. She thought that, unlike the land, he was not rough. But strong – oh, yes, he was that! – and promising.

When they had met during the war she had thought him English rather than South African. He had blended into her upper-class environment with his charm and social skills and her parents and friends were as enchanted with the young pilot as she. Grace recalled her pleasant surprise when Preston's letter had arrived shortly after he had left England. He would soon be visiting her country again, he said, and might he call on her? She had returned with him in June 1919, having accepted his offer of marriage. Now she had just given him a son, whom they had named Barry.

The birth had been difficult and Grace was not surprised when the doctors told her there would be no more. Even Preston, she realised with relief, had taken the news stoically. It was he who suggested they spend a week in Brannigan Bay to help her regain her strength.

Grace tugged gently at a hair that peeked over the edge of his collar. 'You take more interest in that dusty old book than in your son or me.' She smiled to show that her offence was feigned.

Preston snapped the book shut and tossed it onto the table. 'You're right,' he said. 'I'm sorry.'

Refilling his cup with fresh tea she asked, 'What is it about?'

'A diary of the town's development,' he replied, pushing it across to her. 'It was kept by one of the first fishermen. No one seems to know how it ended in the hotel's office.'

As Grace leafed through the book, it was Preston's turn to study her. His wife was a handsome woman, he thought agreeably. Her fair hair was shoulder-length with full, natural curls. A typically English peaches-and-cream complexion completed the picture. He knew that the skin of her body was as smooth to the touch – smooth, soft and yielding. Yet even that could not erase his longing for Magda — no one would ever do that.

That thought had often crossed his mind since he married Grace. Had he been wrong in catering to his father's wishes for him to become settled before he took a greater share in running the business? His thoughts had turned immediately to Grace Connoley when Kevin first broached the subject. Grace had the right background, she was attractive and he liked her. Liked, not loved.

He lowered his gaze when she closed the book, handing it back to him as she said, 'This village fascinates you, doesn't it?'

'Yes,' he replied softly.

'I heard they're launching a new boat in the harbour this afternoon. Could we go? I believe it's a special affair.'

He scowled. 'I don't think you'll appreciate these locals, Grace. They're an unsophisticated lot, I'm afraid.'

'Oh, nonsense! Those I've met have been perfectly civilised. Please, Preston.'

'All right,' he said with an exaggerated sigh. 'But don't expect too much.'

He allowed himself a small smile when she stood up and kissed his forehead. Perhaps Magda would be there.

The boat was twenty foot of carefully seasoned English oak hull. Its mast was silver spruce; the thwarts, centreplate cases, transoms and bottom gratings were made of teak.

The new vessel had pride of place in the harbour. The other boats were already bobbing on the gentle swell near the harbour entrance, their crews waiting anxiously for the virgin to test the rampant power of Brannigan Bay's waters. The first swell would tell: would she move with it or lift herself sluggishly to meet its thrust? Would she be too rigid or too giving? They would soon know.

She stood on two sturdy stocks, painted as white as her hull. Only her innards gleamed red, to conceal the grime and fish blood that would stain her once she had felt the touch of a normal day's work.

The harbour was crowded with women and children also eagerly waiting to see how the newcomer would ride.

Magda held a bottle of champagne, a gift from the builders of *Sea Horse*. Sent with it was a simple letter of good wishes to Jay, which read: 'She will ride well. She has a light heart, is flippant at times, but will mould to a good skipper's ways. She is a good sea boat. God bless her and her crew.'

The sea slurped up the harbour shelf and wrapped round the stocks as Magda said much the same words. 'God bless you,' she ended softly. She brought the bottle down across the rowlock specially positioned near the gunwale for the occasion.

Jay smiled at her as the bottle smashed and the wine frothed and splashed across the bow moments before he gave the command to launch. Eight pairs of stout shoulders heaved, and *Sea Horse* entered the water.

A cheer went up from the assembled crowd as the men scrambled into the water to board her. Oars flashed, bit into the sea and *Sea Horse* moved under the power of the men who would live in and from her.

'She rides!' someone called, voicing everyone's excitement. 'See how she rides to meet the swell!'

The boats outside the harbour had their oars raised in salute. More cheers rose from the watching fishermen as *Sea Horse* met the first swell head on.

'Oh!' The thrill Magda felt inside burst from her lips as *Sea Horse* mounted the swell. With a neat flick of her stern, the boat raced over its pinnacle to meet the next. 'Oh, just look at her!' Magda said to her mother, who stood beside her.

'A fine sight,' Sarah whispered. 'I'm proud for Jay's sake.' She placed her hand on Magda's shoulder.

Tears sprang into Magda's eyes when she glanced down at Vaughn in her arms. 'If only you were older, Vaughn Brannigan, you'd have been there with him. If only you were old enough to remember this day!'

'There'll be other times for him to remember,' said Sarah with a smile. '*Sea Horse* will serve your family for many years to come.' Magda returned the smile and took her mother's hand in hers.

112

On the harbour wall high above, the tourists watched, respecting the intimacy of the moment that belonged to those who made their living from the sea. This was no spectacle arranged for their benefit, but a ceremony of importance.

'One can sense the solemnity of the moment,' said Grace Whitehead. 'Don't you agree?'

Preston shrugged. 'They're simple people,' he replied. 'I suppose they find it necessary to make a fuss of a new boat.'

'Oh, come now, Preston, you're being unnecessarily snobbish about it.'

His gaze returned to the woman with the child in her arms. He had said they were simple people and they were. Yet he had loved one – still loved her. Grace was right: he was a snob.

When he had seen Jay standing beside Magda, their mutual affection obvious in the way she looked at and touched him, Preston had felt a spurt of burning resentment. Everything she was should be his – every feeling, every touch. He had tried in vain to curb his jealousy.

Magda glanced upwards and seemed to stare directly at him. Sanity returned, fought with the terrifying forces that had changed him so. What had he become? Oh, Magda, he thought, it could have been so different!

Preston gripped Grace's elbow. 'Let's go,' he said gruffly, leading her away.

From below, another cheer came from against the cliff face. 'She rides! She rides!'

Three days after *Sea Horse* was already earning her keep, a group of fishermen struggled in the heat with a huge basket laden with fish. It was a long haul from the harbour shelf to the market square where the trucks waited. As they strained under their load, cursing and sweating beneath the blistering rays of the sun and the humidity of the air, they were unaware of the tall, fair-haired man watching them intently, his pale skin protected by the wide brim of his white hat. It was only when they stopped half-way up the steep slope to rest that he moved closer and nodded at them.

They returned his greeting warily, expecting him, like most visitors, to be insensitive to their task and to demand to see and purchase the best of their catch at that very moment. They were surprised when he said, 'There must be an easier way of doing things than this.'

One of them wiped at a layer of fish blood caking his shirt and said, 'Then give us the answer, mister.'

Preston glanced towards the top of the harbour, to where the back of the first truck could be seen. 'The path is pretty steep, but it shouldn't be impossible for the trucks to reverse down one by one. Even half-way down would help.'

The fisherman gave an amused snigger. 'Some answer,' he said to his comrades, straightening his aching back before addressing Preston again. 'We thank you for your interest, mister, but it's already been tried. You know how much a loaded truck weighs? When it's raining, this path is a mud trap.' He turned away and again gripped the rim of the basket.

'A crane then,' said Preston. 'Or a cableway.'

The fisherman shut his eyes for an instant before straightening up. His expression was one of resignation, almost scorn. 'A crane,' he echoed derisively, turning to the others with raised eyebrows. 'A crane, says this man with all the answers. We should build a crane to hoist up the baskets.' He shook his head and said to Preston, 'If you'll excuse us, mister, we have work to do.'

'A winch could be built on top of the cliffs,' continued Preston, unperturbed by the man's response. He pointed at the high cliffs opposite the tip of the jetty. 'There's plenty of parking for the trucks. The cableway could extend down to the jetty.'

The fishermen stopped and studied the cliff top with new interest. 'So,' one of them said, 'how does that help us?'

'You transfer your load while still on the water,' replied Preston without hesitation. 'You dump the fish into baskets, and they're hauled up the cliff by the cable. That way your boats will be lighter when you have to beach them. It means less work all round.'

The men were silent now, gazing alternately at the cliffs and the mouth of the harbour. 'It would also mean,' added Preston, convinced that they were visualising the operation and its benefits to them, 'that you could build cleaning huts up there and demolish the ones in the harbour. That would leave space for more boats if you could level the ground a bit.'

'Hold it,' said the fisherman who had been the spokesman for the group. 'Let's deal with one thing at a time. The cableway first.' He rubbed a coarse hand over his jaw. 'There might be something in what you're suggesting but it would cost plenty, I'm sure. Also, our village council is pretty much opposed to any construction – apart from housing, that is.'

Preston smiled understandingly. 'By spending money on a winch and cables you could increase the volume of catches you can load, making more money in the long term. The village council could advance the money to build it and charge you a loading fee to recoup the costs. You, in turn, could charge a little more for your catches because of the easier loading onto the trucks. As I've said, it'll put more money in your pockets in the long run, apart from saving labour.'

Preston knew he had their full attention now but reminded himself he was dealing with men unaccustomed to long-range thinking or planning. 'I could speak to your council on your behalf, if you like. Perhaps their response might be more positive if it came from someone other than yourselves.'

'From an outsider, you mean,' the fisherman said without rancour. 'Why should you do this for us?'

Preston shrugged and stared at the cliffs. 'I work in a fishing environment so I understand the life of a fisherman. Your harbour is dangerous enough as it is and I don't see why unwarranted hardship should accompany it. That's my only reason for suggesting it,' he added, turning his gaze back to the fishermen. 'I have nothing to gain from helping you.' He doffed his hat and started up the path.

'Mister!'

Preston stopped and faced them.

'What's your name?'

'Whitehead. Preston Whitehead.'

The fisherman smiled for the first time. 'Thanks for the idea, Mr Whitehead. You'll talk to the council?'

'Leave it to me,' he said softly, and walked away.

The warmth of the sun, which earlier he had found uncomfortable, seemed now to blend with the inner satisfaction he felt. It was a small thing, an insignificant start, but a beginning nevertheless. One small group of fishermen would talk and spread his name and intentions to others. Slowly – first with the winch, then with whatever opportunities he could find – he would bring them to his side. When the time was right, they would be with him when he wanted to build his new harbour. They would be with *him*, not with Jay Brannigan and whoever else wanted time to stand still.

Preston went directly to the group of thatched bungalows that served as the village council offices. The men in charge of the town's affairs were always pleased to meet prominent visitors and their hospitality was heightened when they learned that Preston was virtually in control of one of Cape Town's most enterprising fishing concerns. The councillors had reason to respect and even fear the influence and reach of the big companies and thought it wise to listen carefully to what their visitor had to say.

None of them hesitated when Preston suggested they proceed immediately to the harbour to gain a more visual appreciation of his suggestion.

Sea Horse was among the last boats to make its way into harbour. Jay squinted at the shapes of the men on the cliff, unidentifiable against the glare of the setting sun. He lost interest in them as *Sea Horse*'s keel scraped against the pebbles and his men leaped out to haul the laden vessel up the slope.

'A good catch,' he called out to Bull de Vries, who had come in a few minutes ago. His father-in-law merely grunted and beckoned him closer. 'What's wrong?' enquired Jay, seeing the worried frown on Bull's wide brow.

'Your friend's been at work,' he growled. 'That's him up there, with the mayor and some others.'

Jay followed his gaze, shielding his eyes from the sun with his hand as he studied the cliff top again. 'What friend? You mean Whitehead?' he asked abruptly.

'The same,' grunted Bull. 'The bastard's been talking to some of the men about making life easier for them. Says they should build a winch to haul up the catches. The poor fools don't see through him the way you and I do.'

Jay pushed past and began to run up the path. He was only slightly breathless when he reached the spot where Preston and the others stood. A few fishermen had gathered there as well and were participating in the discussion.

Shouldering his way through the group, Jay finally stood face to face with Preston at the front of the crowd. The mayor raised his eyebrows in surprise then, recognising the new arrival, said, 'Ah, Jay, you're just the person whose opinion we need. This,' he said, indicating Preston, 'is Mr Whitehead from Cape Town.'

'I know who he is.'

Preston's mouth pulled into a tight line before he said, 'Yes, Mr Mayor, Jay Brannigan and I have met before.'

'Ah. I see. Yes – well – yes . . . good.' The mayor's gaze flicked from one to the other, sensing the antagonism between them. 'Mr Whitehead has a rather interesting suggestion. He thinks—'

'I know what he thinks. And wants.'

'Ah. The winch?'

'It's madness.' He saw the irritation on Preston's face and realised that he was struggling to curb his own angry response. Yet he knew Preston would not permit their conflict to become too obvious to the others. Whatever it was he hoped to gain from his direct involvement in the affairs of the harbour, he could not risk being denied it by clashing directly with Jay.

The mayor licked his lips nervously. 'Come now, Jay, that's a bit harsh. We all think the idea is worth consideration. There are definite benefits to you fishermen. The only problem would be cost.'

Preston turned towards the mayor. 'I might be able to help,' he said. 'There are plenty of lengths of cable lying around our factories and we may have a smallish winch we don't really

117

need. I could get one of my mechanics to restore it to good working order.'

The mayor glanced quickly at his colleagues. 'That's very generous of you, Mr Whitehead. Very generous.'

Preston inclined his head in acknowledgement. 'I'm sure we could manufacture most of the parts so all you would have to do is arrange transport to collect it from our workshops, then assemble it here. Some more welding might be required, though.'

'We can arrange that,' replied the mayor quickly. He flashed Jay a warning glance and said again, 'Very generous of you, Mr Whitehead.'

Jay flushed hotly with anger. 'A winch?' he demanded. 'Stuck up here on the rocks? It would be unsightly,' he finished angrily. 'And useless.'

'It's obvious,' snapped Preston, 'that Mr Brannigan, unlike his fellow fishermen, has not given sufficient thought to the benefits.' He spoke calmly, staring directly at Jay, whose hands clenched into fists.

A shudder passed through Jay as Preston turned his back to talk to the mayor and the others again as though the matter had already been finalised. Were the others so blind to Preston's scheming ways?

He heard their murmured approval and nods of agreement as he struggled to bring his anger under control. For an ugly moment he had wanted to strike out at the other man, to beat the glint of triumph from his eyes. Yet Jay knew that a physical victory on his part would have been hollow; it would not keep Preston from wanting Magda, or erase him from her mind for ever. Neither would it keep him from whatever it was he wanted of Brannigan Bay. Taking a deep breath he said, 'It won't work.'

The others turned to stare at him. 'Why not, Jay?' asked a councillor. Like the mayor he had felt the antagonism between Jay and Preston but he respected Jay as a fisherman and wished to hear his objections.

'The idea, as I understand it, is that the boats will hover down there, just off the jetty.'

'That's right.'

'If the swells come in from over there, as they usually do, there's no way you'll keep a boat in position long enough.'

Folding his arms across his chest, Preston asked, 'How long does a skilful skipper need? It would take only a few minutes.'

'Too long,' snapped Jay, stung by Preston's sarcasm. 'It's obvious you've never controlled a small boat when the swells are running.'

Addressing the mayor again, Preston said, 'I'm obviously wasting my time trying to help. If Mr Brannigan is speaking for all the fishermen, then perhaps they prefer to stick to the old cumbersome way of doing things.' He nodded briefly and started back towards where his Ford was parked.

'Mr Whitehead!' called the mayor, rushing after him. 'I – ah, I speak for the village . . . and for all the fishermen, I'm sure,' he added with a baleful glance in Jay's direction, 'when I say we'd be grateful to accept your offer. Most generous, as I've said. Certainly worth the experiment. Yes.'

Preston gave a thin smile. 'Very well, I'll get my men onto the project when I return to Cape Town tomorrow. What about my other ideas?' he added quickly. 'The building of huts up here? Enlarging the harbour area?'

The mayor shifted his feet uneasily. He was the son of the first shopkeeper in the village and had never been to sea, did not even enjoy rock angling. He had kept himself and his family aloof from the fishermen and their ways, his relative business acumen and merchant status had assured him of replacing his father as mayor of Brannigan Bay. Now he wondered how far he could test his responsibility for their affairs. All his previous efforts to control the harbour activities – the introduction of licence fees for boats as well as for the curing and gutting of fish – had met with stubborn resistance from the fishermen. Perhaps this time it would be wise to consult them beforehand.

He managed to return Preston's smile and said, 'Perhaps we should start with the winch, Mr Whitehead. I'm sure – well, we'll see what happens after that. Thank you,' he added with a vigorous bobbing of his round head. 'Yes, thank you. Most generous of you, yes.'

With a last hard glance at Jay, Preston climbed inside the Ford.

Most of the townspeople were gathered in the harbour to watch the first trial of the cableway, the lengths of steel strung from near the tip of the jetty to the edge of the high cliffs. The wind, though moderate, whined across the taut steel, jerking it as though resentful of the man-made structure slicing across its path. The cables glittered in the afternoon sun as they swung in the grip of the wind.

'Come the first rains,' grumbled Bull de Vries to his wife, 'the damn things will rust and look plain awful.' He sighed and added, 'Then we'll see what they think of Fancy-pants Whitehead and his schemes.'

Sarah flashed him a sidelong look but did not reply. Over the six weeks since Preston had first suggested the cableway she and Magda had suffered the outrage of their menfolk. Sarah agreed with their sentiments, though her support was based more on her dislike of Preston than any conclusion about his idea. But she had had enough of it; it was done now and there was nothing to be gained by bickering about Whitehead's interference in local matters. All that concerned her was that he leave her daughter alone.

The first of the fishing boats to return with the catch appeared round the base of the cliffs. Bull narrowed his eyes and tried to identify them. He had purposely not gone to sea that day as he wanted to be in the harbour to watch the experiment at close quarters.

He spotted *Sea Horse* among the lead boats just as Sarah said, 'Will Jay be the first to try, do you think?'

'Not bloody likely,' came the muttered reply.

A group of teenage boys struggled with the baskets that would take the boats' loads, dragging them along the jetty to where the cable and its large iron hook were secured. 'Help them, Bull,' said Sarah, but he crossed his arms and did not move.

The mayor, dressed in his best suit, stepped onto the jetty with his councillors. He was smiling broadly and

120

seemed immensely proud, as though the cableway had been his idea.

Preston was among the group. He stood beside the mayor as the boys slung the basket onto the iron hook when the first boat edged nearer the jetty.

The man in charge of the winch on the cliff top started it up and the cables jerked the basket from its concrete perch so that it dangled a few feet above the surface of the water. It hung there, just high enough for a boat to unload its catch.

To the surprise of the watchers – Bull in particular – the first boat to head for the basket was *Sea Horse*. Jay steered her deftly round the tip of the jetty to where the waters were calmer. His vessel nudged the huge basket before his crew drew it closer with a grappling hook.

Spontaneous applause came from the mayor and his group although Preston's face had darkened with rage at the sight of his adversary being the first to try the cableway. Bull saw Jay smirk at Preston and wondered whether his son-in-law would deliberately sabotage the attempt. He thought not; should Jay fail it would reflect badly on him if another skipper was successful. Bull realised that Jay would not permit Preston the pleasure of thinking he was sulking in the background, ready to admit defeat. He found himself whispering, 'Show him, Jay. Show the bastard.'

Though the water was calm, it was an intricate exercise to keep the bobbing boat level with the stationary basket. Twice boat and basket drifted apart, despite the efforts of Jay's men to keep them together with the grappling hook. Each time it caused an armful of fish to be deposited in the sea, bringing a stream of curses from the crew.

'The damn thing's too high!' shouted Jay. 'It should be in the water.'

The mayor's satisfied expression slipped from his face and he glanced at Preston as though expecting an immediate solution from him. A councillor said, 'Perhaps Jay is right. The basket might move with the boat if it was half-way in the water.'

Preston glared at him. 'Let someone else try,' he snapped. 'Brannigan's not going about it the right way, that's all.' No one moved to give the order for Jay to desist.

It took almost five minutes for *Sea Horse*'s load to be transferred to the basket, a time during which the other boats had to wait just beyond the harbour, lurching about on the growing strength of the Atlantic swells.

The signal was given at last and slowly the winch drew the heavy basket up towards the cliffs. As it jerked along, the second cable, working in tandem with the first, brought down an empty basket slung on an identical iron hook.

The cables had sufficient distance between them to allow the two baskets to pass one another, but now the empty one swung precariously in the wind, moving directly into the path of the full, upward-moving basket. As the crowd held their breath and watched, the baskets touched and became entangled, grinding the winch to a halt. The cables strained, shaking as if about to snap. The spectators gasped. Someone laughed.

The man in charge of the winch put the machine in reverse. There was a gnashing noise before the baskets jerked apart. A thin trickle of fish spilled from one side where the wicker had torn, but the baskets started on their way again as Jay's crew rowed *Sea Horse* towards the harbour shelf and the next boat moved into position.

People applauded as the first basket neared its destination. A moment later the sound changed to a sharp cry of alarm as the bottom of the basket jammed on a sharp outcrop of rock just below the cliff edge.

The winch operator was unable to see what was happening and it was only the jarring of the cables and the sudden groan of the engine driving the machinery that warned him something was amiss. By then it was too late; as he slammed down on the winch's brake, the weight of the loaded basket proved too much. It tore from the hook, fell a few inches to a narrow, rocky ledge, teetered there for long, agonising seconds, then tipped backwards and plummeted to the sea. A horde of shiny fish tumbled out to slap against the rocks as they followed the ruined basket's long descent.

The tone of the crowd's groan of dismay seemed to dip in sympathy with the falling mass. The basket crashed into the sea, the impact tearing it apart. The remains lay half submerged in the water.

Silence fell, and all eyes turned to the architect of this ill-fated scheme.

Preston stared at the cliffs as though they would provide a suitable response, some reasonable explanation. At last he said, 'It needs some adjustment. That last rock . . . the weight . . . '

He had spoken to the mayor but his gaze was drawn to where *Sea Horse* lay in the shallows. Jay stood in the rear of the boat, hand on the helm, his wide smile one of fierce satisfaction. The two men held each other's gaze until someone touched Preston's shoulder, forcing him to turn away.

It was one of the councillors. He said, 'I'm sorry, Mr Whitehead, but today was relatively mild. We don't get many this calm, and you saw how difficult it was.'

'We'll lower the basket for the loading,' replied Preston, hating to admit that Jay had been right.

The councillor glanced at the mayor, who gave an almost imperceptible nod. 'It takes too long,' he went on. 'If there's bad weather running the other boats wouldn't dare wait out there as they did today.'

Preston peered at *Sea Horse* but Jay and his crew had lost interest and were busy dragging the boat onto the harbour shelf. The spectators were drifting away, laughing among themselves. He felt the heat on his face. They were wrong to give up. It had only been an experiment, a trial – of course adjustments had to be made! If only it had been someone else who had tried – anyone but Jay Brannigan. He heard the mayor clear his throat and say, 'We don't want to sound ungrateful, Mr Whitehead. But . . . ' He fell silent.

Jay was coming towards them along the jetty. To gloat, thought Preston, tensing himself for the conflict.

'Bad luck, Jay,' a councillor called out when he stopped beside them.

'I had a load of fish when I came in, now I have none. Yet I still have to pay my crew.'

Preston felt the eyes of the group swivel towards him.

'I'll reimburse Mr Brannigan for his losses,' he murmured.

Jay briefly inclined his head. 'An interesting experiment, Whitehead,' he said jovially. 'But, as you've seen, the old ways are best sometimes. In Brannigan Bay, at least.'

The mayor and his entourage shuffled past, allowing Jay to sidle up to Preston. 'I hope you learned something today,' he hissed. 'You can gain nothing here – not things, not people. Just stay away!'

They were standing right up against each other, Jay's bulk blocking Preston from the sight of the other men. The smaller man did not budge. He regarded Jay with hatred and whispered, 'You poor fool to believe that! Even this paltry moment of victory would not have been possible if not for me. Keep clinging to your old ways! Keep believing they'll help you to survive. It makes it easier for me, that's all.'

For a moment Preston thought Jay would push him from the jetty. He saw him raise his hand, the palm outstretched. Then Jay grinned and let his arm fall back. 'Goodbye, Preston,' he said and stepped aside.

Preston moved slowly past him, controlling his steps until he caught up with the mayoral party.

On the wall above the harbour, Magda stood with Vaughn in her arms, watching her husband and Preston on the jetty. 'Don't, Jay,' she whispered to herself, fearing he would explode into violence. She had preferred being up there than with the others in the harbour. It was as if the distance helped shield her from the conflict unfolding below, for she knew it was little more than another round in the intense rivalry of which she had been the cause years ago – the spark that ignited its flame. They had disguised it as two men fighting over divergent ideologies yet obliged her to acknowledge her own part in their enmity.

She too bore scars, but she had learned to live with them. It was over now and she would not be forced into feeling guilt for a single human failing. Yet for Jay and Preston it would never be exorcised.

When she saw Preston move away from Jay, she let out

her breath and shifted Vaughn in her arms, eager to be away from there before either man spotted her.

Starting for home, she almost bumped into Gertrude Kessler who emerged from the path leading to the harbour. The German woman stopped at the sight of Magda, then glanced at the small boy at her side, his hand held tightly in hers. When she looked at Magda again, her smile was anxious.

'Hello, Gertrude,' said Magda, unable to keep herself from staring at the child. He would be three in April, a slight figure with a hint of Magda's dark skin. She tore her gaze from him and smiled at the woman. 'He looks well, Gertrude . . . Happy,' she added to put the woman at ease, finding it strange that Gottlieb Kessler's wife seemed awkward whenever they met, as if she feared that Magda would one day demand her child back.

'The child makes me happy, Magda. Me and Gottlieb.'

Magda could not stop herself from reaching out her hand and gently touching the other woman's cheek. Gertrude Kessler was considerably older than she was but just then she seemed to Magda so very vulnerable.

'You both deserve happiness, Gertrude,' she whispered. 'I could not have wished for better parents for him.' It was true; knowing that Wilhelm received an abundance of love from the Kesslers had done much to alleviate the anguish she had felt at giving up her child.

When she took her leave of them and continued her journey home, she wondered whether her insistence that Wilhelm be adopted by someone in Brannigan Bay had been a mistake. The boy was a constant reminder of her past, further fuel for the hatred that raged between Jay and Preston. If only she had never told Preston about their son! Perhaps then he would have forgotten about her, would have let time ease his grip on an old passion.

She sighed as she entered the sanctuary of the cottage.

Preston's winch and cables were dismantled and stored in a hut for two months until someone came up with the bright idea of mounting the winch on the highest reach of the harbour shelf to draw the boats in once they had beached. Like the first plan, it too proved impractical; the boats could only be handled one at a time, blocking others who were eager to get their vessels to safety. The equipment lay rusting as Bull de Vries had predicted.

For a time, as summer gave way to a cold, wet winter, the affairs of Brannigan Bay continued much as they always had. But with the coming of spring, Illana Brannigan, the daughter Magda had so confidently expected, was born.

The front door of the cottage was open to let the warm December air circulate through the house. Jay heard the squeak of the gate from where he sat at the kitchen table, enjoying his second cup of black coffee since supper.

'Visitors,' remarked Magda, leaning back in her chair to see who it was. 'Evening, Dan,' she called when a man approached the door and she could see his face in the light.

'Dan!' called Jay, surprised that one of his crew should visit so late. 'Come inside. Coffee?'

Dan Robertson was a lanky thirty-five-year-old who had lived in Brannigan Bay for five years and served the last two with Jay. He held his felt hat in his hands, twisting it nervously between his fingers. 'No thanks,' he said with a nod of greeting at Magda. 'Sorry to disturb you after dark.'

'You're not disturbing us, Dan,' said Magda. 'How was your visit to Cape Town?'

'Fine, Mrs Brannigan.' Robertson had taken three days off work to visit relatives.

Magda smiled at him. 'Will you excuse me? I have to feed the baby.'

Robertson nodded, then glanced at Jay who said, 'Is something wrong, Dan?'

The hat twirled between Robertson's fingers. 'Can we talk?'

Jay chuckled in an attempt to dispel his sense of unease. 'Sounds serious,' he said. 'Sit, speak. What's on your mind?'

Robertson took a seat, his gaze fixed on the table as he began, 'I've been with you for two years now, Jay. Two good years, and I've enjoyed being on your crew.'

'It's been good having you, Dan.' Jay found it difficult to curb his curiosity but thought it best to let Robertson say what he had to in his own way.

'I didn't just visit my mother in Cape Town . . . I mean, that was my main reason for going, but . . . '

'Go on, Dan.'

The fisherman at last raised his eyes. Jay saw the guilt in them, almost sensed the words before Robertson spoke them. 'Mr Whitehead sent for me.'

Jay made no response apart from a tightening around his mouth. A cold spot in his stomach started to work its way up inside his chest.

Robertson nervously cleared his throat. 'I wondered what a rich businessman could want with a simple fisherman but I went to see him anyway. He wants me to work on his boat, Jay.' The words came out in a rush as if he could no longer wait to make his final confession.

'On his boat,' echoed Jay. 'In Cape Town?'

The silence dragged on till Robertson said at last, 'No . . . here in Brannigan Bay.'

This time there was movement, a clenching and relaxing of Jay's fists. 'That's impossible,' he said, so softly that Robertson leaned forward to hear. 'That's impossible,' he repeated, more forcefully this time. 'Whitehead has no boats here – never will have, if I can help it. He's lying to you, Dan.'

'No, Jay. He already has the council's permission to operate two boats from the harbour, provided he uses local crews.'

Jay sat in grim silence, unable to accept what he was hearing. It could not be – the council would not allow company boats in Brannigan Bay! It had been tried once before, when his father was still alive, and the request had been denied then. Preston had to be lying, it had to be a desperate attempt to cause dissent among the locals to avenge his defeat in the cableway fiasco.

'I don't think you should trust him, Dan,' he managed to say evenly. 'He's trying to use you to upset me, that's all. We're old enemies, as you know. Whitehead wants control of our waters and he's hoping to gain it by seducing you and others. Don't trust him.'

'It's a shareholding he's offering us. He provides the boats and retains ownership but the crew operate it and share in the profits from the catches. Try to understand, Jay. Perhaps the extra money we make will help us to buy our own boats some day.'

In a way, Jay did understand; he could not blame Dan or anyone else for desiring a better financial situation for themselves and their families. Yet they had to understand what it was that Preston hoped to achieve in the long term.

'Dan,' he started, 'all this will come to eventually is exploitation by the big companies. The first one to get a foot in the door will be followed by others. Next thing you know they'll start cutting prices – they can afford to. We'll all be forced to give up our way of life then. Once they've achieved that, they'll carve up what's left between them and exploit us and the whole bay.' Though he did not say it, Jay knew Preston was counting on him and the other skippers being obliged to follow suit by offering their crews a share of the profits rather than their regular wages. It would place an unbearable strain on already dangerously thin margins. Preston could afford to wait for a return on his investment; the locals could not.

Jay saw the blank look on Dan Robertson's face, a sign that the prospect of being at least theoretical master of his own craft, albeit in a capacity shared by others, had deafened him to his warnings. The others would react in the same way, probably even regard what Jay had said as inspired by his hatred of Preston. The rivalry between them had become a source of gossip ever since the cableway incident, and Jay often felt that the townspeople were watching and waiting to see who would be the eventual victor. He knew they speculated on the origin of the feud but so far no one had dared ask him.

Robertson stood up and carefully pushed his chair back against the table. 'I just wanted you to know, Jay. I didn't want you hearing about this from others.'

'It's all right, Dan. I respect your views but I think your decision is a terrible mistake. Not just for yourself but for us all.'

Robertson did not reply but held out his hand. As he took

it, Jay said, 'I wish you luck, Dan. When does Whitehead plan on sending his boats?'

'January. Good night, Jay.'

'Night, Dan.'

Jay leaned his forearms on the edge of the lower half of the door, letting the panel swing gently back and forth beneath him as he tried to collect his thoughts. He felt betrayed not by Preston's efforts, for he was ready to expect anything from him, but by the village council's silence. How long had they known? He vowed it was not over yet; many would fight with him to prevent it happening, would see through Preston's attempt at control.

When Magda returned to the kitchen, he had disappeared into the night, already working at gathering his forces.

Jay was the spokesman for the majority of fishermen who objected to the council's arbitrary decision to permit company boats to operate from the harbour.

The meeting was brief and acrid, the fishermen's accusations of betrayal countered by the council's claims of having acted in the best interests of the village.

'If that's the case,' demanded Jay, 'then why weren't we consulted? Why was this kept so secret?' He looked from one councillor to the next and saw guilt reflected on some faces.

'We spoke to enough of you to gauge an opinion,' one of them muttered lamely. 'There's no need for us to consult the entire village every time we want to make a decision.'

Jay laughed cynically. 'The ones you spoke to were the same men Whitehead had selected to run his boats. Of course they'd agree – they're blinded by greed, damn you!'

It was the mayor who finally ended the bickering. In an uncharacteristic display of will, he slammed the palm of his hand on the table.

'Enough!' he shouted. The assembled men stared at him in surprise. 'All right, Jay,' he said before gazing at each fisherman in turn. 'Let's stop playing with words and speak openly about this. We're talking money here – the future wealth and prosperity of this community. Unfortunately it means sacrifices have to be made.'

'Yes, our future,' someone muttered, but the mayor ignored the remark.

'Mr Whitehead is not only a wealthy man,' he went on, 'he's also an influential one. He made it clear that he intends building a holiday home here, that he can induce many other wealthy and influential people in Cape Town to do the same. It's such people,' he added, slamming down his palm again, 'who'll ensure our long-term prosperity. Not the harbour, Jay. The fishing might not last for ever, but the land will.'

'You're fools to believe him! Can't you see what he's really after? He wants our town! When he's got it in his pocket he'll walk all over you and build fish factories and God alone knows what else. What will become of your precious holiday resort then, huh? Who'll want to visit a town reeking of fish, the air filled with smoke from chimney stacks?'

'We'd never allow the factories,' retorted the mayor uncertainly, his brief display of authority gone as quickly as it had appeared. He tapped his fingers nervously on the table and glanced at his councillors for support.

The only one among them to have voted against Preston Whitehead's proposal said, 'What you say holds some truth, Jay. There's more to Whitehead's request than operating a few boats from the harbour. As it is, he wanted five, but we approved only two.' Ignoring angry looks from his colleagues, he added, 'Granting him this small concession doesn't mean he'll get his way in future. Meanwhile, the town gains some needed investments and Whitehead thinks he's made some progress. Let's leave it at that and let the future take care of itself.'

Jay pointed a finger at each councillor in turn. 'As long as you understand that the future involves us.'

It was only when he was outside again that he realised this was the first time he had come up against the power of money. It had meant little to him before, beyond the basic security and comfort he demanded for himself and his family. Now it meant so much more, and he did not know how to counter it.

1921

It was only in April 1921, three months after Preston sent his boats to Brannigan Bay, that Kevin Whitehead first learned of his son's actions.

'Who gave you the authority?' he demanded from across his desk. 'Just who the hell do you think you are, Preston?'

'Two boats, for God's sake! The way you're talking, Father, you'd think it was half our fleet.'

'Two boats or twenty,' Kevin shouted, 'what difference does it make? And why there, of all places? Because of your so-called passion for another man's wife – is that it? Do you think this will impress her, that she'll come running to you because you're the big wheel controlling the lives of some fishermen who don't know any better? Is that it, Preston? Control the harbour, then the town and you get the girl with it? When you have it all, what then? Will there be some other obsession on which to spend our money – *my* money?' He was so enraged that he did not notice his secretary quietly shut the door to his office. 'You're a married man, in case you've forgotten. A man with a wife and son.'

Preston was standing before the desk like a schoolboy summoned before his headmaster, his face pale at the vehemence of his father's outburst. 'I don't have to take this,' he spat out, spinning round to leave.

His father's voice seemed to strike into his back. '*Sit down!*'

Despite himself, Preston moved back to the desk and took a seat.

'I'll talk to you any way I damn well please,' said Kevin more calmly. 'You might have a few shares in this business but you're little different from anyone else who works for me. I'll fire you if I have to – do you understand?'

No, don't deny it, you'll just make things worse.'

'For God's sake, Father, I'm your son! I seem to have less say in the business than your clerks! You treat me as though I'm some junior apprentice.'

'That's exactly what you are!' replied Kevin sadly, the rage gone from him now. 'You *are*, my boy, and you're destroying your chance at having a greater say in things with the way you're carrying on. You've done nothing to inspire confidence, nothing to earn additional responsibility. I'm going to give you one last chance, Preston. The shares I've already granted you will remain yours but they'll be all you'll ever have unless you leave Brannigan Bay alone and forget your dream of some grand harbour there.'

His face had slowly returned to its normal colour yet he seemed exhausted by this speech. 'Things are not going well with us,' he said softly, staring at his desktop as though talking to himself. 'There's no spare capital for any grandiose schemes; the big concerns are squeezing prices, hoping it'll force us to sell out. We can hold our own if we're careful. But there's no leeway for expansion. And there's certainly no room for personal vendettas or obsessions! Every step we take must be carefully planned.'

Preston tried to curb his exasperation. Have it your way, he thought, for the moment. If he had to wait until it was all his before he could make things happen then that's what he would do.

The silence in the office dragged on and Preston dismissed himself by standing up and pushing the chair back.

Kevin looked up at him. His tone was placatory when he said, 'Speaking of Brannigan Bay, how's our holiday house coming along?'

'Fine,' came the curt reply. 'They should be finished in the next three months.'

'Good, good. I think I'll take a few weeks off once it's ready – relax and put some finishing touches to it. Your mother needs the break as well.'

Preston did not reply as he left the office.

1924

May

The short, slight man had been seen in Brannigan Bay once before. Then the children who had spotted him seated in his Vauxhall 23-60 had snickered at the sight of the gnome-like figure who could just be seen over the steering wheel.

This time no one was around to be amused when the Vauxhall crunched to a halt on a gravel patch overlooking the western coastline. Climbing out, the man strolled, hands on hips, to the very edge of the rocks. The evening breeze plucked at the few remaining strands of his thin grey hair yet he made no effort to pat them into place. It had been many years since he had displayed any outward sign of vanity.

Brian McDermott was fifty years old, the product of a Scots father who had travelled to the Cape Colony in the 1850s to seek his fortune. The only riches the first McDermott managed to accumulate, however, were the love of a good woman of Dutch stock and a small piece of land in the Karoo from which he eked out a precarious living. Despite a hard life which slowly wore him down, he instilled in his only child his desire for something better.

Brian McDermott was as physically tough as his father, which was a good thing because of his small size. From his mother he inherited a gentle sense of humour as well as a sharp-witted mind that he put to good use as he grew older. Two days after McDermott buried her beside his father's grave, he sold up and headed north to the diamond fields at

Kimberley, to see for himself what he regarded as how the other half lived.

He was disappointed. Not only were the commercial affairs of the town already well under the control of the big conglomerates, McDermott found the dreams of the few remaining diggers too dependent on the whims of chance. He spent two weeks in Kimberley, during which he twice stepped into the boxing ring, proceeding to astound the crowd by beating his bigger and stronger opponents to a bloody pulp. He also cost the spectators a great deal in bets, and McDermott knew his battered body and their sudden realisation of his skills would not permit a third, equally profitable encounter. Adding the earnings from the betting to the proceeds from the sale of his parents' farm, he headed south to Cape Town.

There he bought a second-hand truck, spent twenty pounds and one week restoring it to a roadworthy state, and commenced transporting anything that anyone wanted to move, whenever and wherever they liked.

He had two more trucks by the end of the first year and twelve in total by the second. Though he still frequented bars, occasionally engaging in bouts of fisticuffs for the sheer fun of it, McDermott could measure his business efforts by his growing bank balance.

A reporter from the *Cape Argus*, a regular at a bar McDermott supported, became intrigued by the colourful character who seemed to have sprung from nowhere and persuaded his editor to print an article he had written on the emergent businessman. McDermott's name appeared in print for the first time but it was not to be the last.

The businessmen for whom McDermott transported goods liked and respected the hard-working little man who could converse on an equal footing with them about the intricacies of their operations. Some were wary of a man who seemed to love nothing but business and rock angling, and had what they sensed was ambition to do greater things. A reliable transport contractor now, they reasoned, but likely a canny commercial adversary in time to come.

McDermott, too, considered it was time for diversification. The opportunity arose while he was transporting fish on contract for Whitehead Enterprises. It was Kevin Whitehead himself, with whom he had struck up a firm friendship, who sold McDermott one of his old boats.

'Do I detect,' Kevin Whitehead said when McDermott first raised the subject of purchase, 'that by agreeing to the sale I am launching a future competitor on his way?'

'Damn right,' McDermott replied. 'Competition is what you need. It'll keep you on your toes.' Kevin had laughed, for he knew that his prophecy would come true and that the diminutive McDermott was right. He agreed there and then to the sale.

Other boats followed over the next few years, though no more from Whitehead Enterprises. Despite their continued friendship, the two men became fierce yet honourable rivals as McDermott's company, Deep Sea Limited, went from strength to strength, eventually equalling Whitehead Enterprises in size and income.

McDermott worked like a demon, hiring the best people, paying the highest wages and demanding the most of them. He took a short break to get married to a woman who died five years later without bearing him children, then immersed himself again in his business activities. Deep Sea Limited owned two fish-processing and canning plants on the West Coast but Kevin Whitehead continued to concentrate his activities in Cape Town.

A week before, McDermott had visited his old friend and rival at home where Kevin was restricted to his bed after suffering a heart attack. McDermott had been intending to go but was beaten to it by Kevin's request that he visit him.

The last thing he expected was his friend's proposal that McDermott buy out the majority shareholding in Whitehead Enterprises. 'Why?' he asked in disbelief. 'You have a son! Surely . . . '

Kevin Whitehead had grimaced. 'Yes, with a ten per cent share in the business. Lisa, too, will control her own thirty per cent. But Preston is not right for it, Brian. He's obsessed with other things – personal things. I've worked too long and hard to allow him to destroy my company. And he will, Brian, he will.' He began to cough and

McDermott quickly handed him the glass of water from the bedside table.

When he saw Kevin had his breathing under control, he asked, 'Why me, your business rival?'

'And friend.'

'Yes. Even so . . . '

'Because you understand my business, because you'd love it as if it were your own. You'd keep Whitehead Enterprises strong, build on it, keep it a name worth remembering. Otherwise, I fear it'll be one of the giants who'll swallow up what's left once Preston is through with it.' He laughed drily and added, 'You and I, we're a dying breed, Brian. The old entrepreneurs, you starting out with your rickety trucks, me with my leaky tubs.'

McDermott knew what he meant, for they often decried the changing face of business. Younger, more greedy and ruthless men were now at the helm, who often did not even own the companies they manipulated with fancy schemes learned at university. The real owners, hundreds of faceless shareholders, lacked hands-on experience to enable them to interfere. They were happy as long as the dividends kept rolling in. Few entrepreneurs were left and, as far as McDermott and Kevin Whitehead were concerned, the fun had gone out of it.

'A dying breed is right,' said McDermott with a wry smile. 'Hell, there you lie with your faulty ticker, talking as if I've a whole life ahead of me. Damn it, Kevin, I'm fifty already, wifeless and childless. Another ten or fifteen years from now and I'll be thinking of selling out myself. Preston has his whole life ahead of him. He'll calm down and learn the ropes.'

'Maybe,' came the soft reply, 'but it might be too late. It must be you, Brian. You can sell your shares back to him when you want to retire.'

'You'd trust me?' asked McDermott mischievously.

'We can build it into the contract.'

McDermott laughed. 'I'll think about it, Kevin. Christ knows whether I can afford it, though.'

'Yes, you can. Just hold off building that new canning factory of yours for a while, that's all.'

'You know about that?' asked McDermott with mock incredulity.

Kevin Whitehead mumbled something incomprehensible. When he looked at McDermott again, his expression was serious. 'Speak to my accountants, Brian. I've told them to show you everything. But there's not much time left . . . No,' he said when McDermott protested, 'even my doctor has stopped lying to me. You're going to have to decide fast, or else my sixty per cent goes to Preston upon my death.'

McDermott stood up and patted Kevin's shoulder. 'All right,' he said. 'I'll go over the books. But I think I need to know, old friend, all about this obsession of Preston's. Are you prepared to tell me?'

Kevin let out a long sigh, then nodded. 'Sit,' he told his guest.

Now, studying the spread of Brannigan Bay, Brian McDermott felt saddened that Kevin Whitehead would not be around much longer. What he had said was true: business was no longer the same.

He had spent the days since their conversation poring over Whitehead Enterprises' balance sheets with his accountants. Only once during that time did he meet Preston. The young man had at first reacted with outrage at what he regarded as his father's betrayal, then proceeded to treat McDermott with quiet contempt. He volunteered no information and refused to answer the occasional query even when McDermott asked about the operation of his two boats in Brannigan Bay. 'Those boats are funded out of *my* profits,' Preston had said. 'They've nothing to do with my father or any of his raiders.'

McDermott had let the insult pass, merely stating that the boats in Brannigan Bay bore the Whitehead Enterprises name on their sterns. He had seen it for himself when he visited the village some months ago.

When he had all the facts he needed McDermott headed for Brannigan Bay to mull things over and make a final decision. He had spent the morning fishing from the same spot as he had on his previous visit, but luck was against him. He gave up after a while and drove instead to the harbour where he studied the layout of the enclave more closely while he walked among the boats firmly secured for the weekend.

The harbour had serious disadvantages, he quickly realised; the entrance was narrow and unsafe and the harbour area provided no room for expansion. McDermott reckoned it would suffice for the time being but if the market for fish continued to grow the fishermen would eventually be forced to find and develop an alternative site. Yet did the village warrant a harbour the size Preston had in mind, with factories and canning plants? McDermott thought not.

Nevertheless, he drove himself out to the spot that Kevin Whitehead had described and found he had to respect Preston's choice. An inexpensive jetty and breakwater, decided McDermott, would give the fishermen everything they needed. The area on the high ground where Preston dreamed of erecting factories could be used for other things.

The wind howled in from the sea, jerking McDermott so strongly that he was forced to step back to keep his balance. He looked towards the east, letting his gaze follow the contour of the coastline. He liked the little village. It was quaint, with an abundance of natural scenery and rich fishing grounds for rock anglers like himself. Therein lay the place's future wealth, he decided. Property linked to tourism. It already had a reputation for its healthy climate and abundant fish; with a little development it could offer wealthier tourists – even from abroad – so much more. McDermott's mind went into overdrive at all the possibilities, until he laughed aloud, realising that he was as exploitative as Preston.

He turned his mind instead to the desirability of a retirement home in Brannigan Bay. Ten to fifteen years left before he packed it in, he had told Kevin Whitehead. If he built a place for himself it should be a cosy, comfortable home, one that would perhaps be shared by a woman. He chuckled at the thought. What respectable woman would fall in love with someone like him? He hadn't even tried since Helen's death. There had only been the occasional partner, who usually became bored with his greater interest in his business. McDermott sighed and studied the coastline again, his mind still toying with the idea of a holiday home.

He could come through for weekends and enjoy some angling.

His attention was caught by the setting sun casting its glow on the small hamlet of Clayton across the bay, splaying a golden light over the few scattered cottages. He had been there on his previous visit to Brannigan Bay. *There*, he thought with sudden insight, was where he would erect factories if he needed them. The coast at Clayton was less rugged with fewer cliffs and provided a natural harbour. It was also closer to the Agulhas fishing banks than Brannigan Bay. He wondered whether Preston had ever considered that.

When the wind joined forces with approaching night chilling McDermott on his rocky perch, he stood up and made his way back to the Vauxhall. As he started the engine, he remembered that he had not yet come to any decision on the purchase of Whitehead Enterprises. 'Hell,' he muttered as the engine purred into life. 'Who do you think you're fooling?' For he knew he had made up his mind as soon as Kevin Whitehead had raised the subject.

He would go to him first thing on Monday morning with his offer.

Preston raised his hand to knock at the bedroom door, then slowly lowered it. Gripping the doorknob, he silently turned it.

The light inside the room was dim, exaggerating the pallor of his father's drawn features. Preston stood in the doorway for a long time, staring down at Kevin's sleeping form.

'Why?' he whispered, as if the dying man could hear. 'Why are you doing this to me? You denied me Magda, threatened me with this, yet you've done it anyway. Why?'

He thought back to his acrimonious confrontation with Kevin about the boats he had entered into service in Brannigan Bay. He had not put a foot wrong over the years since then, had concentrated on learning the business and, as far as he was concerned, been an exemplary father and husband.

Husband, he thought darkly, his hand tightening round the doorknob. Marrying Grace had been a mistake – he had no desire to be her husband or anything else. She was just like his mother, an empty-headed dilettante content to perform social duties for her husband, a nervous little filly with no clear-cut identity of her own. How she irritated him!

As for the boy, Grace's son Barry – he was not his *real* son. That child – his and Magda's – had been taken from him even before he had had a chance to acknowledge him.

His gaze had become blurred by the anger coursing through him but again he settled it on his father, the hatred it contained spanning the distance between them as if it could force the sick man to wake.

Three years of toeing the line, of curbing the energies that would make the things he longed for his. Three long, frustrating years, and what had it achieved? His father had not ceded any more responsibility to him. It was nothing less than a betrayal, a prostitution of his birthright.

'You bastard,' he whispered, wishing his father were awake to hear. 'You fucking, betraying bastard. I hope you die.'

In the morning, it was so.

Preston walked slowly from one end of the large office to the other, as if wanting to get the measure of the place his father had filled. It was his now – the office, the boats, the factories. The company. His mother had thirty per cent of it, but she had already indicated that she was content to leave total control in his hands.

When he had stepped inside the office that morning, the first time since Kevin's funeral, he had felt a momentary pang of loss and sense of loneliness but had quickly shrugged it off and reminded himself that he was now in command of the company's destiny. It was time to realise his dreams.

After two weeks Preston had overcome whatever qualms he might have had about succeeding his father. He felt entirely in control.

The soft knock at the office door intruded on his sense of

well-being. He frowned when his secretary entered. 'What is it, Betty?' he demanded gruffly.

'Mr McDermott is here. He's asked to see you.'

Preston slowly capped his fountain pen, answering, 'Very well. Since he's here you might as well show him in.'

Preston was secretly delighted by McDermott's appearance for he had wondered when he would get round to calling. He had no doubt that McDermott hoped, in spite of Kevin's death, to convince him to make the sale anyway.

McDermott stepped inside with a curt nod. 'Good of you to see me.'

'Take a seat, McDermott.' Preston glanced at the large brown envelope in his visitor's hand and knew he had guessed correctly.

The small man gave a wry smile before he pulled out a chair and sank into it. He let his gaze swivel slowly round the office. 'You've made changes,' he said softly.

'There'll be more.'

'I'm sure,' replied McDermott with a short, harsh laugh.

His amusement angered Preston. 'Get to the point, McDermott,' he snapped.

'All right, laddie. You know why I'm here.'

'I can guess – and you're wasting your time. You might have fooled my father but I'm a different kettle of fish.'

'Damn right,' muttered McDermott under his breath. 'I've spoken to your mother about my offer,' he added more loudly. 'She thinks it's a fair one.'

Preston's snigger echoed round the office. 'My mother? What does she know about fair or unfair? She has only thirty per cent. You had no right to approach her.'

'Spare me,' retorted McDermott. He puckered his lips and let out his breath in a low whistle.

Preston glanced significantly at the clock on the wall. McDermott ignored him and said, 'Since Kevin – since your father's death, I've had another look at things. From a different perspective, you might say. My interest in acquiring the majority shareholding in Whitehead Enterprises now has nothing to do with a response to a friend or the challenge to keep it going. It's a question of survival – for both our companies.'

Preston snorted. 'You had a nerve wanting to take over Whitehead when your own company's in trouble.'

McDermott studied him for a long time before he said, 'I mentioned both our companies, Preston.'

'You don't know what you're talking about.'

'Yes, I do. Whitehead Enterprises is over-extended – badly so. Your two fish-processing plants are losing money hand over fist and the big boys are watching and waiting for just the right moment to pounce. They're already squeezing you. You either can't see it, or don't *want* to.'

Preston tried to stop the sudden frown that puckered his brow but the glint in McDermott's eyes showed he had failed. 'Your father knew,' the older man added more gently, 'and he also knew my company is next in line. Merging our interests was the answer. We could rationalise our operations, use our combined capital more efficiently, invest in bigger, more modern boats, for instance. We could— '

'He was thinking of a sell-out,' Preston cut in, 'not a merger.'

McDermott smiled patiently. 'He was thinking of buying time for the name he'd built up. For you, Preston. To achieve that, he needed experienced management – mine. If you'd been less resentful towards me and read the bloody deal I was offering, you'd have seen you had first option on my shares when I decide to get out.'

'At an exorbitant price, no doubt, way beyond what I'd be able to afford on the profits from my meagre ten per cent holding.'

'Christ, but you're one impatient young man! Your mother's thirty per cent would have come to you with time.' He stood up quickly, as if suddenly tiring of Preston's responses. 'I'll leave you this,' he said, dropping the envelope on the desk. 'Think about it objectively once you're over the thrill of your new position.' He started for the door.

'McDermott.'

He turned slowly, his expression revealing nothing.

'I have no need to read it,' said Preston, a small smile playing at the corners of his mouth. 'Not now, not later. Take your miserly offer with you.'

'Easy, laddie, you might come to regret it.'

'No, I don't think so.' He spoke lightly and swivelled his chair so that he stared at the wall. Yet his words were directed at McDermott when he said, 'Whether you're right or wrong about the plants makes little difference to me. I'd planned to sell them off anyhow. I have other things in mind,' he finished, swinging round to face McDermott again. 'Bigger things.'

'Oh, yes, your scheme for a harbour in Brannigan Bay. Yes,' he added, noting Preston's look of surprise, 'your father told me about that – about everything, Preston. You're more of an arrogant fool than I thought if you go ahead on that.'

Preston saw McDermott's gaze move leisurely, deliberately, towards the picture on the wall. It was the one by Magda of him in his airman's uniform on the beach. 'Get the hell out of here,' he growled.

'I'm going, laddie – but first hear me out on this. Building that harbour would mean the end of Whitehead Enterprises. Damn it, man, that kind of development is beyond the reach of even our combined resources! You might just get the jetty laid before the hawks swoop down on you. But the rest of it? You'll never see that, Preston. Not as the owner.'

'What business is it of yours what happens to me?'

McDermott's smile did not reach his eyes. 'As far as you're concerned,' he said without rancour, 'none. But I have a good ten to fifteen years' fight left in me, and I intend to sell out while I'm still doing all right. If Whitehead Enterprises goes there'll only be my outfit left for the big guns to aim at. I haven't got the defence for that kind of hammering, so I'll not stand idle while you play with my future.'

'You can't stop me, McDermott.'

The small man shrugged. 'I'll give it my best try, laddie. Seeing as how I can't do it by controlling you from the inside, I'll just have to work at you from where I am.'

'Are you threatening me?' Preston stood up, his face livid with rage. He moved closer to tower over McDermott.

'You read me right, laddie,' came the calm reply before McDermott slowly left the office.

Preston waited until he heard the door at the end of the passage slam shut before he let out his breath, clutching the edge of his desk as if it would return the power that seemed to have deserted him at McDermott's verbal battering.

It was lies – all lies! It had to be. McDermott had been trying to scare him into taking his offer seriously, that was all. The company was sound, he was sure of it – though it was true that financing a harbour would be risky. But he had always known that and the possibilities for future wealth made the risks worthwhile.

McDermott did not bother him – he was an anachronism, fearful of the large concerns and their modern way of thinking, and Preston knew he could match them. Empty threats, he thought as he tried to concentrate on what he had been doing before his visitor's arrival. Nevertheless, his mind kept returning to what the older man had said about the canning factories. Could they be a shaky operation? He would get his accountants to give him the full facts tomorrow.

Should it be necessary, he would rid himself of them without delay.

1928

May

The boy drew his knees up close to his chest as a wave crashed onto the rocks, sending salt spray into the air and splashing down on the bare skin of his legs. He knew he was dangerously near to the raging water but was thrilled by the powerful pounding of the surf, its angry roar, the tremor he felt through the rock when it struck.

Wilhelm Kessler was eleven years old. Apart from the tingle of fear he felt as the waters rushed towards him, he knew his parents would be outraged if they guessed how he tempted fate. That thought, too, excited him, making him smile when he pictured Gertrude, her round face filled with a mixture of anger and alarm while she scolded him for the risk he had taken. Gottlieb would add words of warning, feigning fury as he puffed at his pipe and tugged indecisively at his belt.

Wilhelm always knew that his father hated having to discipline him with the leather strap, a symbol of punishment, hanging behind the kitchen door.

It had been more than a year since the strap had been used on him. Wilhelm knew that on that occasion, Gottlieb had cried afterwards. He knew too that in their household, *he* was the one who wielded the power, and he enjoyed testing the strength of it.

It was not as if he felt scorn for the gentle German couple, for he loved them dearly in his way. They were simple where he was quick-witted; they were warm and caring towards others where Wilhelm was aloof from both his peers and elders. *He* was the one with strength, the one who could not be touched by the words and deeds of others. Even to his young mind it was a frustration that he had to depend on the Kesslers for care, when it should have been the other way round.

The defensive attitude he exhibited towards Gertrude and Gottlieb had grown even stronger just a few weeks ago. It had started with a simple word spoken spitefully by a boy in Wilhelm's school class. The youth had probably not even known its meaning, a word overheard perhaps from his parents, who were unaware that their son would sense its derogatory nature and store it in his growing vocabulary.

He and Wilhelm had been tensing their bodies in readiness for bitter combat. His body shook with fear, for he knew he was no match for the Kessler boy's natural brutality, so he was relieved when an older boy spotted them and ran over to put a quick stop to it. The youngster poured out his resentment at Wilhelm from behind the protection of the peacekeeper. 'You're a bastard, Wilhelm!' he shouted. 'A bullying bastard!' He ran off with tears in his eyes, his voice carrying across the watching schoolyard as he continued to shout, 'Bastard! Bastard! Bastard!'

It was only later that morning, when Wilhelm asked a teacher, that he learned what the term meant. The teacher was embarrassed for he was aware that Wilhelm was adopted and feared he might upset the boy. He explained carefully but was surprised at the lack of response on Wilhelm's face. 'It's not a nice word,' he added quickly, 'and most people call others that when they're angry with them. That's why— '

Wilhelm had ended his teacher's explanation with a word of thanks before running off. He had no desire to learn the other meanings contained in the word; what he had just heard satisfied him. It came almost as a relief for it clarified so much and explained why he was different from Gertrude and Gottlieb, different from the other children – from everyone else. He was a *bastard*! He was sure that no one else in Brannigan Bay possessed such a status. He was special!

Such was his excitement at this discovery that he did not hesitate to confront his foster parents when he arrived home from school. Gertrude burst into tears, telling him to wait until Gottlieb came in. That evening when Gottlieb entered the house Wilhelm heard Gertrude, crying again, say to him, 'I knew we should be telling the boy. Long ago, I knew we better telling him.'

They called him into the kitchen then, taking turns to explain, leading each other, faltering in their broken English. His real mother was dead, they had said. And his father? he asked when they seemed to have finished. Wilhelm saw the quick, confused glance that Gertrude cast her husband before she said that he had died in the war. Wilhelm sensed it was a lie.

Both Kesslers were concerned at the effect the news would have on him and they talked about how he should disregard what other children said. It was because they did not understand, the Kesslers told him. Wilhelm did and said nothing to reassure them that it had not upset him in the least.

A bastard, he thought now with delight, as the surf roared and swirled over the rocks. Everyone considered it a disgrace, something of which he should be ashamed. Instead he was proud! He would show them all. Some day they would know it had made him a special person, different from them – better than them.

Water splashed across his feet, making him spring back. He drew in his breath at the delicious fear churning through his body as he saw the swells, immense now, harness their force for the next attack on the shore. Beyond them, he glimpsed the fishing boats, sails aloft, running before the storm wind.

Keeping to the rocks, Wilhelm made his way to the harbour. Once, he had to wait for the sea to subside before he could dash across a low strip of rock. Again fear pulsed delightfully through him as he reached safety moments before the next wave crashed in.

When he approached the high cliffs shielding the harbour from the might of the Atlantic, their base was covered in white surf. A pity – it would have been a test of his climbing skills to have scrambled round them. He had done it before but it had been low tide with a calm sea. Today the waves running across the bay were restless and angry, tearing at the cliffs in white, foamed fury. Wilhelm knew he had no hope of getting across and with a frustrated sigh he made for high ground.

A whining wind tore at him as he reached the irregular row of cottages lining the cliffs. A north-westerly, he thought, licking his thumb before holding it up to test the wind's direction. From the high ground he spotted a column of smoke rising on the mainland across the bay. The villagers in the tiny hamlet of Clayton could see the approaching storm before their neighbours in Brannigan Bay and always lit huge bonfires to warn any fishermen plying their trade within the restricted vision of the curving coastline.

Wilhelm studied the group of fishing boats again. There were six, driving in a tight pack towards the middle of the bay. He knew then that they had marked the surging current flicking back from the shore, its ugly power strong enough to turn a small craft and push it to open sea. The fishermen had seen its intent and knew it was safer to spend an extra hour on the swell than follow the shortest course to harbour. They would turn their boats only when they were well beyond its reach, tacking a course parallel to the shore. When they turned for the last time, it would be to rush across the current at a right angle, battling against it for a brief moment before they slipped into sanctuary.

Wilhelm watched them a while longer before he started to walk past the cottages. He noticed Magda Brannigan standing at the wall of her house, her hair protected from the wind by a bright yellow scarf as she watched the boats' progress. He knew that further along the shore, to the west, Gertrude, too, would be waiting and watching.

'Wilhelm!' Vaughn Brannigan came running through the cottage gate. 'You going to the harbour?'

Wilhelm nodded and saw Magda glance at them. He was fascinated by her beauty and the strange way in which she always looked at him, studying him it seemed, as if she knew something that should have been a secret to him alone. Perhaps she was one of those who knew he was a bastard. He lowered his gaze and said to Vaughn, 'You coming along?'

'All right . . . I'll just ask my ma, though.'

'Don't be such a baby! I don't ask my ma when I want to go somewhere.'

The Brannigan boy flushed. He gave Wilhelm a shove that sent him staggering back. 'Don't call me a baby,' he warned.

Wilhelm laughed. 'You want to fight?' He kept a wary eye

on the cottage where Magda was again watching the sea.

Vaughn, too, glanced across his shoulder at his mother. 'All right,' he said, 'but not here, down at the harbour.'

'Ask your ma first,' retorted Wilhelm, but scampered away with a yell when Vaughn lunged for him again. With a last backward glance at Magda, Vaughn ran after the older boy.

Few fishermen lingered on the harbour shelf, only those who had come in earlier that afternoon. Their catch was already loaded on the waiting trucks and now they studied the sea with concerned eyes.

'Let's fight over there,' said Wilhelm, pointing to the drying racks. Vaughn nodded and followed.

Anyone watching the two boys strolling across the uneven rocks would not have guessed their intention. Both appeared relaxed, without anger, two friends whiling away an early winter afternoon. In a strange way they were friends, despite the differences in their ages and personalities. And, like all boys who became friends, there was a strong element of rivalry, envy, and at times animosity between them. Who was the stronger, the faster? Who would take the biggest risk?

The sound of the wind was an anguished moan as they readied themselves for combat, circling each other warily, arms extended. 'You beat me last time,' said Wilhelm and tried unsuccessfully to trip his opponent, 'but I was sick then.'

Vaughn laughed scornfully. 'I always beat you because I'm stronger!' He slapped away Wilhelm's hand and tried to stamp on the older boy's foot.

'Look!' cried Wilhelm suddenly. 'The boats!' He saw Vaughn's gaze dart towards the sea and used his lapse in concentration to strike first.

Moving fast, his arms encircled Vaughn's waist before he tripped him. They crashed down on the hard rock, Vaughn cursing at being tricked, and rolled over and over, their well-matched strength giving each a brief moment of dominance.

Their grunting struggle was observed by a man standing a short distance from the harbour huts. He strode across to them. 'Stop it, you two!' he called out. 'You'll hurt yourselves.'

The combatants released each other slowly and glared at the stranger for disturbing their private trial of strength. 'We're only playing,' muttered Vaughn as he got to his feet. Wilhelm tucked in his shirt and stood beside him. His thick hair, dishevelled by the fight and the wind, stuck out over his ears. He spat on his hands and used them as a brush.

Preston Whitehead smiled as he watched the boy. 'Even if you were playing,' he said, 'it's still dangerous to wrestle here on the rocks. You could hit your head.'

'We've fought on the rocks before,' mumbled Wilhelm, fingering the grazed skin of his knee. 'Once we wrestled on the cliffs,' he added with defiant pride in his eyes.

Preston smiled again. 'Do it once too often,' he warned, 'and you'll be wrestling with the fishes! What's your name?'

'Wilhelm.'

'And yours?'

'Vaughn Brannigan. I'm nine.'

'Brannigan? Jay Brannigan's boy?'

Vaughn stuck out his chest proudly and nodded.

Preston knelt before Vaughn and said, 'Your mother, boy, is she well?'

Vaughn nodded again.

'She at home?'

'Yes, sir.' Vaughn pointed to the cottage overlooking the harbour. 'That's where we live,' he explained.

'And Jay . . . your father – is he home right now?'

Vaughn swung round as if suddenly remembering the storm brewing over the sea. He glanced at Preston across his shoulder and said, 'My dad is at sea. He'll be coming in soon.' He appeared eager to escape the adult's questions.

Preston stood up and placed a hand on each boy's shoulder. 'No more fighting now, you hear? At least not here.' He gave Wilhelm's tousled hair a quick stroke before turning away.

He looked back once as he climbed the steep harbour path. The two boys were standing in the shallows of the harbour, close beside each other. There was little of Magda in him, decided Preston, thinking of Vaughn and recalling the youngster's rough features and rugged frame as he stood

150

beside the other, slimmer, boy. He tried to quell the natural dislike he felt for Jay Brannigan's son.

His gaze was drawn to the row of cottages a short distance away. She was in there, going about her everyday chores, a fisherman's wife who could have – no, *should* have – been so much more. How life had cheated them!

His thoughts drifted back to the time, four years ago, when Brian McDermott had come to see him with his offer to buy the company. He had thought he was on top of things at last but that had been a fleeting phase. Within a few days he had discovered that McDermott had not been lying about the financial plight of his fish factories. Matters were even worse than McDermott had suggested, and Preston quickly realised it was the worst time in which to seek a buyer. The vultures would be able to squeeze him into accepting the unacceptable. The only way out was to try to salvage what he had and get his operations back on an even keel before attempting to sell. That would take time – time during which his dream of a harbour for Brannigan Bay would again have to be relegated to a lower priority. He could not afford the harbour project while he still owned the factories and neither could he afford to sacrifice them yet. A few more years, that was all it needed.

Frustrated still further by the decline in fish prices, it took him until early in 1928 before he was ready to sell. Even then he moved cautiously, putting only one of the two plants on the market as he knew that McDermott had not been exaggerating the avarice of the large fishing concerns. One sale and they would be interested; two and they would scent blood. The price he eventually accepted was lower than he had hoped for but it was better than nothing. He had sufficient capital to initiate his plans but not to complete them and, again, caution ruled the day. Preston contracted a land surveyor to study the terrain at the Brannigan Bay site and provide a report from which the plans could be drawn. The man had been at work for three months already; Preston would meet him later that day.

As he glanced at the Brannigan cottage, he realised it had been some time since he had thought of Magda with

151

any depth of feeling. Almost without realising it, he began to head for the cottage.

Magda shut the front door against the wind and glanced through the kitchen window. From there she could glimpse the bay. A few minutes ago she had seen the boats turn and knew they were through the worst. Relieved, she remembered her daughter and moved across the kitchen to go into the nearest bedroom where Illana, now seven years old, was busy with her homework. Magda watched over her daughter's shoulder as she stroked the child's long, glossy hair.

'I'm hungry,' the little girl said, smiling at her mother in a way that always made Magda marvel at her angelic beauty. Magda had no illusions about her own attractiveness but Illana's appearance had a special quality. Her skin, naturally dark like Magda's, had a velvety texture that made people spontaneously want to touch it. Auburn hair, the red hues more dominant than her mother's, swirled in thick natural curls about her oval-shaped face with its delicate features. The little girl's eyes were an unusually light shade of green, large with a faintly oriental influence in the shape of the lids. Her gaze was candid beyond her years.

'I'll make supper as soon as Daddy is home,' said Magda, kissing her daughter's brow. She saw the flicker of concern in Illana's eyes and added, 'He'll be safe, my darling – he always is. He has *you* to come home to.'

Illana said, 'I've been thinking of him . . . Will he know?'

Magda laughed, thinking of Jay's adulation of his daughter. 'He'll know,' she reassured her, 'because he thinks of nothing else but you.' As she leaned forward to kiss Illana again she hoped that in years to come she would not have to regard her daughter as a rival for Jay's affections. 'He'll know,' she whispered again.

She heard the knock at the door even before she entered the kitchen.

The wind had blown Preston's hair across his forehead, so that when she opened the door it was a few seconds before she recognised him. She mouthed his name but no sound escaped her lips.

'Hello, Magda.'

She stared aghast, wishing she could close the door and shut out all that had happened between them.

'Magda, it's me – Preston.'

His voice broke the strange spell that gripped her. 'Yes,' she said suddenly, opening the door wider.

'It's been a long time.'

She nodded. 'How are you, Preston?'

'I'm well, Magda. May I come in?'

She glanced over his shoulder but the boats were no longer in view.

'He's still at sea,' said Preston. 'It'll be some time before they make harbour and unload the boats. I – let's just talk for a few moments. Please, Magda.'

She settled her gaze on him before she slid back the bolt on the lower door. Preston opened it and stepped inside. 'It's a bitter wind,' he said, closing it behind him.

'Sit, Preston. Coffee?'

He shook his head and sat down at the kitchen table. 'I met your son,' he said, 'at the harbour a short while ago. Vaughn, is it?'

'Yes.'

'I just wanted to see you, Magda. I wanted to know for myself how you were. I've heard things are not going well in Brannigan Bay.'

Magda sighed and took the chair opposite him. 'The fish prices, you mean? Yes, things have not been easy the past few years.' After the glorious start to the twenties, the price of fish had plummeted so that catches of stock fish were sometimes bundled on the waiting trucks for almost no charge at all. Some fishermen had already given up their traditional way of life. Younger people, too, were leaving the town once their schooling was completed, seeking more rewarding careers elsewhere. It was only the tourist trade and the associated building industry that continued to prosper.

'I also know,' said Preston, 'that Jay bought himself a

153

new boat some years ago. With fish prices as they are, it can't have been a very wise investment.'

Magda's mouth tightened, but her voice was even as she said, 'We manage, Preston.'

His arm streaked out so fast she was unable to withdraw her hand before he gripped it in his. 'It could have been so different, Magda,' he whispered hoarsely. 'I could have given you everything! Comfort, love— '

'I have love,' she answered, forcing her hand free. 'I have the comforts I want – and I have a young daughter in the next room, Preston, so please stop this.'

He sighed and leaned back in his chair. 'I'm sorry, I didn't mean to upset you. I . . . Did I tell you I have a son?' he added, his tone suddenly friendly.

'I've heard. How old is he?'

'Barry . . . let me think, eight . . . Yes, he turned eight in March.'

Magda's relief at the change in him was reflected in her light laugh. 'Then he's just a few months older than my daughter.'

Just then Illana came into the kitchen. She seemed about to say something but remained silent at the sight of the strange man.

Magda saw Preston's mouth part slightly. 'That's your daughter?' he asked, disbelief in his voice.

She turned to Illana and smiled. 'Yes, that's Illana – Jay's pride and joy, and my envy.'

'My God, she's beautiful!'

Magda laughed again. 'That's what I mean by envy!' She reached out for the child and drew her gently closer. 'Illana,' she said, 'say hello to Mr Whitehead.' Even as she spoke, she knew she would have to tell Jay of Preston's visit. Illana confided constantly in her father.

'Good evening, Mr Whitehead,' the little girl said politely. She glanced quickly at Magda before she started back for her room.

Preston's eyes were glued on Illana as she left the kitchen. 'She's your daughter all right,' he said. 'She's truly beautiful.'

154

'She has Jay's height,' Magda said quickly. 'She'll be a tall woman.'

Preston's gaze returned to her again. 'I'll be in Brannigan Bay for a few more days, Magda. I've some business here. You heard about my father's death?'

'Yes. I'm sorry.' They sat in silence for a while, till Magda went on, 'Now that Whitehead Enterprises is all yours, you plan to build a harbour here, don't you?'

He stared at her without answering. She said, 'Oh, come on, Preston, everyone knows what that surveyor out at Hagan's Point is doing.'

He shifted uneasily. 'It's the only way, Magda. The independent fishermen can't survive much longer if prices remain as they are. Big boats are needed, boats that can venture out for days at a time, and boats like that need a decent, safe harbour.'

'Those independent fishermen you refer to will fight you on this.'

'You mean Jay, of course.'

'The rest of them as well. So will others – those who don't want to see Brannigan Bay become just another factory town.'

'You're sounding just like them,' he snapped. 'Can't you see the job opportunities this will create, the influx of further wealth it will attract? This town will die without it!'

'Brannigan Bay, as I know it, is already dying, Preston. Most of it is owned by outsiders who come here at weekends or summer holidays to take what it offers. Yet we can live with them, they're people like us. Factories aren't, Preston. We can't live with factories.'

Preston stood up slowly. He stared down at her and said, 'You've become just like him, do you know that? You think and act just like him.'

'Perhaps I do. Perhaps that's because we're the same, because we're both children of Brannigan Bay.'

He turned when he reached the door. 'It's a foolish waste, Magda,' he said quietly. 'Such a waste.'

She remained sitting at the table long after he had left, long after the howl of the wind had turned to a whimper as rain moved in to take control of the dwindling afternoon. She moved only when she heard Illana's shout of excitement and knew the child had seen Jay through the bedroom window.

Jumping to her feet, Magda opened the door. Jay came running through the cottage gate, Vaughn hard on his heels. Both were soaked to the skin.

'There goes my clean kitchen floor!' she shouted as they burst through the door but she flew into Jay's arms and held him tightly.

'Now *that*'s what I call a real welcome home,' he said into her hair.

Illana ran wildly into the kitchen and joined in their embrace, holding on to them both, laughing with relief and joy. Vaughn stood in the middle of the kitchen floor, shaking himself like a dog. Droplets of water spun off him. He slouched his shoulders and grunted, 'Here comes the slimy sea monster!'

The kitchen was warm, cosy, safe from the storm outside, far beyond the reach of the mighty sea.

1933

February

When Preston finally sold his second fish-processing plant, he was forced to use most of the profits from the sale to purchase three new steam-driven trawlers, an outlay that further hindered the implementation of his plans. It was, however, an economic necessity to ensure that he remained competitive with the other fishing concerns.

It bothered him that his available capital and the amount of resources the banks were prepared to lend him did not allow for full completion of the Brannigan Bay harbour project. Ironically, it was Grace who saved him – or, rather, the death of her father. When the news came, Preston gave the matter scant thought; he had hardly known the Connoleys, and even Grace had not taken up his many offers that she travel to England to visit them. It was three weeks later that Grace, an only child, learned of the substantial sum of money she had inherited. Preston immediately adopted a different attitude towards his father-in-law's death. It was a simple matter for him to convince Grace that they were materially well catered for and that her inheritance could be more effectively used to invest in their son's future.

Preston was ready to move.

Barry Whitehead leaned his head against the trunk of the massive oak tree. His eyes were shut while he listened to the sound of his mother's guests' laughter coming from the far side of the large garden.

Opening one eye, he glanced with blurred vision towards the table with its white cloth shifting lazily in the afternoon breeze. If anyone had asked him to describe Grace, Barry would have told of a mother always immaculately groomed and attired while entertaining the wives of his father's business associates. On the few occasions when she came to his room at night, the boy sensed she wanted to be closer to him yet did not know how to achieve it. Preston loved his business too dearly to sacrifice much time to be with his family and Barry came to accept that it would do little good either to indulge in self-pity or resent them for it. He knew instinctively that it would be easier to depend on himself for whatever he needed beyond the basic securities they provided.

Barry sighed – sometimes he thought he had been born lonely.

The voices at the table sounded louder now. He looked their way and saw the group of four women on their feet, checking their handbags before departure. Waiting until they had rounded the corner, he stood up and strolled over to the table. As he had hoped, there remained a generous quantity of cake, though the tea was cold.

He had just stuffed a second slice into his mouth when Grace appeared at the patio door. She stared at him for a moment, then stepped out. 'That's very bad manners,' she reprimanded him. 'You're not some street urchin who has to steal when no one is watching.'

Barry flushed and lowered the slice of cake. 'Sorry, Mother,' he mumbled.

'Have you finished your homework?'

'Yes, Mother. Well, almost.'

'Go and complete it, then. Go on . . . to your room now.' She touched him lightly as he fled past but the gesture was more absent-minded than affectionate.

He entered his bedroom and stared resentfully at the desk set against one wall. When he was seated behind it, he had a clear view of the large, rambling garden. The desk had been a Christmas present from Preston. Barry had wanted a model sailboat like his best friend Lionel Augustine had, and it had taken all his strength to stop tears of disappointment from flowing. For the first time he had come close to screaming his outrage at Preston, who stood behind him with his hands on his shoulders, saying, 'It's from behind this desk, my boy, that you'll learn how to run our business. One day it'll be *your* fishing fleet.' Yet the only part of a fleet the boy had wanted was a simple model sailboat with which to join his friends in play. He shrugged his shoulders and settled down behind the gleaming wood to finish his homework.

A few hours later, he saw Preston's car come up the long driveway. He watched his father climb out, take his briefcase from behind the driver's seat, then enter the house. Barry wondered whether Preston would stick his head inside the room and greet him with restrained politeness, the way he had taken to doing of late.

A further half-hour went by before there was a knock at the door. Barry knew it was not Preston before the door opened to admit Henry, their butler. 'Your father wishes to see you in his study, Master Barry,' the old coloured man said. 'You done something wrong?'

Barry blinked rapidly while shaking his head. 'N-No!' he stammered, falling in behind Henry as he started back down the passage. Henry winked reassuringly at him as he knocked at the study door before ushering the boy inside.

Preston looked up. 'Ah, Barry,' he said as if surprised to see his son standing there. 'Sit down, boy, sit.'

Barry almost fell into the chair in front of the desk. He was in trouble – he had to be! Letting his mind replay the events of the past few days, he tried to recall what he had done wrong.

He was surprised to note that Preston seemed nervous, as if he did not know how to begin what he had to say. Barry shifted his hands from his legs and laid them on the armrest of the chair. His flesh stuck sweatily to the smooth surface.

'Barry,' Preston started, then cleared his throat. 'Barry, your mother mentioned to me that you recently enquired after the possibility of your having a brother.'

Barry stared back, blinking in confusion. Recently? He had not asked about that for some time – not since Lionel had explained how such things came about. Quite interesting it had been too, especially the way Lionel had used his pet Dobermann to illustrate what he was talking about. Since then Barry had merely assumed Grace had not been 'on heat', as Lionel put it, since his own birth.

He concentrated on Preston again and suddenly knew what had sparked off the meeting. They had told his father! He had warned Lionel they would get into trouble, but no, there was no stopping Lionel once he got going on an idea. 'We'll see if she touches it like that woman in my dad's book,' Lionel had said as they hid round the corner of Lionel's home, waiting for the young maid who worked there to make her appearance. They stood quivering with tension, each holding his erect penis, like highway robbers lying in wait with brandished pistols. 'She'll touch mine first – it's bigger,' Lionel had said just as the girl, a few years older than them, caught sight of the two boys with their grey flannels around their ankles and sheepish grins on their faces. Barry had felt the shrinking sensation of surrender between his trembling fingers even before her first outburst of laughter.

Now he was in it – really deep! Why had the maid told on them? She'd found it funny, hadn't she? Preston's voice cut into his panicky thoughts.

'Your mother and I,' he was saying, 'thought you and I should have a chat about . . . well, about things. You know . . . just you and me, man to man, sort of.'

'Yes, Father.' Barry felt the rhythm of his feet as the pace of his swinging increased in tempo. When his shoe thumped against the desk, he immediately drew his legs tightly in under his chair. He studied his father's face but Preston appeared not to have noticed the sound.

'So, I thought . . . Do you know what I'm talking about, Barry?'

'Yes, Father . . . I mean, no . . . Yes!' His feet had started swinging again, as though he lacked control over them. Swish! Swish! Thump!

'Are you swinging your feet, boy?'

'No, sir!' His feet clung so tightly to the underside of the chair that he feared he would fall forward if he released his hands from the armrests. He kept his eyes intently on his father's face, expecting the matter of the maid to be raised at any moment but Preston talked on in textbook fashion about the facts of life. Barry almost felt sorry for his father at not having had a friend with an obliging Dobermann or a maid with a sense of humour. The only item that was new to him was when Preston came full circle to the reason for their discussion: the absence of any brothers or sisters. After Barry's birth, Preston explained, his mother had been unable to have any more children.

Barry felt guilt descend on him. Was that why Grace was not as warm and loving as other mothers? Did she blame him for it? Was that why his father did not play with him or give him the presents he desired? One did not do kind things for boys who were to blame for there being no brothers and sisters.

'Barry!'

'Sir?'

'You're sitting all askew, boy. Straighten up.'

It was as though Barry's immediate response to the instruction caused a change in Preston's mood, for he leaned back in his chair and said, 'I appreciate it must have been lonely for you at times. I had no brother or sister either. Still, look on the bright side: you'll be grown up one of these days and the only one in line to take over the company. Think of that, boy,' he ended with sudden excitement in his voice, sitting forward as if being closer would infect Barry with his enthusiasm. 'One day it will all be yours, Barry – all of Whitehead Enterprises. The name lives on, hey?'

It ended then. Preston sank further into his chair and said gruffly, 'All right, boy, you can go now.'

Barry left the office without knowing what had sparked off the summons or topic of Preston's lecture – for it could not be called a discussion. All that concerned him was whether he had responded according to his father's expectations.

As always, he had no idea just what they were.

Jay arose just as the first rays of sun peered over the mountains to push aside the shadows lying across the sea. The house was silent as his bare feet padded softly down the passage. Even Vaughn was still asleep; he usually got up at the crack of dawn at weekends to earn pocket money by guiding tourists to the best fishing spots.

Jay made coffee while he watched the day grow. It would be mild, a perfect late-summer morning. While he waited for the water to boil he readied his fishing rod and packed fresh bait, spare sinkers and a gutting knife in a large canvas knapsack.

Magda watched him sleepily when he returned to the bedroom to dress. 'What's wrong?' she asked.

'Nothing. I thought I'd try my luck on the rocks, that's all. It's a beautiful day.'

'It's Sunday, Jay. It's been a long time since we attended church together as a family.'

'Perhaps next week. It's just so perfect outside, Magda.' He kissed her and said, 'Don't keep breakfast for me.'

The sea lay like a placid lake as he made his way over the rocks past the harbour. Three others had beaten him to it, two local men and a stranger to whom Jay called a friendly greeting.

He chose a spot on the rocks lining an area known as the Cove. As he cast his fishing line in deep, he wondered whether he shouldn't have asked Bull de Vries to join him.

The sun warmed him while he waited for a fish to nibble at his bait. Near him, the low tide crept lazily up the damp sand. Further along the beach, a few holidaymakers were already out to make the most of the superb weather, their umbrellas bright circles of colour against the stark whiteness of the sand.

A few hundred yards from the rocks where Jay sat, a huge house overlooked the breakers, its shape softened by the early-morning haze drifting off the sea. Jay knew it was Brian McDermott's house. He found it strange that they had never met, especially as McDermott had been coming to the village for many years now and was reported to visit almost every weekend since having the house built a year ago. What was even more surprising was that McDermott seemed to have no interest in their harbour; he appeared content to have nothing more than his large, fancy house where he could spend his weekends. That was as it should be, thought Jay.

He knew that Bull had met the businessman once or twice

when he was out angling and that he thought McDermott 'an interesting and honourable sort'. Even Vaughn spoke proudly of having helped him with his fishing, receiving generous payment for his services.

As Jay stared at the house, he realised someone inside was watching him. A short, wiry man appeared through the door that led out onto a wide veranda, walked across the lawn, then leaped nimbly over the low wall bordering the edge of the property. McDermott?

Jay watched him come closer, all thoughts of fishing now gone from his mind. McDermott was still some yards away when he smiled and said, 'Jay Brannigan, if I'm not mistaken?'

'That's right,' replied Jay, his own question contained in the tone of his response.

McDermott chuckled as he made his way up onto the rocks. 'Someone pointed you out to me a while ago,' he explained. 'McDermott's the name,' he added, stretching out his hand. 'Brian McDermott.'

'I'd reckoned as much,' said Jay, returning the firm handshake. 'You're up early for a Sunday.'

'So are you.'

'I'm always excited at the prospect of a beautiful day. I wanted to get in some early-morning fishing.'

McDermott smiled again and said, 'I've been meaning to talk to you for some time now.'

'What could we have to talk about, Mr McDermott? I'm just a simple fisherman.'

McDermott laughed. 'I've yet to meet a fisherman who's simple,' he replied, studying Jay before he added, 'I think we have much in common that warrants discussion. Preston Whitehead, for instance.'

Jay tried in vain to conceal his interest. After a lengthy silence McDermott said, 'Did you know he has the finance he needs to get going on a new harbour? Oh, yes,' he added, finding the answer on Jay's face, 'he has the money and he has the government's blessing to proceed. All he needs now is the village council's approval.'

When Jay still did not respond, McDermott got to his

feet with a grunt and said, 'I'm told I make great coffee. Like some?'

'I think it's just what I need,' replied Jay, reeling in his line.

March

The village council called a special meeting to discuss the prospect of a new harbour. It was held in the dance hall of the Crystal Lodge, the only venue large enough to accommodate the many townspeople who came to debate the issue.

Apart from every fisherman who owned or operated a boat, there were the town fathers and the prominent merchants, as well as a sprinkling of holidaymakers who were also landowners in Brannigan Bay.

The general feeling among those attending was that it was a straight fight between profit and tradition, with Preston Whitehead, most of the councillors and the local merchants in favour of the former. Opposing them were Jay Brannigan and the majority of the fishermen.

At the invitation of the mayor, who presided over the meeting, Preston was the first to present his case to the assembly, appearing relaxed as he stood up and surveyed the crowds. Without any preamble, he spoke directly to the group of fishermen crowded around Jay, warning them bluntly that their way of life was coming to an end. Ignoring the angry murmur from the men he raised his voice, saying, 'Just think of your situation over the past few years. The lowest prices ever, your children choosing different ways of life. And it's going to get worse. My harbour can save you – can keep you and your families alive! My boats will provide you with work – different from your old ways, certainly, but work that'll allow you to feed and clothe your loved ones.'

Preston used the silence in the hall to press on with his arguments, making the merchants his target this time. 'Along with a safe haven for the boats, I plan to build factories for cleaning the fish – and supplies for the building of my factories

164

will come from local merchants. The factories will need people to operate them, people with money to spend locally.'

A few questions were fired at him, all of which he managed to field with ease, causing Jay to grunt in reluctant admiration.

When Jay stood up to speak, he followed Preston's example and plunged straight in. 'He's pleading for a larger, safer harbour, one used by big boats with immense nets that scoop up tons of fish at a time, boats big enough to roam deeper waters once the supply of fish within the bay is depleted. The same fish, gentlemen, which attract the tourists in growing numbers and cause many to purchase property and homes.'

Preston interrupted him. 'I fail to see where this is leading. My proposed harbour affects only the fishermen and the commercial aspects of Brannigan Bay. It has nothing to do with tourism.'

'Ah, but it has, it most certainly has.' Jay stepped closer to Preston, his hands in his pockets. 'Most come here to enjoy the fishing – from rocks, not boats. If the smaller fish have been scooped up by nets, the larger ones that feed on them will no longer come into the bay. Without fish, there'll be fewer tourists . . . and *less* money spent among our local merchants.' He was pleased to see the owner of the Crystal Lodge rub his jaw thoughtfully before bending his head close to that of the man who had recently built a bakery in town.

'Earlier, you spoke of building factories – factories with sanitary conditions, I think you said. Does that mean no fish entrails will be thrown back into the sea?'

'Exactly.'

Jay faced the crowd again. 'Just the other day,' he said casually, 'I was looking at an American magazine.' He glanced at Brian McDermott, who smiled encouragingly leaving Preston in no doubt about the source of the information. 'In it I saw an article on two coastal towns, fishing hamlets like Brannigan Bay, where these so-called sanitary conditions were implemented. What followed after a short time was a scarcity of fish in the nearby waters. They had moved off to find replacement food for the fish entrails that were no longer thrown into the waters.'

'That's rubbish!' burst out Preston. 'It's never been proved!'

Jay ignored him. 'What *is* true is that a new, larger harbour will be used by big boats with the capacity for larger catches. They use immense nets that scoop up tons of fish at a time, and they're big enough to roam deeper waters once the supply of fish within the bay is depleted. But . . . that's progress.'

McDermott was on his feet before Jay had a chance to answer questions. 'I have some plans I think you should all know about.' Everyone leaned forward. 'Just last week,' he continued, satisfied he had their undivided attention, 'I received permission from the government to build a factory at Clayton, your neighbouring village across the bay.'

The silence lasted only seconds before the assembled crowd broke out in a confused babble. Everyone had questions, it seemed. Bull de Vries glanced at Jay, who wore a smile of deep satisfaction. The mayor slammed his gavel repeatedly on the table but it was only when he got to his feet that some measure of order was restored.

Preston had gone pale. 'You're arguing against yourself, McDermott!' he shouted. 'It makes no damn difference whether there's a factory here or across the bay.'

'It's for shark oil,' came the steady reply.

'Shark oil?' someone echoed from the back of the hall.

McDermott nodded. 'That's all I'm interested in catching and processing. A rather smelly affair,' he added with a laugh, 'but that's not Brannigan Bay's problem.'

'And trawlers?' asked the mayor. 'Will they be allowed to operate from there?'

'Only if they're fishing from the Agulhas bank. No boats will be allowed to lower their nets inside Brannigan Bay. Not from *my* harbour,' he added significantly.

'Well,' the mayor said, his broad forehead gleaming with sweat, 'apart from the other arguments against a new harbour for our town, there doesn't seem much point in having two of them in one bay, does there?' He pointedly avoided meeting Preston's angry gaze.

When they put the matter to the vote, Preston's proposal was unanimously rejected, and the meeting closed.

Jay was talking to some supporters near the back of the hall as the crowd filed out, excitedly discussing McDermott's bombshell. Preston, his face livid with rage at his defeat, moved over to them. 'I should have guessed,' he said, glancing at McDermott and Jay in turn.

'Yes,' replied McDermott, 'and you should have remembered what I told you, Preston. I warned you I would stop you however I could.'

Preston's voice was bitter when he said, 'It's not over yet, McDermott.' He pushed angrily past them, staring intently at Jay with hate-filled eyes.

He's right, thought Jay. All that had been won was this round.

June

The three boats chugged through the early-morning mist, breaking the sea's calm, flat surface so that it rippled under their bows.

On the lead craft, Olaf Svenson leaned his head against the protective glass of the wheelhouse, his eyes narrowed against the glare of the sun pushing at the mist 'Keep her steady,' he told the helmsman. 'That outcrop of rock is not far away.'

The Swede tried to recall the rock's structure, its reach, the curve of land beyond it. He had been past it many times before but now his memory was hazy.

It was almost six months since Svenson had joined the Whitehead Enterprises fleet as a skipper. Not an intelligent man, he nevertheless realised that he owed his position to Preston's awareness of his hatred for Jay Brannigan. It was a long time since the night Jay had beaten Svenson on the rocks after the episode with Gottlieb Kessler, but the humiliation had not left him.

At first he could not believe his luck in being given command of one of Preston's newest and largest steam-driven boats. He had wondered why his crew was made up of the roughest men on the payroll of Whitehead Enterprises. Now he knew.

Preston Whitehead's orders had been clear: they were to

avoid entering the bay from the open sea from where their approach could be seen. When the Brannigan Bay fishermen became aware of their presence, the boats from Cape Town must already be in position within the waters of the bay, their nets out.

The mist had slowed them. The local fishermen would not be daunted by it and would be at sea when the intruders arrived. It would soon be too late for what Preston wanted to achieve.

'It's somewhere dead ahead,' Svenson told the helmsman, trepidation tightening his voice. He leaned out of the door and saw the blurred shapes of the other two boats following them.

The sun thrust determinedly through the mist and again a shaft of dazzling light struck through, seeming to point to where a strip of grey rock jutted from the Atlantic. Svenson saw its weathered crevices clearly. The water swirled lazily round its base, helping to conceal the danger lurking below its placid surface.

'Swing, damn you! Swing!' he shouted as the helmsman cursed and jerked hard on the rudder. The boat shuddered as it turned, the low growl of its engines changing into an urgent whine as power was increased. Svenson's heart thudded as their slow turn eased them frighteningly close past the rock.

He tried to bring his breathing under control. 'You can turn back on course now,' he said. 'It's a straight run from here on.'

The mist had begun to dissipate when Svenson recognised the more familiar parts of the bay. He scanned the sea but detected no sign of any boats. 'What's the time?' he asked.

'Seven-thirty,' replied the helmsman.

Svenson gave a satisfied grunt. 'Looks like we're in luck – they're not out yet.' Jumping to the deck, he gave the waiting crew instructions. A group of them hurried to ready the dinghy that would haul the large nets behind the parent boat.

The boats and their dinghies worked in unison, cordoning off a section of sea to be swept by their nets. 'What happens now?' a crewman asked the helmsman.

The Swede turned to face the cliffs around which he knew the fishing boats would appear. Maliciously he replied, 'Now, we work. And we wait. They'll be here soon.'

He began to move away but turned back to the man and said, 'Fetch my rifle.'

The mist was not the reason that the fishermen of Brannigan Bay were late. For the past three days the town had been celebrating the Festival of the Sea, an annual thanksgiving for the bounty yielded by the ocean. Special church services were held daily, old family recipes dug out from dusty files and sea foods prepared in the traditional way. The festive period culminated in a dance held on the cliff tops, and it was that which caused the fishermen to linger in their beds.

'My mouth feels like it has barnacles in it,' groaned Jay, rubbing a hand across his bleary eyes.

Gottlieb Kessler leaned his head wearily on the gunwale. He straightened up after a while and glanced at the boy watching them from a little distance away. 'Jay,' he said, 'Wilhelm is old enough to feel the oars. He wants to go with.'

Jay shifted his gaze to Wilhelm Kessler. The boy met his look defiantly. As always, Jay felt himself tense at the sight of Magda's child. Wilhelm was sixteen, slim and wiry, though the anger ever present in his eyes made him appear older.

'Does the boy know how it's done?' he asked Gottlieb.

The German nodded.

Though most of the boys were out in the boats from a tender age, they were fifteen or more before they were permitted to become a crew member. Then they had to 'feel' the oars – row all day until their hands bled and their muscles ached agonisingly when they returned to harbour. It was a challenge all boys aspired to, sometimes with fear at the thought of this test of manhood.

Jay saw no fear in Wilhelm Kessler. 'He can come,' he said softly.

Pockets of mist clung stubbornly to the cliff face when they launched *Sea Horse*. Wilhelm clambered in and took the place usually occupied by Gottlieb, who tried hard to conceal the

169

pride on his face as he moved to the back of the boat, taking a seat beside Jay at the helm.

'You're a clever swine,' said Jay, 'bringing your son along on a day when you have an almighty hangover.' Gottlieb made no reply, his gaze and thoughts riveted on Wilhelm.

Wilhelm's eyes held a determined gleam, and his jaw clenched as he strained at the oars. Jay noticed a fisherman wink encouragingly at the boy but receive not a flicker of response from him.

Turning away to study the sea, Jay thought about Vaughn; his son would now be more impatient than ever to take his test at the oars. Jay longed for the day when Vaughn would take his place among the crew.

His eyes on Wilhelm again, he saw the boy had a natural rhythm, his body moving in an easy flow as he pulled at the oars. *Sea Horse* snaked over the calm sea and rounded the base of the cliffs.

'Jay!'

He started at the urgent note in Gottlieb's voice, then swung round and looked to where he was pointing. 'The bastards!' he said in a low voice. 'Those are Whitehead's boats – they must be!'

'Dragging the fish from our sea,' said Gottlieb angrily.

'Keep rowing,' commanded Jay as the crew stopped to watch. 'Let's get over there.'

There was something familiar about the big man standing beside the wheelhouse of the first boat but it was only when *Sea Horse* came alongside that Jay recognised Svenson, who smirked as he stood looking down at the smaller craft, his hands on his hips. 'So, Brannigan,' he called out above the throb of the engines, 'I see the whales haven't got you yet.'

Jay ignored the remark. Standing up, he spread his legs as *Sea Horse* rolled on the light swell. 'What are you men doing here, Svenson?'

'What does it look like we're doing, Brannigan? We're fishing – in a *real* boat!'

The smell of burning coal from Svenson's boat was in Jay's nostrils. 'Get out of our waters, Svenson.'

'*Your* waters? Do you think you own the sea, Brannigan? On

this boat, I'm the master. I'll fish where I want, so get out of my way before I ram you!' He turned and barked an order at the helmsman. The threatening note of the engines increased as the big boat began to move sluggishly.

'He means it,' said Jay, ordering his men to take to their oars.

'We run for harbour, Jay?' asked Gottlieb in dismay.

'No! We'll cut their nets, that's all.' He hauled out his gutting knife and signalled his intentions to the other skippers. Within moments all the boats were heading to where the wide semicircle of corks bobbed on the surface of the water, the heavy nets suspended beneath them, and before Svenson or the other Cape Town skippers had realised what the locals planned, *Sea Horse* had already reached the perimeter of the nets. Jay and his men leaned over the gunwales and slashed through the ropes securing the nets to the corks.

'Move fast!' Jay shouted, knowing that Svenson would soon recover and retaliate. The other local skippers had joined them now, each boat selecting a section of net along which to wreak havoc.

Shouts and curses resounded from the Cape Town men as they watched their nets sink towards the sea bed. The crews fought uselessly to drag the nets back onto the decks, and already Svenson's boat had begun its slow turn, skipper and crew bent on revenge.

'*Now* we get back to harbour,' shouted Jay. Oars clawed at the water and the boats headed closer inshore where the bigger vessels could not follow.

As *Sea Horse* mounted the quickening swell that rushed forward to pound the shore, Jay noticed a crowd of villagers watching the mêlée from the rocks. But when he looked back over his shoulder, he saw that Svenson was ignoring the dangerous surf and coming after *Sea Horse*, a rifle in his hands. The Swede was steadying himself against the side of the wheelhouse and taking careful aim. There was a light puff of smoke before a bullet whined past dangerously close to Jay's head.

Jay's crew stopped rowing to stare, shocked, at their pursuer. The two other Cape Town boats had remained in

171

position, their skippers not prepared to risk moving closer inshore.

Another puff of smoke from Svenson's rifle – and Jay saw him take aim again. Seconds later splinters of wood flew from *Sea Horse*'s stern as the bullet hit home. The crew spun off their thwarts and hugged the deck in fright. Jay remained at the helm, caught between the danger behind him and the imminent threat of the surf ahead.

'Keep rowing!' he shouted and swung hard on the helm, but the boat veered broadside to the next swell, sliding clumsily forward on the wave. Beside him, Gottlieb was using his fists to restore discipline and Wilhelm was the first to take up his oar again. Slowly *Sea Horse* responded to their efforts to turn her from the shore.

The other fishermen had realised what was happening and descended on Svenson's boat. Bull de Vries's vessel was the first to come alongside, taking advantage of the sluggish movement of the larger boat as it was forced to turn back from the tug of the inshore current. Svenson was struggling to reload his rifle as Bull and half his crew scrambled aboard, quickly disarming the Swede and throwing his rifle overboard.

As *Sea Horse* nosed alongside Svenson's craft, Jay readied himself for the jump to the deck a few feet higher than their own gunwales, followed by Gottlieb, holding a club.

Bull pulled him aside as he stepped onto the trawler. 'This must stop,' he said. Even as Bull spoke, the Cape Town boats hove to some distance away, obviously deciding they had had enough.

Jay knew Bull was right. It would serve no purpose to carry on fighting; what had happened today would have to be resolved in some other way.

Next to the wheelhouse, Gottlieb moved away from Svenson, who was on his hands and knees on the deck. A trickle of blood flowed from the corner of Gottlieb's mouth. He caught sight of his skipper. 'I got the bastard Swede, Jay!' he shouted in triumph.

'Gottlieb!' The German spun round at Jay's warning shout. Behind him, Svenson was back on his feet, a knife in his hand. Though still dazed, he lunged forward. Gottlieb stepped back,

172

but not quickly enough to avoid the blade slicing across the flesh of his forearm. Blood spurted onto the deck as he reeled back and tripped across a pile of rope. He fell heavily and lay helpless at Svenson's feet.

'Pa!'

Wilhelm's anguished cry brought Jay into action. He rushed forward but the boy was faster. Wilhelm hurtled across the deck, the sun glinting on the blade of a gutting knife in his hand.

'No, Wilhelm! No!' Gottlieb's shriek mingled with Svenson's surprised cry of pain as the knife was buried up to the hilt in his side. The Swede was rocked back by the impact of the stab and the boy's weight. He stood there, disbelief on his face as he clutched at the wound.

Wilhelm struck again. And again.

Jay reached his side and gripped the boy's wrist just as Svenson staggered up against the gunwale, teetered there for a moment, then toppled headlong into the sea.

Wilhelm stood silently, pinioned within Jay's arms, his lips twisted into a macabre grin of satisfaction as if he was acutely aware of what he had done – and had enjoyed it.

'Fish him out,' said Jay, but the men who had remained on the boats had already rowed towards where Svenson drifted, a red stain swirling in the water near him.

'It's over,' said Jay, releasing Wilhelm. 'We're leaving now – and so should you,' he added to Svenson's crew.

Gottlieb's face was ashen white, but Jay knew it was because of the shock of what Wilhelm had done not because of his wound. 'It's a shallow cut,' murmured the German, staring at his son as if at a stranger. 'The Swede?' he asked.

Jay did not answer. Like Gottlieb, he could not take his eyes off the boy. Wilhelm was grinning dazedly, the trembling of his shoulders the only sign of what he had been through. A moment later the men in *Sea Horse* hauled Svenson's body aboard. Jay glanced at Gottlieb's anxious face before he turned to a fisherman who was taking charge of the Cape Town crew.

'We'll take Svenson with us,' he told the man. 'There'll be an inquiry . . . ' He shrugged.

The man nodded, his expression grave. 'Whatever our

differences,' he said, 'we'll say the boy protected . . . That is his father, isn't it?'

Jay nodded.

'Well,' the fisherman continued, 'that was the truth of it.'

Jay's quick smile conveyed his thanks. He studied the man who, only a few moments ago, had been their enemy. 'Why did you come?' asked Jay.

The fisherman glanced at the Cape Town boats moving slowly closer. 'We were told we were heading for a fishing bank,' he replied, 'not some bloody bay. They said—'

'They?'

'Svenson. And the big boss.'

'Whitehead?'

'Himself. They said there might be trouble. We thought it would be Port Elizabeth boats, snooping too far south.'

'But you must have known,' argued Jay. 'You were hugging the shoreline.'

'We were only told the truth once we'd left Cape Town. And a skipper's a skipper – you do as he tells you.'

Jay had no answer to that. Instead he told his men to return to their boats. As they rowed away, the intruders hauled in the remains of their nets before turning the boats towards Cape Town.

Magda and Jay sat in the quiet kitchen. 'What will become of him?' she asked, raising her cup to her lips. Her fingers trembled.

'There'll be an inquiry, of course.' Jay sighed, reached out and covered her hand with his. 'I don't think they'll punish Wilhelm too severely.'

'He's still a boy!'

'A boy who stabbed a man many times.'

'Defending his father!'

'He stabbed Svenson several times.'

'Wilhelm was upset, confused . . . in shock!'

'He *enjoyed* it, Magda. I was there when it happened . . . I saw the look on his face when he plunged that knife into the Swede.'

'The child was shocked – distraught! Of course he'd seem strange! He's probably haunted by what he was forced to do!' Her voice was shrill, with a touch of hysteria, a sound Jay had never before heard from her.

'I'm not the only one who saw it. He was provoked,' he continued, 'I don't deny that he acted to protect Gottlieb. But, Magda, that boy enjoyed what he did! He stuck that knife in three times – smiling while he did it!'

'You're lying! You're lying because you still resent—'

He wanted to cringe away from what he saw in her eyes. 'Ask your father if you don't believe me. *He* saw it. Gottlieb as well. We all did.'

She moved towards him, her body rigid. 'Are you trying to tell me I gave birth to a killer?'

'No, only that you – that we should accept Wilhelm enjoys violence. I think I'm trying to warn you that Wilhelm will live and die by violence.'

Her face was white as she stared disbelievingly down at him. 'You're a fool, Jay Brannigan. An arrogant fool!'

As she tore, sobbing, from the room, Jay sighed into his hands and wondered if she was right.

The boy and girl sat close beside each other on the rocks as they warily watched the waves.

'Aren't we too close?' she asked when foaming water crashed upwards, booming and hissing, spraying them with its touch.

Vaughn Brannigan placed a comforting arm about his sister's shoulders. 'We're quite safe,' he told her. 'The tide's already turned.'

Illana was twelve, a tall girl with small, budding breasts. The beauty she had had as a tiny child had been refined now that she had shed her little-girl plumpness.

She enjoyed the feel of Vaughn's arm about her, the way she always enjoyed his touch. Illana was a spirited girl but there were times when she needed the comfort and security of her large, muscular brother. Sometimes, when she felt depressed, it was Vaughn, with his easy smile and gentle manner, who cheered her again. She adored him, would do anything to prevent him from ever changing.

There were times when she thought him almost too gentle and forgiving, when it had been she who had taken revenge on his behalf – like the day that a strict teacher, frustrated at Vaughn's slowness in solving an arithmetic problem she had written on the blackboard, had taunted the boy in front of his peers. Illana had been furious on learning about it at mid-morning break when a girl from Vaughn's class teased him. Although younger and smaller than her brother's tormentor, Illana leaped on the girl and forced her to the ground, punching her, scratching her face and tugging her hair. It had cost Vaughn all his considerable strength to pull his sister from her victim.

She studied him now, saw his eyes half closed against the glare of the sea. Nudging him in the ribs, she asked, 'Did you read my story?'

His lips framed a small smile before he nodded.

'And?' She knew he was teasing her by delaying his verdict. 'And?' she prompted again. 'What did you think?'

'Not bad this time.'

'Not bad? *This* time?' She tried to pull free, but his grip was too strong. 'Vaughn Brannigan – you said the last one was the best you'd read! Were you lying?'

'No, little sister,' he said, bringing her closer so that he could kiss her cheek, 'I'm lying now . . . It was terrific – better even than the last one.'

The anger and doubt disappeared from her face, softening her features when she beamed at him. 'You mean that, *boet*?' she asked, affection apparent in her use of the diminutive meaning brother.

'Of course.'

He was always the first to see anything she wrote – school essays, poems, her short stories – and no one else's approval meant as much as his.

'You still want to become a writer some day?'

'I want nothing else! And you, *boet*? Do you know what you want?'

'I wish I did,' he answered softly, shifting position to ease his

176

cramped muscles. 'In Brannigan Bay you're either a fisherman or you work in a shop. I don't know what else there is.'

'You could be a teacher,' ventured Illana.

Vaughn laughed. 'A teacher? Come on, sis! You know I can hardly pass my class tests! All I have is strength.'

'A wrestler then!' she said and punched his arm. 'No, maybe not,' she continued. 'I wouldn't like to think of you doing that.' Sighing loudly, she added, 'Besides, you're not ugly enough.'

Vaughn was silent for a few moments, then said, 'Perhaps I could be a strong man who showed off his muscles – like this.' He giggled, pushed back his shirt sleeve, curled his hand into a fist, and flexed his biceps. 'See? Big, isn't it?'

A voice from behind made them spin round. 'Showing off again?'

Vaughn lowered his arm. 'Hello, Wilhelm,' he said sheepishly, quickly rolling down his sleeve.

Illana could not stop staring at the strange boy who had become a man in the eyes of the village children – because he had taken a life. Though the three had grown up together, it seemed to Illana that she was seeing him for the first time. The arrogant swagger that had often irritated her was suddenly terrifying.

Wilhelm's mouth twisted into a sneer as he stepped from the rock and came to stand in front of them. 'I have to go before some inquiry or other,' he said, nonchalantly. 'Someone's coming from Cape Town to find out what happened.'

Illana lowered her eyes to the rocks at her feet. She, like most Brannigan Bay children, knew that Wilhelm was not the Kesslers' real son – neither he nor the Kesslers made any secret of it. It amused the kids, though, the way he affected their German accent as if trying to prove he was different. He had acquired his parents' clipped speech patterns and guttural consonants, like an Afrikaans speaker who seldom used English. Wilhelm's idealisation of the Kesslers' fatherland was an open secret. Illana often wished that he and Vaughn would end their friendship as her father wanted. Once she had heard her parents arguing about the relationship between the two boys.

'When is this – this inquiry?' Vaughn asked.

'Monday.'

'What are you going to tell them?'

'The truth. That Swede tried to kill my pa. I was too fast and strong for him, though.'

Illana saw Vaughn studying Wilhelm strangely. His face held none of the awe she had seen in other boys when they saw Wilhelm or spoke of what had happened. He said, 'The killing must rest heavy on your mind. If it were me, I wouldn't sleep.'

Wilhelm laughed scornfully. 'I'd do it again if I had to,' he said. 'You're always so soft, Vaughn.'

'He's not soft!' Illana blurted out.

Wilhelm widened his eyes in mock surprise. 'Oh,' he mimicked Illana's voice, 'the little sister has a tongue, does she?' Before he could say anything else, Vaughn jumped up and positioned himself between her and Wilhelm.

Illana sprang to her feet and clutched Vaughn's shirt. 'Don't fight him, Vaughn,' she pleaded. 'Not because of me. It's all right. I don't mind being mocked. Really!'

She need not have worried; Wilhelm had already stepped back from Vaughn, who was stronger and heavier though an inch or so shorter. 'Come on, Vaughn,' he said, laughing nervously. 'I was only teasing.'

Turning away, he clambered to the top of the rocks, looking back once at Vaughn, whose face still expressed protective anger. 'Vaughn,' he said almost gently, 'will you come with me to the inquiry Monday?'

Illana saw the anger drain from her brother's face. She knew even before he spoke that he would agree. He always did.

'Yes,' he replied.

Because of the influence of people like Preston Whitehead and Brian McDermott and the testimony of the local fishermen and Preston's crews, Olaf Svenson's death did not result in legal action. The issue was resolved instead by a one-man commission of inquiry who visited Brannigan Bay and reprimanded Jay and Gottlieb, as he had Preston Whitehead in Cape Town, for the part they had played in inciting the violence.

That same day, Barry Whitehead sat behind the desk in his bedroom and watched the rain trickle down the window pane. He thought about the conversation between Preston and some guests in the lounge the previous evening. Had a boy from Brannigan Bay really killed one of his father's fishermen?

It was only recently that he had learned of Preston's plans for Brannigan Bay and from what he had understood of last night's talk, he suspected that that was what had led to the killing. Barry hoped he was wrong; he liked Brannigan Bay, its narrow streets, old houses, rocks and beaches. With factories it would surely be little different from Cape Town or any other city.

He shut his eyes, opened them again, and tried to concentrate on his homework.

Part Three

1939–1942

1939

January

Jay stood on the cliffs overlooking what had once been a natural cleft in the coastline. It was little more than a swath of raised rock forming a barrier against the Atlantic swells.

The enclave was larger now, transformed by huge blocks of concrete, the unfinished jetty like a fat grey finger. It covered a low reef jutting into deeper waters and much remained to be done before it became the harbour Preston Whitehead had wanted for so long.

Things had changed rapidly since the meeting in which Preston's attempt to build his harbour failed. No one, including Brian McDermott who was the first to admit his actions might have foreseen such rapid development. It was as if the world, suddenly aware of the health benefits associated with shark-liver oil, feared that its source would vanish overnight. Boats, specially converted into shark fishers, sailed in from as far afield as America and Scandinavia. Their quarry was the *vaalhaai*, with the female most sought after because of the higher quality of her liver. One night's catch, the fishermen using hand lines, easily numbered a few hundred and the price for livers quickly exceeded two shillings a pound.

Other factories were hastily erected in Cape Town and elsewhere to process the catches, but it was to the harbour at Clayton that the boats turned for safe berth while they worked the shark-infested waters around Brannigan Bay. It was too much for a small harbour to handle and there were renewed calls for a large harbour at Brannigan Bay. The village council, cracking under the pressures of big business and a growing demand from local fishermen, considered itself honour bound to grant the concession to Whitehead Enterprises. There were, however, to be no factories.

Jay's eyes burned as he studied the harbour, silent today as it was Sunday. Sighing, he walked rapidly away along the footpath winding across the top of the cliffs.

As he entered the village centre, he saw Vaughn standing on the café veranda. At twenty, Vaughn was taller and heavier than Jay. He leaned back casually against a pillar as he talked, typically relaxed, to a girl among a crowd of young men.

Jay wondered what would become of his son once the new harbour was complete and the old fishing ways slowly died. His dismal train of thought was interrupted when Vaughn saw him and waved. Jay raised his hand, smiling when he saw the disappointed look on the girl's face as Vaughn deserted her and strode across the road.

'Hello, Dad.' Wide smile, open face, eyes a deeper blue than Jay's. His thatch of sandy hair was in need of a trim, reminding Jay of Bull de Vries when he had been a younger man. He was suddenly struck by how strong the resemblance was between Vaughn and his grandfather. Both were physical giants and easy-going men seemingly at peace with the world. Vaughn had not, however, inherited his grandfather's quick temper and rarely exerted his strength on others.

'Son.' Both men were at ease in each other's company.

'Out walking?' asked Vaughn.

Jay nodded. 'To that damned harbour they're building. They're moving fast.' Vaughn's expression was understanding, for Jay had tried to instil in him his own hatred of the new harbour and that its coming should be seen as a personal defeat for the Brannigans. Yet Vaughn had never questioned the source of the feud with Preston Whitehead.

Jay again glanced towards the young men across the street. Wilhelm Kessler was leaning against a balcony support, tense and unsmiling. Taller than average, yet slim and wiry, he had retained the aloofness and arrogance of his childhood. Loved only by the gentle German couple who had adopted him – and intensely loyal to them – he was not popular, befriended only by Vaughn. Jay was relieved that Wilhelm had chosen to work on another boat; he would have found it difficult to refuse a request from Gottlieb.

Watching Wilhelm, Jay was reminded that one other person

loved him, but the memory was so bitter he drove it instantly from his mind and spoke to Vaughn. 'What are your plans for today?'

'Some of the girls want to pick flowers on the mountain slopes. I suppose I'll go along.'

'Does your mother know? She'll be annoyed if you miss lunch.'

'I've told her. Wilhelm and I had tea with her a little earlier.'

'Well,' said Jay, disguising his instant resentment with a squeeze of his son's arm, 'I'd better get home before *I'm* the one in trouble. Where's Illana?'

'At Uncle Brian's. Some last instructions before she leaves for Cape Town.'

Vaughn's words brought home again to Jay how little time he had with his daughter. In a way he feared losing her more than he did Vaughn, though the different love he felt for each was equal in intensity. He tried not to imagine her in Cape Town and the men, sophisticated and worldly, who would covet her beauty and spirit.

When he arrived home Magda was seated in the sun outside the front door of their cottage. Though a faint touch of grey now showed among her thick auburn hair she still appeared younger than her forty-two years. She was as slim as he had always known her – almost fragile. Jay thought that, for the wife of a fisherman, Magda Brannigan, *née* de Vries, had borne the years well.

She had no need to ask where her husband had spent his morning. Since construction of the harbour had got under way, Jay was drawn there every Sunday as if on some self-torturing pilgrimage.

'Illana's at Brian McDermott's,' she told him when he sat beside her.

'I know. I spoke to Vaughn in the village. Will she be back for lunch?'

Magda nodded. 'I'd better prepare it,' she said. 'The sun made me lazy.' She stood up and went inside.

Jay sat a while longer, letting the sun ease the lines on his face. He felt tired, exhausted by too much anger and passion.

He sensed that more was to come.

Illana Brannigan stared at the wall behind Brian McDermott and smiled. 'One of my mother's,' she said, tilting her chin towards the charcoal drawing.

McDermott glanced over his shoulder. 'Yes, I bought that from her when I was new to the village. Hardly knew your dad in those days.'

Illana's gaze remained fixed on the sketch. It was of the harbour, the sea grey and moody, so that the white sails of the boats captured there seemed almost out of place. Illana knew that Magda lacked formal training, merely exercising a natural talent that had been finely tuned over the years, as if life's experience had allowed her to interpret and express what others might overlook.

'Illana.' She turned her attention back to McDermott, who was shaking his head at her wayward thoughts. 'You're not listening to me, girl,' he gently admonished her.

'Sorry, Uncle Brian.'

'You won't turn into a fine journalist if you don't learn to pay attention – and that would disappoint me, as your benefactor.'

'I'll work on it,' she replied, flashing him a disarming smile that immediately produced a forgiving shake of his bald head. 'I owe you so much!' she whispered. It had been Brian McDermott who, on first learning of Illana's desire to enter journalism, used his influence to ease the way for her. Calling on his old friendship with a reporter he had met in his pub-crawling days, McDermott had persuaded him – now a senior member of the *Cape Argus*'s management – to create a junior position for her on the newspaper. She had cried with happiness, for she knew how difficult it was to break into that field – especially for a woman. McDermott's faith in her made her even more determined to be a success.

'I'd better be going,' she said and stood up. 'Thanks for all the advice, Uncle Brian. I promise I'll— '

'Sit, Illana girl.' He had spoken softly, yet his expression made her obey without question. McDermott waited until she had resumed her seat before he continued. 'I'm not your

186

father,' he said, 'so perhaps it's not my place to say what I'm about to.'

'Uncle Brian,' began Illana, leaning forward to rest her hand on his knee while she spoke, 'I know what you're trying to say and why. You're worried about me, as Mum and Dad are, and it makes me feel loved to know that. But although you think I've been very sheltered here in Brannigan Bay, you're forgetting that wicked and charming men – that was what you were going to talk about, wasn't it? – admittedly as boys, have been coming to this town almost every holiday. I know what I'm up against – really I do!'

McDermott gave up. He stood and hauled Illana to her feet, drawing her to him. 'Give the old man a hug,' he said.

Illana squeezed him with all her strength. She was a good few inches taller than McDermott, so that her long hair, auburn and thick like her mother's, fell across his head. She pulled slightly away and kissed his forehead.

McDermott held her at arm's length and studied her face intently. 'You'll do, Illana girl – you'll do just fine!'

The days to Illana's departure for Cape Town were suddenly past and Vaughn carried her luggage through the gate to McDermott's car, for the old man and Magda were driving her to Cape Town.

Jay stood motionless, his expression revealing his fear that once Illana passed through the garden gate she would be gone from his life for ever. Bull and Sarah de Vries were near the gate, the last to say goodbye to their granddaughter.

Illana held her brother's face between her hands. He was the only one who was smiling, and she was grateful for that amid the gloom of the others. How like Vaughn: she could always rely on him. She wished he could come with her to offer the support she would need while she experienced so much that was new.

'Goodbye, *boet*,' she said now, using the endearment for the first time in years.

Vaughn clasped her so tightly that she was unable to breathe. 'I'll miss you, sis.'

When he pulled her tighter still, she wondered what would become of him. Yet now was not the time to try again to establish his plans. She had tried more than once to talk to him about them but it was the one subject he was hesitant to discuss with her. Sometimes it seemed as if Vaughn knew that something awaited him. There was no need to plan; it had already been done for him.

She kissed him one last time then glanced at Jay.

Her father smiled gamely back at her, though he could not hide the sorrow he felt at her leaving. 'Dad?' she said softly and went to him.

Jay opened his arms. She moved into them, rested against his chest, smelled on him the familiar scent of the sea. 'Oh, Dad!'

'Come, my darling girl, no tears – remember? We promised.' Despite his words, she felt the tremble in his body. Though Cape Town was only eighty miles away, she knew that to him it would seem like another continent.

'Take care, my sweetness,' he said into her hair. 'I love you.'

'I love you too, Dad. Always have, always will. My number one man. Always.'

She flew back against him, then drew away and strode towards the gate before he could see the mistiness in her own eyes.

When she hugged Bull and Sarah she made no effort to curb her tears. Then she was past them, with only the open car door ahead of her. She slid inside, struck by the tangy leather smell of the seats.

Just once, before Brian McDermott eased the car round the first corner, she glanced back at the house. They all stood at the gate, their hands raised yet unmoving, the men's shoulders slumped.

McDermott stopped in the main road to buy cigarettes, leaving Illana and her mother chatting desultorily. A sharp rap on the closed window at Illana's side of the car made them jump. Wilhelm Kessler stood outside, a smirk across his lips. Illana tensed, as she always did when he was near her. She had tried to like him, to understand him for Vaughn's sake, but had failed. The only thing she found in his favour was that he never pestered her – although the way she sometimes caught him studying her made her skin crawl.

'Hello, Wilhelm,' she said, managing a smile as she wound down the car window.

'You on your way then?'

'Yes.'

'Have fun.'

'I'll be working, Wilhelm.'

His smirk became a leer. 'Sure,' he replied.

She began winding up the window, but his hands on the glass prevented her. 'Don't worry about Vaughn,' he said, his face so close to hers she felt his breath on her skin. 'I'll look after him.'

Illana stared at him, then pushed at the window handle again. The glass shifted an inch and Wilhelm released his grip on it.

'Goodbye,' he said through the rapidly closing space.

'Bye.'

Magda had been watching Wilhelm oddly, in a way Illana had often witnessed whenever he was near. It had been like that ever since she could remember. She could never define her mother's expression, for at times it seemed one of concern, at others almost of fear – yet fear of what?

The return of McDermott stopped her from dwelling on it. Let's go, she urged silently. She did not return Wilhelm's laconic wave when the car jerked forward. Her mind turned instead to the road winding ahead – to Cape Town and her future.

The south-easterly was almost gale force as Barry Whitehead peered through his bedroom window, as outside, leaves and twigs swirled in the gusts.

It was calm in his room on the upper level of the old house in Rondebosch, though the wind screeched and rattled the windows. Barry sat behind his desk, pushed right up to the window for a view of the magnificent garden, his mother's pride and joy. As he watched the tall oak trees sway, he realised that she seldom used it for her own pleasure. The only times he had seen her go into the main grounds were when she entertained.

Now it no longer mattered to him, for the next day he was leaving for England to go to Cambridge later in the year. He would be away from Grace and Preston and their empty life and big house and lovely garden that no one used. Even now he felt no bitterness, just relief that he would at last be on his own – for a few years, at least, because as usual Preston had not discussed with his son what Barry wanted from life. He took it for granted that Barry would join the company at the conclusion of his studies, just as he had decided that the boy wanted a desk for Christmas.

At the memory Barry pushed back his chair and stood up, his hands deep in his trouser pockets as he stepped towards the window. He pressed his forehead against the pane, as if to try to clear his mind.

When he left the room with its packed suitcases and empty cupboards, he found Grace sitting in the living room, a fragile figure among the vast space and bulky furniture. She was unaware of him as he studied her.

'Mother.'

'Oh . . . hello, dear.' Slight jerk of the shoulders, rapid blink, nervous smile. 'All packed?'

'Just about.'

Nothing to say even now that he was leaving.

'I was wondering . . . '

'Yes, dear?'

'It'd be nice if you could go over with me. Just for a while. You haven't been back to England since you married Father, have you?'

Grace laughed nervously, a short, shrill sound. 'Goodness, Barry! What an odd thought.'

Odd? Was that what her life had been reduced to? Perhaps if she came with him, could think for herself for just a little while, many things would be less odd for her. Just for a while, just to be away from *him*, even at this stage of her life with her hair that had been done too often, the skin on her face that had formed premature wrinkles. Even now, though he owed her nothing but life itself, Barry wanted her to escape with him.

190

The imminence of his departure brought out his resentment of his father. He wanted to shake Grace, to tell her how pathetic she had allowed herself to become. But all he did was touch her arm and say, 'Mother, would you walk with me through the garden?'

Grace glanced quickly at him, then returned to the magazine she had been reading. She shuffled through its pages as if seeking something to shield her from his words, answering, 'Really, Barry, in this wind? You are silly today. Really odd.'

Those were the last words she spoke to him in private for their farewell at the docks next day took place under Preston's watchful eye. Barry sailed on the *Arundel Castle*, the third ship in the Union Castle line to bear that name. Preston had insisted he go first-class, ignoring Barry's protestations that he would have little chance of meeting people his own age that way.

Only when the tugboats had turned the ship in the direction of the harbour entrance did Grace and Preston thread their way through the throng of relatives and well-wishers lining the edge of the docks. Grace glanced back one last time before Preston's hand on her elbow moved her on again.

'He'll be all right, won't he?' she asked as they approached their car.

'Of course,' replied Preston curtly. 'It's about time the boy learned to stand on his own two feet.'

'England will be so strange to him, so unsettling. I've never known whether Barry has any real confidence in himself.' She stopped and let Preston open the car door for her. He shut it crisply without reply.

The wind, though less gusty than the day before, snatched at his coat and lifted the lapels of his dark jacket into his face. He cursed as he slid into the driver's seat.

The silence of the woman beside him, the way in which she seemed to draw herself into a tight ball of self-pity against the side of the car, made him clamp his fingers tightly round the steering wheel. How she irritated him! Worse than that – how he despised her.

At times when Preston thought about his treatment of her, he realised he was being unfair. Grace had not forced him into marrying her; if there were blame, it was his for having married a woman he did not love. If she had fought back, threatened to leave him, perhaps the slow slide into one-sided antipathy would not have taken place. Preston knew she felt trapped but she was afraid to leave him and afraid that it was too late for her to start again somewhere else with someone new.

In a sense what he felt towards Grace was transferred to Barry as well. As the boy matured, Preston took his withdrawn manner to mean that the son had assimilated the defeated ways of his mother. It had come as a shock to discover, just over a year ago, that what he had taken for timidity or reservation on Barry's part was in fact rejection.

After his first sense of outrage had passed, Preston felt relieved to discover that the boy at least had a mind and spirit of his own. But it was too late for him to exploit this discovery. It was good that Barry was off to England; Preston had no place for a rebel in his home, nor the patience to tame one. England would do that for him – England and new friends. Perhaps when he finished his studies and returned, Barry would be ready to be moulded into the future role he would play in Whitehead Enterprises. But it should have been his *real* son who took over the company – not a creation shared by that woman who posed as his wife.

His real son, he thought again, the boy Magda had given him. Perhaps some day . . .

September

It was an exciting time for Illana Brannigan, though her first few months as a junior reporter on the *Cape Argus* had not been easy. Many of her colleagues suspected her appointment had been gained through influence at high level and resented a woman entering a traditional male domain.

Though her physical appearance made a few of the younger, more junior journalists overcome their displeasure – giving rise instead to an intense rivalry to see who would be the first to bed her – the majority went out of their way to see how much ill-treatment the newcomer could take before she fled in tears.

They underestimated someone who had grown up with some of the toughest males around. Illana was no stranger to dirty hands and when an especially demeaning task was imposed on her she gazed at her tormentor with undisguised scorn, wondering how he would fare on the boats of Brannigan Bay.

What helped, too, was a rapidly developing maturity that enabled her to understand their actions and steel herself to overcome their barbed words and hostility. Illana was determined that they should tire of their malicious game long before she did.

She was right – but by then the new war diverted their attention.

The outbreak of hostilities caused its own divisions within South Africa. A large proportion of Afrikaners, many of German descent, was opposed to taking up arms against Germany, as apart from their kinship with the land of their forebears, there lingered the bitter memory of thousands of Afrikaner women and children who had died in British concentration camps during the Anglo-Boer war early in the century. But in spite of this, Jan Smuts, the deputy prime minister, persuaded parliament to ally with Britain and was asked to form a new government. Full conscription was not introduced but tens of thousands of South Africans of both language groups responded to the call for volunteers.

With the declaration of war came Illana's first break – in the form of Rafe Turner, a respected journalist, who strolled across to the tiny wooden structure that served as her desk, and said, 'Come with me.'

He had gone some yards down the long room before Illana realised he had spoken to her. 'What?' she asked, staring quizzically at her equally dumbfounded colleagues. Every pair of eyes in the room focused on her and Turner.

He put his hands on his hips with an exaggerated sigh. 'I said you're to come with me.'

Illana gaped at him. Unlike the others Rafe had not insulted and humiliated her. After scrutinising her figure intensively when she arrived at the *Cape Argus*, he had simply ignored her – though she had often felt him watching her reactions. Now he had summoned her to accompany him – but where to and why?

'Miss Brannigan,' he said in his deep, husky voice, 'I don't have all day. Are you coming or not?'

Illana jumped up but Turner's voice stopped her. 'Miss Brannigan,' he said, 'bring lead and a sheaf of papyrus. How else will you take notes?'

Pencil . . . paper – her hands scrabbled among the disarray on her desk, searching. Could he be offering her her first story? She spun round breathlessly and ran after Turner, who had already disappeared into the corridor. As she raced past the men's desks, Illana did not fail to notice the surprise on their faces. She knew instinctively that she had won; Rafe Turner had let everybody know that the war against her had ended.

She caught up with him half-way to the ground floor. 'Where're we going?' she gasped, trying to keep pace with his long stride.

'To the docks. I thought we might find a human angle on this new war of ours.' He smiled as he spoke, slowing his pace when he saw her struggle to keep up with him. She thought, too, for the first time, that Rafe Turner was a rather handsome man.

Tall and thin, Rafe was thirty-three. Over the next few weeks, as he involved Illana increasingly in the articles he planned to write, she found that beneath his overt cynicism lay an easy humour, as if the world and those who occupied it were one big joke. Illana liked him, and she knew then that she wanted him as her first lover. She sensed it would be easy with Rafe – uncomplicated yet pleasurable.

They started going out together at night, for a quiet dinner in interesting out-of-the-way places, to small parties where the guests were either journalists or artists. Illana found that she liked the people and the ambience but although she circulated freely among the guests, listening avidly, she always left with Rafe. On their walks home along darkened streets, he shared with her his experience as a journalist, inspiring her to strive for that elusive greatness that only came with time and hard work. Not once did he touch her although, subtly, Illana made it clear that she was not averse to intimacy between them. Rafe's reticence made her like him even more, for she sensed that he was being considerate of her youth.

After six weeks of constant companionship and an easy relationship in the company of their colleagues, it was she who made the first move.

Rafe had taken her to a Portuguese taverna not far from the dockyard, an area she viewed with dismay. When they went into the taverna though, the intimate warmth and pervasive sense of welcome dispelled her reservations. She drank more than usual yet when Rafe called for the bill her head was clear. 'Rafe,' she said, 'I want you to take me home with you.'

He smiled, a lopsided grimace that she found attractive, and continued to riffle through his wallet. When he had handed over the money to the waiter he turned back to her, his eyes soft, almost sad. 'Illana . . . these past weeks with you . . . It's not what I was after.'

'I know. But it's what I want.'

It was the first time she had seen him appear uncomfortable. He lowered his eyes and took a cigarette from the pack, his fingers shaking as he held a match to it. Squinting at her through the smoke, he said, 'For a nineteen-year-old, you have a way of stating your mind, don't you?'

It was better than any vision she had entertained of them together. Rafe was gentle, curbing her impatience, easing her anxieties. Afterwards, she lay close to him, enjoying the sound of his voice against her hair when he spoke to her, her mind and body drifting on the edge of sleep.

Over the following weeks, thanks largely to Rafe's influence, she received increasing responsibility in discovering and writing her own stories. She was aware that without his support and guidance, she would have had a frustrating time. With the outbreak of war, the use of newsprint was severely curtailed, with the *Cape Argus* printed on eight pages three days a week, which meant that many regular features were dropped. As all writing, including photographs, was uncredited, it was more difficult than ever to build an individual reputation.

Under Rafe's tutorship, mostly in the cosiness of his small flat in Greenpoint, she learned the finer skills of writing. Gradually, less of her work was rejected by the sub-editors and stories, now recognisable as near to her original submissions, began appearing in print.

'You're getting there, lady,' Rafe whispered as he passed her desk after her report on a train derailment was accepted unaltered. Illana had to stop herself from hugging him right there in front of everybody for all he had done in accepting her talent and offering unstinting support.

The year ended, Christmas came and Illana headed home to Brannigan Bay.

'Those fancy clothes make you look terrific, sis,' said Vaughn, placing his arm about her shoulders. 'A real film star!'

Illana hugged him, finding his bulk so different from Rafe's slimness. Only three days away from him and already she missed him, she thought wryly. Had he come to mean more to her than she realised?

She and Vaughn were strolling slowly over the rocks near the old harbour, catching up on the year that had passed since she had left. It was her first time alone with Vaughn for Magda and Jay had monopolised her since her arrival.

'Cape Town must be full of broken hearts,' he continued, releasing his hold on her to help her down a high outcrop of rock. 'Is there someone special?' He picked her up and placed her on the ground beside him.

Illana glanced away and did not answer. She knew she could trust Vaughn, that he would understand if she explained about her and Rafe. Yet even as she said, 'There is someone . . . sort of,' she knew she could not explain what she herself did not fully understand.

Vaughn pointed to a boat in full sail out on the bay. 'I wonder for how long we'll still see that,' he said, 'now that building of the new harbour has gone ahead.'

Illana stared at the brightly coloured sails. 'What are your plans, Vaughn? You staying on, or thinking of joining up?'

'I don't quite know,' Vaughn replied slowly. 'I don't feel this is my war. Perhaps that's wrong, perhaps one should take a stand.'

'There's no need to choose sides,' she told him. 'There are many who feel the way you do. You'll carry on fishing with Dad then? For now, anyway?'

Vaughn walked on before he replied. 'I don't know . . . I've been thinking about moving to Johannesburg. A job in the mines, perhaps.'

'No carrying on the Brannigan tradition, then?' she asked gently.

'Fishing isn't for me, sis. I enjoy it but wouldn't like to make a life of it. With this new harbour the only future will be that of skipper on some company-owned boat.'

'Then I'm glad I've already flown the nest. Dad might have tried to enrol me as one of his crew to replace you.'

Vaughn laughed with her but the sound was wistful. 'Anyway,' he said softly, 'there's no need for me to rush into any kind of decision. I'll wait another year or so, then see how things stand.'

The calm manner in which he had spoken made Illana feel again that her brother had some knowledge that his life was already clearly mapped out, beyond his own influence.

She wanted to hold him, to believe that her presence could help them always be together, as they had always been until now. But she knew his life was not hers to influence. It was beyond her reach, just as she had moved beyond the confines of her childhood and Brannigan Bay.

Barry Whitehead's first Christmas in England was a disappointment. He realised it was due partly to the war, yet also he could not help longing for the sunny skies of Africa. It was not that he was homesick, for he seldom missed either of his parents. He wrote to them dutifully, telling of life at Cambridge and of weekends in London. Perhaps it was nothing but the war that caused his melancholy – after all, it was almost the sole topic of conversation nowadays.

Barry spent most of the Christmas period in London, where the days flashed by in a constant whirl of parties until the time came to return to Cambridge and his studies.

1940

Hester and Manfred Muller's second son, Rudi, was born on 16 March 1908, on a farm in the then colony of German West Africa. His brother Neels was twelve years older, an easy-going individual who enjoyed something akin to hero worship from Rudi.

A staunch supporter of the Afrikaner cause in neighbouring South Africa, Manfred Muller felt it only right that his sons share his beliefs and that they do whatever they could to help overthrow the yoke of British authority. 'First it must be Neels,' he told his sons, smiling at Rudi, 'because he is the eldest. Your turn will come.' A disinterested yet obedient Neels left the farm early in 1914, destined for the mines in the Transvaal where he would meet with old friends of his father.

Although he was more interested in the worldly ladies of Johannesburg than passionate causes, Neels was among the miners caught up in a brutal conflict with the authorities after widespread strikes. On the run with a group of ringleaders, he joined an Afrikaner group opposed to alliance with Britain in 1914.

Led by Major Kemp, Neels and his comrades rode across the Kalahari Desert for German West Africa, planning to meet with German forces there, then move south to harass government troops. The journey was harsh and tiring yet Neels consoled himself with the thought that he would soon see his parents and young Rudi again.

Rudi never forgot that hot dry day when a rider came out of the shimmering heat and dust, shouting to his father that Neels and the others had arrived in the colony.

'I must ride to meet him,' his father had said excitedly, then immediately packed his saddlebags for the long ride to the border. As he mounted, he saw the expression on six-year-old Rudi's face. 'Come with me, son,' he said with a smile. 'Let's ride to welcome your brother.'

Rudi's excitement and pride at being considered worthy to accompany his father had helped ease the rigours of the long journey south. He would see Neels – and soldiers!

Then a disappointment: the soldiers were not resplendent in bright uniform as he had imagined. Instead, confronting him was a motley collection of tired, dirty men, raggedly clothed, often weaponless. Neels seemed small and frail, with a sparse, downy growth of beard. Gone was the ready smile Rudi remembered so well; in its place a nervous tic played constantly at the side of his mouth.

'We ride south!' their father had shouted jubilantly, undeterred by the sorry state of the commando. Arrangements were quickly made for Rudi to be escorted home by the older men in the welcoming contingent and Manfred Muller rode joyfully off in search of combat.

The commando had a few successful skirmishes with government troops along the border, always managing to disengage before being overwhelmed by numerically superior forces. Then bravado took them as far as Upington in the northern Cape, where Neels, still a reluctant rebel, was wounded and dragged to death by his horse.

Manfred returned to his farm a broken man, robbed of his fighting spirit by the loss of his favourite son. He took to disappearing for days at a time, riding into the veld with minimal supplies. Gradually he began to take Rudi with him and they sat beneath the starlit sky while Manfred spoke of the injustices perpetrated by the British in their government of South Africa. Where Neels had been influenced by his father to hate the British, Rudi inherited Manfred's obsessive desire for revenge.

Having lost all interest in life and the farm, Manfred left most of the chores to his wife and Rudi. Neither felt great loss when he died the day after Rudi turned twenty. Though eager to follow in Neels's footsteps, Rudi remained at home, eking out an existence sufficient to keep himself and his mother alive.

Hester followed her husband barely a year later. It was while going through her papers that Rudi found a pile of letters that had passed between his mother and her sister in South Africa. It had been many years since Hester had mentioned his aunt Gertrude and her hope, long extinguished, of the day that they would attempt the long journey south to meet the Kesslers. Rudi glanced idly at a fading photograph of a smiling woman, plump like his mother, standing close beside a serious-looking Gottlieb. Throwing the photograph and the letters onto a growing heap of oddments, he scooped everything into his arms, threw it on a heap of rubbish in the yard and set it alight.

He accepted an offer for the land the same day, packed his few belongings and headed for South Africa. There, at least, he could act against the British – somehow avenge Neels's death. There was little he could do from a tiny scrap of land set in semi-desert terrain.

At first in Johannesburg, he was just another citizen, but Rudi determinedly wormed his way into an extremist Afrikaner group more intent on anarchism than on providing an alternative to continued British rule. Yet, for a while, it satisfied Rudi's need for action.

In 1938 he came into contact with the Ossewa-Brandwag, the 'Ox-wagon Sentinels', known as the OB. Claiming to be a cultural organisation established to preserve the traditions of the Voortrekkers, the OB proclaimed itself above party politics yet preached a policy of an authoritarian state, along the lines of German National Socialism, and called on all opposition elements to stand together against the leadership of Jan Smuts. Its structure was modelled on paramilitary lines and it had its own army, the Stormjaers, a body of men hand-picked from within its ranks. It was exactly what Rudi was looking for.

When war was declared, he had already become a minor official within the OB, harbouring heady ambitions for a brighter future. His main task was to find suitable young men to join the organisation and enter the ranks of the Stormjaers.

Rudi was aware that the OB had asked Germany for aid in overthrowing the newly formed Smuts government, offering in return the use of air and sea bases once this goal had been achieved. The pragmatism acquired over time made him view this as an unrealistic ambition, one to which Germany would not respond.

Without his being aware of it, Rudi's logic followed the same course as that of the German High Command, who felt the OB could be used to greater effect by causing dissension on the home front, weakening Smuts politically and forcing him to the polls. Once a government sympathetic to the German cause was in place, the proffered opportunities could be exploited.

Whatever his doubts, Rudi applied himself zealously to his allocated tasks and was rewarded with an extra responsibility: to seek out persons sympathetic to the German war effort in the hope of persuading them to pass useful information to the OB. Realising that it would be both safer and produce speedier results, he concentrated first on acquiring the services of persons already inclining in that direction. He contacted Germans resident or working in the country as well as South Africans of German descent. It was not long before his success in establishing a widespread ring of informants in the Transvaal led him to spread his efforts to other provinces.

Rudi decided to make first for Cape Town, as he realised that the city would grow in significance with the increased usage of the Cape sea route by British war and merchant ships. It was the ideal city in which to have informants, for the Germans would need details on naval and military movements. He already had contacts there . . . among them his aunt Gertrude in Brannigan Bay.

In October 1940, when he boarded a train to Cape Town, a thousand miles from the OB headquarters in the Transvaal, he did not suspect that, like other, more visible members of the organisation, he was already under surveillance by military security.

For a time, Illana wondered whether she had made a mistake in choosing newspaper reporting as a career. As the war dragged on the availability of newsprint became increasingly restricted.

The print was set in smaller type and the traditional eight columns reduced in width to make nine. Text was pruned to the bare minimum, advertising space reduced and very few illustrations – only in black and white – appeared. No reference to the weather was permitted as this was thought to constitute a security risk and even the social columns detailing travel movements of socialites were carefully scrutinised for coded messages. It was not an easy time for someone to try to make a name for themselves in journalism.

Yet, backed by the indefatigable Rafe Turner, Illana turned a potentially frustrating situation into one of challenge. She worked hard, ruthlessly paring excess words from her reports and articles. 'It won't do you any harm,' Rafe told her one night when she read him the full text of an article she had written, complaining about what would have to be cut. 'Trimming as we have to,' he continued, 'teaches us to be more concise and to assess a situation better.'

Illana had moved in to his flat three months before. She was still not sure if she loved him, but she was content, at ease in their relationship. They were well matched in lifestyle and temperament. They never argued and were not overtly jealous if either received undue attention from someone of the opposite sex. They never discussed the future beyond how it affected their careers. There were times when Illana wondered how long it would last – for, on her side at least, there was no passion.

When she was summoned to the editor's office and told that they wished to transfer her to the *Star*, their sister paper in Johannesburg, Illana felt a sense of relief competing with her excitement and satisfaction at her superiors' faith in her. Then followed guilt.

She did not accept immediately but promised to give her answer the following morning. First she must discuss it with Rafe – she owed him that.

Illana sat tensely beside him on the bus going home. When she prepared supper – it was her turn that night – she twice stopped herself entering the little lounge where Rafe sat sipping a brandy, flicking idly through a magazine. She could not bring herself to hurt him but she had already made up her mind to accept the offer. The opportunity might not arise again and, besides, she wanted it. But she would miss him . . . because she cared for him. *Cared*, she repeated silently. Cared – not loved.

As she pushed a stray curl from her forehead, she sensed him behind her. Though he was smiling, Illana had never before seen him so sad.

'You made up your mind yet?' he asked softly.

'You know,' she said flatly.

'For some weeks now. They asked me what I thought about the idea.'

'And?'

'I told them they'd made the right choice.'

'Oh, Rafe . . . '

'I didn't want to say anything to you,' he went on, turning away from what he saw in her eyes. 'They hadn't made a final decision, you see. I was afraid I'd get you all excited for nothing.' He pretended to study the contents of the saucepan.

They stood side by side, mere inches apart yet it was as if there was a solid wall between them. 'Rafe, I— '

'I think it's for the best, Illana,' he interrupted softly. 'For you and for us.'

'For us?'

He nodded, his lips twisted into the lopsided grin that had first attracted her to him. The humour contained in the grimace was now directed against himself. 'Perhaps we should have talked about it,' he said. 'I don't think it would have ended well for us, Illana – not the way it's been going. We're too . . . just too comfortable with each other, I suppose.'

'Rafe— '

'No, don't deny it – God, are we having our first fight?' His laugh sounded brittle.

Illana turned away from him and from the truth he had spoken; the very sentences he had used were the ones she had voiced in her thoughts.

'Illana?'

She turned slowly, and this time he reached for her,

touching her with the gentleness that had always been his way. 'I'll miss you, my girl,' he whispered as she moved against his chest. 'Terribly.'

'I was happy with you, Rafe.' Tears were just behind her closed eyelids.

'Then that's something to remember me by,' he said and held her away from him. His smile was less sad now. 'I'll always be here for you,' he added. 'If you ever have need of me – or just a friend.'

'Rafe!' She threw herself back at him, held him tight as she let the tears flow.

'Come now, old girl,' he said into her hair. 'Let's not turn this into the Last Supper, shall we?'

But it was.

Illana moved out the next morning, for they knew it would be better that way.

It was two weeks before Rudi Muller had completed his task in Cape Town and was able to leave for Brannigan Bay, making his way to the village by bus after disembarking from the train at Bot River.

Arriving at the bus terminus late in the afternoon, he collected his single battered suitcase and walked to the centre of town, admiring the quaint cottages he strolled past. He was in good spirits when he checked into one of the smaller hotels.

After changing into more casual clothes, he strolled to the old harbour. The sea was deep blue and flat, the air mild and refreshing though dusk was approaching. A pretty town, he thought, and stretched lazily. Even if he had little success with his mission here, the journey would have been worthwhile. It had been some time since he had allowed himself to relax.

Rudi felt satisfied with his efforts in Cape Town. He had recruited five informers, two of them ideally placed in the operations division of the South African Railways and Harbours. From now on the reports he passed to the German Consul in Mozambique would be far more accurate.

He had had second thoughts about coming to Brannigan Bay; he knew little about the Kesslers or how loyal they would be to their old fatherland – or even if they were aware of his existence.

Shrugging off his doubts he told himself that even if he failed to locate them or they refused to help he would find someone else, someone who had contact with the many wounded servicemen recuperating in the village. They would be a valuable source of information.

He smoked a cigarette while he studied the fishermen cleaning their catches. Then he returned to the hotel, put on a jacket and tie, and asked for directions to the Kessler home.

Gertrude Kessler glanced at her adopted son when he walked out of the kitchen door with a brief wave of his hand. 'Will you be home for supper?' she asked in German.

Wilhelm, a jersey slung carelessly across his shoulder, turned slowly to stare blankly at her. His cheek bore a bruise from a fight earlier that week. 'No,' he replied in the same language, 'I don't think so,' and walked out of the house.

Gertrude called after him, 'No more fighting, you hear?' There was no reply.

She returned to her knitting, though her thoughts remained on the young man she and Gottlieb had raised as their own. Gertrude knew how difficult Wilhelm could be, how unpopular he was with most villagers. Yet he had always been devoted to her and Gottlieb, protective almost, and nothing could change the love she felt for him.

Gertrude was used to him getting into scraps – it was almost a way of life for the young men of the village. But this time it was different. The fight had not been caused by women or liquor or merely high spirits; it had been sparked off by which side men took in the war.

It worried her that Wilhelm, regarded by most as being as German as his foster parents, should have become involved. With the talk about internment camps for Germans resident in the country and the government warnings on informers, the elder Kesslers wanted nothing but to be left in peace. She sighed and lowered her knitting to her lap, plagued by her sombre thoughts.

The soft knock at the door made her jump. The top half was open and when she leaned back she saw the man standing there.

'Frau Kessler?' he asked as he stepped closer.

Gertrude tensed at hearing the unexpected German, the sound so familiar, yet spoken in a different accent from the one she was used to. '*Ja?*' Her voice sounded breathless, uneasy.

He moved closer still, smiling as he rested his hand on the edge of the lower half of the door. 'I am Rudi Muller,' he said, still in German. 'Hester's son. Your nephew.'

'Hester's boy?' Gertrude stared at Rudi in disbelief, her gaze quickly scanning his black, close-cropped hair, the short, stocky build. Could it be . . . was it possible? 'Hester's boy?' she said again and rose to her feet.

'Yes, Aunt Gertrude. May I come inside?'

Now she saw the resemblance to her sister, the same thin smile and direct gaze. 'Yes – oh, yes! Come in, come in! Gottlieb!' she called out and rushed forward to pull back the door bolt. 'Gottlieb!' she shouted again. 'It's Hester's boy! Rudi! He's here!'

Gertrude was as tall as her nephew and even broader. He almost disappeared from view when she embraced him, crying happy tears of disbelief as if it were her sister herself resurrected from the dead.

Gottlieb came into the kitchen, his eyebrows knotted in question. He watched his wife drag the stranger inside, trying to talk and kiss him at the same time. Latching onto Gottlieb's arm, she pulled him into their embrace. 'It's Rudi,' she sobbed and thrust the men towards each other. 'Hester's son!'

Rudi grinned awkwardly at the uncle he had never met before. Gottlieb, too, seemed uneasy, though he stuck out his hand and bobbed his head. 'Hester's son?' he asked, as though he would not be satisfied until the stranger confirmed his wife's hysterical outburst.

'Yes, Uncle,' replied Rudi, shaking Gottlieb's hand. 'It must seem strange, my appearing like this. But— '

'Come . . . sit,' interrupted Gertrude, almost pushing him into the nearest chair.

Rudi looked at Gottlieb who had remained near the door. 'I was in Cape Town,' he explained, 'on business. It seemed like a good time to meet my family. At last,' he added.

Gertrude's eyes still brimmed with tears. 'Just look at him, Gottlieb,' she said. 'See him and you see Hester.'

Gottlieb stared at Rudi and blinked. For the life of him he could not remember what Gertrude's sister had looked like, only that she had been rather plump and of sour disposition. He had never liked her or her husband – but, then, he had hardly known either of them. 'So,' he said, scraping a chair closer, 'you are Hester's boy.'

Rudi hid his amused smile at the Kesslers' constant repetition of that fact. 'Yes, Uncle Gottlieb. Her flesh and blood.'

Gottlieb nodded slowly as if he had finally come to accept that it was so. 'We've often wondered what became of you.'

'Well, as you can see, I'm no youngster any more. Thirty-two, to be exact.'

Gertrude had herself under control by the time she served them all coffee. 'A rusk, Rudi?' she asked, then immediately enquired whether he had eaten supper.

'No,' he replied, 'but I'll get something at the hotel, thank you.'

'Hotel? No nephew of mine will be staying in any hotel while he's in Brannigan Bay,' she said firmly. 'You'll get your things when you've had your coffee. Wilhelm will help. You can share his room.'

When Rudi frowned, Gertrude proudly said, 'Wilhelm's our son – your cousin. He's twenty-three. A good boy, tall and strong.'

Rudi smiled and sipped his coffee. Stay there with them? It would curtail his freedom of movement yet could ease his task of getting them on his side. The Kesslers were his first priority, he reminded himself; if they agreed to help he would have no need to search elsewhere. Once he had accomplished what he had come for he could relax for two or three days before returning to Johannesburg.

'I couldn't impose on you like that,' he said at last, then saw the firm set of Gertrude's jaw; his aunt was going to have it no other way.

'Gottlieb,' she snapped, 'go to the bar and find Wilhelm.' She stopped and glanced at Rudi, saying, 'The boy does not really drink that much, but he's a fisherman. He likes to mingle with his friends.'

Still issuing orders to Gottlieb, she said, 'Tell Wilhelm to meet his cousin and help carry his bags.'

'There's only one suitcase,' objected Rudi, but Gertrude appeared not to have heard. She ushered her husband from the kitchen with a further string of commands.

When Gottlieb had dutifully departed, Gertrude returned to the kitchen table. She sat down and smiled at Rudi as if he were some long-lost lover. 'Now,' she said, 'tell me everything.'

Rudi could feel the young man's eyes on him as he unpacked his suitcase, storing his few clothes in the drawer Wilhelm had made available for his use. 'You can have more space if you need it,' Wilhelm said from his bed. The paraffin lamp on the bedside table cast flickering shadows across the small room, conveniently hiding his expression.

Rudi smiled and shook his head. 'This will do fine, thanks.' He was surprised at how well the youth spoke German.

He busied himself with storing his clothes and thought about his cousin. He had not been aware of his existence till now. An adopted son, his aunt had told him while they were alone, yet he seemed even more German than his foster parents.

When he had met Wilhelm at the hotel, Rudi had been amused at Gertrude's description. A 'good boy', she had said. A mother's blind love, Rudi had thought then, for when he stared at his cousin he realised that Wilhelm was probably the exact opposite. He sensed the young man's bitterness, the tension that showed in his stance and movements, the inherent cruelty lurking behind the flat, expressionless eyes. Yet Rudi had felt a certain kinship with Wilhelm; there was something attractive about him.

'So,' came Wilhelm's voice from behind him, 'you're in agriculture.'

Rudi slid the drawer shut, turned and nodded. He had told the Kesslers he was employed by Southern Agriculture, a company that acted as agricultural consultants to large co-operatives as well as the government. It was true in a sense for he was on the company's payroll and in their personnel dossiers. What he did not explain, was that Southern Agriculture was owned by the Ossewa-Brandwag, providing a convenient source of finance for some of its activities and a useful cover for travel.

Rudi sat on his bed and started undoing his shoelaces. He grinned at Wilhelm and said, 'And you're a fisherman.'

The younger man's lips pulled into an answering smile though it did not reach his eyes. He's like ice, thought Rudi as he removed his shoes and pushed them under the bed.

He felt tired, both from the long journey and endless chatter Gertrude had demanded of him. Rudi had purposely refrained from bringing up the subject of the war in the hope that it would be raised by either Gottlieb or Gertrude and reveal where their sentiments lay. But the conversation had centred mainly round his family and his present situation and Rudi had been acutely aware of Wilhelm's gaze, as if the young man were weighing him up or trying to place him.

'What's that little badge on your lapel?' asked Wilhelm when Rudi removed his jacket.

Rudi glanced at him, then folded the jacket neatly so that the badge faced upwards. It glittered dully in the dim light. About an inch and a half in diameter, the national crest was embossed in its centre and the words 'On Service' and the Afrikaans equivalent, '*Op Diens*', surrounded it. Suspended below it was a small orange flash.

'It's for what they call Key Men,' explained Rudi, 'those who are prepared to fight, yet prevented from doing so by the strategic nature of their work.' Rudi hated the badge but, as with his cover as an employee of Southern Agriculture, the badge removed the threat of conflict with volunteers and even patriotic businessmen with whom he occasionally came into contact.

When he turned to Wilhelm again, the youth's earlier smile had changed into a twisted sneer of derision. 'So,' his cousin said, 'you're a volunteer.' The words were almost spat out.

Rudi felt a stab of excitement at the young man's hostility. Earlier in the evening he had wondered why Wilhelm should have chosen to stay on as a fisherman, then reasoned that he might be like many other youths, particularly those from rural towns and villages, who had no strong feelings either way about the war. What he now saw on his cousin's face made him reconsider yet he knew he must tread carefully. 'Haven't *you* thought about volunteering?' he asked, curious to hear his cousin's response.

Wilhelm snorted loudly and shifted on to one elbow, his eyes glowing with scorn. 'My parents are German,' he said forcefully, 'as yours were. It's the arrogant British who started this war. I refuse to take up arms on their behalf. So should you.'

Rudi's thoughts were racing. Be careful, he reminded himself. All Wilhelm had revealed was how he felt about fighting for the British against Germany not how deep his feelings were about actively opposing the former. Yet all Rudi's senses screamed at him to risk exploiting the situation for the opportunity might not arise again.

'I wasn't prepared to take up arms,' he said softly.

'Why the badge then?'

He glanced at Wilhelm and saw a slight softening of his expression. 'It's simply a question,' he went on quickly, knowing that he had gone too far now to avoid giving some kind of explanation, 'of the badge being a convenient tool, let us say. It avoids arguments, conflicts.'

'Aren't you prepared to stand up for what you believe?' snapped Wilhelm.

Rudi knew then that he had guessed correctly regarding the young man's aggressive temperament. Standing up, he began to undo his trousers. 'More than prepared,' he replied, slipping them off and facing his cousin again. 'And you,

Wilhelm?' he asked quietly, tension tight in his stomach as he took the final plunge. 'Are you prepared to *do* something for what you believe?'

The two men were silent for some time before Rudi sat down again and said, 'Wilhelm, have you ever heard of the Ossewa-Brandwag?'

Wilhelm did not go out with the fishing boats the next day. No one thought anything strange of his wanting to spend the day showing his long-lost cousin around the village.

They left the Kessler cottage shortly after breakfast, watched by a beaming Gertrude who was thrilled to see how well the two cousins got on together. Wilhelm led Rudi to the nearby rocks where they could talk freely and observe anyone who might approach them. 'Tell me more about the Stormjaers,' he demanded when they sat down.

Rudi gazed at the calm sea. 'It's still in its infancy stage,' he explained. 'For now, the Stormjaers are used to maintain order and discipline at OB meetings. I think that'll change with time.' He saw the intense concentration on Wilhelm's face. 'As the Germans have their SS, so the OB has its Stormjaers, a body of hand-picked men from within our own ranks. They'll be used when the time is ripe.'

Wilhelm said nothing, eyes focused on the horizon, deep in thought. Rudi watched him and thought back to their lengthy conversation lasting into the early hours of the morning. Though Wilhelm's intense interest and excited response had pleased him, Rudi had given only a sketchy outline of the OB's aims and activities. Yet the more he talked, the more he was convinced of Wilhelm's suitability. His cousin asked penetrating questions, displaying a particular interest in the Stormjaer movement. At last Rudi had considered it safe to reveal the true reason for his visit to Brannigan Bay.

'Don't speak to my mother or father about that,' Wilhelm had warned him, adding that the Kesslers had lived in the country too long to act against the authorities. 'The only tie they have to their fatherland is their language. That, and their fading memories of life there.' He had offered to pass on information useful to the OB but made it clear that he wished to be more active within the ranks of the organisation.

'You wish to join the Stormjaers?' asked Rudi.

'Yes.' It was said without any hesitation. 'Right away – I can leave with you.'

Rudi shook his head. 'No,' he said firmly, 'the time isn't right. There are those among us who must still work at shaping the Stormjaers to become what we wish it to be. Only then will it suit you.' He smiled and added, 'You see, even within an organisation such as the OB there are divisions within the ranks. There are those who talk and those who act. We, the doers, must first entrench ourselves.'

'You'll send for me?'

Rudi nodded. 'For you and for any others who think and feel as you do.'

They smiled at each other before shaking hands.

It was then Rudi realised that he was being watched. A man standing on the rocks above began to walk quickly away. There was something vaguely familiar about him. Disquiet settled on him as he watched the stranger attempt the pose of a nonchalant stroller. Where had he seen him before?

It came to him then, bringing with it a stab of fear. The stranger had been on the train with him from Johannesburg. Rudi had seen him in the dining car, always sitting alone, never mixing with the other passengers. Even then he had felt the man watching him.

He tried to appear casual when he asked, 'Wilhelm, when is the next bus to Cape Town?'

'This evening. Why?'

'I . . . I've just remembered there's something I have to do there before I return to Johannesburg.'

At five o'clock that afternoon, Rudi Muller settled himself onto the bench at the rear of the bus from where he could watch the road behind. Even if he was followed by car to Cape Town he was confident of losing whoever was so interested in his movements.

Now that he knew of the tail he would lose it.

*

The noise of the air-raid sirens seemed to penetrate Barry Whitehead's brain as he scurried after other frightened men and women towards the nearest bomb shelter.

He glanced upwards as he ran, hating the feeling of helplessness against the enemy on high. Greater than his anger at Preston was the shame he felt for not having had the courage to ignore his father's wishes and join up anyway. Like many of his fellow students at Cambridge, Barry had been more than ready to abandon his academic career. An impassioned plea made to Preston in a letter, the first communication from son to father of any consequence, was met by a stern refusal: Barry was first to complete his studies. After that, they would see.

They, thought Barry now as he ducked into the shelter entrance; there had never been any *they*.

As he pushed his way to the depth of the shelter, an elderly woman standing beside him saw his dark frown. She smiled and said, 'It'll be over soon, lad. Them Jerries are only good for hit and run, they are.' She smiled again before edging further into the crowded mass of humanity.

Barry stared in dismay at her departing back. She had thought he was scared! Here he was, angry as all hell, and an old woman had thought him scared.

Glancing furtively about him, he wondered who else had the same impression. The others paid him no heed, were involved in casual conversation with those nearest them, seemingly oblivious to the downpour of bombs, the sound of which crept steadily closer. Barry was suddenly painfully aware of how few young men were there besides himself. He wanted to shout out his rage and frustration, to tell them how his father was making him suffer.

At last the barrage was over. Barry followed with leaden feet as the Londoners poured from the shelter to resume their interrupted activities.

The area surrounding the shelter had escaped the carnage, though smoke and flames poured from a building just two blocks away. The bleating of sirens filled the streets, causing scurrying pedestrians to pause briefly before going about their business. The citizens of London had learned that unless you had family or friends in an area that had been hit, your presence was merely an obstacle to those involved in bringing relief to the victims. Next time, it might be you who prayed anxiously for hasty aid.

After a few moments of indecision Barry began to try to find his way in the gathering dusk. Although he had visited London several times, it had always been with friends. He was alone that weekend, staying at the house of a fellow student who had gone away with his parents. He had looked forward to exploring London on his own, yet now felt the need for company and bustling life about him. When he came to a pub he did not hesitate to go straight inside.

The bar was not as crowded as he had expected – probably due, he thought, to the early hour of the bombing. Most of the patrons were in uniform, making Barry feel even more conspicuous. He ordered a beer, studying people's reflections in the long mirror against the back of the bar.

The barman handed him his beer. 'Caught in the raid, were you?'

Barry nodded, the images of his shame fresh in his mind. 'Didn't last long, though,' he muttered.

Three women walked into the pub just as he reached for his wallet. Even if he had not spotted them in the mirror, the sudden hush would have made him turn to look.

They were all more or less the same age – about twenty, he guessed – very pretty and obviously flattered by the reaction their arrival caused. Two men in air force uniform moved towards them, using all their charm to persuade the newcomers to join them at their table. Barry could not help feeling envious again; he felt so out of place in his civilian clothes. He watched the girls order drinks, then turned his attention back to his beer, downing half of it in a few gulps.

'Barry? It is Barry, isn't it?'

The sound of the woman's voice close to his shoulder made him turn in surprise. It was one of the three who had entered the pub just moments ago. She was vaguely familiar but Barry could not recall where they had met.

'That's right,' he said at last, then realised his lips were caked with beer foam. Wiping the back of his hand across them, he added, 'I'm sorry, but I . . . '

Her easy laugh saved him from further embarrassment. 'That's all right, I didn't expect you to remember me. We were such a crowd that night. Christmas Eve . . . The party, remember?'

'Of course, yes!' She had been the one who helped him drag his drunken friend upstairs to a room. Joan . . . Jean . . .

'Jenny,' she said, rescuing him again. 'I couldn't help noticing your reflection in the mirror as I walked in. I've a pretty good memory for faces,' she added, smiling disarmingly.

Barry laughed. 'I'm afraid I wasn't all that sober that night.' Now he remembered chatting to her for a short while. She had had a partner with her, if he remembered correctly.

'You on your own?' she asked, glancing at the empty stool beside him.

'Yes, in London for the weekend.'

'Want to join us? I'm here with two friends.' When Barry glanced across her shoulder to where the two other women were taking seats at a vacant table, Jenny laughed and said, 'I see they've managed to put off our ardent admirers in uniform.'

He laughed with her, pleased at the invitation and relieved there would not be any servicemen present to bring on his unease again. After paying for his second beer he followed Jenny to her table.

Barry found his gaze riveted on the girl at the far side of the table. She was not beautiful or even especially pretty but there was a sensuality about her that he had discerned in very few women. Lowering his eyes, he took the chair beside Jenny.

He said a general 'Hello', felt himself blush and twirled his beer glass nervously between his fingers. Despite a natural shyness, Barry was not unused to female company for he was handsome with the build of a natural athlete. Now, though, he felt awkward and knew that it was caused by more than his not wearing a uniform.

When Jenny introduced the girls, he was again struck by the young woman sitting opposite. She was watching him. 'This is Lesley,' Jenny was saying, 'and that's Alice on your left.'

Barry grinned sheepishly and felt himself blush violently when Lesley smiled at him. 'Hello, Barry,' she said, her voice throaty. He saw then that he had been mistaken about her age; she was older than the others.

He took three nervous sips of beer and hoped the shaking of his hand was not obvious.

'You not in the services, then?' asked Alice.

'I— '

'Barry's at Cambridge,' Jenny answered for him, surprising him with how much she recalled from their brief earlier acquaintance. She and Alice fell into conversation about Alice's thwarted visions of going to university. Barry made a contribution now and then but his gaze was constantly drawn to Lesley. She caught the look each time, causing heat to rush into his cheeks. She seemed so . . . amused, he thought and wondered how old she was. Twenty-four or thereabouts.

Once, when Jenny drew Lesley into their discussion, Barry had the chance to study her more closely. Her dark brown hair was thick and glossy, curling attractively on her shoulders and some time later when she stood up to go to the ladies' room joined by the other two, Barry saw soft curves and a full bosom.

He noticed that Alice had followed the custom that had become popular since silk stockings had disappeared from shop shelves. Her legs had been smeared evenly with cream and, using a dark brown eyebrow pencil, she had drawn a thin line up the back of them to simulate the seam of a stocking. From a distance, particularly in dim light, it looked like the real thing.

He went to the bar and ordered a round of drinks and returned to their table, all the time keeping his eyes fixed on the door to the ladies' room. He wanted to enjoy watching Lesley walk. His attention was focused solely on her as she came back. The pub had filled up considerably over the past half-hour and every male in the place seemed to be doing much as he was.

A group of soldiers tried to waylay the girls, loudly

pleading with them to accept a drink. Barry was relieved to see the offer sweetly yet firmly declined by a smiling Lesley. She moved on, her hips swaying gently. He watched her and knew her movements were not deliberately provocative; there was no need for that.

He rose to his feet when they reached the table, then almost fell back in surprise when Lesley, instead of resuming her seat at the other side, took the chair next to his. He could almost touch her. He tried to slow his whirling thoughts, to find something to say instead of sitting there, mute like a dummy. All he could think of was what it would be like to touch her, to feel the soft creaminess of her skin against his.

She rescued him by saying, 'You're not English, are you? Your accent, it's different.'

He held her gaze this time, though a spear of heat stabbed deep within him. 'South African,' he replied at last.

She nodded slowly. 'At first I thought you were Australian, but it's not quite the same.'

'No.' What to say next? He couldn't leave it all up to her. His mind seemed drained by her overwhelming nearness and her constant, forthright gaze.

'I'm a student,' he said suddenly, hurriedly, 'at Cambridge. I . . . What am I saying?' he added with an embarrassed chuckle. 'You already know that.'

She laughed with him, the sound light and gay. 'When do you hope to finish?'

He found himself explaining Preston's attitude towards his joining up and his frustration at being left out.

'I don't think you should feel guilty about it,' she said gently. 'I mean, it's not as if you don't *want* to fight.' She added, 'I think what bothers you more is going along with your father's wishes and not doing what *you* want.' She touched his hand understandingly as she spoke, mutely asking him not to take offence at what she had said.

Barry smiled at her, finding it hard to believe that this lovely stranger, at a chance meeting in a London pub, could see through him so clearly. She removed her hand and glanced at her wristwatch.

'Must you leave?' he asked quickly, his spirits falling.

218

'I really should,' she replied, her eyes holding his boldly.

'Can . . . May I walk you home?'

Across the table, Jenny caught his eye and raised an eyebrow. 'We'll be here for a while,' she told him, 'if you decide to come back.'

'I . . . Of course. I mean . . . '

'It's not far,' said Lesley. 'Thanks very much, Barry.'

Her ready assent made his mind spin wildly when he stood up with her, helping her slip the mandatory gas mask across her shoulder. He stood waiting while she said goodbye to her friends. 'See you later,' he called to Jenny who flashed him a thumbs-up sign when Lesley's back was turned, causing him to blush again.

The crisp air outside was a welcome relief from the pub's smoke-filled atmosphere. Barry glanced at the dense blanket of cloud hiding the moon and said, 'Let's hope the raiders don't come again tonight.'

Lesley gazed upwards but made no response. He felt suddenly immature. What to say – what to do – once they reached her home? He must have been mad to accompany her.

She walked close to him, their shoulders touching as they moved. Their dangling gas masks threatened to become entangled so Barry shifted his to his other shoulder.

'I notice you blush easily,' she said suddenly. 'It's very attractive. Most men are so full of themselves.'

He knew he should have returned the compliment but was unable to speak. Her forthrightness surprised him. He felt himself tensing again, his jumbled thoughts wondering what she expected when they arrived at her home. His sudden doubt at proving adequate for her was amusing in a way and made him smile in the dark despite his nervousness.

It was not as if he was inexperienced sexually but Lesley was different . . . older. She liked him, he was sure, but it did not mean she had any desire for him.

His thoughts were interrupted when she began to laugh. Barry looked up quickly and saw why. A short distance ahead three men walked side by side, their white shirt-tails hanging over the backs of their trousers. Ever since the blackout had come into force in September the previous year and motorists been forbidden to use their headlights, there had been a rapid rise in accidents involving pedestrians. The dangling of white shirts below jackets or blazers was a prudent precaution adopted by vast numbers of men.

'I should be used to it by now,' said Lesley, 'but I always find it funny.' Barry laughed with her and wondered whether she would find it amusing if he opted to do the same. He didn't chance it, though.

They reached her place a few minutes later, a block of flats with one section showing some minor bomb damage. 'It happened last week,' she explained. 'Luckily no one was hurt.'

They started across the dark street. She was a production clerk in the War Office, she told him, liaising with manufacturers of munitions and other war material. Barry thought it an unusually senior position for a woman, particularly one so young. The flat, explained Lesley, was a special arrangement made by her employers, a perquisite she could not have afforded under normal conditions.

Barry slowed as they neared the entrance, wondering what to do. Would she interpret it wrongly if he offered to accompany her to the door of her flat? Or should he say goodbye on the pavement?

Lesley was ahead of him as they reached the entrance. She turned so that they stood face to face, she only an inch or so shorter than he. They stared at each other before she said, 'Coffee? Or are you in a hurry to get back to the others?'

He shook his head, not trusting himself to speak. A light breeze wafted from the corner of the building and moved her hair, displacing a soft curl so that it clung to her cheek. Barry reached out slowly, pushing it back in place, his fingers lightly stroking her skin.

She smiled, said, 'You have gentle hands,' and laid her fingers over his. She took his hand, then, to lead him inside the building.

The flat was not large, with a single bedroom, lounge and a small kitchen. It was tastefully though sparsely furnished and Barry settled himself on the sofa while Lesley busied herself making coffee in the kitchen, talking to him all the time. He closed his eyes and let her voice wash over him.

'Jenny,' she was saying, 'works for one of our suppliers. We go out together occasionally. Alice is a friend of hers. We met for the first time tonight. As did you and I,' she added, peering round the corner to smile at him. 'Are you asleep?'

His eyes flew open and he said, apologetically, 'I was listening to you – to your voice. It's nice.'

She leaned against the doorway and stared down at him with her intense eyes. The soft light from the kitchen outlined the curves of her body. 'You're nice,' she said softly.

Barry wondered whether his nervousness showed on his face for she quickly added, 'I don't normally pick up strange men in pubs, Barry. There is someone . . . He's in the army somewhere in Europe. I haven't seen him for more than a year now. He writes occasionally.'

'Lesley, I didn't think— '

'But,' she overrode him, 'I feel lonely and scared sometimes. Like tonight. I don't want to be alone tonight.' She held his gaze a moment longer before turning back into the kitchen.

They drank their coffee in silence and Barry felt himself relax again. He wanted her – had wanted her from the first moment he saw her and he was content just to let things happen.

Lesley took the lead and, again, Barry was content to follow. She was skilful, gently assertive, with experience that she shared slowly and gradually with him.

'Relax,' she whispered as he lay on his back on her bed while she traced her tongue down the length of his naked body, making his flesh tremble and flutter from the intense pleasure. 'You're beautiful,' she said, taking him gently between her fingers. Her touch was light, yet firm.

She left the bedside lamp on. 'I want to see you,' she said when Barry reached out to switch it off.

He watched as she moved lower, sliding her body close to his so that he could feel her heat and the traces of her juices against his skin. Naked, she seemed more shapely than her clothes had led him to believe, with rounded hips and large, firm breasts.

She closed her lips softly around him. Barry groaned and feared he would explode within her mouth. She felt his first spasm, released him and moved back against his chest.

'It's all right,' he whispered as he felt himself regain control.

He felt her breath against his skin when she said, 'Everything's fine, Barry. Everything.' She stroked his belly in slow, circling movements.

They lay touching and stroking each other for a long time, keeping their passion at bay. Then she moved again, straddling him this time so that her heavy breasts were all he could see. She moved expertly, taking him inside her with a slight shift of her hips. The heat of her as he thrust upwards was so intense that his need for release became a bitter-sweet agony.

She was talking softly, murmuring his name but the sound seemed to come from far away as he struggled to hold back. Opening his eyes, he watched their movements, the breaking of light and shadow as she slid slowly up and down him. The world consisted of nothing but Lesley moving above him. Barry was aware of the bed squeaking beneath him and tried to concentrate on the sound. She moved faster, her breath coming in short gasps as her body slammed aggressively into his and the sound of her climax was a primitive growl of satisfaction.

'Please!' she shouted down at him. 'Now!'

There was a brief pause of the most intense, exquisite agony and then, crying out, Barry caught her hair in his hand and jerked her roughly to him, crushing her lips to his. Her breasts were squashed against his chest as their warm breath and cries mingled with their kiss.

Slowly Barry relaxed, though he continued to pulsate with powerful spasms, encircled by the warm firmness of her arms.

'Jesus!' he said in a loud exhalation of breath.

Though her body slowly relaxed, she forced her legs between his so that they remained tightly locked together.

'Lesley . . . '

'Mmm?' Slowly she released him and rolled onto her side, flinging a leg casually across his. He could feel the flutter of her heart against his chest.

'You were . . . wonderful.'

He felt her lips pull into a smile against the skin of his neck. '*We* were wonderful, Barry.' She let out a long, contented sigh before raising herself on one elbow to study his face. Her gaze was as open and frank as when he had first seen it, though now her eyes seemed lazy with the warm afterglow of their lovemaking. 'You are the first,' she whispered, 'since Michael.'

'Is that his name?' His voice sounded unusually deep and Barry realised that there was much more in sex than he had either experienced or imagined. 'How old are you?' he asked suddenly.

'Twenty-four and yes, his name is Michael,' she replied with a laugh. 'He's twenty-eight.'

'I'm twenty,' he said softly, surprised he no longer felt ashamed of it. 'You could be accused of cradle-snatching.'

She leaned closer and kissed his forehead.

'Do you love him?' asked Barry after he had lit each of them a cigarette.

'Michael?' Smoke wafted over him when she spoke. 'I don't think so. I miss him, though, and I'm frightened for him.' She dragged on her cigarette again before saying, 'I think it's easy to confuse love with liking when there's war.'

'And lust.' He immediately regretted his words when he felt her stiffen beside him. 'I'm sorry,' he said quickly. 'I didn't mean it to sound like that. Not about us.'

'Perhaps you're right,' she whispered. 'Perhaps tonight was more lust than liking. I'd like to think not, though.'

'Why me, Lesley? You could have any man you wanted.'

She stared back at him as if mulling over her answer. 'Perhaps it's because you're young,' she said, tracing her finger over the outline of his jaw. 'Young and gentle. I sensed that from the start and perhaps gentleness was just what I needed. Whatever the reason, I'm glad you're here.'

'So am I.' He kissed her, with growing passion. When they made love again, he was the aggressor although their coupling was slow and relaxed. Only at the very end did they thrash about while she held him locked within her, pulling at his buttocks as if she wanted more of him, though she cried out at the depth of his penetration.

Afterwards, when their breathing had returned to normal she refused to release him, as if his withdrawal would leave her lonely and alone again.

Much later, he said, 'I suppose I should go.'

'Must you?' Her voice sounded almost desperate, so that Barry pulled her tightly to him and smothered her lips with his.

'No,' he said into her hair. 'I don't have to and I don't want to.'

'Then stay. Just tonight, Barry. Be with me when I wake.'

The German bombers returned that night, as they had every night since 7 September. Barry and Lesley lay, holding each other and listening to the terrible drone, the thump and crash of bombs. She reached for him then, as if he could oust the danger. They made love silently, sharing life while death rained down from the dark skies.

Barry left her flat before eight the next morning. As she walked him to the door, he realised they had not talked about meeting again.

She seemed to sense his confusion for she said, 'I leave for Coventry in ten days' time. I'm to be stationed there for a few months. At the Vickers Armstrong Works.' She kissed him, gently and without passion. 'I'll still be here next weekend. That's if you . . . '

He squeezed her hand and said, 'I want to see you again, Lesley.'

The station sounds meant different things to different people. To some they spelled welcome, a return home or the longed-for departure to one. To others they were the stark sounds of parting, the prelude to loneliness or the beginning of something new. To Illana they were a bit of each.

She was pleased she had managed to persuade Magda and Jay not to see her off; it would have made things even worse. It had been difficult enough when she had gone to Brannigan Bay the previous weekend to say her farewells.

She stood alone on the platform, waiting to board the train that would carry her northwards across the arid plains of the Karoo to her new life. Just then a train pulled into the adjoining platform, announcing its arrival with a long blast of its whistle. Steam plumed white and thick from the locomotive's side. A sudden breeze swirled the air, scattering the steam and smoke. One by one the station lights came on and the raw screech of wheels on rails filled Illana's ears as the great locomotive drew to a halt.

The train doors swung open, conductors waved their flags and overhead a loudspeaker crackled out an announcement as passengers poured onto the platform to be embraced by loved ones or to stare forlornly around in search of them.

The loudspeakers called for Illana and her fellow passengers to board their train. A porter helped carry her bags to her compartment, which she was pleased to learn she would have to herself. After he left she opened the smallest suitcase and unpacked the items she would need on the thousand-mile journey.

Passengers were still milling around the train that had arrived earlier. Illana glanced through the window and watched them, wondering how she would feel when she arrived in Johannesburg. Someone from the newspaper would meet her but she knew she would still feel apprehensive and lonely.

The crowd had thinned now, most of the new arrivals walking away with those who had met them. Their faces were relaxed and smiling, their voices mingling with the shouts of porters and the hiss of the steam locomotives. Only a few still stood aimlessly beside their luggage as though they did not know what to do next. Illana wondered what had become of those supposed to meet them.

Someone rather familiar stood on the platform, his hat pulled too low over his eyes for her to see his face. He stood stiffly, hands buried deep in his pockets, newspaper tucked under one arm. Illana let out a small cry when she recognised him. There was no mistaking the dark brown jacket with its leather elbow patches. It was Rafe.

He seemed to relax when he realised that she had seen him. His shoulders sagged, and the newspaper slipped from beneath his arm. Pushing it back, he started towards her.

'Illana . . . ' His face was almost level with hers though the platform was much lower than the compartment window. 'I didn't want to come . . . I – oh, Jesus, Illana – I just had to see you. Just once more.'

She reached out and laid her palm gently against his cheek. His skin was rough and unshaven. 'I'm glad, Rafe,' she whispered, meaning it.

They stayed like that as the seconds passed, neither saying what they felt for it was all in their eyes. At last he placed his hand over hers, lightly stroking her fingers.

'You are so very beautiful,' he whispered, 'so precious. Too precious for me to own. I always knew that . . . '

'Rafe – I'm sorry!' She cried but her tears were for herself as well as for the man she was leaving behind.

A whistle blew, the sound a jarring end to their moment of parting. There were other sounds now – the blaring of loudspeakers, a burst of laughter from the adjoining compartment. A cloud of steam drifted from the locomotive one carriage away from Illana's, cloaking Rafe for a moment before it moved on.

'Train's about to leave,' he said hoarsely.

'Yes.'

A sharp jerk broke their touch before the train moved slowly from the platform. Rafe took a few steps forward, keeping pace with it, then stopped.

Both reached out at the same time. He clung to her fingers for an instant before the train drew them apart.

'I was happy with you, Rafe,' she called out.

He smiled but although she could not hear what he said

above the screech of the train's wheels she knew it was 'I love you.'

The four men who came for the Kesslers reached Brannigan Bay late on a Friday afternoon. They arrived in two black cars, one a 1938 Dodge, the other a Plymouth registered the week before.

The men were dressed in dark suits and hats and seemed bored by the task that awaited them. Their first stop was the small police station where the sergeant in charge shook his head in disbelief. 'The Kesslers?' he asked. 'Are you sure?'

The senior of the four men stared at him expressionlessly; he had been asked similar questions many times over the past month when more and more persons of German citizenship or extraction had been arrested and interned. All he said to the sergeant was, 'They were seen meeting with a known subversive.'

'Here? In Brannigan Bay?'

Four heads nodded slowly. 'We lost him in Cape Town,' one of them said, and was treated to a baleful glance from the leader.

'But the Kesslers have lived here for years,' the sergeant argued. 'Everybody knows them. They're good, decent people!'

The senior man shrugged. He was merely carrying out instructions; the background of those he had to arrest held little interest for him. 'You must come with us,' he told the policeman.

The sergeant hesitated a moment, just long enough to whisper 'Fetch Jay Brannigan,' to a young constable listening in wide-eyed awe to what was being said.

The constable ducked out of the back entrance, ran back inside to grab his bicycle clips, quickly placed them round the edge of his trouser legs, then hurtled outside again. Within seconds he was on his Rudge bicycle, pedalling furiously down the gravel road.

Jay had been home only a few minutes, having left Vaughn to take care of their day's catch. When he saw the breathless constable in the doorway, he jumped up from where he had been sitting at the kitchen table. Before he had time to collect his thoughts the constable blurted out his tale.

Magda entered the kitchen. Her hand flew to her mouth and she stared at Jay in alarm. His eyes held confusion.

'It must be a mistake,' he said, 'Gottlieb . . . They would never . . . No, it *must* be a mistake.'

'There were four of them, Mr Brannigan,' the constable spluttered, trying to catch his breath after his frantic ride. 'Security police or something like that. They were – well, they sounded like they meant what they said.'

'Where are they now?'

'With the sergeant. They told him to go with them to the Kesslers but he ordered me to fetch you, Mr Brannigan.'

'Stay here,' Jay told Magda. 'I don't want too many of us around, it'll just draw attention.' He patted the constable's shoulder and said, 'Let's go.'

Magda stared at the door when it shut behind them, unable to believe what she had heard. Internment for the Kesslers? At some camp, Koffiefontein, she had heard someone say when the first arrests started. It was ridiculous to think that Gottlieb and Gertrude – Wilhelm! Her legs suddenly felt weak and she gripped the back of a chair to steady herself. They couldn't take him. It was bad enough to think of Gottlieb and Gertrude locked away but Wilhelm was too young to be kept captive like some animal.

Without further thought she dashed out of the cottage and ran for the harbour, praying she would be in time. She hurtled wildly down the steep path, the hem of her skirt flapping dangerously round her ankles.

Sea Orchard, the boat in which Wilhelm served, was already pulled up on the harbour shelf. Vaughn noticed her when she was half-way down the path. Dropping the fishing lines he was working on, he ran to meet her but though Magda saw him coming her eyes searched desperately for Wilhelm.

'Ma! Ma?' She heard her son's shout as he reached her, holding out his arms to stop her wild flight.

'Wilhelm!' she called as she ran full tilt into Vaughn, almost knocking him over.

'Ma, what is it?'

She was trying to wriggle free. 'Wilhelm,' she said again, her voice almost a whisper this time. 'Where is he?' Taking a quick breath, she relied on Vaughn's strength to keep her upright as she scanned the men remaining within the harbour. One or two watched her curiously but most busied themselves with their tasks.

'They've come for Wilhelm – for the Kesslers,' she told Vaughn and saw the confusion on his face. 'Internment!' she said more firmly. 'He must get away. Now!'

'Internment? Why?'

She tried to break free again, but his grip on her forearms was too strong. 'Let go!' she cried, ignoring the hurt look on Vaughn's face.

It was only when he said, 'He's here, Ma – he's safe,' that she relaxed.

Taking her by the elbow, Vaughn steered her towards the nearest cleaning hut. It was dark inside but Magda could discern the dim shape of someone bent over a large basket used by the fishermen to store their equipment.

When Vaughn said his name, Wilhelm turned and straightened. Vaughn took his mother's arm and pulled her inside.

Even in the dark Magda could see the effect of her words on Wilhelm. His face was pale, his lips set. 'Who are they?' was all he asked when she finished.

'Security police,' she replied. 'That's what the constable thinks. Why would they— '

Wilhelm hissed, 'Because we're German – they need no reason other than that.'

'*You*'re not!' exclaimed Vaughn.

Wilhelm turned away from them and hauled out his oilskins from the basket against the wall. 'They'll not get me,' he said. 'I'll die before I let them take me!'

Vaughn moved closer and laid a hand on his friend's shoulder. 'I'm sure they'll let us explain.'

'No. It's not explanations they want.' Wilhelm seemed excited now, recovered from his initial shock.

'They'll realise they've made a mistake once we all talk to them,' persisted Vaughn.

'No, there's no mistake.'

Glancing at Vaughn, Magda said, 'It doesn't matter – just go now, Wilhelm! They'll know you're here.' She clutched Vaughn's shoulder so tightly it made him flinch. 'Son,' she whispered, 'it doesn't matter what they think, whether they're right or wrong! You must help him get away from here – to one of the coves across the bay. They won't find him there.'

'Ma, I can't! We'd be breaking the law!'

'Yes you can! You can,' she added more calmly. 'First he must get away safely, then we can find out what's going on.'

Vaughn glanced at each of them in turn. 'They'll see the boat. We wouldn't get very far.'

Wilhelm's hand was on his arm. 'I can escape across the rocks,' he said, 'and hide out near the beach. You can fetch me there later after dark. Will you do it, Vaughn? Will you help me, old friend?'

Magda kept her eyes on Vaughn when he turned to her as if seeking advice. 'Do it. Please.'

He held her gaze and she saw the disapproval in his eyes before he let out a long sigh. 'Go,' he whispered to Wilhelm, 'but don't run till you're out of sight of the harbour.'

'I'll stay against the edge of the water,' came the reply. Tucking the oilskins under his arm, Wilhelm added, 'You'll find me where the rocks meet the beach.'

Vaughn nodded. 'Go,' he repeated, quickly squeezing Wilhelm's shoulder before the other slipped from the hut.

The only sound was Magda's laboured breathing. At last she said, 'Thank you, son.'

He smiled and placed his arm about her. 'I was just about done on the boat so let's go home. It wouldn't do for the police to find us here. And they'll come, I'm sure of it.'

As they walked up the sloping path, Vaughn glanced back once but detected no sign of Wilhelm. The only movement he spied in the gathering dusk was the splashing of waves over the rocks. High tide, he thought, already planning the best route to follow that night. He must make sure to be unobserved when he took out a dinghy for everyone would know what he was up to once they learned about the Kesslers.

Studying the sky he was relieved to see a dark bank of cloud moving in from the south-east. Good. It would make things easier for without a moon it would be difficult to spot a boat moving out across the bay.

Jay had not returned when Magda and Vaughn reached the cottage. Vaughn went outside to wait for his father, then realised it might be less suspicious if he were seen somewhere in town. He decided to go to the café where there were sure to be others; he could wait there until it was dark enough to fetch Wilhelm.

He moved off, watching the approaching cloud layer anxiously.

'No,' said Jay, 'I won't allow Vaughn to help.'

Magda watched him hunch his shoulders in defiance, his face revealing his outrage at what had happened to the Kesslers as well as his dismay at what she wanted done.

'Jay, he—'

'No, Magda! I cannot let Vaughn take the risk. It's not right. There's no need for it. I've told you the Kesslers' side of things – they're sure to be released once the police have completed their investigation. How were they to know their nephew is a subversive?'

'I can't take that chance, Jay,' she replied, her voice strangely calm. 'Wilhelm is my son.'

'You'd risk *our* son to help him escape? A criminal? You said yourself he didn't deny doing anything wrong.'

'He's not a criminal, just a confused boy. You know how he's always felt about Germany, how he resents this war. So did you, once.'

'That was a long time ago, Magda,' he snapped back. 'I didn't break the law.'

'Neither has Wilhelm – yet! All he and the Kesslers have done wrong is to meet with a subversive. The man is his cousin, Jay!'

'Then let him explain that to the police. His running away will only make matters worse for Gottlieb and Gertrude. Can't you see that?'

'I know! I know!' Her anger left her and she reached out to touch him, trying to make him understand. He did not move away but neither did he respond.

Magda said, 'Perhaps you're right, perhaps the Kesslers will be cleared. But Wilhelm . . . He's angry and embittered, Jay. I'm frightened of how he would behave if the police had him. He could make things even worse for himself and the Kesslers. I can't let them get him, Jay. I can't.'

Moving away from her, he leaned against the wall. 'No,' he kept saying, the echo of the word hammering into her repeatedly, compelling her to accept his refusal.

'Let's free him, Jay! Let him go. Don't leave me to think of him in a prison cell. For God's sake, Jay – Wilhelm is my *son* . . .'

Her voice trailed off as she saw Jay stiffen, his gaze on the open kitchen door.

Magda swung slowly round. Vaughn stood there, his hand on the doorknob as though to close it and shut out the words she had spoken.

But it was too late for that.

'Shall we light a fire?' asked Vaughn.

Wilhelm shook his head. 'Not tonight. Tomorrow I'll see whether I can find a better hideout across the dunes.'

Vaughn hugged himself to ward off the chilly air that had accompanied the clouds and wind. Their flight across the bay had proceeded relatively easily. It was only when they approached the opposite shore with its low hills and scrub that they had had to move cautiously. Fortunately the swells ran lightly so that there was little danger of their boat overturning in the surf.

They found somewhere for the night in the lee of the first dunes, which would provide shelter from wind and rain. Vaughn had brought along a strip of canvas for Wilhelm to make a rudimentary shelter.

While Wilhelm gnawed at the cold chicken Magda had packed for him, Vaughn studied his half-brother in the shadows cast on the white sand. He could not decide whether he regretted having gone home early, whether he should have heeded the warning that sounded in his mind as he moved closer to the kitchen door, his mother's voice drawing him onwards. He remembered only being intent on quelling whatever it was that raged between his parents, of telling Jay that it was his own decision to help Wilhelm escape.

Learning the truth had provided a quiet satisfaction. It explained the curious kinship that had always existed between Wilhelm and himself and much else as well: the concern his mother had always exhibited for the other boy; Jay's resentment and disapproval of their childhood friendship.

He had stood there, watching the consternation on his parents' faces as they stared back at him. Vaughn had been more anxious about the pain his learning the truth was causing them than about his own reaction to the news.

Even now he could not define whether he felt any differently towards Wilhelm, if the knowledge of their shared blood bound them any closer. He certainly did not resent him. In the same way he had been at pains to make Magda understand that it changed nothing about what he felt for her and how much he admired and respected her. But in Jay's eyes Vaughn saw only shame and distress and he knew they must talk.

Wilhelm's voice interrupted his thoughts. 'You staying the night?'

Vaughn gazed intently at him without answering. His half-brother – his and Illana's. He almost wished he had not promised Magda that he would never share this knowledge with either Illana or Wilhelm. He wanted to reveal it now, to use it to try to stave off the strange, dark madness that seemed to have sucked Wilhelm into its grip. But his promise had been made.

'Hey! Have you gone deaf?' Wilhelm's words blended with the light wind that whipped over the dunes scattering grains of sand against their clothes. 'I asked whether you're staying with me tonight.'

'No, the men who arrested your parents are out searching for you. The police as well. They might want to question my parents so it would seem strange if I wasn't home.'

'Where are they? My parents, I mean.'

Vaughn scooped up a handful of sand and let it sift slowly through his fingers. 'At the police station,' he replied.

'In the cells?'

Vaughn nodded. He could almost feel Wilhelm's rage. 'According to my dad,' he said, 'it's because they met someone opposed to the war, someone who wanted them to act as spies. Is that what you meant this afternoon when you said there had been no mistake?'

Wilhelm traced his finger through the loose sand, forming a pattern that had meaning only to him. 'There *was* someone,' he whispered, his words barely audible above the wind. 'He's my cousin but my parents knew nothing of why he was here.' He gave a disgusted snort and added, 'Can you imagine them doing anything against the law? Only the fools who arrested them could think that!'

'It was you who helped him?'

Wilhelm was still playing with the sand as he said, 'Rudi is with the Ossewa-Brandwag.' He told Vaughn everything then, about what he had learned of the OB and the Stormjaers, about Rudi Muller's promise that he would be sent for when the time was right. 'My parents know nothing about it,' he repeated.

Vaughn sat silently, trying to understand the events that had led to his being on a deserted beach with a childhood friend. No, he quickly corrected himself, with his mother's son.

Wilhelm leaned forward suddenly and gripped his arm. 'Come with me,' he said in a low voice. 'Come and fight against the bastard Smuts and his government!'

'This is not a game!' snapped Vaughn, jerking his arm free, suddenly resentful of Wilhelm's ignorance. If he knew the truth, then perhaps he would realise what pain he was capable of inflicting on those who cared more than they dared reveal. He lowered his voice to a whisper as though someone nearby might overhear them. 'I want nothing to do with this damned war. I don't hate the Germans but neither do I want to fight for them.'

'And for your own country? For its future and the people who should be ruling it? Are you prepared to fight for them?' Wilhelm pushed his face close to Vaughn's, the way he often had as a boy when they were about to wrestle. 'What kind of man,' he asked, 'is Smuts, to arrest gentle people like my parents? Is that the kind of man you want to let do as he pleases with our country?'

Vaughn stared back at him in the dark. 'It's only because they suspect them,' he began. 'Your parents will be released soon, I'm sure of that. It's no reason to want to go to war, Wilhelm. What you should do is go to them now, help explain things. Your running away is making matters worse.'

Wilhelm's lips were twisted into a sneer. 'Is that what your dad thinks?'

'Yes. I agree with him.'

'If it were *your* parents? What would you say then, Vaughn? What would you do?'

'I – I don't know.'

Wilhelm gripped his wrist, the touch gentle yet firm. 'Come with me,' he pleaded. 'We've always been together. It mustn't end now.' But Vaughn pulled free and pushed himself to his feet.

'I'll come again tomorrow night,' he said without answering Wilhelm's question. 'Do you want cigarettes?' he asked, handing over his packet without waiting for a reply.

Wilhelm's face was angry as he followed Vaughn back to the boat that lay pulled a few feet up the beach, the surf lapping against its stern.

They pushed it into the water and turned its bows. Vaughn clambered in. He gripped the oars and glanced over his shoulder. 'Till tomorrow,' he said.

'Yes.' Wilhelm's voice was almost drowned by the sound of the ocean. He gave the boat a final shove and Vaughn readied himself to plunge the oars into the water.

Overhead the moon had appeared through a gap in the clouds, casting a strip of light across the sea as if to show the course he should follow.

The Brannigans kept Wilhelm hidden for two weeks until the initial frantic efforts to locate him were over.

Vaughn brought him back to Brannigan Bay late one night,

then drove him out of town in Brian McDermott's car, borrowed on the pretext of wanting to impress a new girlfriend.

He stopped the car alongside the road on the outskirts of the town of Grabouw, leaving the engine running. Vaughn kept his eyes fixed ahead, waiting for Wilhelm to move.

The other grunted but remained in his seat. 'You sure this was what Rudi wanted?' he asked.

'Yes.' At Wilhelm's urging he had telephoned Muller the week before and explained his cousin's predicament. The OB man had said Wilhelm should go to Grabouw, to an address that he gave Vaughn and from there he would be taken to Bloemfontein by road. After that, he, Muller, would find a way for them to meet.

'I think it's best,' said Vaughn now, 'if you go from here on foot. It'd be wrong if Mr McDermott's car was seen in the town. You have the address?'

Wilhelm patted his shirt pocket in reply. 'Well, I suppose I'd better get going.'

'Yes.'

'Relieved?' Wilhelm asked, his tone and expression mocking Vaughn. When there was no response he added, 'I'll send word once I'm settled – in case you decide to come to Johannesburg. Will you?'

Vaughn met his gaze for the first time since they had stopped. 'Yes,' he said. Even as the single, abrupt word echoed within his head, he wondered whether his verbal agreement had been prompted by his recent speculation about moving to Johannesburg to find a career for himself or because he now knew who Wilhelm was. He told himself it no longer mattered; he would be going – he was certain of that.

Wilhelm's teeth gleamed whitely as he smiled in the dark and held out his hand. Moments later he disappeared into the thick brush beside the road.

It was Barry's third visit to the London pub where he and Lesley had met. As he ordered a beer, his stomach tightened at the memory of their being together, then seemed to pitch

236

upside down at the knowledge that he was to see her again the next day. During the journey from Cambridge to London, he had had to keep reminding himself it was true, that only one more night separated them. Just another night before he would see and touch her again.

As the barman placed his beer before him, Barry was tempted to share his joy with him, to say, 'I'm seeing my girl tomorrow,' as if speaking the words aloud would further reinforce their truth. But the barman turned away without responding to Barry.

He sipped his beer slowly, hoping it would calm the butterflies fluttering in his stomach. It had been the same when he came to London to see her the second time, although his nervousness then had been caused more by doubts about how she would react to him arriving on her doorstep. He had spent the week since their first meeting reliving their time together, trying to recall each word, each expression. Had Lesley meant what she had said about wanting to see him again or had she just been polite, relying on him to interpret what she really felt? The week had dragged past as he weighed up his recollections of her, each hour bringing with it a conflicting conclusion.

In the end he decided to let fate lead him where it would, and arrived at Lesley's flat long after dark on the Friday night. A myriad of doubts plagued him as he found his hand reaching of its own accord to knock timidly at her door.

Lesley was at home and she was alone. Barry's whirling mind had assimilated all that as he stood staring at her, unable to speak. Yet he was not too numb to note her welcoming smile or to hear her say, 'Barry, you came. I knew – oh, I'm so glad!'

It was a dream come true, beyond even his fantasies. They talked, they probed, they listened and they came to know and understand each other until the time came to part – Lesley to start her new job in Coventry, Barry to return to his studies at Cambridge. Now, at last, he would soon see her again.

Barry planned carefully so that he could slip away from Cambridge on the Thursday. He had arranged to spend the night in London with a friend's parents and would leave for

Coventry early next morning. He and Lesley could be together for the whole weekend.

'You planning to nurse that beer all night?' The barman's voice jerked him from his reverie. 'Seems you've plenty on your mind, then,' he added when Barry grinned and reached for his drink.

This time Barry said, quite loudly, 'I'm seeing my girl tomorrow.'

Coventry was bathed in bright moonlight when at 7 p.m. 450 German Heinkel III and Junkers bombers dropped the first of their deadly load.

It was a raid like no other and in the hours that followed, 1500 high explosive bombs and 30,000 incendiaries fell destroying 60,000 buildings, killing 600 people and leaving 1200 more injured. It heralded the first of the major raids on Britain's provincial cities and it also introduced a new word into the English vocabulary. From then on, any city that suffered badly in raids was deemed to have been 'Coventrated'.

Barry heard of the raid next morning while waiting for his train to leave. He had been in the station waiting room at 8 a.m. when a wireless broadcast announced a successful British air raid over Berlin. The report following was about a heavy German air attack on one Midlands town in particular. Barry thought immediately of Coventry as for some time the city had been a target for air raids. None of his fellow passengers could provide him with more information.

His concern for Lesley's welfare increased when they were still some miles from Coventry and he caught his first glimpses of the damage to the surrounding areas. The train came to a halt on the outskirts of the smoke-shrouded city and Barry learned that the rails in the station had been torn up by bombs.

Passengers panicked in their fear for the safety of loved ones. They scattered from the train, and Barry followed, hoping that he would find a bus or tram still working.

The trams were not operating – there were power cuts and most of the lines had been destroyed in the raid. He succeeded in fighting his way onto an overcrowded bus headed for the city centre. From there he would somehow get to the Priory Row cottage Lesley had said she shared with two other girls.

The bus's progress was slow, hampered by immense craters, piles of rubble and workers trying to locate and defuse the horde of unexploded bombs littering the streets.

Barry's fear for Lesley's safety increased as his journey progressed. The bus passed horrifying sights: ragged brick-work and broken walls lined the road and the crash of falling concrete and roofs could be heard from inside the moving vehicle. Telephone wires were strung like tangled fishing lines across the streets, forcing people to pick their way carefully through them. An acrid pall of smoke mingled in the air with the morning mist. Worst of all were the pitiful scenes of bewildered families scratching through the remains of what had once been their homes, searching for something of value – sentimental or otherwise – that might have survived. Others, already reconciled to their homeless state, walked in groups as they deserted their city for fear the raids would be repeated that night. Their faces wore dreamlike expressions. Some carried small bundles of personal possessions tightly under their arms, others pushed bicycles or prams.

Barry was one of the first to get off when the bus finally stopped in what had been the city centre of Broadgate. The central area was almost completely flattened and ruined; it was difficult to imagine how anyone could have survived.

'The city centre,' said a man beside Barry, 'took a proper pasting.' His words deepened Barry's despair and sense of helplessness.

He saw the remains of the old cathedral, now without pillars or roof, smouldering beams still crashing to the ground. When he began to walk, the sound beneath his feet was of crunching glass.

Spotting a police station, he went inside, asked for directions to Priory Row and ran out again.

As he tore along, heart thumping in his chest, the smell of charred wood and rubble was momentarily displaced by the distractingly strong and unmistakable aroma of tobacco.

A tobacconist must have caught fire during the raid . . . but the impression was short-lived and his only thought was to find Lesley.

Less than five minutes later Barry stood before what had once been a row of timber-framed cottages. Apart from two units that were miraculously unscathed, little was left but blackened bricks. He stared at the remains and knew, even before a smoke-stained fire warden spotted him and came closer with a list of names in his hand, that he would never see her again.

'Are you looking for someone, lad?' the warden asked, laying a hand gently on Barry's arm. His voice was scratchy from smoke and his eyes showed the ravages of the previous night – the grisly sights he had been forced to endure. Yet his voice was filled with compassion when he said, 'Have you got a name for me?'

Barry could not speak. He saw only the smoking ruins before him, felt only the light grip of the warden's hand. Reaching into his breast pocket, he handed over a slip of paper on which Lesley had written her name and new address. His gaze was mesmerised by the fine, feminine scrawl of her handwriting as the warden took it from him.

'We got them all out early this morning,' the warden was saying as he studied the note.

Barry felt the increased pressure of the hand on his arm. I already know, he wanted to tell the man. I think I knew all along.

The warden saw his face and turned away. 'I'm sorry, lad. Was she your sister?'

Barry shook his head. 'No, just a friend.' His voice cracked.

He was walking away, blindly, numbly, when the warden's voice coming from afar said, 'You all right? Come and have a cuppa. It always helps.'

His voice answered the man, like an echo springing back at him from the ruins. 'Just a friend,' the voice said. 'That's all she was.' Tears cast a thick curtain of mist before his eyes and he stumbled over some debris in the road and almost fell. His dazed mind wanted to command his legs to give way beneath him so that he could lie on the ground and cry till the pain left him.

But he walked on, saying repeatedly, 'Just a friend.'

Jay stared at the harbour jetty, covered now and then by the pounding surf. He sighed, turned to Vaughn and said, 'Are you sure of this, son?'

Vaughn studied the white-capped waves in the bay. The wind blowing up the cliffs made his hair stand stiffly on end. 'I don't quite know, Dad, but I want to go. I feel I have to find out for myself—'

'What life beyond Brannigan Bay offers,' Jay finished for him. He had known it would happen eventually for Vaughn was not a fisherman at heart.

Though Vaughn had been aware for some time that he would leave Brannigan Bay he wondered how much his promise to Wilhelm had hastened the planned move.

It was a while before Jay spoke again, saying, 'Promise you won't go to work on the mines. It wouldn't seem right.'

Vaughn smiled and nodded although he had already considered the mines as an option – he had heard that the wages were high. 'I promise,' he said softly.

'And you'll try to find out about the Kesslers?'

'It'll be the first thing I do. Illana can help with that, too.'

Jay grunted. 'You'll be seeing *him*, I suppose. You owe Wilhelm nothing, Vaughn. Any debts were settled when we helped him escape. Even your mother accepts that now.'

Vaughn thought it better not to respond. 'I was thinking of leaving after New Year. Will that be all right?'

'That'll be fine, son.' Jay straightened up, threw an arm round Vaughn's shoulders and said, 'Come, let's go home. Your mother's going to have to be told some time.'

1941

Vaughn wandered round the small apartment, smiled inwardly and said, 'It's great, sis. Really . . . modern.'

'It's tiny,' retorted Illana, 'and becoming even smaller while you're standing there looking all gawky. Sit, will you?'

Vaughn did as he was told, settling into a chair that seemed barely capable of holding him. 'So, are you an award-winning journalist yet?'

'No chance of that while there's a war on. Everything is censored – not even any by-lines put to articles. Still, I'm working on some challenging projects – and some frivolous things too,' she added with a chuckle.

'Such as?'

'Well, I get to mix with the socialites, reporting on what they get up to. Their fund-raising efforts for the various war charities, the gambling parties— '

'Gambling?'

'Oh, it's all very proper! The parties are to raise war funds and usually held by wealthy people. Attendance by invitation only, you understand. Full-dress affairs, actually,' she added in society tones which made Vaughn laugh.

'You go to them?'

'But of course, my dear! People who spend their money like that love to see their names in print. I've even been offered gambling chips by a guest,' she said.

'You turned down the offer, of course.'

'Of course,' Illana replied primly. 'He was rather old and running to fat.'

'No big romance, then?'

Lowering her eyes she said, 'No. Not yet.'

Her response, almost too quick, made Vaughn wonder

but he decided not to probe and Illana stood up to make tea. Instead he told her what had happened to the Kesslers.

'I had a letter from Ma,' she told him from the kitchen. 'She was a bit vague, though. I'll see whether I can find out what's become of them. I'm in a better position to sniff around than you.'

'I was thinking much the same,' said Vaughn. 'Could you get into the camp? Perhaps do an article on it?'

'No chance! There must be another way – I'm not completely without influence,' she added with a little smile as she handed him his tea.

'Did Ma mention we helped Wilhelm escape?'

Illana almost choked. 'Helped him escape? Ma?'

'And me. Dad, too, though he wasn't happy about it.' He explained the full chain of events, fighting the urge to tell her who Wilhelm really was.

She was shaking her head in disbelief. 'It's so unlike Ma! She's always so . . . so calm and controlled. I can't imagine her doing a thing like that!'

She sat down, thoughtfully stroking her chin. 'This subversive who came to see the Kesslers. You say he's Wilhelm's cousin?' When Vaughn nodded she asked, 'What's his name?'

'Rudi Muller,' Vaughn replied reluctantly, perturbed by the gleam that sprang into Illana's eyes.

'Muller? Of course. He's an obvious choice for the job of recruiting informers!'

'You know him?'

'Of him. I'm part of a team of journalists who investigate the OB's activities to establish whether the organisation is as ominous as the rumours suggest. It *is*,' she finished firmly, 'and Rudi Muller is one of the driving forces behind it. He's also actively involved in recruiting Stormjaers.' Before Vaughn could speak she went on, 'You know what became of Wilhelm, don't you?' Her tone was demanding and Vaughn felt resentful.

Placing his empty cup on a nearby table, he heaved himself to his feet. 'All I know is that he's somewhere in Johannesburg.'

'Here? You've kept in touch with him, haven't you? That's dangerous, Vaughn! You could— '

'I said that's all I know about him,' he snapped, angry with himself for lying to her. 'You sound just like Dad,' he added with a quick smile.

She studied him carefully, then said, 'He's with the Ossewa-Brandwag – he must be. I wasn't exaggerating when I said they're a bad bunch. Stay away from them, Vaughn.'

'I'd better get going,' he mumbled and made for the door.

Sensing she would get nothing further from him, she followed quickly. 'Stay a while longer,' she pleaded, sad that their first meeting should cause tension between them. 'Please stay, Vaughn.'

'I've a job interview,' he replied. 'It's nothing grand – truck driver for a clothing factory.'

'It's a start. Think you'll like it?'

'It's long distance. Deliveries to Natal and the Eastern Cape. New places, long open roads.'

As he went towards the door, she flung her arm round him. 'Let me know how it goes. If you have no luck I can contact a few people I know. Is that room you rent all right? You could have shared with me, you know.'

'It's fine, sis. Thanks for the offer.' Since arriving in Johannesburg three days ago, Vaughn had stayed in a single room in a boarding house in Kensington to the east of the city centre. The rent was reasonable and included breakfast and an evening meal.

As Vaughn opened the front door, Illana said, 'How about dinner tonight? My treat. There's a little restaurant— '

'Sorry, sis, not tonight. I promised I'd join the others at my place on a pub crawl. It'll be my first night out in the big city. Some other time?'

She nodded and raised her face so that he could kiss her, troubled by the way he had evaded her eyes while he spoke. It was not like the Vaughn she knew.

Only later, while she was preparing a fresh pot of tea in the hope that it would dispel her sense of unease, did she know for sure that he had lied to her. And she was convinced that she knew where he was going and that Wilhelm would be there.

It was the OB's first public meeting that year and considered so important a display of its growing strength that it was to take place in the City Hall. The OB's new leader, Dr van Rensburg, formerly administrator of the Orange Free State, would address the members in his capacity as Commandant General. Illana would have attended but her editor, fearful for her safety, had insisted that one of her male colleagues go in her place.

Was it possible that Vaughn was one of them, she thought now, that he was more under the influence of Wilhelm than she had believed? Illana shut her eyes tightly, trying to still the beginnings of pain pounding inside her skull. She had come to understand the workings of the OB well over the past few months and could comprehend the sentiments of the vast majority of its members. For the most part they were Afrikaners disenchanted with petty squabbles among their politicians who saw the OB as a means of retaining their cultural identity. Most were ignorant of the growing militaristic element. They knew nothing of the hard core of men like Rudi Muller and his Stormjaers who were secretly building a private army, training their men with arms stolen from railway sidings and dockyards with the help of more militant supporters. As far as most members were concerned, the Stormjaers existed to keep order at meetings. They did not share Illana's growing knowledge of the brutal beatings of dissenters within the ranks or of the suspected murders of police informers.

Illana knew, too, that Prime Minister Jan Smuts was painfully aware of the disapproval of many Afrikaners of South Africa's alliance with Britain in the war. It was a major reason that he was hesitant to act against the OB and its leaders.

Illana was aware, as were her colleagues on the *Star*, that a special investigative squad had been established by the police and that the names of most OB members were listed on their files.

She could not help wondering if Vaughn's name would not soon be added.

Vaughn left the factory's recruitment office flushed with success: he would start work on Monday. Filled with a sense of well-being, he opted to take a trolleybus to Kensington instead of walking. He enjoyed the almost silent ride and wondered how Jay would react to his new employment. At least he had kept his promise about not seeking a position in the mines.

After freshening up and changing his clothes, he resisted the temptation to take the trolleybus back to the city and instead walked the few miles.

The late-afternoon streets were still busy as he made his way to the Waverly Hotel where he and Wilhelm had arranged to meet. The hotel was situated opposite the City Hall and just before Vaughn went inside he noticed that a small crowd had already gathered on the steps. They seemed tense, reminding him of a conversation overheard on the trolleybus when someone mentioned that trouble was expected. The event was billed as a cultural concert yet Vaughn could not shrug off the feeling that the stranger's prediction might well be proved true.

A gum-chewing woman seated behind the reception desk peered up as he walked past. She studied him from head to toe, the look so brazen that Vaughn blushed.

He went upstairs to a wide veranda overlooking the city hall. It was stuffy: the summer heat clung to the streets although the dark blue of the sky was already streaked with indigo as the sun slipped towards the west.

Ordering a Castle beer, he felt in his jacket pocket for his cigarettes. The packet was empty. As he glanced round in search of the waiter from whom he had ordered his drink, his gaze settled on an advertising poster pasted against the opposite wall. MEN OF THE WORLD SMOKE MAX, it declared. He ordered a packet from the waiter when he brought the beer, the sides of the glass coated with condensation. The waiter gave an approving nod, making Vaughn wonder whether he also paid attention to advertisements. 'A box of matches as well,' he called after the retreating figure.

Settling back, drink in hand, Vaughn realised he was early; it was still half an hour before his half-brother was due. He wondered if Wilhelm was not taking a risk by being seen in public; the only letter he had received from him, addressed to a friend's home, had spoken boastfully of the police not daring to arrest him now that he was with the OB. Wilhelm had added that the OB had many police supporters and that he was confident the search for him was over.

The bar was slowly filling up and Vaughn suddenly regretted his arrangement with Wilhelm. He was starting to enjoy the atmosphere of the city and it would have been fun just to sit there and watch people.

Glancing out at the street he saw that many more people had arrived at the hall. Some were already filing inside while in the street cars cruised by, trying to find parking. Several policemen hung about on the pavement, some mingling with the OB members. Vaughn mused again about what Wilhelm's letter had said of widespread police support for the OB. He knew they were forbidden to join but the way those standing outside the hall chatted and laughed with the OB members seemed to confirm Wilhelm's claims.

The waiter returned with his cigarettes. 'One and six, sir,' he said. Vaughn paid him with a two-shilling piece and told him to keep the change. It was an extravagance he could not really afford – as was smoking – but it made him feel good.

Brannigan Bay seemed a million miles away when, a while later, he ordered a second beer thinking he would have enough time to drink it before Wilhelm arrived.

A group of three soldiers and two women walked in, seating themselves at the table beside his. They glanced at his civilian clothes – arrogantly he felt. He was struck by an unfamiliar flush of resentment but kept his gaze fixed on his beer glass. From the volume of their voices, he guessed the soldiers had already had a few drinks before coming to the hotel.

It had turned quite dark. Only a few men remained outside the hall but the police were still present.

A woman's shrill laugh made him jerk his eyes towards her. She was sitting at the next table and, like her male friends, her face was flushed with liquor. 'Leave the *Boere* alone,' she said loudly, referring to the OB members. 'Let them have their silly meeting.'

The ruddy-complexioned soldier sitting beside her straightened in his chair. 'Silly?' he roared. 'It's not bloody silly at all!

Those Nazi bastards are doing everything they can to sabotage what we're fighting for up north. I get more pleasure bashing their faces in than I do from killing Germans!'

'OK, OK!' the woman said quickly, holding up her hands in a placatory gesture. 'It's just that I thought you guys would find Helen and me more fun than beating people up.'

'Of course you're more fun,' another soldier said, 'but that has to wait till later. Our mates are at the Victoria Hotel waiting for the meeting to end. That's when the action starts.'

Vaughn's heart pounded while he pretended to concentrate on his beer. There *was* going to be trouble. He thought of all the women he had seen accompanying their menfolk into the City Hall and dreaded the terror they would experience at the sight of hordes of soldiers preparing to assault them. His innate dislike of any intolerance surfaced as anger and he had to restrain himself from shouting at the group beside him. He knew, though, that they were in no mood to listen to reason; they wanted blood.

He glanced towards the veranda entrance in search of Wilhelm, shuddering when he thought of how he would have reacted had he heard the soldiers.

The idea of leaving the bar was suddenly appealing; he could wait for Wilhelm at the hotel entrance or cross the street and warn the policemen.

He started to get up although he knew it might seem suspicious to go so soon after what the soldiers had said. Already he had heard one warn the others to keep their voices down.

Moving carefully round their table, he quelled the urge to look at them. When he heard a soldier say, 'No tin badge on him,' Vaughn knew they were referring to the 'On Service' badge he had seen worn by many men in Johannesburg.

Wilhelm entered the hotel's front door just as Vaughn reached the foyer. They shook hands, Wilhelm seeming genuinely pleased to see him. Both spoke at once, Wilhelm trying to relate everything that had happened to him since leaving Brannigan Bay, Vaughn attempting to warn him of the threat of violence. He succeeded in overriding Wilhelm and quickly described what he had heard.

'It's what we expected,' Wilhelm responded, with what sounded to Vaughn like keen anticipation. 'We're ready for them.'

When Vaughn began arguing Wilhelm silenced him, saying, 'You needn't get involved – there're more than enough of us.'

'That's not what I meant,' Vaughn snapped back. 'Why fight each other like a bunch of children? We could tell the police about it, let them take care of things.'

Wilhelm sneered. 'We take care of things ourselves,' he replied. 'You'll learn that.' Starting for the door he turned and added, 'You can watch the proceedings in the hall, then slip out before the end. Just give me your address. I'll look you up over the weekend.'

Despite the rage he felt at Wilhelm's arrogance, Vaughn told him. 'Wouldn't it be easier if I met you somewhere?'

Wilhelm shook his head. 'I'll collect you. I drive an OB car now.'

The policemen eyed them suspiciously as they crossed the street, making Vaughn suspect that they were fully aware of the threat of violence. It worried him how few of them were on duty and he considered breaking away from Wilhelm to warn them. The moment was lost and he was forced to follow him into the great hall.

Dr van Rensburg was already addressing the meeting. 'He's been to Germany and met Adolf Hitler,' Wilhelm whispered as they stood at the rear of the hall.

Though the stage area was some distance away, Vaughn saw that van Rensburg was a large man, somewhere in his mid-forties. His hair was close-cropped, German style, and, unlike many present in the hall, he wore no beard. Since the Great Trek celebrations in 1938, it had become popular for Afrikaners to sport long beards. Many innocent men had been assaulted by soldiers for no other reason than that they wore beards and were automatically assumed to be OB members.

A large flag adorned the wall at the back of the stage; it was about six feet wide, brilliant white and in its centre was a black eagle, its tongue, wing-tips and breast feathers depicted in harsh red. The eagle's claws rested on what Vaughn recognised as the wheel of an ox-wagon. Half the wheel was accurately portrayed, while the lower half enclosed an ox-wagon against the background of a mountain. The only thing missing, he thought wryly, was a picture of Adolf Hitler and the sound of German marching music.

It was eleven o'clock when the meeting finally ended. The crowd rose to their feet just as Vaughn realised he had lost his last chance of avoiding getting caught up in the conflict threatening outside.

He was tense as he made his way towards the exit, eager to be among the first to get out. Wilhelm's grip on his elbow stopped him. 'Vaughn,' he said and pointed to a short, stocky man standing beside him, 'I'd like you to meet my cousin, Rudi Muller.'

Rudi glanced at Wilhelm then stared steadily at Vaughn. 'So, you are my cousin's friend,' he said, holding out his hand. His grip was firm and dry within Vaughn's. 'I'm grateful to you for having helped him escape,' he said, stepping back as if to study Vaughn from a better angle. He gave what seemed like a nod of approval, then said, 'You found tonight interesting?'

Vaughn nodded. It was true.

'Good,' said Muller. 'Afrikaners everywhere want what the Ossewa-Brandwag can offer them – a one-party state built not on class but on race.' He sniggered as if his words were a well-rehearsed statement with which he did not necessarily agree. 'Smuts knows how the people feel – that's why he dare not arrest any of our leaders. Also, hundreds of policemen are members of the OB. They keep us informed of any planned move against us.'

'I thought the police are not permitted to support any particular organisation.'

'Of course they aren't,' Muller replied, 'but their patriotism goes deeper than their duty to the police force.' He seemed about to say more but was interrupted by a shout from the door. 'It's started,' he said and left rapidly followed by Wilhelm.

After a moment's hesitation, Vaughn went after them, hoping that it would not be as bad as he thought.

Illana's heart beat wildly as she made her way through the excited crowd gathered in Loveday Street, which ran at a ninety-degree angle to President Street and the City Hall. As she pushed through the fringe of the crowd, her alarm increased at the sight of the crude weapons clutched by those standing further forward. Many had armed themselves with sticks, clubs and metal laths. Others were using whatever they could find to pry loose cobblestones and pieces of concrete pavement to use as missiles once fighting broke out.

She stopped, frightened. The mood around her was ugly. She was jostled roughly as men pushed to the front. A soldier, his eyes bleary from alcohol, leered and made a grab at her. She whirled away, stepped on someone's foot, then lowered her head and pushed through the ranks of men, ignoring their curses and groping hands.

At last she managed to break through the mass and found herself on the pavement, her back squeezed up against the cool glass of a shop window. Inside, a dummy had been decorated in the latest female fashion: fairly short skirt, square-shouldered jacket, wedge-shaped low-heeled shoes. Illana felt absurdly relieved at the sight of another, albeit lifeless plaster figure of a woman amid the male madness surrounding her.

The storefront provided temporary sanctuary but Illana feared she would be swamped by the crowd and forced to move with it if she tried to escape. It had been a mistake to come – yet Vaughn was there, inside the hall.

She had been unable to still her terror since he had left her that afternoon. As darkness fell, seeming to heighten the stillness within her tiny apartment, she knew she could not wait all night without knowing if he was safe.

The angry shouts grew suddenly louder and the crowd moved sluggishly forward. A man near Illana stumbled and fell. No one stopped to help. Then she was caught up in the movement, forced to go with the human tide.

Although she was still some distance from the front rows she could see the entrance to the City Hall. People were streaming out, spreading across the steps to spill into President Street. Scuffles began almost immediately as they clashed with the crowd assembled there. Illana noted a second group of soldiers moving in from the direction of Harrison Street.

Suddenly the combatants moved apart as if by some unspoken signal. Shouted taunts echoed and both sides broke into rallying songs. The police moved between the adversaries, batons at the ready.

Illana could not see Vaughn among the crowd flowing from the hall – too many people were blocking her view – but as she watched, two soldiers ran forward and attacked a policeman, kicking him when he fell to the ground. Some OB men rushed to his aid, knocking his assailants down the steps.

Illana's stomach turned at the sight of the violence and again she wanted to run away but the crowd was packed solidly behind her and there was no way to go but forward.

'Nazi bastards!' came a shout from just behind her. As she whipped round towards the source of anger she suddenly spotted Vaughn from the corner of her eye. He stood at the edge of the crowd, his head swivelling round as he surveyed the scene before him.

'Vaughn!' Her cry was like a whisper against the roar. She started forward, pushing against the backs of those in her way. If she could just break through and cross the street she could reach him, lead him away from the ugliness. But her slow progress was suddenly reversed. She was pushed backwards so fast that her feet did not touch the ground. Through a sudden break in the crowd she saw policemen charging the front ranks of soldiers with their batons. They struck out indiscriminately, injuring curious bystanders scattering to escape the violence.

Illana found herself shoved hard against the shop window again, this time with such force that she thought the glass would shatter. Then she was spun round as the crowd frantically tried to escape the swinging police batons, and her face squashed against the glass. The female dummy was before her eyes, taunting her with its fixed smile and unruffled appearance, just for a moment before she was toppled to the rough, broken concrete. Someone stepped on her ankle, causing a brief stab of pain before the raw burning of her grazed elbows claimed her senses. Her cries went unheard in the mêlée until a blow in the small of her back silenced her. She lay still, crumpled in a heap on her side, facing the shop's wall like a derelict in a drunken stupor.

Illana rolled onto her back just as a soldier hurtled past, blood gushing from a vicious cut above his eye. Someone struck out from the crowd and the soldier stumbled and fell in front of her. A policeman chasing him grinned maliciously and raised his baton.

She pushed herself to her knees, too confused and frightened to attempt to stand. Her stockings were torn at the knees and she experienced hysterical concern at the loss of an item already in short supply.

Hands gripped her shoulders forcefully. 'You all right, miss?' It was a soldier, the confusion of the moment registered on his young face. 'You all right?' he asked again as he helped her to her feet.

Illana nodded weakly and knew she would have collapsed if it were not for his arm about her shoulders. He propelled her forward, keeping close to the wall, his head turned away as he watched what was happening in the street.

The soldier stiffened and Illana swung round to see what was happening. A policeman's baton seemed to sweep towards her with the speed of a lightning bolt. She screamed.

The baton struck the young soldier across his right shoulder, narrowly missing Illana's face. He cried out and slumped against her, bringing her off balance. She teetered with him in her arms for a few, clumsy steps, then fell back against the wall before dropping to the pavement, dragged down by the weight of the dazed soldier.

The policeman had moved with them, his eyes reflecting a glazed madness as he viciously prodded the soldier in the ribs with his baton. Illana shouted at him, though she doubted whether he heard or whether he even noticed she was a woman. There was blood on his face and the crazed gleam in his eyes told her he had gone beyond the point of self-control.

The baton was raised for the next indiscriminate blow. It started its swoop, then stopped in mid-air. The expression on the policeman's face changed to one of surprise as he stared down at the large hand clamped round his wrist.

Illana, too, stared up at his assailant, her saviour. A wordless gasp escaped her lips as she saw Vaughn standing there, his face flushed with anger. As she watched, still pinned to the ground by the soldier's weight, Vaughn wrenched the baton from the policeman's grasp. Bringing it down across his knee, he snapped it in two. The policeman stared at him in disbelief, then realised he was now without weapon and facing a powerful man. He started to back away as Vaughn stepped towards him, then turned and ran. Vaughn let him go.

The soldier began crawling away from Illana just as Vaughn leaned forward to lift her to her feet. 'Oh, Vaughn!' she cried, feeling his arms about her, as strong as she remembered them from childhood.

'It's all right, sis,' he whispered and held her tightly, breathing a silent prayer of thanks that he had located her in time. He and Wilhelm had become separated in the furore awaiting them when they left the City Hall. As the fracas round Vaughn had developed, he decided to get away before being caught up in it. Yet he had been unable to move, his attention riveted on the sudden violence. His main concern had been for the women among the OB supporters but recognition had spurred him into instant action; he had raced down the steps and through the fighting men as he saw the policeman attack again.

Illana was shivering in his arms. 'Come,' he said and started them moving. 'Let's get away from here.' He scanned the area round them for the safest escape route. There was fighting everywhere now, pieces of kerbstone and cobbles being hurled about by both sides.

Before Vaughn could make up his mind, there was a sudden lull. In its place were shouted insults.

'Nazi bastards!'

'Smuts's lackeys!'

Chanting came from further down President Street. 'We want the OB! We want the OB!' The arrival of army trucks, their engines growling ominously, seemed to bring about a momentary calm. At first Vaughn feared the trucks were bringing more soldiers to join the fray, then saw they were empty, with officers at their head.

Keeping to the wall as he began moving away, he shielded Illana behind him, relieved to see that the officers were succeeding in controlling the soldiers. Many reluctantly boarded the waiting vehicles but a number slipped into the dark streets, ready to continue the battle once their superiors had departed. Civilians, too, began drifting away and the trucks crawled off, the soldiers in the back singing and shouting insults at the OB men remaining on the hall steps.

The walk to Illana's flat seemed endless and more than once he thought she was too shaken by her experience to carry on. She had not said a word to him and was trembling violently. Vaughn decided to stay with her that night.

Along the way he saw more army vehicles and officers trying vainly to round up their men and end the hostilities. Once, a car slowed and seemed to want to stop beside them. Vaughn did not glance at its occupants and was relieved when it accelerated away. He thought briefly of Wilhelm and wondered what had become of him. Then he plodded on, holding Illana tightly to prevent her from stumbling.

For the first time since arriving in Johannesburg, he longed for the sanity of Brannigan Bay.

When Illana woke early the next morning, Vaughn was pleased to find that she had recovered fully from her fright of the previous night. He hugged her, promised to contact her once he was settled in his job and then let himself out of the flat.

Wilhelm arrived at the boarding house shortly after nine. He seemed proud of the cut he sported above his eye, explaining that sporadic outbursts of violence had continued throughout the city until after one o'clock that morning.

'Where're we going?' asked Vaughn as they drove off in a large brown Buick.

'Thought I'd show you a little of the city.' A moment

later he added, 'Rudi wants to offer you a job with us. Took an instant liking to you, it seems.'

'I already have a job,' replied Vaughn, irritated at Muller's assumption that his having helped Wilhelm to escape arrest automatically meant that he sympathised with the OB and its ideals. 'I start Monday as a truck driver.'

Wilhelm laughed. 'That's what he wanted you for,' he said. 'As a driver.'

'Tell him thanks but no thanks.'

'There'd be free board and lodging. Rudi and I share a large house with a garden and live-in maid – all the comforts you could ask for!'

Vaughn shook his head, staring out of the window as Wilhelm added, 'Think about it.'

They stayed off the subject for the next hours, during which Wilhelm pointed out various sights and landmarks. It was only when they stopped at Zoo Lake that he spoke about the OB again.

'I've been accepted as a Stormjaer,' he said with undisguised pride. 'There's to be a swearing-in ceremony,' and he explained how each new Stormjaer recruit was expected to take an oath while a comrade pointed a pistol at his head.

Later, as they drove back through the city, Vaughn noticed groups of African labourers clearing away the stones, sticks and other evidence of the night's fighting. Their refuse barrows were piled high with debris.

Wilhelm told him that more trouble was expected that night. 'We think they're going to attack our headquarters but we'll be ready for them if they do,' he said, relishing the prospect of more violence.

When they stopped outside the boarding house, he asked, 'So, how's your reporter sister? She moved to Johannesburg a while ago, didn't she?'

Vaughn hesitated, then said, 'Yes, she's working for the *Star*.'

'You've seen her?'

'Yesterday. Just to say hello.'

'The *Star*,' muttered Wilhelm, tossing his head angrily.

'They blame us for every damn thing happening these days. You want to watch what you tell her, my friend.'

Vaughn turned angrily in his seat. 'What the hell do you mean?'

'She's a reporter, she'd love to learn about the OB from you. She knows about us, doesn't she?'

'Us? There's no "us", Wilhelm! I'm not part of the OB! Attending one meeting doesn't make it so. Anyhow, I went there to meet you, not because I wanted to hear what your precious OB had to say.'

'Hey, take it easy! All I meant was that Illana will try to find out what she can.'

'She's my sister, damn you!'

'She's still a reporter. I'm just saying you should take care, that's all.' He gave a short laugh and added, 'So, when do I get to see her?'

'Just leave her alone, Wilhelm. You've never liked her so why the sudden need to see her?' He told himself he was wrong, that he had no right to keep Wilhelm from seeing his half-sister. Yet the previous night's experience made him want to keep them apart. Illana's interest in the OB was dangerous enough; direct contact with a member might make things even worse.

Wilhelm was watching him steadily. 'My, but we are touchy, aren't we?'

'Just leave her alone, that's all.'

'Whatever you say, my friend, whatever you say.' His eyes were cold in spite of his smile.

'Thanks for the tour,' said Vaughn and climbed out, slamming the door.

Wilhelm leaned forward so that he could see him through the open window. 'When do I see you again?'

'I'm doing my first delivery run with another driver,' Vaughn told him. 'I'll be away the whole of next week. After that I go solo.'

'Next weekend, then?'

Vaughn hesitated. He would need to rest and would want to see Illana. 'The one after that,' he said.

'Good! Same time on the Saturday morning. I'll show you the house. You could spend the night.'

'We'll see.'

Wilhelm watched him enter the boarding house, then shifted the Buick into first gear and let in the clutch. He trod hard on the accelerator as he pulled away, thinking that with time and patience he would persuade Vaughn to involve himself in some OB activities, in something that would commit him fully to their cause. It would be good if the two of them were together again, the way they had been as children.

He could neither explain nor understand the need he had for Vaughn. It had always been like that, as if Vaughn provided him with some link to the normality he scorned. Illana was different, he mused. She had always been high and mighty, thinking herself too good for him. Now, though, she might be of use to the OB. Once he had secured Vaughn's commitment, he could be used to pass false information to her – which might embarrass the *Star* and perhaps make them abandon their witch hunt. Or he might even get Illana to support them.

It would take time and careful planning.

Jay studied the newspaper reports of the Johannesburg riots, feeling a fresh wave of relief that Illana and Vaughn had not been caught up in them. Illana had telephoned the morning afterwards, saying that Vaughn had arrived safely in Johannesburg and spent the night with her. Neither of them had been anywhere near the trouble, she added.

Jay wondered whether that were true; an earlier letter from Illana had told proudly of her new responsibility for reporting on the OB. He grunted; at least she was unhurt, that was all that mattered. And Vaughn would already have started his new work. A truck driver . . . Still, it was better than being in the mines.

A car stopped outside just as he folded the newspaper and laid it on the table. Leaning back to glance through the kitchen door, he saw Brian McDermott's black Pontiac. McDermott seemed troubled as he opened the gate and came rapidly down the path towards the cottage. Jay sighed and rose to meet him.

'Jay,' the short man said curtly and stepped inside.

'Evening, Brian. Something wrong?'

'Damn right something's wrong,' muttered McDermott under his breath. He slumped into a chair. 'Your bloody chum's been busy again.'

'Preston?'

The older man rubbed his hand across his bald head. 'The bastard has somehow got permission to build a factory.'

'Here? In Brannigan Bay? But—'

'Not shark oil,' McDermott interrupted quickly. 'Abalone.'

'What?'

'Canning abalone. He plans to export it. The concession is through and it's a clean process – no smell, no messy waste. The only thing he'll dump will be the shells and that won't be a problem. It's a good idea, when you think about it. No, my friend,' he added with a sigh, 'he's got his way on this one.'

Jay stared through the open door as if the fading blue of the sky would provide him with the answers he sought.

McDermott's voice made him turn back to his guest. 'The bastard beat us in the end, Jay. He hasn't got everything he wanted but in a way he's won.' Smiling thinly, he patted Jay's shoulder and left.

Later that night, when they were in bed, Jay relayed the news to Magda. 'Somehow I feel I'm the real loser in all this,' he said bitterly. 'The new harbour came in spite of my efforts to stop it, and now this factory.'

She leaned across him and caressed his cheek. 'Don't think that, Jay,' she whispered. 'No one lost and there's no winner. It's time, that's all, it's change.'

But she could tell that he was not convinced.

October

The house Wilhelm Kessler and Rudi Muller shared was old but freshly painted, with a well-tended garden. Situated at the top of a rocky ridge with its closest neighbour lower down the slope, the back of the property bordered on the edge of the ridge, affording them the privacy their activities required.

Vaughn had been there before, usually on Saturdays when he returned from one of his long-distance hauls. He and Wilhelm usually went out at night, either dancing or visiting bars. Only once did Wilhelm try to coax him into attending an OB function but he backed down at Vaughn's vehement refusal and did not ask again.

Though he knew the house and its grounds well, Vaughn paused to survey the vast expanse of lawn as Wilhelm's Buick halted in the driveway. From there a path wound its way through tall trees to a summerhouse. The place was designed for a big family, thought Vaughn wryly. It was a house that warranted the sound of laughter, parties; it did not seem suited to men involved in illegal activities.

It upset him that Wilhelm bragged about the robberies he had taken part in, defending his actions by maintaining that his purpose was to raise funds for the OB and not personal gain. 'Many of our members lose their jobs for no more reason than being OB members,' Wilhelm had told him during the drive to the house. 'We take care of them with money stolen from those who oppose us. How can that be wrong?'

Vaughn had not responded. He was exhausted after having been on the road for almost two full weeks in a row, and did not want to argue about the OB's motives. He intended, though, to discuss it with Wilhelm at an appropriate time. Vaughn regarded their activities as wrong and felt that Wilhelm must be made aware of the possible outcome of his growing involvement. He wondered whether his half-brother had taken part in any of the vicious beatings of RAF personnel stationed in and about Johannesburg. The attacks were widely reported in the newspapers and Illana had filled Vaughn in on the appalling details missing from print. The OB was openly accused of being behind the assaults for they had publicly threatened to take action against British men who consorted with African women.

Noticing Vaughn studying the house, Wilhelm said, 'You should bring Illana round some time. I'd like to see her again.'

'She's busy at weekends,' Vaughn replied and started

for the house, relieved when Wilhelm merely grinned and followed him inside.

They lay chatting idly in the sun at the back of the house, moving indoors only when the late-afternoon air began to cool. While Vaughn poured them each a brandy, Wilhelm ordered supper from the African housekeeper.

Her obvious fear of the young man upset Vaughn. He knew her only as Anna, a soft-spoken woman whose husband was not permitted to live on the premises. Vaughn doubted whether she saw him more than once a month when he came to the city to visit her with their two children. There was so much evil in the country, he thought sadly, realising anew that such injustice was perpetuated by Ossewa-Brandwag with their ideals of racial 'superiority' and 'purity'. Picking up his brandy, he walked quickly from the kitchen to the spacious lounge.

'Where's your cousin?' he asked when Wilhelm joined him a few moments later. Muller was seldom there when he visited.

Wilhelm answered him with a shrug but his expression contradicted his feigned disinterest. After a pause he said, 'My dear cousin seems to think everything he's involved with is a secret. I no longer ask questions.' He drank deeply from his glass, almost finishing the brandy in one gulp.

Vaughn had witnessed the growing gulf between Wilhelm and his cousin before. He knew that Wilhelm and many younger Stormjaers thought Muller and some of the other leaders too conservative. They wanted more action, more violence, direct confrontation with the Smuts government. As Vaughn sipped his drink, he decided again that it was time he and Wilhelm parted ways; his half-brother was too extreme to be influenced. Neither had Vaughn any wish to land himself in trouble for it would only cause his parents pain. Wilhelm was his own man now; there were limits to the responsibilities demanded by their shared blood.

Gulping the rest of his drink, he said, 'I think I'd better get going. There's no need for you to drive me. I'll get the bus just down the road.'

Wilhelm looked annoyed. 'What's up with you?' he

demanded. 'I thought you were coming to the party? I even lined up some spare girls.'

'I'm tired – haven't had much sleep over the past few weeks. Sorry.' Vaughn stood up and took his jacket from the back of his chair. 'Enjoy it,' he said as he went towards the front door, hoping that Wilhelm would leave matters there.

It seemed he would. All he asked was, 'Will I see you next weekend?'

Vaughn hesitated at the door. 'Let's not make a firm arrangement,' he replied slowly. 'I'll call you.'

There was no response as he closed the door and started down the driveway, already looking forward to a quiet evening on his own. He really was tired and an early night would do him good. Perhaps he would give Illana a call, arrange to have lunch with her the next day.

Wilhelm watched Vaughn leave, frustrated by his early departure. The girl he had organised for Vaughn that night was an OB member and she had declared herself more than willing to bring him under her spell – whatever it took. It had become obvious to Wilhelm that the direct approach in trying to get Vaughn involved was meeting with little success. Perhaps sex would work where his other efforts had failed.

He turned away, his gaze falling on the front page of the *Star*. He also had the other Brannigan to deal with, he reminded himself, kicking aside the newspaper with its front-page article on the OB. Illana had become one of their most zealous critics, one he would love to silence. But Muller had made it clear she was not to be harmed. Wilhelm had no intention of hurting her . . . A little scare should be enough.

Turning on the wireless he wondered whether he shouldn't stay home to listen to the Radio Zeesen transmission from the German Broadcasting Company. They put out propaganda material in German, English, Afrikaans and Portuguese. The South African broadcast, under the banner of 'Greetings from the Fatherland', normally took place around 11 p.m. and carried instructions in code to the OB and German agents operating in Southern Africa. It invariably urged all Afrikaners to join the OB.

Though Wilhelm knew that Muller understood the codes

used in the Zeesen messages his cousin had not revealed them to him. It irked him that he was not yet fully trusted, and he promised himself that that would soon change.

Wilhelm had gradually come to lose his earlier awe of Muller, seeing him now as another van Rensburg. They were not men of action dedicated to striking at the Smuts government when the time was ripe. The country could have been theirs by now but people like Muller and van Rensburg clung to their dream of supplanting Smuts by indoctrination. With most South African troops fighting up north, it would have been a relatively easy task for a few thousand well-trained and determined Stormjaers to act in unison and bring the government to its knees. Rumours – increasing daily – were circulating that van Rensburg was a Smuts man merely posing as an OB follower to keep it in line.

What kept Wilhelm going was his renewed hope of ousting the Smuts government through Robey Leibbrandt who had firmly entrenched himself as an alternative to van Rensburg. The thought of Leibbrandt brought a tight smile to his lips. A South African boxer who had taken part in the 1936 Berlin Olympic Games, Leibbrandt was fervently anti-British and an ardent admirer of Adolf Hitler. Carefully nurtured by the Germans as a potential agent for them in South Africa, Leibbrandt received a thorough grounding in the theory of National Socialism when he was invited to study at the Reichsakademie for Physical Culture in Berlin.

Aware of the strong divisions within the country, the German High Command had little doubt that toppling the Smuts regime would be a demoralising blow to Britain. If Jan Smuts, a trusted adviser of Winston Churchill, were to go, the way would be free for a sympathetic government to invite them to occupy their harbours and airfields. It would give Germany access not only to the strategic Cape sea route but also provide them with the mineral supplies they needed.

They named the plan Operation Weissdorn and Leibbrandt was the man they chose to carry it out. His mission was the assassination of Jan Smuts and other leaders, particularly the Jews who controlled the mining industry, men like Sir Ernest Oppenheimer.

In June 1941 Leibbrandt returned to his home country in the *Kyloe*, a yacht which the Germans had seized from the vanquished French. He landed on the barren West Coast of South Africa with a transmitter capable of reaching Germany, US$14,000 and £300 in South African currency. He had a pistol, explosives and the means to detonate them.

After burying his equipment near his landing point, he made his way to Cape Town where old friends helped him meet with local members of the OB. At first he was treated with suspicion – his naturally abrasive manner was off-putting – especially as he claimed to be the only true representative of the Führer.

It was some time before he went to Pretoria to meet van Rensburg. The OB leader agreed that Leibbrandt could join the organisation but stressed that it should be on their terms. He would not allow him to proceed with his plans to stir up civil war.

Leibbrandt ignored the OB leader's warning and began to select suitable recruits – many of whom were already Stormjaers – to implement Operation Weissdorn. He named his faction the National Socialist Rebels. Each recruit signed an oath in his own blood – the Blood Oath – and many were eager to do so.

It was inevitable that Leibbrandt and van Rensburg would clash. This conflict was so heated that van Rensburg decided to neutralise Leibbrandt. News of his activities was leaked to the police but it was some time before they took the rumours seriously enough to act.

Meanwhile, Leibbrandt taught his recruits how to make time bombs and use them. He laid plans for the theft of arms and ammunition caches. At camps across the country, up to five hundred men at a time were taught how to use Bren guns and hand-grenades. They received lectures on tactical street fighting and how to take control of key points. At a farm outside Bloemfontein a workshop was set up with the necessary equipment to manufacture bombs and even hand-grenades. The two men living there were employed by the South African Railways, using their workshops to turn out bomb casings.

The news of Leibbrandt's raids and sabotage thrilled many Stormjaers although the more traditional members of the OB resented the implication of their apparent complicity. More information was leaked to the police, who continued to regard it as an OB smokescreen.

Without his cousin's knowledge, Wilhelm attended many of Leibbrandt's meetings, was introduced to him and finally took the Blood Oath.

Soon, Wilhelm told himself going to the kitchen to pour a fresh drink, things would change.

Illana waited for the kettle to boil and wished the man in her flat would leave.

She had met Ian Parker two months ago at a gambling party. He was forty, but like many monied men he appeared younger and was in peak physical condition. She doubted whether he had ever lacked anything in his life or even had to struggle to get what he wanted. He was one of those men to whom everything came easily.

Knowing what he was like had not detracted from the instant physical attraction she had felt for him. Nor did it diminish his charm, nurtured as it had been by a life of easy conquests.

Ian Parker was fabulously rich, his world one of which Illana had only read in books or encountered among people she wrote about. While they allowed her only glimpses, Ian hauled her into his world and shared it with her, wondrous events full of exciting people, opulent mansions, expensive cars and the latest fashions. At first Illana had balked at his demands on her but gradually she became accustomed to the social set into which he had introduced her.

Now he had arrived to collect her for dinner. Illana wished he had called beforehand but realised she should not have allowed him to dominate her life. Ian and his confident, frivolous circle of friends were not what she needed.

He stood near the window in the lounge, gazing down at the street. He was so different from Rafe, she reflected wistfully. As with his zest for all the good things in life, so did

Ian Parker approach sex. Experienced and expert, he aroused in her sensations and an awareness of her body that she had not thought possible.

'Ian?' she said softly.

'Is coffee ready?' he asked. 'We must get going.'

Illana felt a flash of resentment pass through her. How like him to dismiss what she had told him when he arrived that evening.'I meant what I said about wanting to stay in tonight.'

He stroked his pencil moustache thoughtfully, towering over her. 'Of course you did, my dear, but you'll soon feel differently. The whole crowd will be there. Can't afford to disappoint them now, can we?' he added. 'Come on, pour the coffee and let's be on our way.'

She stepped away from him, turned down the gas-ring and said, 'Ian, haven't you heard what I've been telling you? You never listen, do you?'

His self-assured smile vanished, and in its place she saw the familiar annoyance he displayed whenever someone thwarted him. 'Oh, come now, Illana,' he said, placing his hands on her shoulders. 'You're being a little over-sensitive.'

'No, I'm not.' She tried to pull away when he lowered his head but he held her firmly and kissed her neck, his lips soft and sensuous against her skin. Despite her anger, she felt a shiver pass down her body. 'Ian . . . don't . . . '

'Mmm? You love it – I know you do, my Illana. There . . . What's that little tremor? Loathing – or lust?' He laughed arrogantly when he pulled her to him, thrusting himself against her groin.

'No! I don't want to— ' She tried to regain her earlier anger, to use it to overcome his hold on her, but its remaining flame was a mere flicker against the new heat overtaking her. She shut her eyes, hating herself for the weakness that revealed itself as a stifled moan.

He moved her easily, pushing her against the kitchen table. She felt him lift her dress, felt the touch of his hands on her skin as he drew down her pants. She leaned back on the table, lifted her legs and worked them over her shoes.

She groaned as he gripped her hips, lifted her and pushed

her down on the table. The surface was cold against her back. Ian undid his trousers and leaned over her, holding her breasts so tightly she cried out.

Afterwards there was nothing but the familiar feeling of degradation that so often filled her when they were done with each other. She rested her cheek against the hardness of the table, slowly relaxing her legs.

As Ian withdrew from her, he ran his hand between her thighs and said, 'Now we're really going to be late.' He gave her leg a quick pat before doing up his trousers and leaving the room. She heard him go into the bathroom.

Illana felt as if she could not move. She lay there, the lower half of her body as exposed as when he had taken her. She thought of Rafe, of the gentleness that had always followed their love-making. Forcing herself upright, she smoothed down her dress and threw her pants into the washing basket in the corner of the kitchen.

Ian was back in the lounge. He smiled when she walked in but she avoided his eyes and went into the bathroom, locking the door behind her.

When she came out he was standing at the window, casually smoking a cigarette. 'Have a quick bath,' he said with an offhand glance at her. 'And put on something elegant, will you?'

'I'm not going, Ian. I told you that.' She felt naked without underwear, as though he could see through her dress.

He crushed out his cigarette in slow, deliberate movements. 'All right then, have it your way.' Despite his attempt at nonchalance, Illana saw the anger in his face as he left.

She remained in the middle of the room, undecided about what to do next. She wanted to bathe, to wash away her humiliation, but her body seemed too drained of energy to move towards the bathroom. The door to her bedroom stood open beckoningly, offering the sanctuary of rest and, hopefully, sleep. Still she did not move.

It was only when she felt as if her legs would buckle beneath her that she went back into the bathroom, roughly pulled her dress over her head and started the taps running.

She slipped into the hot water and lay motionless for a

long while. Soon it would be Christmas – she wished she could go away. A few weeks away from Ian in the soothing peace of Brannigan Bay were just what she needed. But she had already decided against it; her colleagues were expecting something newsworthy to break soon about the OB. Robey Leibbrandt had caused too much friction for things not to come to a head over the next few months. The newspaper, like the police, had been leaked information – by the OB, no doubt – connecting Leibbrandt and his followers with several violent crimes. Something had to happen soon and Illana was determined to be there when it did.

Anyway she wanted Vaughn to go home with her but his leave was not due until he had completed a full year of employment. They had more or less agreed they would both save their leave and visit Brannigan Bay together the following December. Illana hoped she could last that long.

While she soaped herself she thought of how Wilhelm Kessler's name had surfaced recently in various pieces of information. She had not told Vaughn when he telephoned that evening to invite her to lunch the next day although she had intended to. Illana decided that she would not raise it at lunch tomorrow; mention of Wilhelm always made the atmosphere between them tense and she and Vaughn saw too little of each other for that.

A holiday, she thought again, and let the warm water trickle down her skin. It would have been so welcome.

December

Preston Whitehead strolled slowly through the shell of his abalone-canning plant. Construction had started months later than planned; he had been obliged to wait for the arrival of equipment imported from the United States and he saw little sense in investing funds in plant that would lie idle. His resources were severely stretched as it was, and it would be years before the harbour showed a return on investment.

He stared out through a window at the jetty below, deserted

on the Sunday afternoon, the trawlers moored to their berths rolling idly on the gentle swell. Up against the mainland was the semi-cleared area where he had hoped to build a dry dock. That idea, too, had had to be scrapped because of inadequate funds.

He pressed a hand to one side of his forehead as if that would still the pain throbbing within. The harbour had been a mistake from the start – he was prepared at last to admit that. His father had been right all those years ago: he had allowed a youthful obsession to grow with him into adulthood, disguising it as a business need. All he had to show for it was an expensive, half-completed harbour and a small canning factory that was still a liability. Two fish-processing plants in Cape Town were gone, sacrificed to provide capital for his obsession. He still had the original plant but he had borrowed heavily against it when Grace's inheritance had proved insufficient.

A harbour and a small factory – was that all he had to show for the years of hatred and bitterness? He had a wife he did not love because he had never tried to. Now it was too late. And his son? The acrimonious letters that flowed between Barry and his father made it obvious that the boy hated him for refusing to allow him to volunteer.

Boy, thought Preston. Barry was no longer that. He was twenty-one and would be leaving Cambridge soon. Preston wondered whether his most recent letters would stop his son from joining up. He found it strange that he suddenly wanted to try again with Barry. It was too late for Grace but with Barry there was still a chance. Before, he could not have cared less whether his son stayed on in England after completing his studies but, now he wanted him back. He was not prepared to lose Barry to the war or anything else and would do everything in his power to prevent it.

A shadow fell across the open doorway. Preston's eyes widened in surprise at seeing Jay Brannigan standing there.

Jay seemed equally bewildered to find his old adversary inside the building for he glanced over his shoulder as if wanting to escape.

'Jay . . .'

'Preston.' The nod was abrupt, his expression discomfited.

'I was . . . strolling around. Didn't expect to find anyone here.'

Preston crossed his hands behind his back. His fingers twitched nervously. 'I was doing much the same,' he admitted. 'Thought I'd see how far the builders had progressed.'

Both men studied the building avoiding each other's eyes. They gazed at the ceiling, the unpainted walls, the marks and grooves on the floor indicating where the equipment would be installed. Finally Preston said, 'The builders have closed shop for Christmas.'

'Yes.'

'Should be going again by mid-January, though.'

Neither man moved, apart from the swivelling of their heads as they again pretended to inspect every nook and cranny. 'It's smaller than I thought,' said Jay.

Preston shrugged. 'It'll do to start with.'

'Uh-huh.'

Forcing himself to look at Jay, Preston said, 'It's not what you once feared would happen . . . not what you and I fought over. There's no mess and it involves divers, not trawlers.'

'The trawlers are here anyway, Preston.'

'They would have come whether I built the harbour or not, whether it was McDermott or someone else who built a plant over at Clayton. You know that, Jay.'

Jay grunted before saying, 'Perhaps, perhaps not. But I don't like this harbour, nor this shed of yours. I don't like any of the change they've brought to Brannigan Bay.'

Change, Preston thought wistfully. Even without Magda that would have put Jay and himself on opposite sides of the fence. Perhaps then it would just have been the intensity of their enmity that differed.

'The war would have brought about its own kind of change,' he said. But when he turned back, Jay had gone.

He wiped his forehead with his handkerchief, then left the building, stepping carefully over the rubble just outside the door.

1942

As global war raged on, the war that split South Africans at home reached boiling point, much as Illana and her newspaper colleagues had predicted.

It started on Christmas Eve in 1941, when an under-cover police agent who had managed to infiltrate the ranks of Robey Leibbrandt's National Socialist Rebels was the cause of his being taken into custody.

The arrest of Leibbrandt and other prominent rebels exposed their mass subversion plans. Barely a month later the police raided the first of many farms to discover not only documents but gelignite, fuses and detonators – as well as stocks of two-inch water piping used in the manufacture of grenades. There was no telling how much could be attributed to the OB and its Stormjaers or to the Rebels.

January 1942 also saw police efforts focused on the arrest and questioning of hundreds of their colleagues on the Witwatersrand. Among them were members of the railway police, traffic police and prison service. Their names had been found in a loose-leaf book detailing the structure of a police battalion within the OB. It was a blow to the morale of a police force that prided itself on its loyalty to the state instead of to any political party or institution.

Despite their setbacks, the Stormjaers went on a sabotage spree, blowing up electricity pylons and cutting telephone and telegraph wires across the country. Early February brought the first bomb blasts, which heralded the final break in the tenuous relationship between the National Socialist Rebels and the Ossewa-Brandwag.

*

When Barry's time at Cambridge was almost at an end, he was still undecided on whether to volunteer or return to South Africa.

His mind was made up for him a week later when he was summoned to the Dean's office and introduced to a stern-faced man wearing a brown raincoat. There was some small talk about the high standard of his work at Cambridge but then the visitor, with a rather condescending smile, told Barry that he was entering service with an organisation he referred to as BP.

'BP? Is that something to do with bombers?'

The visitor shook his head.

The Dean cleared his throat and said, 'There are plenty of ordinary young men to serve on the fighting front, Whitehead. A Cambridge graduate can serve in different, yet equally important, ways.'

'Such as?'

'Figures,' their visitor quickly replied, glancing at the Dean. 'That sort of thing.'

'Figures?'

'You're good with figures and you have an analytic mind, too.'

'I *hate* figures.'

'Nevertheless, it's a talent that can't be wasted. And,' added the man, more severely this time, 'in times like these we can't always choose what we'd like to. It's our duty to serve as best we can.'

'Tell me more about this mysterious BP,' persisted Barry.

The Dean and his visitor exchanged a look before the latter began to explain. During the First World War, he told Barry, a small cryptoanalysis bureau had been set up. By 1939 it had come under the auspices of the government Code and Cipher School. The department moved from its old premises to Bletchley Park, a large country house in Buckinghamshire, and was referred to as BP. All information gathered there was passed on to the Operational Intelligence Centre, the OIC, which served as a centre for collection, co-ordination and evaluation of information that had a bearing on the movements of enemy maritime forces. The OIC, Barry's visitor added pointedly, also co-operated with their opposite numbers in the Allied Forces when it came to the exchange of information.

A lengthy silence followed when the visitor finished explaining.

'Do I have any say in this?' asked Barry as the tortuous silence dragged on.

The visitor stared back at him. 'You're a South African, a guest in this country. You've completed your studies . . . '

Barry gazed into eyes that lacked so much as a trace of the threat that the words had contained. So they were prepared to send him back home if he refused to co-operate. He realised suddenly that it was not his so-called talents that were required. They cared neither what he did nor what he thought. The man in the raincoat was just doing his job because – *damn* his father! – that was the favour asked of high officials by Preston Whitehead, an old friend from the First World War, a business friend of Britain. It had to be Preston – treating his son as a child, determined to keep him out of harm's way by getting him placed somewhere safe.

Barry's face flushed with rage, his knuckles whitening as he gripped the arms of his chair and grappled with the choice before him. He could give in again and spend the rest of the war in some drab little office shuffling figures or whatever else they could find to keep him occupied. Or – and his spirits lifted at the thought – he could pretend to agree to return to home and, once there, join the South African forces. Anything to get away from Preston's control.

His euphoria lasted only a second as he realised that if Preston could reach across the Atlantic and rule his life, he could do the same – far more easily and effectively – back home. He'd been beaten, he thought, and rubbed a hand wearily across his brow, beaten by a father who was too powerful for him and because he, Barry, was too weak.

When he raised his eyes again, the visitor and the Dean were watching him. He saw their impatience and thought he detected scorn, too, as if they had read his mind and agreed with his conclusion. He started to get to his feet, then sank back in his chair.

'All right,' he said slowly.

The visitor gave a satisfied nod and said, 'I'll be in touch concerning the arrangements.'

Barry ignored the man's outstretched hand, nodded briefly at the Dean and made for the door. He already had it open when the visitor said, 'Don't talk about this to anyone.'

Barry turned and stared down at him. 'About what?' he asked. 'You've not told me much, have you?'

'You'll find out soon enough,' the visitor replied softly.

When Barry finally arrived at Bletchley Park he found an organisation with thousands on its staff. Ponderous mechanical machines, operated almost exclusively by Wrens, were used to speed up the mathematical calculations needed to decipher German codes. The women worked long hours and, because of the security restrictions, were permitted only limited social contact. It was not much better for the men.

In spite of his resentment at being manipulated by his father, Barry was unable to prevent himself from tackling his training with his usual competence. Such was his return to normality that he struck up casual relationships with some of the women who shared his work environment able, for the first time since Lesley's death over a year ago, to become aroused by others. At times when he left the confines of Bletchley Park to return to the flat he rented nearby, Barry wondered if he was clinging to a romantic illusion about her but at others he felt sure he would never find anyone else like her nor would he ever love anyone as much.

After only a short spell at BP his natural aptitude for analysis led to further training in the broader spectrum of intelligence work at the Operational Intelligence Centre. It was during his stay at the OIC that Barry learned of the organisation's belief that German U-boat activities would be extended to the waters round South Africa, off Cape Town in particular.

He also heard, for the first time, of the Ossewa-Brandwag and its aims. The OIC knew that the South African security police suspected that a powerful wireless, capable of transmitting and receiving messages to and from Germany, had been installed by the OB. Already aware that the OB was passing on details of maritime and military activities gleaned from informers, OIC recognised that, with the means to transmit, it became a substantial threat to Allied shipping.

It came as little surprise to Barry when his superiors told him that he was the ideal man to act as liaison between their office and South Africa. At first Barry wondered if it provided them with a handy excuse to rid themselves of him and the favour someone owed Preston Whitehead. Later he realised, with humility, that his performance had impressed his superiors. Despite his youth and lack of field experience, they sincerely believed he had been a good choice.

It was only later, as he finalised his arrangements for his departure the following month, that he came to think of his posting as a challenge. Though he would be stationed in Johannesburg, a city he did not know, he would be on home ground.

His task would be to keep the OIC informed of OB activities, to provide his analysis of what they added up to and decode any radio messages intercepted by the South Africans.

He would, he thought as he entered the final phase of his training, at least be his *own* man from now on.

September

Lately, Wilhelm Kessler found himself thinking frequently about the plans Robey Leibbrandt had had for Jan Smuts's demise. Leibbrandt's ideas could still come to fruition if someone carried out the assassination. It would be the signal for many inside the OB, who were frustrated by the plodding leadership shown thus far, to rise and bring the country under Afrikaner rule. Wilhelm visualised himself marching at the head of a column of determined Stormjaers into the internment camp at Koffiefontein. Smuts's 'lackeys' would throw down their weapons and surrender, knowing that the battle was over before it had begun.

Then would follow the greatest victory of all: the freeing of Robey Leibbrandt. He would be the one to invite their German brothers to come officially to their aid. It was his right.

These thoughts of glory occupied him while he concentrated on the beam of his car lights filling the road ahead. He drove slowly and wished his cousin would tell him what had been discussed that night.

Wilhelm and Muller were on their way back from Vereeniging where ten OB leaders had gathered. Wilhelm, like the other junior officers and bodyguards, had not been permitted to participate in the discussions. His exclusion rankled with him for he considered himself above the rank and file of OB members. The relationship between him and his cousin had become even more strained of late. There were times when he wondered whether his cousin had learned of his being a secret member of Leibbrandt's Rebels.

Muller had brooded silently throughout the journey back to Johannesburg. Even in the dark Wilhelm could see the pinched look on his face. Something was very wrong. Another defector? There had been many of those lately.

Glancing at Muller again, Wilhelm resisted the urge to prompt him into speaking. He turned his thoughts instead to visions of himself being the one to unlock the barred cell holding Leibbrandt captive.

The vision faded when Muller said, 'Speed up, will you? I want to be home before midnight.' Wilhelm flashed him a scornful glance, though he pressed down his right foot, making the powerful Buick surge forward.

As they entered the outskirts of Johannesburg, Muller spoke again. 'The British are sending one of their men, an intelligence officer, to investigate us.'

Wilhelm sneered in the dark. Now he knew what had been bothering Muller and what had been discussed that night. 'So?' he asked. 'Our own police have been investigating us for years and what have they achieved?'

Muller studied him. 'The more they search,' he replied

276

slowly, 'and the more of them searching, the greater the chance of them taking action some day.'

'Act? They would have done so long ago if they'd had the nerve. No, Smuts won't dare raise a finger against us. He knows he'll have a civil war on his hands if he does. A few arrests of unimportant individuals, yes, nothing more.'

Muller shook his head sadly. 'Even a man like Jan Smuts will eventually lose patience.'

'If he lives long enough.'

Muller's head snapped round at the vehemence in Wilhelm's voice. 'Don't talk such rubbish,' he said harshly. 'You sound just like that madman Leibbrandt.'

Wilhelm's hands tightened on the steering wheel, but he bit back his angry retort. He and Muller had argued bitterly over Leibbrandt in the past, to the point where Muller had threatened to have Wilhelm expelled from the OB if he continued to support him.

They drove in silence then, and it was only when they neared the house that Muller said, 'I'm told we should have the parts we still need for the transmitter in a week or so. Then we can start sending messages. The first will alert Berlin about the arrival of the Englishman.'

Wilhelm smiled. Once it had become known that Leibbrandt's radio transmitter had failed to function properly, Muller had made the first moves to have one built for the OB, one powerful enough to reach Berlin. They secured the services of a radio engineer of German descent but the man made it clear that his skills would not be enough; parts would be needed, and they would not be easy to obtain. Within the following week a diathermy machine was stolen from Bloemfontein hospital and the engineer had most of what he needed to go ahead with the project.

Glancing quickly at his cousin, Wilhelm asked, 'Are the OB really concerned about this Englishman?'

Muller shrugged non-committally.

Wilhelm did not need to ask how news of this latest threat had been acquired; the number of OB supporters among the police force had grown dramatically, as had the flow of information from that quarter. 'We can take care of the Englishman if he becomes a nuisance,' he said and swung the car into the long driveway leading up to the house.

Muller hissed, 'There have been enough people "taken care of". That's been the cause of most of our present problems.'

When Wilhelm brought the car to a halt, Muller stayed in his seat, staring at him. 'You must stop thinking along such lines,' he said more calmly. 'An element in the OB thinks it can solve everything through violence. They're very quick to "take care of" people.' He squeezed Wilhelm's shoulder. 'Don't be misled by them, Wilhelm. They're often little more than gangsters hiding behind our cause.'

Wilhelm moved against the door and Muller's hand fell from his shoulder. 'You yourself have given the order for men to be killed,' he reminded his cousin.

'Yes, but they were never easy decisions, and they certainly gave me no pleasure.' He watched Wilhelm closely but the young man jerked out the Buick's key and opened the car door.

Muller sighed. It was true, he had been responsible for taking men's lives and still lived with the haunting knowledge of it. But he would do so again if necessary.

He climbed out of the Buick and followed his cousin.

The night was cold, and Illana was thankful that it was only a short walk from the tram stop to her flat. Though it was already nine o'clock, the extra time spent at the office had been worthwhile.

It had been an unusually exciting day for Illana and her colleagues, starting with the news that a man's body had been found in the burnt-out wreck of a car, his identity confirmed only when dental records were checked. He had been a policeman before joining the OB. When the journalists had sifted through the evidence in their possession, they were convinced that the latest murder had been initiated by the OB – or, at least, by one of its factions.

Had the murdered man been a police agent? He would not be the first to have been exposed and executed. With dissension growing daily within police ranks, former colleagues and friends became bitter enemies and betrayal was commonplace. Illana had phoned her contacts in the force about the latest killing but they had been tight-lipped, confirming her suspicions that the dead man had been linked to them. The newspaper report had had to be carefully worded but Illana was satisfied that the public would clamour for action against the OB. It would be a further signal to the organisation that not everyone was indifferent to their violence.

As she walked, Illana realised that the day's events had exhausted her, and hoped Ian would not appear later. He had sounded irritable when she telephoned to tell him she would be working late that night but she had been too tired to care or to remind him of the many times he had changed their arrangements at short notice.

She stopped and checked the traffic before crossing the street. A battered Ford was coming down the road but it had slowed as if to park. Illana crossed the road, anxious to get home, and have a cup of tea and a warm bath.

She reached the pavement and rounded the corner. The entrance to her block of flats was twenty yards ahead.

Car lights splashed across the street, lighting up the day's debris lining the gutters. Illana felt sorry for the street cleaners who still had their job to do in the cold.

A car cruised slowly past. It was the Ford she had seen in the main road. Two men sat inside, neither of them looking her way when it stopped a few yards further on. The door on the passenger side swung open but no one climbed out.

Illana was beside the vehicle when suddenly a man jumped out, clamped her hands behind her back with one of his and the other over her mouth, muffling her scream. She was lifted effortlessly off her feet and pushed roughly through the rear door, which had been opened by the second man.

Her assailant flung her on the back seat, using his weight to keep her there. He was a big man and she lay powerless and terrified beneath him. The car moved away from the pavement, the driver taking his time as though nothing untoward had happened. The man above her moved so that he could slam the door shut. His hand across her mouth smelled of grease. Forcing herself to meet his eyes, she was shocked to see him slip a black hood over his head. The car was moving faster now. She felt them go round a corner, then a second one. The glow of the street lamps faded.

The pressure on her face diminished a little when the Ford stopped.

'Miss Brannigan?'

Illana's eyes widened with fear. They knew her, had probably been watching her for some time.

'Miss Brannigan,' the man above her repeated, his voice heavily accented. Afrikaans-speaking, she realised and told herself to remember to pass that detail on to the police – if she lived to talk to them.

'I'm going to remove my hand now,' the man said. 'Don't scream. You'll only make it worse for yourself. Do you understand?'

She tried to nod but her head would not move inside his grip. She mumbled and he slowly took away his hand. The taste of grease lingered on her lips.

'We want to talk to you, that's all,' the masked man said. 'Keep quiet and you won't be harmed.' This time she nodded, trying to move away from him.

The man in front shifted round in his seat so that he could see her. He, too, wore a mask. 'Let her get up,' he told his companion.

At first Illana's captor seemed reluctant to obey, then he moved back, pulling her with him. She was pushed against the seat. He kept his hand clamped firmly round her arm. Though she wanted to glance about her, she was terrified they might think she was planning her escape, but from the little she was able to see she could tell they were parked in a dead-end alley.

The man in the front spoke again, and Illana had the impression that he was the leader. 'You've been saying some bad things about the OB, Miss Brannigan,' he said. He spoke better English than his companion, yet she knew he, too, was Afrikaans.

A shocking thought struck her. How did they know she had written the reports? No by-lines were used during the war.

'I report things as they happen,' she replied, terror vibrating in her voice.

'Oh, yes,' said the masked man in the front, 'you journalists always report the truth, don't you? The only problem is *you*'re the ones who decide what the truth is.'

Illana made no reply for fear she might antagonise them if she tried to argue.

'Tonight's little drama merely serves to show how easily we can get to you. Think of it as a little lesson to help guide your search for the truth. Do you understand what I'm saying?'

She had herself under a measure of control now, and she concentrated on the man's voice, determined to identify it again.

'I asked you whether you understood, Miss Brannigan.'

Her reply stuck in her throat as she felt the man beside her slip his hand beneath her coat to grip her thigh. She tried to squirm away, but his hand on her arm held her firmly in place. 'I – I think so,' she managed to squeak. 'You want me to stop writing about the OB.'

The driver sniggered, making the mask tremble. 'On the contrary,' he said, 'we'd be very happy if you continued to write about us. It's just the stance, shall we say, of your reporting we'd like you to reconsider.' He added, 'Think about it on your way home, Miss Brannigan. We'll see from tomorrow's edition just what decision you came to.' He reached out suddenly and slapped away his companion's hand. 'Leave her,' he snapped in Afrikaans. 'She already thinks we're nothing but a bunch of pigs.'

The man beside her grumbled before removing his probing hand.

'You're free to go,' the driver told her. 'Oh, one more thing. Don't run to the police.'

'I wasn't! I— '

'Oh, yes, you were. It won't help, you see. Even if the man you speak to isn't one of ours, we'll know you've been to see them. It might make us less inclined to be patient. Now go, Miss Brannigan. And think carefully about what we've said.'

Illana was unable to move. She sat, mesmerised by the dark eyes showing through the slits in the mask. It was only when

281

the man beside her leaned across and opened the door that she scrambled out but before she got away she felt his hands again, squeezing her buttocks before she pulled free and shut the door. His crude laugh sounded before the Ford's engine coughed into life and the vehicle reversed rapidly past her, forcing her to flatten herself against the wall.

The sound of the Ford faded rapidly into the distance. Illana's legs trembled so much that she sank onto her haunches and thought she would vomit. Taking deep breaths of cold air, she remained like that for some minutes. When she felt a little better Illana stood up and wondered which way to go. She knew they had not taken her very far from her flat but it was only when she had walked to the end of the alley that she knew where she was.

She broke into a run, finding strength as the sudden realisation of the horror she had just been through hit her.

The Ford was parked nose to nose with Wilhelm Kessler's Buick in Rissik Street in central Johannesburg. The three men leaned casually against the Buick, smoking idly, looking like friends, to any passer-by, who had happened to meet along the road.

'Do you think she'll listen?' Wilhelm asked the Ford's driver, a man named Kriel, older than Wilhelm, and the third man, Louw. He rubbed his hand across his hair to flatten it after taking off his mask.

He shrugged and said, 'We'll have to wait and see. We certainly gave her a scare, though.'

Louw sneered. 'I could have scared her a lot more,' he said, rubbing his groin suggestively.

Wilhelm leaped forward and grabbed his shirt but the other man stepped between them and said, 'Take it easy. Louw became a little ardent, that's all. No harm done.'

Wilhelm glared at them both but relaxed back against the side of the Buick. Flicking his cigarette into the street he said, 'OK. Remember this is just between the three of us. Muller mustn't know.'

'No one will know,' Kriel assured him and indicated to his companion that they should leave.

The screeching of the train's brakes woke Barry. He peered through the window but could not see a station sign. Probably a farm siding, he decided and tried to get back to sleep. He was exhausted but excitement kept snatching him from much-needed sleep.

He had arrived back in South Africa that morning on a flying boat after four days of travelling during daylight only. His apprehension had increased as the pilot steadied the plane for the landing at Durban.

The sea, which had appeared calm from high altitude, was quite choppy and the plane bounced off the surface the first time its hull met the water. They touched down again, lifted off, then settled firmly. The rush and thump of the water was deafening as the plane skimmed over it at full speed. At last it slowed and taxied towards the harbour.

Barry left Durban the same day aboard a train for Johannesburg. Tomorrow, this journey would be over although another, far different and more dangerous, lay ahead.

'It's a good one, Illana. As always. All of you did well.' The man who had spoken, a senior editor of the *Star*, nodded at the assembled journalists. He patted the report and said again, 'A good one.'

Illana's eyes remained focused on the desk when she said, 'I don't know . . . I – I wonder whether we aren't jumping to conclusions. Sometimes we're too quick to accuse the OB of anything that happens. I – I just don't know.'

Her colleagues stared at her in disbelief. The night before, she had been the one who urged them on, even accusing them of being too soft on the OB. 'You're not serious?' one of them asked, banging down his pencil on the table top. 'Jesus – you are too!'

Illana could not look at them. She had not slept at all that night. At first, after a bath and many cups of tea, she felt searing anger about the way in which she had been treated. To hell with the OB, she had thought. She would not let herself be scared off by a bunch of thugs. Yet as the night drew on, she recalled the murders that had taken place, often for no other reason than that their victim opposed them. When dawn finally showed through her bedroom curtains, she was still undecided about what to do. Now the decision had been made.

She felt the editor's eyes on her. He said, 'The rest of you get going. I want to speak to Illana. Alone.' A moment of silence followed before they left the room, slamming the door behind them. Illana couldn't blame them. If it had been one of them she would have felt betrayed.

'Illana.'

She looked up.

'They got to you, didn't they? It's written all over your face. You're terrified.'

'No, that's not it—'

'Illana.'

'Oh, Jesus, yes!' She covered her face with her hands and swallowed against the flood threatening to burst from her.

The editor moved closer. 'When?' he asked gently.

'Last night. Two of them.' She told him what had happened. 'You're right,' she added, 'I *am* terrified. So much for honest journalism.'

'You have every reason to be frightened – those people mean what they say. It also means that what we've been reporting has got them panicky. Come,' he said and patted her shoulder, 'we'll talk to the police. They'll give you protection.'

'No! Not the police. The OB will learn about it – they warned me!'

The editor rubbed his jaw, knowing she was right. After a while he said, 'I know someone who can be trusted He's definitely not OB – he's at the head of a special team investigating them. It was one of his men who brought about Robey Leibbrandt's arrest.'

When Illana still did not move, he held out his hand and said, 'I'll take you to him myself.'

The detective's name was Willy Meyer. He looked about sixty but was actually fifty-one. His special task for the past two years had been the investigation of crimes believed to have been committed by members of the Ossewa-Brandwag. It was not an easy assignment and it saddened Meyer that the greatest obstacles were within his own ranks. He had always been harshly aware of the divisions among his countrymen but had never dreamed they would filter through to those charged with upholding law and order.

At least he was sure of his team. He had chosen them carefully, taking his time in investigating their backgrounds and activities until he was satisfied. Most were young, keen and dedicated.

And there was the Englishman, Barry Whitehead. No, not an Englishman, he corrected himself. 'Let's just hope he hasn't picked up too many arrogant English ways,' he grumbled aloud, putting a match to his pipe and pacing the office. From the brief meeting he had had with Barry, who had been brought straight from the railway station to Meyer's office, Willy Meyer doubted whether that would be the case. The young man seemed pleasant – certainly intelligent – and had made no pretence about his inexperience.

'Sir?'

Meyer turned slowly and raised an eyebrow. The young brown-haired man standing in the doorway went on, 'That newspaper man who phoned you is here, sir. There's a lady with him too.'

Meyer grunted round the stem of his pipe. 'All right, give me a few minutes before sending them in. And get that new bloke Whitehead to come here, will you? We'll get him to earn his keep from day one.'

A few yards from Meyer's door, Illana, sitting beside her editor, glanced up when the detective who had met them approached her. She felt strained and nervous; any one of those men moving through the offices could be OB on the look-out for her.

Five minutes later they were ushered into Meyer's room. Illana shook hands with him, then turned to the other man present, whom Meyer introduced as Barry Whitehead. 'If you don't mind,' added Meyer, 'I'd like him to hear what you've got to tell us.'

'Not at all,' she replied.

Barry smiled at her, said, 'Hello,' then resumed his seat against the wall.

It struck Illana how exhausted he looked. In need of a proper shave as well, she thought, mesmerised by his piercing blue eyes.

After half an hour of intense questioning by Meyer, Illana decided her visit to the police had offered little comfort. 'There's almost no chance we'll track them down,' Meyer told her. 'They wore masks, and you didn't get a look at the car's registration number – the car was probably stolen in any case. They spoke Afrikaans,' he ended with an expressive shrug.

Illana knew he was right; she had thought much the same during the drive to police headquarters.

'The latest newspaper report you mentioned will appear this afternoon,' Meyer went on, 'so if they're going to act, it'll most likely take place in the next few days.' He assured her that men would be positioned near the entrance to the flats and that someone would follow her to and from work each day.

'And you,' he added to her editor, 'had better clean up *your* house!'

'What do you mean?'

'How else would they know Miss Brannigan is involved in the reports on them? You don't use by-lines these days.' Illana smiled her thanks at him; she had forgotten to mention that.

'Someone working for the *Star*?' her editor asked, in consternation. 'That's ridiculous!'

Meyer smiled indulgently. 'Is it, old friend? We would have said much the same thing about the force just two years ago. Think about it.'

Illana was reflecting that the only person outside her work circle who knew about her involvement was Vaughn. She had pleaded with him not to mention it to Wilhelm – or anyone else for that matter.

'Something on your mind, Miss Brannigan?' asked Meyer, surprising Illana with how observant he was. She shook her head.

Barry spoke for the first time. 'I don't want to sound melodramatic, but it might be a good idea to have your men empty Miss Brannigan's post box for her. They can leave her mail under the door to her flat.' He had no need to spell out the possible use of explosives by the OB. Meyer regarded him with new respect.

Illana looked at him for the first time since sitting down, though she had sensed his eyes on her all along. It was an unsettling feeling. She thought, You poor man – you're dead on your feet.

Meyer's voice drew her attention again. 'I'm sorry, Miss Brannigan, but I need to ask a few more questions. Very personal ones, I'm afraid.' He tried hard to appear fatherly and his discomfiture was apparent.

'All right,' she said softly, guessing at what was to come.

'We need to know about any regular visitors to your flat. People who stay overnight, perhaps.' Meyer tugged at his collar.

'There's only one person,' replied Illana without hesitation, feeling herself blush and wondering whether the presence of the man in the corner had anything to do with it.

'We need a name,' Meyer prompted gently. 'And a description, please.'

'Of course. Ian Parker. He – he stays overnight from time to time.'

Meyer had started writing but lifted his pen and frowned quizzically at the mention of Ian Parker. Illana was not surprised that Meyer knew of him; Ian's name appeared often enough in the social columns. 'Do you need a description?' she asked, nevertheless.

Meyer shook his head and went on to enquire about female friends who visited her. While Illana spoke she looked surreptitiously at Barry again, but he seemed to be concentrating on Meyer's rapidly moving pencil. She wondered why she was bothered about what he or the others thought. They were professional policemen, after all. Why should they care about who she slept with?

Her editor smiled reassuringly. 'It's almost over,' he whispered, misinterpreting her frown.

She was pleased when he took her arm and escorted her from the office.

Illana arrived home after five that afternoon. As she approached the entrance to the building, she glanced along the street, curious to see whether the detectives would be in position yet. Willy Meyer had promised he would send them immediately. A few cars were parked along the street, none of them occupied. Illana wondered whether she would have been able to spot them anyway; if they were any good at their job they should not be noticeable.

As she entered the foyer of the building she passed the pigeonhole bearing her apartment number. Had it been emptied? She must break the habit of going directly to it every time she came home.

Her mail lay on the carpet when she opened the door. Did the detectives slip it under the door or had they entered the flat? Though they had no key, they were surely capable of getting in anywhere they chose; she would have to get used to the loss of her privacy.

The late-afternoon sun angled through the windows, and Illana moved closer to enjoy its fading warmth.

The sudden knock at the door made her jump. 'Who is it?' she called out, forcing her voice to sound calm.

'Me. Ian.'

Illana leaned briefly against the wall. She didn't want him there with her; she longed to be alone.

Sighing, she opened the door.

October

The house was in Westcliff, one of the most elegant suburbs of Johannesburg. Rows of cars, many of them the latest models, crammed the long driveway curving up the rocky slope dominating the area. More cars lined the street at the foot of the hill.

Barry was fortunate to find a vacant parking space just as he entered the winding road. He slowed the Studebaker provided by Willy Meyer and eased the car into the space. As he switched off the engine he heard the faint sound of laughter coming from beyond the walls of the mansion.

A black man smiled in welcome as he opened the wrought-iron gate when Barry approached. He was old, his black hair peppered with grey.

Lights glowed brightly in every room of the large house, creating a sharp contrast to the London night life Barry had become accustomed to. The tinkle of piano music floated out, mingled with laughter and conversation.

Barry paused outside the front door and wondered whether perhaps he should not have come. The gambling parties held at the houses of the wealthy to raise money for the War Fund were tolerated if not publicly approved by the authorities. He knew that the gambling – usually roulette, Crown and Anchor or *chemin de fer* – was strictly controlled by those who administered the activities. And, he reminded himself, despite his current undercover role, he was not a policeman.

He lit a cigarette, preferring to stay outside a little longer. He had not really wanted to come this evening but had found it difficult to refuse without offending the hostess. Barry knew he should have felt honoured: attendance at the gambling parties was by invitation only with the number of guests strictly limited. Still, he felt out of place amid the opulence of his surroundings. He smiled wryly, thinking that as Preston Whitehead's son he should have been accustomed to it. His years in England had changed him more than he had realised.

The woman who had invited him was a Mrs Penelope Roberts, an old friend of the Whitehead family and a member of the committee controlling the gambling. Barry had not seen her since his early teens when she had moved from Cape Town to Johannesburg. However, when he had written to his parents to tell them he was returning to South Africa and would be based in Johannesburg they had insisted he contact her to pay his respects.

Dragging deeply on his cigarette, he realised he would

eventually have to go to Cape Town to visit Preston and Grace. That would have to wait though; first he had to make some headway in his investigations. In the month he had been in Johannesburg he had achieved little apart from becoming informed on the scope and impact of OB activities. He had passed on some information he had gleaned from men and women he had interviewed in the internment camps yet so far there had been nothing of any significance to report to his superiors in England. It was early days, he reassured himself.

Dropping his cigarette to the ground, he crushed it beneath his shoe before entering the house, straightening his bow tie as he walked through the door.

The hall was a treasure-trove of antique furniture, rugs and artefacts. Looking as old as her surroundings, Penelope Roberts sat behind a table that served as a registration desk and purchase point for gambling chips. A full glass of what Barry knew was whisky and very little water rested in her hand.

'Dear boy,' she called and took a quick sip. 'Come inside, come inside! Goodness – I still can't believe what a handsome man you've turned into. Come, a kiss for your Aunt Penelope.' She proffered a wrinkled cheek and waited for the caress.

It was a few minutes before he could escape, promising to return soon to purchase chips. Penelope introduced him to two young women who wandered into the hall, their faces flushed with excitement and the effect of liquor. They readily agreed to her request that they take charge of Barry and look after him.

Pale, scented arms were thrust through his and he was led between them, chattering together, to wide doors opening onto a large room bustling with activity. Barry scanned the crowd, relieved that his dress suit was reasonably new as the other guests were resplendent in the latest fashions. One or two people less involved in the gambling eyed him as he walked in but otherwise his arrival aroused scant interest.

One of the girls at his side suggested a drink. Barry readily accepted, eager for the opportunity to take stock before mingling with the guests.

He was led to a ten-foot-long bar manned by a short, middle-aged man who served him whisky and soda with considerable flourish. He watched expectantly as Barry took a first, small sip. It tasted no different from any other he had drunk before but he accorded the barman a nod of approval.

His two caretakers were both talking to him. Barry studied them: they were in their early twenties, pretty and obviously spoilt. Neither appealed to him.

'So,' one of them said in a shrill voice. 'Mrs Roberts says you've studied in England. Oxford?'

'Cambridge.'

'Oh. My brother is at Oxford.'

'Bully for him.' He immediately regretted his sarcasm and smiled at her. She seemed not to have noticed and chatted on about her plans to go to England. She would have gone already, she added, but Daddy wanted her to wait until the nuisance of the war was over.

'Daddies always know best,' replied Barry despite his earlier resolution. He sipped his whisky, trying to quell the sudden urge to get very drunk.

A burst of laughter from the other side of the room caught his attention – particularly a woman's laugh. Barry felt a pleasant tug of excitement in his stomach when he recognised Illana Brannigan, the only woman among the group of men standing near a roulette table. She was talking now, her face animated as she gestured with her hands in the air. She was not dressed as formally as most of the other women in the room but her simple yet chic yellow dress accentuated her figure and thick auburn hair.

Though he had not thought of her since their brief meeting in Willy Meyer's office a month ago, seeing her now brought back the effect she had had on him. Her unusual beauty had attracted him, as it would any man, but it had been more than that which fascinated him. She was a female journalist – a rare breed – what she had experienced would have been difficult enough for anyone – let alone a woman. He admitted that the way she had held his eyes had been the real cause of the tingle that had rippled across his stomach.

The girls beside him were watching Illana, too, envy

on their faces. One of them saw him watching her and said, 'She's a reporter on the *Star* – that's why she gets invited to these parties.' The comment and her tone made it obvious that she and her friend felt Illana Brannigan did not really belong there.

Barry asked, 'You mean to say she's not rich?'

'Goodness, no! I mean – she's working, isn't she? I believe she's a fisherman's daughter,' she added with obvious relish while she raised an eyebrow at her friend. 'Any money she has she gets from Ian Parker – Oh, there he is now! He's so divine!'

Barry followed her gaze and saw a tall man approach the group. So this was who Illana had mentioned that day. Her lover. He felt an unreasonable flush of resentment as Parker placed a proprietary arm about her shoulders to draw her closer to him. The other men moved slightly away in silent acknowledgement of his presence.

Barry concentrated on what he had just learned about Illana. A fisherman's daughter . . . and a Brannigan. Coincidence? He thought not and was conscious of a sinking feeling inside him. It would be easy to check out.

Illana's eyes suddenly met his and rested on him for a moment. She smiled and although she was talking to Ian Parker, she continued to watch Barry.

His fingers tightened round his glass as he returned her smile. Parker turned to find out who was enjoying her attention. His mouth narrowed to a thin line as he studied Barry and his brows knit in a frown. He leaned towards Illana, and Barry could tell that he was the subject of their exchange.

The other men were talking among themselves now, moving about so that Barry could no longer see Illana's face. He turned away, finished his whisky and handed the glass to the barman. The little man produced a fresh glass and filled it. It was stronger this time.

When Barry looked back again, Parker was in conversation with another man. Illana had moved off and was standing near a roulette table, watching the play, her back to him. He wanted to go to her but was nervous of how she would react. After all, their meeting in Willy Meyer's office had been both brief and official. He should feel flattered she even remembered him.

One of the girls with him excused herself to join Parker's group, making her interest in him quite clear. Barry studied him again, instinctively disliking him.

'What does Ian Parker do?' he asked his remaining hostess, wishing she would join her friend. He wanted to be alone and free to watch Illana.

'Ian? Oh, he's involved in a number of things. No one knows for sure but he has masses of money. A jolly good polo player as well.'

'Hello.'

Her voice made his heart lurch. 'Miss Brannigan,' he managed calmly.

Illana glanced at the woman beside him. 'Hello, Dianne,' she said, but Barry's caretaker merely gave a flicker of a smile before moving off without apology.

'Oh dear,' said Illana, amusement in her voice. 'I wonder what it is about being a reporter that makes me such anathema to your friends.'

Barry laughed at the obvious lack of concern on her face. 'They're not my friends,' he assured her.

'Ah! Are you here on official business, then? It's Mr Whitehead, isn't it?'

'Yes. Barry Whitehead. Journalists obviously have a knack for remembering names,' he added.

'You remembered mine well enough,' she quipped. 'Policemen obviously share the same skill.'

'I'm not really a policeman,' Barry countered.

'No?'

'No. I was a guest that day you came to the office.'

She fingered her lip, her eyes teasing him when she said, 'Do you mean to say I bared my soul in front of someone with no reason to be there?'

'It's not *that* bad,' he replied. 'I'm . . . well, a sort of unofficial police officer, you could say. I liaise with the detectives.'

'Ah. Tell me more. You're talking to a journalist, remember?'

Barry was remembering just that; he would have to be

careful about what and how much he told her. Then, again, no one had said he should keep his work secret. Surely Illana Brannigan was the last person who would pass on information to the OB? Still, it would be wise to be cautious.

'It's *that* secret, is it?'

'No,' he replied, 'but I don't think what I do is newsworthy.' For a moment he was tempted to ask her whether she was one of *those* Brannigans but resisted the urge. He did not want to risk spoiling the moment with her.

They stood in silence for a few seconds until Illana tilted her jaw at the barman. 'His name's Charlie,' she said. 'Did you know he's a millionaire? He does this for fun.'

Barry contemplated him, polishing glasses in a corner of the bar, like someone who had just discovered his true métier.

Illana's voice made him turn to her again. 'I still maintain you could provide something of interest – even if I'm not allowed to write about it. Could we discuss it over lunch some time?'

Barry could not believe his ears but heard himself say, 'That would be nice. When?'

'I'll have to check. I know where to contact you. Or have they moved you somewhere more secret?'

He laughed and said, 'No, I'm still to be found in the same place.' The smile left his face when he saw Ian Parker approaching them. The tall man stared sneeringly at Barry when he came to stand beside Illana. As he had earlier, he put his arm round her shoulders and pulled her to him. Barry felt a flicker of satisfaction when he saw her flinch before introducing them.

'So,' Parker said, 'I see Illana's watchdogs take their job seriously. Not gambling then, Officer? It is Officer, isn't it?'

Barry ignored the gibe but before he could reply Illana said, 'You're mistaken, Ian. Mr Whitehead is not one of my watchdogs, as you call them. And you know very well it's been some weeks since surveillance was called off.'

'Quite. You chaps satisfied she's safe?'

'My colleagues believe the OB won't take things further.'

'What *I* believe, old chap, is that the OB is capable

of anything. Then again, you policemen should know that all too well. After all, you need only talk to some of your colleagues to find out what they're prepared to do for the organisation they support.'

'Ian! That was uncalled for!'

'Was it? Oh, so sorry, old chap.' He dismissed Barry with a smirk and tightened his grip on Illana. 'Come on,' he said, 'you've been polite to all your admirers long enough now. Let's take in some gambling, shall we?' He did not wait for a reply but steered her away from Barry. She smiled apologetically before allowing Parker to lead her to the tables.

Barry swallowed his whisky as if it would drown the rage that Parker had provided. When he placed the empty glass on the bar, Charlie reached for it automatically but Barry shook his head and left the room, deciding he had had enough of the likes of Ian Parker.

He made his excuses to Penelope Roberts who continued loyally to man her desk in the hall, was obliged to kiss her cheek again, then fled gratefully into the fresh night air.

When Illana telephoned Barry to set a date for their lunch, he could scarcely conceal his delight when it appeared they could only meet in the evening.

They found each other in the foyer of the Carlton Hotel in central Johannesburg. 'I'm starved,' she told him and made for the dining room. She was not really very hungry; the excitement she felt at seeing Barry again had diminished her appetite.

She was intensely aware of him and wondered what it was that attracted her so much. As a rule she did not enjoy the company of men her own age. She found them brash and immature and knew that it was not merely her exposure to Ian Parker and his lifestyle that made it so. But Barry Whitehead was different.

She let him order the wine and complimented him on his knowledge. 'My years in Cambridge,' he explained.

'Cambridge. Hmm, you're definitely no ordinary policeman, then.'

He considered the tablecloth. Illana watched him and thought, it's his smile. The almost lazy grimace, half shy, half amused, which she had noticed the first time she saw him. 'Not ordinary at all,' she added softly, surprised to find herself speaking her thoughts aloud.

'There's really nothing secret about me and what I do,' he said, playing with his wine glass. 'I'm afraid you're going to be disappointed if it's a story you're after.'

'Oh, well,' she teased. 'I'd better make the most of the meal then. It's on expenses!'

Her remark broke the tension between them, making them both laugh. Barry offered her a cigarette, lit it, then relaxed back in his chair. 'I enjoy your company, Miss Brannigan,' he said.

'And I yours, Mr Whitehead.'

They were smiling lazily at each other, both of them relaxed now but intensely aware of the attraction between them.

Barry looked away, knowing he was going to spoil things by what he was about to say. Yet it had to be done. 'Illana,' he started, frowning now. 'That night at the gambling party . . . that woman with me said something . . . '

'About me? It's probably true,' she said lightly.

'It was about your being a fisherman's daughter.'

'What?'

'You're Illana Brannigan, of Brannigan Bay. Jay Brannigan's daughter. It was easy for me to check.'

Illana sank slowly back in her chair. 'Oh, God. *That* Whitehead.'

'Yes.'

To his surprise, she smiled, then began to laugh, the sound throaty as it was when he had first heard her at the party. 'Oh, dear,' she said after a while. 'Should we get up and walk out on each other?'

'No! That's not what I meant. I just thought you should know. It's not my feud.'

'It's not mine either, Barry. What happens next?'

He saw her amused expression and realised how serious he had sounded. He laughed too, more at himself than with her, and said, 'You get some more wine, for one thing. Then we order our dinner. These true confessions have made me ravenous!'

'Done!' she sang out, pushing her glass forward. 'Drinking with the enemy – exactly the depraved sort of thing we journalists thrive on. God forbid my father should ever know!'

They talked easily then, almost rushing to share the backgrounds that had so sharply separated their families.

They were among the last to leave the dining room. By then Illana knew all about Barry's childhood, his strained relationship with his father, how Preston had influenced his activities even in England. Barry had even told her about his brief relationship with Lesley.

In turn Illana told him about her wanting to escape Brannigan Bay, about her move to Johannesburg and how she became involved with Ian Parker. She did not speak of the physical attraction that had bound her to him or of how impossibly difficult one found it to give him up. Neither did she tell Barry about Rafe. There would be time for that later for she did not doubt that the evening they had shared was the first step to much more. During the drive home, Barry said, 'I'd like to see you again. Is that possible?'

Illana touched his hand lightly where it lay on the steering wheel. 'If you don't stay in touch, I'll concoct some sordid exposure of your being a super-spy. Front page news on the *Star!*'

Barry was pleased to discover that her flat was only four blocks from where he lived. He helped her out of the car and walked with her to the entrance. They stopped and studied the entrance hall and the steps leading up to the flats. Then Barry turned her lightly towards him and said, 'Since Willy Meyer's men are no longer watching . . . '

She smiled against his lips when he drew her against him and lowered his face to hers. 'A pity,' she murmured. 'I thrive on scandal.' Then she opened her mouth to his.

Their kiss was gentle, as if he thought her too fragile for the passion she was sure he could feel flooding through her. He held her face between his hands as he said, 'Good night, Illana Brannigan. I'll be seeing you.'

Illana drew the curtains, walked quickly to the kitchen to check on the state of the meal she was preparing for Barry and went back into the lounge. She giggled at how excited she still felt, weeks after she had met him. Even the business of cooking a meal for him instilled in her a sense of anticipation for she was acutely aware that it was the forerunner to the love-making that ended their meetings.

The thought of it stirred her now. His physical presence made her feel almost delirious. She wished she could tell the world about what she and Barry had found in each other. A front-page editorial, she thought. What would her parents say when they knew she was in love with Preston Whitehead's son? She would have to tell them some time, of course, though it could wait until she saw them again.

She thought, too, of how glorious it was to be in love, and as she returned to the kitchen, she whispered to herself, 'Hurry to me, my love.'

'Their transmitter is working,' said Willy Meyer, glancing at the assembled detectives.

His gaze rested on Barry who asked, 'There's no longer any doubt?'

Meyer shook his head. 'Our colleagues found the body of a German this morning. He'd been badly burnt, but identification was still possible. He was a competent radio engineer. That, his nationality, and the burning, all point to the OB. Obviously they no longer had any use for the poor bastard, and he might have become a security risk.'

Barry let out his breath. 'So all we have to do now is track the damn thing down.'

'Easier said than done,' someone muttered and lit a cigarette from the butt of one he had just finished.

Meyer glared at him and puffed at his pipe. 'We'll start by doing tests in the vicinity of the OB houses we know of. All informants are being contacted as well, just in case someone knows anything. I doubt it, though, or we would have picked up something about the radio's construction by now.'

Barry nodded, recalling when news of the OB's quest for a radio had been passed to him and his colleagues at the OIC. No information had come in since the theft of the diathermy machine and the police believed that only a select few were aware of the plans to build the transmitter.

Meyer kept his men for a further half hour, during which they were assigned specific responsibilities. The air in the room was thick with smoke when they filed out.

Barry started to go after them but Meyer's voice stopped him. 'A moment, Barry,' he said. 'Close the door, will you?'

Barry frowned when he saw how uncomfortable the older man seemed as he sat down behind the desk. Meyer blew smoke, grunted, then said, 'I understand you and Miss Brannigan have been seeing each other.'

Surprised, Barry answered, 'That's right.' His reply was curt but he wondered what business it was of the police. He did not even think to ask how Meyer knew of their relationship.

Meyer shook his head and waved his pipe in the air, trailing a thin trickle of blue smoke behind it. 'No, no,' he said quickly. 'It's none of my business who you associate with. There's just something I thought you should know.'

'About Illana?'

'Her brother. Vaughn Brannigan. Has she ever mentioned him to you?'

Barry tensed. 'Yes. He works in Johannesburg but I haven't met him. He's a long-distance truck driver, I think she said.'

'Mmm. And did she tell you he sometimes visits an OB member?'

'What?'

'I know – it seems unlikely that someone like Illana Brannigan, who has done her best to expose the misdeeds of the OB to the public, might have a brother on the other side. Perhaps she doesn't even know about it – although someone who's as familiar with the organisation as she is could hardly be unaware of something like that.'

'You're sure of this?' Barry shifted uncomfortably in his chair.

'I said he *might* be with the OB. He's been to Rudi

Muller's house several times and spends the occasional Saturday night there. There's a younger man living there as well. Wilhelm Kessler.'

Barry felt sick. While he knew all there was to know about Rudi Muller, he had come across Wilhelm Kessler's name just recently in one of the many police files on the OB. 'Kessler,' he said now and rubbed his jaw. 'He's suspected of involvement in robberies, isn't he?'

Meyer grimaced. 'He's also from the same town as Miss Brannigan and her brother.'

Barry nodded slowly, his mind reeling as Meyer went on to fill him in on the Kesslers' arrest and Wilhelm's escape. 'The parents are completely innocent, I'm convinced of that,' he said. 'If it were up to me they'd be free by now. By the way, Wilhelm Kessler and Rudi Muller are cousins. Once we knew he was with Muller,' he continued, 'we thought it might prove more useful to us in the long run if we didn't arrest him. He was small fry at that stage but things have changed over the last year or so. Kessler's name has been linked to more than one robbery – to murder as well – but there's never been definite proof. One of my men has tied him to Robey Leibbrandt's faction, too.'

'Vaughn Brannigan may just be a friend of Kessler's.' Barry was silent for a while, trying to focus on the terrifying thought that had gripped him. 'Willy, is it possible . . . the attack on Illana . . . '

'That it was her brother who initiated it?' Meyer finished for him. 'He must have known what role she played at the *Star*.' He shrugged and sucked his pipe noisily. 'He obviously knows where she lives.' He leaned closer and added, 'Does she know what you are – what you do?'

Barry rubbed a hand wearily across his eyes. 'Only that I'm with Military Intelligence. She's smart enough to find it strange that someone attached to a British organisation should be seconded to a police force in another country. She hasn't asked me about it, though. For Christ's sake, Willy, Illana's not some spy for the OB!'

'That's not what I'm saying or thinking, Barry. But she is Vaughn Brannigan's sister and he, in turn, may or may not be an OB member. If he is, then we can take it for granted she's aware of it.'

'And that she'd warn him if she knew what I was. Is that what you're saying?'

Meyer's eyes were apologetic. 'There's Kessler as well, Barry,' he said. 'Same town . . .'

Barry sighed. 'What do you want me to do, Willy?' He glanced up and saw sympathy in the other man's eyes. If he did not tell Illana what the true scope of his activities was it would be because he felt he could not fully trust her, that he feared her loyalty to her brother might prove stronger than her love for him. Telling her everything would provide an equal test of her loyalties.

'It's the nature of the work we do, Barry, that sometimes makes us ask ourselves painful questions. I have wondered how my wife would feel if she knew there were times I couldn't trust even her.'

Barry's feelings were in turmoil when Meyer added, 'It's your decision, Barry, but if her brother was the one who set up the attack on her, then she has a right to know about it.'

'And if he's innocent? If he's not even an OB member?'

Meyer thought for a while, then said, 'If that's the case, then neither of them will have any cause for worry. If he is with the OB, I can't see Vaughn Brannigan being anything more sinister than a messenger boy. The worst she'll do is warn him that we know about him and that might scare him off – save him from trouble later.'

'I'm to tell her then, about what I am and what I do?'

'As I've just said, the worst that can happen is she might warn her brother – perhaps Kessler as well. But *he*'s sure to know about our being aware of him.' He sighed and stood up. 'When will you see her again?'

Barry pushed himself wearily out of his chair and said, 'Tonight.'

Barry hesitated at the top of the steps and stared at the door to Illana's flat. He sighed, walked on and knocked softly.

She was in his arms as soon as she opened the door, her body soft and pliant.

'Today dragged,' she whispered into his neck. 'Did it for you?'

He nodded and ran his lips across her thick silken hair. Since leaving Willy Meyer's office, he had struggled with how to tell her, how to hide that he was watching for her reaction when she learned his suspicions of her brother – and he had to find out if she had lied to him.

'You're very quiet tonight,' Illana said while they were eating. 'Is something wrong?'

'Just tired, that's all,' he replied, hating his cowardice.

'Well,' she said, leaning towards him, 'if the man is tired, perhaps he should lie down. Preferably on my bed.' She started to get up, pulling at his hand.

'Illana, there's— '

'No talking. You're wasting energy. Come with me.'

Her need overwhelmed his hesitancy and it was easier to lose himself in her and let waves of delight wash away the guilt. 'Illana.' He rolled off her and lay on his back, his chest heaving.

'I'm not complaining,' she whispered, snuggling against him, 'but I can't help noticing you weren't joking about being tired tonight.'

'No, I'm . . . Illana, I . . . '

'Why so serious? There's something bothering you, isn't there?'

He concentrated on the glow of street lights that showed dimly through the closed curtains. 'The police know about Vaughn.'

'Know what?'

The tension in her voice plucked at him. Could she be lying?

'They know about his being in the OB,' he said softly and sat up against the pillows. She moved with him yet away from him so that their bodies no longer touched.

'They're mad,' she hissed.

'They've seen him visiting a house where OB members live, Illana. Where Wilhelm Kessler lives.' He turned his head so that he could see her and whispered, 'Please,

302

my love, please don't deny that you know who Kessler is.'

Her eyes were closed and she was shaking her head from side to side as if the movement would shut out his words. 'I know who Wilhelm Kessler is,' she whispered, then her voice rose in fury and she shouted, 'I know who all of them are, damn you! I also know that Vaughn is not one of them! He and Wilhelm were childhood friends, that's all.'

Barry waited, expecting more, but she did not speak or move. 'Then tell him to stay away from them, Illana – for *his* sake! Wilhelm Kessler is dangerous.'

Illana's rage was almost palpable. She was only inches away from him but Barry felt as though they were separated by a chasm.

'Just who are you, Barry Whitehead? What is it you do? You must be well trained to bed a woman as if you love her when all the time you know everything about her. Everything . . . who she knows, who her brother knows, where he goes. Have you been using me all this time, hoping I'd be a useful source of information?' Her voice was like ice.

'Illana— '

'What else do you know about me? Do you know what Ian Parker and I were like together? How we fucked on my kitchen table? On the floor . . . in the bath? Right here in this bed where you used me, too.'

'For God's sake, Illana, don't!'

'Leave me. Go.'

He started to get out of the bed but turned and gripped her shoulders. She drew back but his hold on her was too strong. 'I *had* to tell you, Illana. There was a chance he might have been the one who prompted the attack on you.' This time she jerked free, sprang off the bed and went to the window. As he had earlier, she stared unseeingly at the glow of lights through the curtains.

'I knew nothing about Vaughn until this afternoon – I swear it!'

'It doesn't matter any more.'

'It does! *You* matter to me. What you think, what you feel matters to me more than anything in the world. I love you!'

'Leave me.'

He stood immobile for what seemed like a long time, then started to dress. 'You asked what I am,' he said as he pulled on his shirt. 'My function here is to report the actions of the OB to my superiors in England. But I did not know that the police suspected Vaughn.'

When she made no reply, he did up his trousers, slipped into his shoes, picked up his jacket and opened the bedroom door. Pausing briefly, he could discern her outline dimly in the dark. The light from the windows reflected the trace of tears on her cheeks.

'Speak to Vaughn,' he said, 'Tell him to get away from them and from Kessler. The police won't bother him.'

He waited but when she still did not look at him, he left her flat. There was no longer anything there for him. It had not even come to a test of loyalties, he thought miserably. By telling her what the police suspected about Vaughn, he had cast himself in the role of accuser. Worse, her response had been to view *him* with suspicion.

Monday

Vaughn's hand shook as he reread the letter, his face filled with pleasure at seeing Jay's familiar handwriting.

His father had written of his plans to use *Sea Horse* as a diver's boat to collect abalone. Jay would be at the helm on the surface, controlling the machine that provided air to the diver below and he wanted Vaughn to dive. It made sense, of course; Vaughn was painfully aware of Jay's struggle to find and keep suitable crew now that the new harbour was fully operative.

He scanned the letter again, smiling at Jay's mention of how ironic it would be to work for Preston Whitehead. He was surprised that Jay had come to accept that the old ways could not last for ever.

The reasons for his change of heart did not matter, Vaughn thought with a light heart; what counted was that Jay seemed to *want* it. It was what Vaughn wanted – to be back in Brannigan Bay, where the horizon of sea and cloud stretched away endlessly instead of to a bend in some grease-smeared road. He folded away the letter, knowing he would read it again later that night. He felt as if he finally knew where his life was going.

He began visualising *Sea Horse* – almost as old as he was – in her new role. They'd have to fit her with an engine, of course. He could help pay for that; he'd saved most of his salary.

Jumping from the bed, he hurtled into the passage, leaving the door wide open behind him. He had to tell Illana – had to tell Jay and Magda he was coming home.

In his haste to get to the public telephone booth on a nearby street corner, he almost bowled over his landlady as he sped down the passage.

'Vaughn,' she rebuked him gently, for of all her ten boarders he was her favourite, 'it's not like you to rush about like some maniac. What's wrong?'

He gripped her shoulders and nearly kissed her. 'Nothing's wrong, Mrs Botha! I'm going home . . . to Brannigan Bay.'

Her smile slipped a little as she took in what he had said. 'I'm glad for you, Vaughn,' she said and he knew she meant it. 'You've talked of it often enough. But I'll miss you.'

This time he did kiss her, a quick peck on her wrinkled forehead. 'I'll miss you too, Mrs Botha. I'll probably leave at the end of the month.' He frowned suddenly. 'Depending on when my employers will let me go.'

Making his excuses he rushed on, pausing briefly once he was on the grass verge of the street to check his pockets for small change. He was out of breath when he reached the telephone booth.

The coins clattered onto the stand as he quickly counted them. Not enough for a call to Brannigan Bay, he decided; his meagre supply would be depleted by the time the neighbour managed to summon Jay or Magda to the telephone. First Illana, then, but as he swung the handle he vowed that a telephone for his parents would be the first thing he would spend his money on when he was home.

As he asked the operator for Illana's number, he hoped she would be at home – she would give Magda and Jay a call to tell them he was coming. A week or two – a month at the most!

'Hello?'

'Illana! It's me – Vaughn!'

She was talking before he could announce his news. 'Oh, Vaughn – I was praying you'd call! It's the police – they know about you seeing Wilhelm. They think you're one of them – one of the OB. But it's Wilhelm they're after! Stay away from him, Vaughn. Please! Promise you won't see him again.'

His excitement fell away as he learned of the attack on her and he listened in stunned silence to what Illana told him about police suspicions that he might have had something to do with it. Why hadn't she told him before? It must have been Wilhelm, he felt sure.

Vaughn's shoulders sagged when he heard her talk about Barry Whitehead. She was saying something about an argument they had had but his mind was trying to focus on the implications of what he had just learned. Illana and Barry Whitehead – Preston Whitehead's son, Wilhelm Kessler's half-brother, as he and Illana were. There was no shared blood between them – at least he could grasp that – but it was wrong because of Magda. Poor Illana, she had no idea. Her only guilt lay in associating with the son of their father's enemy, their mother's – '

'Vaughn? You still there?'

'Yes, I'm here.' He spoke so softly he knew she had not heard him. 'Illana, wait!' he said more forcefully when she started to speak again. 'Just wait! You can't— '

'Vaughn? What is it? You sound strange.'

'You mustn't see Barry Whitehead again.'

'Vaughn, I— '

'Not ever, do you hear?'

'Haven't you listened to anything I've said?' He heard anger in her voice now. 'I think he wanted to warn me but I was too shocked to think clearly. I wanted to blame somebody for frightening me. His being there made it easy for me to pick on him. I was wrong, Vaughn, but I'll speak to him, make it up— '

'No!'

There was a brief pause before she spoke again, her voice low this time. 'What happened between our fathers has nothing to do with us.'

Vaughn rested his head against the cool glass of the booth. Oh, yes, it does, he wanted to shout, but all he said was, 'I'll explain everything tomorrow.'

'You're taking sides in this, aren't you? You're against Barry, even though you've never even met him. Just because— '

'Illana,' he interrupted, 'I said I'd explain. Tomorrow after work I'll come to your place.' He hung up before she had a chance to say anything else.

He walked slowly back to the boarding house, wishing he could regain his earlier euphoria. That was impossible now; he would have to betray Magda and Jay to tell Illana what she had to know. Rubbing a hand across his eyes he decided he would not try to influence her final decision. If she wanted to see Barry again after what he had to tell her, then so be it. But at least she would know. It was her right.

As he stopped in front of the gate leading to the boarding house, Vaughn stared at the last tips of sunlight on the dark red tiles of the roof. Wilhelm, he thought wearily. He was at the centre of them all, binding them together yet keeping them apart.

Did he owe *him* anything, in the same way that he felt he owed Illana the truth? He was too exhausted to find an answer; it could wait until tomorrow.

Rudi Muller exhaled heavily before he growled, 'I think you should postpone the robbery. There's too much police activity.'

Wilhelm did not bother to reply. What his cousin thought did not concern him as the money he planned to steal was not destined for the coffers of the OB. He had developed other plans since the day the police captured Robey Leibbrandt, gaoling him like some common criminal. The fools. Did they think bars could hold a man like Leibbrandt? Not while people were willing to risk everything they had to free the land and its rightful rulers from the yoke of British domination. He, Wilhelm, was the one who would do it. Leibbrandt might not even remember their brief meeting but he would never forget the man who had transformed his vision to reality.

'Wilhelm! Did you hear what I said?'

Wilhelm's eyes were cold as he studied the man he had once trusted and believed in. Soon would come the time of reckoning for those who had ignored the wishes of the people they were supposed to serve.

'What?' he asked at last.

'The robbery,' Muller repeated. 'I think we should call it off.'

Wilhelm snorted derisively. 'It's too late,' he snapped. 'My men will be here at dawn and it'll take place as planned.' He saw the look on Muller's face and smiled at his cousin. '*My* men,' he repeated deliberately.

Muller sprang to his feet, his face flushed. 'Soon,' he growled, 'you and I must talk – before you go too far, cousin.'

Yes, thought Wilhelm. Soon we will have our talk.

Tuesday

Vaughn lay awake listening to birdsong, still tired after a restless night. He could not help wondering how he would feel when the day ended. Dressing swiftly, he paused to wash his face but planned to return to shave before going to work.

He left the boarding house at a brisk trot, slowing only when he reached a busier road where he hoped to pick up a lift. Ten minutes later he was ensconced in a battered Morris belonging to a factory shift worker on his way home.

The sleepy-eyed man dropped him just over a mile from Wilhelm's house. Vaughn ran the rest of the way, relieved that he had decided to perform this last service for his half-brother in warning him of the danger threatening him. Vaughn didn't care whether or not Wilhelm chose to heed it but the warning would have been delivered and that was what mattered. After that, he would owe Wilhelm nothing.

The men with Wilhelm were the same two who had helped him attempt to frighten Illana. They had both taken the Blood Oath but were unnerved by the anger they saw in him. The robbery he planned was dangerous enough but it was his other plan that worried them.

Wilhelm cursed, kicking at the two cars parked in the driveway, his Buick and the dark green Chevrolet in which the other two men had arrived. The third had not been at home when the others went to collect him. The Chevrolet had been stolen the night before and its registration plates changed. It would be dumped after the robbery had taken place.

'Where the hell can the bastard be?' he snarled. 'He can't just disappear.' They could manage without him but the risks would be greater.

'Perhaps the police got wind of what we're up to,' the one named Louw said. He glanced at Kriel, who was chewing a thumbnail, unable to contain his nervousness.

'They might have taken him in, Kessler – might even be questioning him right now.'

Wilhelm shook his head angrily, although the same thought had crossed his mind. 'No,' he said, 'the bastard's probably too scared to go through with it. To hell with him – we'll do it alone.' He got into the Chevrolet, failing to notice the anxious glances exchanged by his two accomplices, and slammed the door. He knew it would take little persuasion for the men to withdraw their support and he was thankful Muller was not at home. His cousin had been called out the night before to an emergency meeting in Voksrust, and was not due back until later that morning.

'Let's get a move on,' he growled as Louw and Kriel hesitated outside. Louw shifted behind the steering wheel while Kriel climbed into the back. Louw began reversing the Buick down the drive then stopped. 'Someone's coming,' he muttered.

Wilhelm jerked but his anxiety changed to relief when he recognised Vaughn. 'Who the hell is that?' demanded Kriel.

A slow smile spread across Wilhelm's face. He opened his door and said, 'I think we've found our fourth man.' As he climbed out he whispered, 'Whatever you do, don't mention the robbery in front of him.' He started down the drive towards Vaughn, meeting him a few yards from the cars.

'Vaughn,' he said and smiled widely. 'You're up early! I haven't seen you for so long I was beginning to think you'd gone back to Brannigan Bay.' He laughed, but there was no change in Vaughn's expression.

'That's exactly what I plan to do. I *am* going back.'

Wilhelm was not surprised; Vaughn had never adapted to living in the city. He was reminded of his former desire to win over his friend to the OB but Vaughn was not right for it. He still believed in the inherent goodness of people and Wilhelm had felt relieved when Vaughn curtailed his regular visits to the house. Now, however, his appearance was a godsend. He must tread carefully, though, as Vaughn seemed tense.

'So,' he said, 'you've come to say goodbye.'

Vaughn nodded. 'That – and to warn you.'

'Warn me? What's wrong?'

'It concerns the police. I learned— '

He stopped when Wilhelm's hand shot out to rest on his shoulder. 'Listen, Vaughn, I've got to see that these two chaps with me get to a certain place quickly. We're already late. Why don't you come along? You can tell me all about it while we drive.'

Vaughn stepped back from his touch. 'No. I must go back and get ready for work. This won't take long.'

Wilhelm reached for him again, tugging him gently towards him. 'All the more reason to drive with me,' he said. 'I'll have you back at your room much sooner than you'd make it by bus. Come on,' he said and smiled encouragingly. 'We'll quickly drop off these fellows then head straight back to your place.'

Vaughn glanced at the men inside the Chevrolet before agreeing reluctantly. Wilhelm introduced him and told Kriel to move to the front so that he and Vaughn could talk in the back. 'It's all right,' he told Vaughn and indicated the two men. 'You can speak in front of them.'

While they drove, Vaughn filled him in on his telephone conversation with Illana. Wilhelm nodded once or twice while Vaughn spoke.

'What you're telling me is not really news,' he said, lighting a cigarette without offering one to Vaughn. 'I've been aware of the police interest in me for some time. As for this Whitehead fellow, I've known about him even before he left England. Didn't know his name, though,' he added. 'You say he's related to that Whitehead who was always interfering in Brannigan Bay?'

'His son. I told you that.'

Wilhelm gave a high-pitched giggle. 'Fancy our little Illana having the hots for— '

'I didn't come here to talk about Illana,' Vaughn snapped. 'All I want to do is warn you that the police are bound to move against you soon. It obviously doesn't worry you.'

Wilhelm was no longer listening to him but instead leaned forward to whisper in low tones to the men in the front. Vaughn was irritated by his nonchalant attitude. Or was it a façade?

He knew they were somewhere on the East Rand, and concentrated on his surroundings, spotting a sign that told him they were passing through Boksburg. The streets were fairly empty, and most of the pedestrians were Africans who still had many miles to walk before they reached their places of employment.

They headed out of town for about four miles before turning onto a dirt road. Two miles further on, when they turned off again, Vaughn glimpsed mining switchgear in the distance. 'Where are we going?' he asked, suddenly feeling an unease caused by the brooding silence within the car.

'To a nearby mine,' replied Wilhelm non-committally.

The road curved sharply before descending steeply to cross through a dry, badly rutted river. Louw stopped the Chevrolet at the top of the hill, then slowly manoeuvred it in among the thick brush alongside the road. Vaughn felt his shoulders knot with tension and he knew then what Wilhelm and his comrades were planning. It had to be a payroll robbery.

Before he could protest, Wilhelm swung back to him and smiled. 'The boys thought of something on the way – something you can help us with.'

Vaughn stared back at him, outraged. 'You lied to me,' he said. 'This was all planned. It's a robbery, isn't it?'

'I need your help. I'm one man short.'

'I want no part of it.'

Wilhelm's face tightened. 'You're here now, so you might as well do it. Come on, Vaughn,' he pleaded. 'No one's going to get hurt and what's one week's wages to a rich mining company? There'll be a share for you too.'

'I don't want it and I don't want any of this. Why— '

Louw had turned in the front seat, a pistol in his hand. It was not pointed directly at Vaughn but the sight of it silenced him.

Wilhelm gently pushed aside Louw's hand. 'There's no need for that,' he said, his eyes cold and hard when he turned back to Vaughn. 'My old friend here will help us – he knows I wouldn't ask if I could avoid it.'

'No.'

'What does it matter to you? You're leaving soon. Just this once, Vaughn. No one will be harmed, I promise.'

'Once is one more time than I want, Wilhelm. I plan to leave here with a clear conscience.'

'Just this one last favour. To an old friend.'

Vaughn recognised the false earnestness on his face and was sickened by it. Wilhelm felt nothing for him and probably never had. He was incapable of feeling anything for anyone.

He remained in the car when the others climbed out. Wilhelm bent down and peered inside. 'All you need to do,' he said, 'is stay by the car. Start it when I give you the signal.'

The other men had begun covering the back of the car with loose brush. Vaughn let out his breath and climbed from the Chevrolet, studying the terrain around them and wondering if he could make a getaway through the thick brush and, if he did, if Wilhelm would permit one of the others to shoot him. They all held pistols and Louw was standing close enough to stop him if he tried to run.

Wilhelm walked a short distance down the hill to check that the Chevrolet was properly concealed. He gave a satisfied nod and came back to where the others waited. 'We'll take them when they're in the middle of the river,' he said, 'when they're moving slowly. Kriel, you move into the road once they're past. They won't be able to turn round, but might try reversing back up the hill. Stop the bastards if they do.'

Vaughn asked, 'How many guards will there be?'

The other men turned and stared at him as if surprised to hear him speak. 'There are always three,' replied Wilhelm, 'but they're old men. There won't be any problem.' He opened the boot of the Chevrolet and handed each of them a black cloth hood. Vaughn turned the thing round in his hands, loathing the thought of putting it on. None of the others had and he presumed there was still time before the payroll vehicle was due.

The sun was rapidly overcoming the crispness of the early-morning air as Vaughn reached into his pocket for a cigarette, then noticed that no one else was smoking.

They heard a car approaching from the direction of Boksburg. 'They're early!' shouted Louw. Quickly he donned his mask. Vaughn did the same.

Wilhelm said, 'It might be some other car but get ready, just in case.' Louw had already started running down the road to take up position. Wilhelm turned to Vaughn and snapped, 'Duck down beside the car on the driver's side,' as he ran after Louw, joining him where he lay flat on his stomach in the brush beside the dip in the road.

Vaughn tried to still the pounding in his ears. He was barely able to discern the sound of the approaching vehicle. Kriel crouched a few feet away from him, clasping his pistol.

A thin column of dust appeared beyond the crest of the hill moments before the car came in sight. The driver slowed and engaged a low gear before beginning the descent. Dust from the car's wheels stung Vaughn's eyes, making him choke when it found its way inside the mask.

As the vehicle passed their hiding place, he saw three men inside. It was the right car.

Kriel stood up, followed by Vaughn. The car was almost

in the dip now. As its front wheels descended into the deep rut, Wilhelm and Louw jumped into the road with their pistols pointed straight at the occupants.

Wilhelm had been right; the road was too narrow for the car to turn round and the river bed made it impossible for the driver to attempt an escape into the bush. He did exactly as Wilhelm had anticipated; he crunched the car into reverse and the wheels spun as they sought purchase on the loose gravel, sending up a spray of dust and pebbles as the car tried to claw its way back up the hill.

Kriel jumped into the road. 'Start the engine!' he shouted at Vaughn, who reached for the Chevrolet's door. His attention was fixed on what was happening down the road.

The driver spotted them and stopped the car. The only sound was the idling of the engine. Wilhelm and Louw had run after it and now stood one on either side.

'Switch it off!' Wilhelm shouted at the driver. He jerked open the door when the engine noise died. 'Get out!' he shouted. 'All of you!'

The driver was quite young while the other two were in their sixties. They seemed terrified but opened the boot of the car at Wilhelm's command and hauled out four money bags which they dropped in the dust.

As Vaughn began to climb into the Chevrolet, he heard the sound of a second car, approaching from the direction of the mine this time. The others had heard it, too, and the young security guard seized the opportunity created by the diversion to leap at Wilhelm, trying to grab hold of his gun hand. The two men fell over backwards.

Vaughn flinched at a sudden gunshot. He saw the young guard jerk and realised Wilhelm had shot him. Wilhelm got up, pointed the pistol at the guard, and fired again.

Vaughn shouted, 'No!', but the only sound that left him was a hoarse croak. Bile rushed up his throat.

Wilhelm stared down at the dead man. A thin tendril of blue smoke curled from the barrel of his pistol.

Vaughn was suddenly pulled out of the Chevrolet by Kriel who said, 'You help them – I'll get the car.' He was inside before Vaughn could react.

The approaching car appeared at the top of the opposite hill. Its driver tried to brake when he saw the men and the car in the road, but his vehicle's tyres lost their grip and it skidded. Slipping broadside down the hill, it smashed into the payroll vehicle, sending Wilhelm and the others scattering.

Vaughn ripped the mask from his head and ran down the road. Behind him, Kriel reversed the Chevrolet out from the brush, pointing its nose in the direction they had come from.

A cloud of dust was settling slowly where the vehicles had collided. The driver of the second car staggered out, his forehead streaked with blood, and fell to his knees.

Time seemed frozen as Vaughn saw one of the guards, his face twisted in fear, pull a revolver from inside his jacket pocket. He raised his hand, pointing the weapon at Wilhelm who was watching the injured newcomer.

'No!' Vaughn yelled. The security guard spun round, his face revealing confusion caused by the new threat. The sound of a gunshot, the flicker of flame that emerged from the barrel, the crushing blow that robbed Vaughn of breath all seemed to take place in a sickening compression of time.

Vaughn felt himself moving, his feet seemed no longer to touch the ground. He was floating, a weird sensation of weightlessness, as if the ground that rushed to meet him was an illusion. There was a second shot, louder this time. He saw earth, sky, then dust everywhere as he rolled over and over, sliding across the gravel.

Complete silence surrounded him and the buzzing in his ears sounded like the roar of surf. Brannigan Bay, he thought and wondered why he was suddenly there. Wilhelm, too? That was his face, wasn't it? Yet so far away, so very, very far.

There were other sounds now, sounds outside himself. A voice . . . Wilhelm's?

'Vaughn? Vaughn? Shit!' Wilhelm's face was closer now, almost touching his. 'I got the bastard! Vaughn?'

'Leave him, for Christ's sake! He's dead – let's get the hell out of here, Wilhelm!'

Wrong. Not dead.

There was movement, but he could not see it. More voices,

shouts, the sound of feet. An engine? Dad's new *Sea Horse*? But a boat and dust?

Dust . . .

When news of the robbery came over the wireless in Muller's office, he cursed loudly, slamming his fist on the desk. Two security guards and one of the robbers killed, the report had said.

When Muller telephoned the house Wilhelm's casual response intensified his indignation. 'More than ten thousand pounds,' his cousin stated proudly, as if nothing had gone wrong.

'To hell with the money,' growled Muller. 'Who did we lose?'

'Vaughn.'

The news that Vaughn had been involved came as a shock to Muller. Outrage overtook surprise as Wilhelm's cool tone made him realise how little the death of his cousin's friend had affected him.

'You left him there? Didn't you think— '

'I had no choice.' Wilhelm overrode him. 'The mine was only a mile or two away and the sound of the shots was sure to have drawn attention.'

'You fool! We'll have the police to deal with now.'

'So?' snapped Wilhelm. 'Do what you usually do and deny your precious organisation had anything to do with the robbery. Tell them it was a group who acted on their own. Men with guts.'

'Guts? You're even more of a fool than I thought! I'm finished with you, Wilhelm. I've had enough. Get out – out of the house and out of the OB.' He heard Wilhelm snort derisively before he slammed down the receiver.

Muller remained standing for a long time, staring down at his desk as if it would provide him with the answer to his predicament. It would be easy: one telephone call to the right people and Wilhelm Kessler would cease to be a problem. But his hands remained thrust deeply in his pockets. One last chance, he told himself, for Wilhelm to run and escape the wrath he deserved.

A little later he reached for the telephone and asked for the number where he knew he would find Captain Willy Meyer. While he waited for the detective chief to come to the telephone, Muller felt a final twinge of guilt at what he was about to do. He told himself he had no alternative; it was a choice between his cousin and the organisation and it had always been the latter that had served him loyally. Wilhelm Kessler had declared himself the enemy.

The grunt in his ear told him Meyer was on the line. 'Captain, this is Rudi Muller. I have some news for you about this morning's robbery. I know who was behind it.'

Wilhelm threw his clothes into a suitcase haphazardly. Things were going against him. If only the security guard had not attacked him. But it had felt good firing the pistol, to see the look of surprise on the man's face, to fire again, to feel the thrill of control and power. To take life.

The killing of the second guard, the old man who had shot Vaughn, had not been as satisfying; the reaction had been too spontaneous.

The thought brought a sudden pang of loss as the full realisation of Vaughn's death struck him. A vision of them as children filled his mind, the two of them running across the rocks, calling out challenges to each other, but the emotion and the memory lasted only a moment for there were things to be done. Closing the lid of the suitcase, he glanced round the room to see whether he had missed anything, then went downstairs.

From the lounge he could see Louw and Kriel leaning against the side of the Buick, smoking cigarettes while they nervously watched the entrance to the property. Wilhelm knew they were eager to get away.

Soon they would, he thought. They would leave with him, taking the stolen payroll with them, some of which would be used to achieve Wilhelm's ideals. The time was right to attain Robey Leibbrandt's goal. Nothing – not the police, nor the OB – would prevent it from happening.

He went towards the front door, thinking that he should

317

try to get word to Leibbrandt of his plans. It was right that their leader be aware of what was to happen.

As he was about to step outside, he stopped and glanced at the telephone. There were arrangements to be made, people to be contacted before he could act but it would be safer to do that somewhere else, in case Muller was angry enough to send his men to the house.

Nevertheless he moved towards the telephone. Placing his suitcase on the floor, he pulled a slim notebook from his pocket and leafed through it. He owed Vaughn this, at least.

The switchboard operator who answered the call said, 'Good afternoon. The *Star*.'

The newsroom in which Illana sat was empty. Had others been there when Wilhelm's call came? She was not sure. It made no difference: she was alone now, more alone than she had ever been in her life.

She wondered why she could not cry.

Vaughn.

She saw her brother as a boy, his face as she walked beside him, and then as an adult. They had spent too little time together and there was no time left to catch up.

Willy Meyer replaced the receiver, frowned at the telephone and glanced at Barry. 'They've confirmed the identification,' he said. 'It's Vaughn Brannigan.'

'Oh, no.'

Meyer studied the anguish on the young man's face. 'Go to her, Barry,' he said gently. 'You should be the one to tell her. *Why* couldn't it have been Kessler instead?'

Barry sat down. He and Meyer had just returned from seeing Rudi Muller at the OB offices. 'Have our men found Kessler yet?' he asked.

Meyer shook his head. 'Some of his stuff was still at the house but they think he's made a run for it. He must have suspected Muller might betray him.'

'Do you think Muller was telling the truth about Vaughn's not being a member of the OB?'

'He has no reason to lie. Why should he cover that up if it were true?' He thumped his fist lightly on the desk and said, 'I'm sure it was Kessler who did the shooting. The shots that killed the guards were fired from the same weapon and no gun was found on Brannigan.'

'What was he doing there?'

'I don't know. You heard Muller. Brannigan hadn't been to the house for some time. Perhaps Kessler forced him into it.'

'The mine manager who arrived on the scene – didn't he see anything that could help us?'

'He hit his head on the windscreen and was too dazed to notice. Anyhow, the guard who survived said they all wore masks.'

Barry let his breath out slowly. 'Muller must have known about the robbery before it took place.'

'Oh, for sure! Maybe he even condoned it. He's sacrificing Kessler for the sake of the OB, that's all. There's no proof to tie the organisation to the crime and he knows it.'

'You're going to let them get away with it?'

Willy Meyer smiled patiently. 'Not Kessler. As for the OB, well, let's look at it as another nail in their coffin. Eventually the government must act. I think we should have another chat with Muller though, perhaps squeeze the bastard a bit. He might have a few ideas about where Kessler is hiding.'

Rising from his chair he laid a hand on Barry's shoulder and said, 'Go to her.'

Barry went directly to the *Star* offices but Illana had already left. He climbed back into his car and drove to her flat.

There was no one with her when he knocked at her door. He noticed her swollen eyes and said, 'You know.'

'Yes.'

'I – Oh, Illana – I'm so sorry!' He wanted to touch her, to hold her, but he remained in the open doorway, unable to move towards her.

'That's what *he* said as well. That he's sorry.'

'Who?'

'Wilhelm.'

'Kessler? *He* told you?'

She seemed hardly aware of his presence, as if she were talking to herself. 'He telephoned. He killed the guard who shot Vaughn, did you know? He seemed proud of it. More proud of that than saddened by Vaughn's death.'

She moved back woodenly when he stepped inside, her hand clinging to the doorknob as though she would fall without its support. Her skin felt clammy when Barry took her hand and he was frightened by her terrible stillness.

'Your parents,' he asked as she walked stiffly away. 'Do they know?'

She nodded and stood in front of the window, her back to him. 'I called them.' Her sudden brittle laugh was out of place.

'Illana . . . Don't . . . '

She turned round slowly. Her gaze held his but her eyes were those of a stranger. For a moment Barry thought she was about to accuse him of causing what had happened, that his revelation to her about the police suspecting Vaughn being involved with the OB had been the catalyst of the tragic event. All she said was, 'I want Wilhelm Kessler to pay for what happened to Vaughn.'

'Illana. Wilhelm didn't kill him.'

'You're wrong!' Her voice was high-pitched and angry. Barry moved closer but still did not touch her.

'Wilhelm seduced him with friendship,' she went on. 'He might not have pulled the trigger, but he's the one who killed my brother. He must pay.'

'We'll find him, I promise. He won't get away with it.'

'No.'

'We'll find him,' he said again.

He held out his hand towards her but she moved even closer to the window until her back rested against it. 'Barry, I – I need to be alone a while longer. Later, perhaps, we can talk.'

He nodded slowly and let his hand fall back to his side.

'I can help with the arrangements. Vaughn will be buried in Brannigan Bay?'

'Yes.' She seemed about to reach out to touch him but turned her face away again. 'Will you call me? Tomorrow?'

'Yes,' he whispered. 'Illana, Vaughn was not one of them. The OB confirmed that.'

'I know. Wilhelm told me. He said . . . he said that Vaughn did not even know there was to be a robbery.'

'Kessler told you that? We wondered— '

'It was as though he wanted to apologise to me. He said – oh God, Barry— ' Tears fell from her eyes and she flung herself into his arms. Her body trembled against his and her voice shook when she repeated Wilhelm's story. 'I told Vaughn your suspicions. That's why he went there – to warn Wilhelm.'

'It's all right, my love. It's all right.' He held her tightly to him, sharing her pain yet feeling joy that she needed him.

It was silent in the cottage. The last of the many villagers who had called throughout the afternoon to express their condolences had long since gone. Though he had been numb with shock, Jay thought of how quickly the news had spread. The reports of Vaughn's death had contained only sketchy details of his having been shot and killed at the scene of a robbery. There was no mention of his being involved. Illana, too, had been vague about what had happened although she had told Jay about the part Wilhelm Kessler had played.

He sat at the kitchen table with Magda opposite. Her eyes were dry for her crying had ceased for the moment. Jay knew, though, that the night would bring more tears.

'He would have come home, Jay. I know it.'

'I wonder whether he even received my letter.'

She did not reply for she could not. She waited and wondered when Jay would talk of what had happened to bring her two sons together in a crime that had led to the death of one. Perhaps he would wait until Illana was home and could provide them with all the details. Magda hoped so.

They sat silently until Jay sighed, stood up and walked

slowly to the door. 'I'm going to the harbour,' he said, so softly that Magda hardly heard the words.

'Jay . . . '

'It's all right, my girl. It's all right. I'll be back soon.'

The cat, Ginger, which had been Vaughn's since it was a kitten, lay on the still-warm porch. Its coat was rough and patchy and it was blind in one eye. It yawned and stretched when Jay bent down to stroke it. 'He would have come home, Ginger,' he whispered. The cat understood the touch of the hand on its fur though the words meant nothing to it and curled onto its back, inviting Jay to tickle its stomach.

Jay left the cat, stepped through the squeaking gate and walked towards the edge of the cliff. He glanced back once to see if Ginger was following but, as he had guessed, the cat was too lazy to move from the porch.

When he got to the harbour he found himself contemplating the wooden racks full of fish left to dry in the sun. He shook himself and looked up and out to sea. It was calm and inviting. There were no sea horses on the bay, and his *Sea Horse* lay twenty yards from the water's edge, a painful reminder of a new future that had been snatched from Jay and his son.

'Vaughn!' The cry burst from deep inside him when he fell to his knees.

It was dark when Magda found him there.

Wednesday

Barry sat with Willy Meyer in the detective's office. Though they hardly spoke, both shared their frustration at the lack of information on Wilhelm Kessler's whereabouts.

Meyer's hands were clasped tightly before him on the desk. 'I know Kessler's up to something – but what? No one seems to know a thing.' He sighed and lowered his balding head onto his hands, mumbling, 'I'm *convinced* Muller really doesn't know anything more than he's already told us.'

Barry sympathised; apart from interrogating Muller, Meyer's men had tracked down every known Rebel and every noteworthy OB member. No one knew anything but Barry wondered if they weren't too scared to talk.

Meyer rubbed his tired eyes. Neither he nor Barry had had much sleep lately. 'Have you heard from Illana yet?' he asked.

'The train reaches Cape Town tomorrow afternoon. She'll probably call from there or when she gets to Brannigan Bay. Her brother's body is on the train as well.'

Meyer nodded wearily, then jumped when the telephone rang. Snatching up the receiver he barked, 'Yes?'

His eyes widened as he listened. 'Damn,' he muttered. 'OK. Just stay on it, try to pick up his trail again.' He hung up and turned to Barry. 'Kessler was spotted in Cape Town but the detective who recognised the Buick wasn't near his own car at the time. He couldn't follow.'

'Where was he seen?'

'In the city centre. Three men were in the car and he swears one was Kessler.' He reached for the telephone again but stopped and said, 'Barry, I'm going to need you there. In Cape Town.'

'I'll leave right away.'

'An army plane could get you there a lot quicker than anything else. It's late but I'll see what I can fix.'

'I'll pack meanwhile. You'll call me at my flat?'

Meyer nodded. 'Take care of yourself,' he called and smiled.

Barry waved before leaving the office. Mixed with the satisfaction he felt at their having moved a step closer to their quarry was the excitement of going to Cape Town.

It was just eighty miles from Brannigan Bay and Illana.

Thursday

The military aeroplane, a Dakota, left Waterkloof air base in Pretoria early on Thursday morning. There had been no problem gaining clearance for Barry to accompany the flight. When they landed at Cape Town he thanked the crew and then greeted the detective who had come to meet him. Klaus Deetlefs was a beefy, middle-aged individual with an easy smile. 'Welcome to the fairest Cape,' he said, grabbing Barry's holdall.

Deetlefs chatted ceaselessly while they drove to the city. 'The old man,' he said, referring to Willy Meyer, 'told me your parents live down here. Like to surprise them?'

Barry glanced at him. Visit Grace and Preston? The idea appealed. Since he had been back in the country he had only spoken to them on the telephone. Despite the tension which still existed between father and son, Barry knew he was now free of Preston's influence and control. Yes, he decided. He wanted to see them.

'I'd like that,' he told Deetlefs.

'There's no need for you to go back to the office with me,' replied the detective. 'I'd have heard from Meyer by now if he'd learned anything new. Just leave me your telephone number and I'll call you if there're any developments. Otherwise I'll pick you up round lunch-time.'

'If it's no trouble, then fine.'

Deetlefs grinned. 'No trouble at all.'

Rudi Muller sat behind his desk and brooded.

It had not been an easy morning. There had been a further visit from the police – the third since the robbery and Vaughn Brannigan's death, although this time it had been a different team. Muller knew they were Meyer's men and that the detective was hoping that he would contradict himself in the endless interrogation or let slip where Wilhelm Kessler was.

He had no idea where his cousin could have disappeared to and his surprise at being told Wilhelm was in Cape Town was genuine. Muller had sworn that he did not know where Wilhelm would head for in Cape Town or what he planned to do there. But it was different now.

Muller was relieved that the telephone call had come after the police had left for he doubted that he could have concealed his shock at the news relayed to him.

The man who had called had been a disciple of Robey Leibbrandt for a few months, then gradually been disillusioned by his wild ideas and arrogant posturing. Muller had persuaded him to remain with the breakaway faction and, as he listened to what his informant had to say, he was pleased at his foresight. Though he had known for a while that something was brewing, he had been unable to establish the exact details.

The man told him that the call had come for all who had taken the Blood Oath to be ready. Whispers, too, were circulating of what was planned.

He had listened without replying but afterwards, he speculated on what he had learned. The information about the rebels' plans had merely confirmed what he had come to suspect although the real shock was in learning who was behind it. He had underestimated his cousin. How could he have been so blind?

The chances of Wilhelm and his followers achieving what they planned were slim yet not impossible. They were desperate, misguided men. Whether they succeeded or not, they would cause immense harm to the OB and the official Stormjaer movement. They could not be allowed even to attempt to carry out their crazy plan.

He would speak to the OB leadership and to Dr van Rensburg himself but doubted that they would have the courage to act in time to thwart the rebels. Muller feared they would want to talk and talk would be wasted on these men. Firm action was required – action that should have been taken a long time ago.

He wondered whether he should try to deal with it himself. He could call in the help of those Stormjaers who were still loyal to him and who had eliminated other problems before.

The alternative, though, was to hand it over to the police. If he did that, at least the OB would be seen as having distanced itself from what the Rebels planned. Muller sat motionless while he considered and then reached for the telephone.

'I want to speak to Captain Meyer,' he said into the mouthpiece.

'You look well, Mother.' Barry's words were the truth; Grace Whitehead had aged since he had last seen her, yet she appeared more relaxed and more at peace with herself than he remembered.

She pushed back a stray strand of greying hair and smiled. 'You're in fine shape too, Barry,' she said. 'I always knew you would turn into a handsome man.' Her eyes held his a moment longer before she glanced at her wristwatch. 'Your father should be home any moment now. You're lucky you caught him. He's leaving for Brannigan Bay this afternoon. You should have warned us you were coming, son.'

The mild rebuke made Barry smile. How could he have warned them? While Deetlefs had driven him there he had considered what and how much he would tell his parents. Nothing, he had decided.

'You're not going with him?' he asked Grace.

Her sudden shrill laugh was as Barry remembered it. 'Oh, you know . . . he'll be fishing and so on. Some business meeting, maybe.'

Preston arrived five minutes later. 'Johannesburg seems to agree with you,' he said as he came forward to shake Barry's hand. 'You've filled out.'

'I'm surprised. Police work is rather a case of odd hours and snatched meals.'

While Grace fetched tea, Preston asked, 'So, what brings you to Cape Town?'

'An investigation.'

'Hmm. For how long?'

'Don't know. A few days, most likely.'

'You'll spend the night at home?'

'I think not. I'll have to be on call.' While it was the truth, Barry was relieved he need not spend more time here. He wondered momentarily whether he was being unfair – callous, even, to feel not the slightest guilt about it.

'Well,' said Preston, 'try to stay the weekend if you can. I'm leaving for Brannigan Bay this afternoon. You could come through when you can get away. We could fish . . . talk about our plans for the future.'

Our plans, thought Barry, but smiled and said, 'I don't think so, I'm sure to be pretty busy.'

'Pity. I'll be meeting Smuts. He's a regular visitor there.'

'The Prime Minister?'

'Yes. I've come to know him pretty well – a fascinating man. Not many men your age would get the opportunity to meet him. It could be a useful introduction for you, Barry.'

'As I said, I— '

'Well, see what you can arrange. I'll be there till Sunday evening.'

Barry nodded but the gesture was more to get his father off the subject than an indication of acquiescence. He had no desire to spend time with Preston, and neither did he relish the confrontation that would undoubtedly arise once Preston broached, as he had put it, *their* plans for the future.

It therefore surprised him when he said, 'I'm in love with Illana Brannigan.' Barry had no idea what had sparked off the statement.

'Illana Brannigan.' Preston's voice contained a deep anger.

'Yes. Jay Brannigan's daughter.'

'You young fool.' The words were spoken with scorn.

'Father, I'm no longer— '

'You bloody fool! What do you know about love? What do you know about the Brannigans?'

'I know you hate Jay Brannigan, that there's always been some sort of rivalry between you two. It has nothing to do with Illana or me.'

'It has *everything* to do with you! Her mother . . . ' He fell silent as Grace entered the room, followed by a maid bearing a tray of tea.

Preston glared at his son, his face still suffused with rage. Then he turned away and concentrated on the tea the maid offered him, looking up only when Barry told him and Grace about Vaughn Brannigan's death.

By the time Deetlefs arrived, there had been no further opportunity for Preston to finish what he had begun to say about Illana's mother. As Barry left, he regretted, after all, that he could not spend more time with his father. He said, 'We need to talk, Father. I'll try to get away and join you in Brannigan Bay.'

Preston nodded curtly and went back inside, leaving Grace to say goodbye to their son.

As Barry and Deetlefs arrived at police headquarters, a young detective came running towards them. 'You're to phone Johannesburg immediately,' he told Barry. 'Ask for Willy Meyer.'

Meyer's voice was excited when he told Barry about Muller's call.

Barry interrupted him, saying, 'Does he know where Kessler is?'

'No, but he thinks he knows what he's up to. You remember the rumours about what Robey Leibbrandt planned to do?'

Cold shafts of fear worked their way into Barry's chest. 'He plans to assassinate the Prime Minister? Kill Jan Smuts?'

'Yes. We've already contacted the Prime Minister's office. We're waiting to hear what his movements are over the next few days. Barry — you still there?'

'Yes.' Another lengthy silence. Then, 'Willy, there's no need for you to wait. I can tell you exactly where Smuts is. Where Kessler will be.'

Since arriving in Cape Town on Wednesday, Wilhelm and his men had used a house in the suburb of Goodwood as their base. It was a rundown cottage set well back from the road, hidden by trees and overgrown shrubs in the unkempt garden. It belonged to a man in his sixties, an ex-bodyguard of the Prime Minister, who had also taken the Blood Oath. His name was Chris de Wet.

De Wet sat with Wilhelm and the others in the kitchen. The place smelled of stale cooking, and dirty plates and utensils cluttered the sink. De Wet had just returned from making a telephone call at the corner café and he glared morosely at the mess his guests had made of his kitchen.

'So,' said Wilhelm. 'Your contact says Smuts has already left?'

De Wet confirmed this with a grunt. At least it meant his visitors would soon depart. He did not like Wilhelm and had come to doubt that it was right to support them.

'Are you sure you can trust him?'

'He has no reason to lie. I often speak to him.'

'He doesn't suspect why you asked?'

'Of course not. He's used to my asking after the health of Smuts. He volunteered the information without my even having to ask about the old man's movements.'

Wilhelm watched him steadily. 'You like Smuts, don't you?'

De Wet held his gaze. 'He was good to me.'

'Yet now you're prepared to betray him.'

'No!' said de Wet quickly. 'I'm doing this for my country, not out of vengeance against Smuts.'

Wilhelm watched de Wet as the big man stood up and began washing the dishes. Five minutes later he was still busy at the sink. Louw stood to one side of him, keeping his attention occupied with banal chatter. De Wet did not hear the soft footfalls behind him as Wilhelm moved closer, a pillow in his left hand, the pistol in his right pushed into the soft casing. The last sound de Wet heard was the crash of the plate that fell from his hands when the pillow was slammed against the side of his head.

The noise of the plate smashing as it hit the floor mingled with the smothered shot before de Wet died.

Wilhelm threw the pillow onto the body and turned to his men. 'Let's get going,' he told them.

They collected their luggage, loaded the Buick and headed out on the road to Brannigan Bay.

Magda and Illana followed the coastline westwards as if drawn to the soft hues of the setting sun that still cast fingers of light across the placid waters of the bay. They walked close to each other, their hands sometimes touching, yet never holding.

A misty haze clung to the rocks below the path they followed. It curled up against the incline but lacked the power to flow over and cloak the street and houses. Illana wished it would envelop her as though its tendrils could ease the pain burning inside her.

She glanced at her mother, surprised to see that Magda's

expression was calm, as if now that she had left the sanctuary of the cottage she would not permit her mourning to be witnessed by others. But the fading light revealed shadows and lines round her eyes that Illana could not recall seeing before.

'Ma?'

Magda stopped walking when Illana slowed her pace. They turned and faced each other. Illana opened her mouth to continue, found she could not and walked on again.

Magda's gentle hold on her forearm stopped her. 'Talk, child,' she whispered. 'Our silence will change nothing.'

'Oh, Ma . . . '

Magda pulled her close. Neither woman wept, but Illana's eyes were tightly shut.

'You and Vaughn were always close,' said Magda and reached up to stroke back a lock of hair that had fallen across Illana's forehead. 'Closer, I sometimes think, than he and I ever were. I envied you that.'

'No, Ma, he loved you and Dad more than anyone else. He was coming home, his landlady said so. He was coming home because he wanted to be with you.'

Magda's smile was wistful. 'I was never that close to either of you, was I?' she said as though Illana had not spoken. 'Not like you and Jay.'

'Ma . . . '

'It's true. There was always something . . . ' She shivered and fell silent. Illana reached out to her.

'You're wrong, Ma, very wrong. I always . . . I don't know, I suppose I felt content and secure with you – because I felt loved.'

She was surprised when Magda laughed and said, 'You never even discussed boy problems with me!'

'Is it too late now, Ma?'

'For us, no.' Illana saw the flash of pain in her mother's eyes, although Vaughn's name had not been mentioned. She followed when Magda walked on again and told her about Rafe Turner and Ian Parker.

Magda forced thoughts of Vaughn away and concentrated on what Illana was telling her. But elements of their earlier conversation continued to echo, making her wonder whether she hadn't too easily given up Illana to Jay, as if she had always known she could not have what father and daughter shared. And poor Vaughn, she thought, losing track of what Illana was saying. He had had less than any of them. Magda remembered with stark clarity the evening she had run to the harbour, panic-stricken at the thought that Wilhelm would be arrested with the Kesslers. When she had implored Vaughn to help him, perhaps she had been prepared to sacrifice his safety for Wilhelm's and even looked on him as Jay's and not hers.

'Ma? Are you all right?'

Magda was unaware that she had stopped walking. 'Yes,' she replied quickly, shakily.

She heard Illana say, 'He's a sort of policeman . . . well, more than that, actually. In the secret service, I think.'

'Ian, is it? Parker?'

Illana rolled her eyes in mock exasperation. 'I've lost you,' she said. 'It was while I was still seeing Ian that I met this other man. I'm in love with him.'

Magda smiled. 'He's a lucky man, my darling. Who is he?'

'Ma, I'm sorry. His name's Barry Whitehead. Preston Whitehead's son.'

Magda knew she was still smiling, for the grimace seemed to tug painfully at the corners of her mouth. Yet she felt cold inside, the pull of her lips a betrayal of the effect of Illana's words. She heard herself say, 'Yes. He's about your age. A few months older, I think.'

'Preston Whitehead's son, Ma,' said Illana more forcefully. 'Dad's enemy.'

'Yes.' The word was flat, spoken tonelessly. Preston's son – not hers. 'Yes,' she said again.

'There are times when I feel almost a traitor to Dad. I know that's not fair to myself, but, oh, Ma, I can't *help* loving Barry!'

Magda felt a pain, fleeting but intense, within her heart. Illana's words took her back to her youth when she had been torn by love. But suddenly the pain was gone, bringing in its place a determination that her daughter should not suffer as she had.

'Go with it, Illana,' she said, her voice strong again. 'Love him and take all that he can give in return. Don't even think about what went before or what might follow. Time is too precious for that.'

Friday

A south-easterly wind screeched in across the bay tearing at the three figures as they climbed out of their car. Leaning into the constant buffeting, they made their way to the wall above Brannigan Bay's old harbour.

Wilhelm glanced to his right, to where the shapes of the cottages, among them Jay's and Magda's, lay ghostly white in the growing dawn. For a brief moment he wanted to go to them, to tell them himself how Vaughn had died, but he shrugged off the impulse and started for the harbour, Louw and Kriel a few steps behind him.

It was fitting that it ended here, he thought. No, he corrected himself. It was here where it would all begin again. It was only for Jan Smuts that it ended.

The clothes the three men wore were rumpled. They had arrived on the outskirts of the village late the previous afternoon, had hidden the car in dense bush and spent the night inside it.

The sea was uneasy as Wilhelm led his men down the harbour path, its surface whipped up by the wind. Huge swells rolled continuously towards the rocks where they burst in an explosion of restless energy.

The boats had been dragged high above the high tide mark to lie at an angle on their sides. The stench of fish clung to the air, and the wind howled across the taut lines securing the boats in place.

Heading past the slipway, Wilhelm led them to the rocks beyond the harbour, to where many fishermen had trampled a rough path between the rocks and bushes at the base of the cliffs. 'Watch your step,' he warned his men. 'It's pretty rough.' He wondered whether they had heard him: the noise along the coastline was deafening, a continuous cacophony of booming and hissing.

The spot at which he finally stopped was in the lee of an outcrop of rock. Looking round, he nodded in satisfaction, then studied the path they had been following. It lay only a few yards from their hiding place. If he moved back a few feet, he could see all the way to the harbour. Anyone approaching could be easily observed.

Wilhelm was completely relaxed as he took out his handkerchief to wipe down his pistol, the weapon large and ugly within the slimness of his fingers.

Louw watched him for a while, then asked, 'You sure you don't want to use the rifle? It'll be more accurate.'

Wilhelm shook his head briskly, his eyes emotionless. 'He'll be close enough,' he replied. 'I want him to see me, to look into my eyes as I pull the trigger.'

They settled into position, Louw and Kriel to the rear of Wilhelm. Each man had a view of the harbour, and Kriel, lying furthest back, could watch the top of the cliffs overlooking the rocks.

It was another ten minutes before Louw whispered, 'Where is he? Why doesn't he come?'

Wilhelm did not reply at first. Had de Wet lied about Smuts's habitual early-morning walk across the rocks?

'He'll come,' he replied at last. 'Smuts will come.'

Outside the cottage where Jan Smuts was staying, the wind whipped at Barry's hair. He had hardly slept that night and his eyes were red-rimmed from tiredness. It was the tension and thrill of the chase that kept him going; he had Kessler now – he was sure of it.

He, Deetlefs and a team of detectives had left Cape Town in a frantic rush, pausing only to alert the local police to what was happening. Barry had urged them to go straight to the Prime Minister's lodgings and stay there until Barry arrived.

Deetlefs's men, with the assistance of the local constabulary, had spent what remained of the daylight scouring the village for signs of Wilhelm Kessler's presence. They had found nothing so stood watch around the Prime Minister's house that night in case the Rebels were bold enough to attempt an attack.

The lack of information on Wilhelm's movements frustrated Barry. If the Prime Minister continued to be guarded by such large numbers, the Rebels would undoubtedly learn of their presence and move off to try again some other time. He longed to go to Illana, just a few hundred yards away. Apart from wanting to see her, he was sure that whatever she could tell him about Kessler the man would give him some understanding of the way Kessler's mind worked. Intuition told him that to Wilhelm Kessler's way of thinking, there was some moral irony in carrying out his plan in Brannigan Bay. Perhaps he saw it as some personal revenge, that killing Smuts in the same place that had sparked off his course of violent crime against society would be an act of justice. The clues to the answers came at around midnight when he was brought inside to the telephone. It was one of Deetlefs's colleagues in Cape Town. The caller told him of the discovery of de Wet's body in his Goodwood house. When he added that de Wet had once been a bodyguard of the Prime Minister, Barry knew that Kessler or one of his men must have killed him. He realised, too, that de Wet must have been a source of information on Smuts's movements.

Though Barry knew Smuts was still awake and reading in his bedroom, he refrained from going to him personally and instead questioned all the staff present at the house. They were again asked about the Prime Minister's regular habits – if he went to the village each morning, to any particular shop. Someone mentioned that he went daily for a walk at dawn.

Now, Barry gripped the collar of Smuts's coat, pulling up the flaps so that they hid most of the face of the man wearing it, a detective similar in build to Smuts. Barry grinned at the nervousness on the young man's face.

'It'll be OK,' he said. 'I'll be playing the role of bodyguard and I'll only be a few steps behind you. The others will be somewhere ahead of us on the cliffs. They'll signal if they spot Kessler. Then you stop and we'll take it from there.'

The detective smiled but it was clear that Barry's words had not eased the anxiety he felt at being a walking target.

One of Deetlefs's men burst through the gate just then. 'We've found it!' he shouted triumphantly. 'The Buick! It's parked above the harbour.'

'Cocky bastards,' muttered Deetlefs. 'I suppose they planned on a quick getaway.' He waved at Barry and led his men round the back of the house, heading for the cliffs from where they would try to pinpoint the ambush.

Barry waited a few minutes more, then tapped his companion's shoulder.

'Let's go,' he said.

Preston Whitehead stopped his car on the market square, parking close to the only other car there, a Buick with a Johannesburg registration number. Tourists, he thought as he climbed out, wondering whether they, like himself, were out for some early-morning fishing.

He opened the boot of his car and took out his fishing tackle. Rock angling was not for him that morning; when he had decided to come to Brannigan Bay for a few days to check on the progress of his factory, he had arranged for a fisherman to take him out on the bay in a small boat. He liked doing that occasionally.

While he checked his gear he glanced towards Magda's cottage. He felt genuine pity for her – for Jay as well – for he could imagine how he would suffer if Barry had to die. When he had arrived in the village the previous afternoon, he had been tempted to go to them and express his condolences, but had decided against it in the end; their anguish would still be too raw.

As he slammed the boot shut, he wondered whether he should tell Magda and Jay about Barry and Illana. It was probably better not to; it was something he and Barry had to sort out first. He felt a flush of irritation at how he had reacted when Barry had told him.

He had handled his response badly, he realised now, as

he had handled everything with Barry badly. All his good intentions of how he would tell him how much he had come to need him, as a son and as a business partner, had vanished at the sight of the confident young man waiting for him at home. Barry had seemed like a stranger to him, the animosity he felt towards his father obvious. Preston had immediately slipped back into his old style of communication, for he did not know how to react to the stranger. But he should have been more restrained when Barry told him about Illana. He should have held back his anger and kept it in check until they had the opportunity to talk about it as mature individuals. The discovery of Barry's relationship with his old enemy's daughter had brought an irrational resentment bubbling forth inside him. How could his son have the daughter of a woman he had himself once wanted and had possessed only fleetingly? Not the daughter Jay Brannigan had sired. It would be a betrayal – it would almost be incest.

He had calmed down during the drive to Brannigan Bay, and hoped that it was not too late for them to settle their differences. Preston promised himself that if Barry came to Brannigan Bay – and he prayed that would happen – he would do everything in his power to break down the barrier between them.

He had been astonished when he arrived at Jan Smuts's house the previous evening to keep his appointment with the Prime Minister and found the police there. And then, strolling from inside the house, tall and confident and very much in control of things, Barry had appeared.

'I don't think you should bother the Prime Minister now,' he told Preston after briefly explaining the situation. Preston had nodded numbly, stunned by the news and by how much older Barry appeared than at their meeting earlier that same day, as if the added responsibility of the affair he now controlled had bestowed further maturity on him. He is beyond me now, Preston had thought with despair. I can no longer hope to reach him. Yet he said, 'When this is over, can we talk? We need to talk.'

Barry had stared at him for what felt like a long time, then said, 'Yes. I'll come as soon as I can.'

Now Preston shook his head at what was happening in Brannigan Bay. Wilhelm Kessler, Barry had told him. Could it be the same youth – the one who had killed Svenson, the Swedish skipper, so many years ago?

He knelt and felt inside his haversack. His hand found the pistol he always carried with him on fishing trips out on the bay to use on troublesome sharks who might venture too close to the boat. He let the weapon drop back inside and straightened up.

Slinging the haversack across his shoulder, he decided he would first try to find the fisherman and get him to help carry the rest of the equipment. As he turned, he caught sight of two men walking a few yards apart from each other. Even before he recognised Barry, he knew that the slight figure in the oversized coat was Jan Smuts. He raised his hand and was about to call out, then stopped himself. Surely it was too risky to allow the Prime Minister to be so exposed?

Preston stayed where he was, realising that something strange was taking place, that he should not interfere. He was curious, though, and once the two figures had disappeared down the path to the harbour, he started forward, wanting to watch what happened from the wall.

The haversack bumped against his back as he walked.

Wilhelm could hear Louw shift awkwardly behind him. 'Christ,' came the muttered voice, 'these rocks are bloody hard.'

He was about to warn him to be silent when he spotted the two figures making their way down the harbour path. 'It's Smuts!' he hissed.

'There's a bodyguard with him,' whispered Louw. 'As we thought.'

'You take care of him,' replied Wilhelm. 'Leave Smuts to me. Move only when I do.' He glanced at the cliffs to see whether anyone was watching from there, but the only movement was that of the coastal brush jerking within the clutches of the south-easter. He shifted position slightly so that he could move rapidly when Smuts walked by.

The first of the figures had reached the rocks now. He stumbled awkwardly as he stepped onto them and the wind whipped the sides of his coat open. He took another step, then stopped.

'He's turning back,' Kriel hissed, his voice trembling with tension. 'The bastard is turning back!'

'Shut up! He's resting, that's all. Don't move.'

On the rocks, almost a hundred yards from where Wilhelm and his men waited, Barry Whitehead frowned and said, 'What's wrong? Keep going, damn you!'

'It's my ankle,' the young detective whined. 'I think I've sprained it.' He knelt and gripped his hand round it.

'Oh, for Christ's sake!' Barry let his gaze travel rapidly across the rocks, suppressing the urge to gaze up at the cliffs where Deetlefs and his men would be. Should he go on alone and try to flush Kessler out?

'Try to take a few more steps,' he pleaded with the crippled man. 'Come on, just a few slow ones.'

'It hurts like hell!'

'Try, damn you!'

The man took a hesitant step, then gave an agonised yelp and turned back to Barry. 'It's no good,' he said, his face twisted in pain.

Barry shut his eyes to hide his frustration, then said, 'All right, you stay here. I'll go on alone.' He started past the detective who sank to his haunches on the rock.

Wilhelm's eyes were stiff in their sockets as he focused on the crouching figure. 'He's hurt his leg or something,' he told the others. 'We can still get him, though.'

'The bodyguard's coming on alone,' said Louw, then gave a sharp intake of breath. 'You know who that is? Remember that photograph one of our police contacts gave us? It's that Englishman, the one your friend warned you about! It's a fucking trap!'

Wilhelm swung his gaze to the figure drawing rapidly closer. He did not recognise Barry, though he had studied the photograph intently to see what his enemy looked like. It *was* a trap – Louw was right. If that were really Jan Smuts crouched out there on the rocks, his bodyguard would never leave him alone.

Wilhelm was rigid with anger and frustration. They knew about his plans – they had to know! Muller? But how had he found out? There was no time to dwell on his predicament for Kriel jumped to his feet and took aim at Barry just as Wilhelm spotted a movement on the cliffs above them.

Someone shouted, 'There they are!' but the sound of it was drowned by the crash of Kriel's pistol, the noise deafening within the enclave of rocks.

A second shot sounded and Kriel toppled backwards, his pistol clattering onto the rocks as it dropped from his hand. He stared at Wilhelm as if in disbelief at what had happened to him, then clutched at the wound in the centre of his chest before he lay still.

Louw stared down at him, the rifle in his hands half raised to fire back at the cliffs. When he finally turned to shoot, the rifle moved only a fraction of an inch before he too was brought down by a well-aimed bullet. He fell back against the rocks, cursing as blood pumped from a shoulder wound.

Wilhelm did not hesitate. He burst from cover and ran for the base of the cliffs where those above could not see him. He glanced sideways as he ran, trying to see what had become of Barry. There was no sign of him. Had he been hit by Kriel's one and only shot?

Keeping close to the cliffs, he made his way as fast as he could towards the harbour. He had to make it back to the Buick before the police reached it.

Just as he leaped over a rock, Barry rose to his feet a few yards ahead, his gaze directed towards where Wilhelm and his men had been hiding. Wilhelm fired a shot in his direction, but even as he pulled the trigger he knew he had missed. He tried to take aim again, but his foothold was unsteady, giving Barry precious seconds in which to swing round and raise his pistol. As Wilhelm desperately tried to regain his balance, he saw Barry slip from his perch. He fell heavily, his pistol flying out of his hands.

Wilhelm gave an animal-like cry of triumph as he righted himself and charged his enemy. So intent was he on this single moment of revenge for having been thwarted, that he didn't notice the figure racing across the rocks towards them.

Wilhelm stopped when he came to a rock above Barry, and grinned down at the stunned look on his victim's face. A trickle of blood coursed brightly down Barry's forehead where he had hit it during his fall. His eyes met Wilhelm's and tried to focus.

Steadying his pistol, Wilhelm aimed its barrel directly at Barry's chest. His finger tightened on the trigger.

'No!' The voice came from mere yards away. Only Wilhelm's eyes moved. He saw the man standing there, a haversack clutched to his chest. There was something familiar about him but Wilhelm deliberately ignored him and turned his gaze back to his victim.

He did not see the sudden hole that ripped the haversack open, leaving a charred ring around its perimeter. He felt only the sharp pain that struck at the side of his chest, tearing at him, robbing him of his strength so that he was unable to keep his arm outstretched. It sank slowly to his side, the pistol still in his hand. Then he was on his knees, unable to breathe, yet acutely aware of Barry lying near him.

Wilhelm felt his lips twist into a grin, as though he no longer had control of them. Even when he collapsed slowly onto his side and slid from the rock, he felt the grimace pull at his mouth.

Preston's legs were shaky from the run and the shock at what he had done but he stepped closer and knelt beside Barry. 'Son? Son, are you all right? Oh, God, I thought he was going to kill you!'

Barry was nodding silently. He held onto Preston when he helped him to his feet. 'I'm OK,' he said shakily. 'Just winded. I fell pretty hard.' He gazed towards where Wilhelm Kessler's leg twitched a last time before he lay still. Then he turned back to Preston and said, 'You saved my life.'

Preston stared back at him, feeling for the first time real warmth between them. But why had it meant taking a young life to achieve it? He glanced at Wilhelm's body and shivered. If he hadn't decided to follow Barry at a distance instead of waiting and watching from the top of the harbour, it could have been his son lying dead on the rocks.

The other detectives arrived then and after a cursory enquiry as to Barry's well-being, rushed to where Wilhelm's men were.

Preston stared down at the ruined haversack in his hands. He wished he could throw it into the sea where it would sink to the bottom and never remind him of what he had done. But he could not; the police would need it as evidence. He let it fall to the ground, the pistol still inside it, then stepped a few paces away. He began shaking uncontrollably as the full impact of what he had been forced to do struck him. His mind was filled again with the old memory of a teenage youth who had stared defiantly at him when he stopped a fight between him and Vaughn.

The light touch on his elbow made him jerk. 'Dad? Are you all right?'

Preston smiled quickly, wondering whether Barry's answering smile was also because he had realised that this was the first time he had called him anything but 'Father'.

'Yes,' whispered Preston, 'I'm fine. I think it's shock, that's all.'

'You go on home, I have to stick around here for a while, I'm afraid.'

'You'll come and see me later?'

'When I can.' Barry was alarmed at Preston's state. He appeared dishevelled and there was an uncertainty in his gaze that Barry had never seen before. He touched his father's shoulder lightly, said, 'Go now,' and watched Preston walk with slumped shoulders back towards the harbour.

As Preston approached the path, he noticed that the police were keeping at bay a horde of curious villagers drawn to the harbour by the sound of shots. He saw Jay standing near the front of the onlookers, a young woman of spectacular beauty at his side. Illana, he guessed, remembering the little girl he had seen all those years ago when he had visited Magda at her cottage.

Illana . . . Jay's daughter . . . Barry's woman. A sudden weariness added itself to his drained emotions and he stopped

341

walking as if he did not have the energy to take even one more step.

He stared towards where Jay stood leaning against the harbour wall, a puzzled frown on his face at seeing Preston there. Preston could not help thinking that not very many years ago he would have taken pleasure in announcing to Jay that his son was bedding Jay's daughter. But not any more, not after today. He thought, Let it end here, with the boy's life. Let the children make their peace where he and Jay had neither the will nor the courage to make theirs. It was over, ended. He started slowly forward again.

Jay moved closer as Preston reached the top. 'What's happened down there, Preston? Were you involved?'

Preston turned and looked back across the rocks to where the detectives were carrying Wilhelm's body to the harbour. Further back a second body was being hauled from behind the rocks, while a third man, holding his shoulder, walked between two detectives.

He did not answer Jay, glancing instead at Illana who stood a short distance away from them, her gaze focused on the men far below. 'Jay,' he started then, shocked to hear his voice rasp, 'Your son . . . I'm terribly sorry.'

Jay nodded his thanks. 'It's hard on Magda.'

'Yes, I can understand that. Jay? Your daughter . . . my son . . . Do you know?'

Jay's eyes did not leave Preston's face. 'She told us,' he said softly.

'I won't stop it, Jay. I won't even try to. They have their own lives to live, it would be unfair to burden them with our shortcomings.'

For the first time since they had fought over Magda so long ago, Jay smiled at him. 'Magda and I told Illana pretty much the same. We'd like to meet him.'

'That's him over there,' said Preston, pointing to the men on the rocks. 'He's been in charge of this whole affair.'

'What happened?'

Preston told him what he knew of the plan to assassinate Smuts. 'The police laid a trap, I think. God, Jay, he was about to shoot my son! I didn't even think – I just fired. I killed him.'

Jay touched his arm as if concerned that Preston might collapse before his eyes. 'Take it easy,' he said. 'Who was he? Do you know?'

'A local. You'll probably know him – Kessler, Wilhelm Kessler.' He felt the tightening of Jay's grip on his arm, the sudden intake of breath. 'What is it, Jay?' There was pity in the other man's eyes before Jay looked quickly away. 'Jay?'

'God, but I'm sorry, Preston.' His voice was a whisper. 'You couldn't have known . . . '

'Known what?' He felt a terrible foreboding blend with his battered emotions as he stepped closer, holding onto Jay for support.

'He . . . Wilhelm was your son.'

'No! No . . . there's my son— Oh God, *no*!'

'Yes. Magda's son.'

There was a growing heat inside Preston's chest, a burning sensation of such magnitude it made him want to lie down on the ground and roll into a tight ball until it had passed. The crowd surging near them seemed to spin dizzily as he tried to focus on Jay.

The sounds were clear and harsh, a babble of excited voices, the faces of strangers staring at him, Jay shouting at someone to get help. But the strongest sound was the pounding inside his chest, flowing and overflowing to touch and surge with brutal, tearing force through his whole body.

He felt himself begin to fall, felt strong arms embrace him – Jay's? The pain faded as unconsciousness overcame him.

A police car rushed Preston to Cape Town. Barry went with him, holding his father's head in his lap as the car raced towards the hospital.

In Brannigan Bay, knots of people gathered to discuss the day's events. First the killing of Wilhelm Kessler, then Preston Whitehead's heart attack. What had transpired between him

343

and Jay Brannigan to bring it on? Frequent curious glances were cast towards Jay's and Magda's house, but no one dared venture in to find out what had happened that morning.

In the kitchen, Jay sat silently, his hands dangling limply between his legs. Magda had not moved from her chair at the table. She was no longer crying and a cold absence of emotion had taken the place of her tears. Her trancelike state frightened Jay.

'Magda?'

He had expected her not to hear but she turned to him, her eyes empty and as devoid of feeling as her voice when she said, 'Somewhere, sometime, I must have sinned terribly. Two sons in one week, the one the cause of the other's death. Was it that one mistake, Jay? My son, my sin – was that it?'

He moved swiftly to her side, placing his arms on her shoulders as he knelt beside her. 'No, my love,' he whispered, 'it was no sin. I was the one who tried to make it so. You have never sinned, Magda. Never!'

'Then why?'

'Because of me,' he said thickly. 'You're paying because of me.'

'Jay, no! That's not true!'

'If I'd had the strength to overcome my bruised pride I could have allowed Wilhelm to be raised as our own. Perhaps then he would have turned out differently. He should have had my love, not my resentment. Perhaps then . . . Oh God – why am I always too late?'

Now it was her hands that comforted him, stroking his cheeks, wiping away the tears coursing freely down them. She laid her head lightly against his and kissed his hair. 'Jay, Jay, your only sin was in being human. I understood – believe me, Jay, I always understood. And it's only too late for them. There's still us . . . and Illana.'

He slowly raised his head, unashamed at his display of tears. 'Yes,' he said, 'we'll start again.'

'Call Illana, Jay. Let us tell her . . . as we should have told them all right from the start.'

The cold Benguella sea current nudged the Cape coastline, putting fingers out towards the harbour where the lone couple strolled, as though daring them to test its strength.

'My father wants me to run his abalone factory,' Barry told Illana. 'It's all he has left, poor man. I had no idea how shaky the company was.'

Illana stopped walking and turned towards him. 'Will you?'

Barry gazed out at the waves breaking over the little jetty. He was exhausted, both from the events of the past few days and the time he had spent at Preston's hospital bedside. He had arrived back in Brannigan Bay that afternoon, just in time to attend Vaughn Brannigan's funeral.

'The doctors say he won't recover fully from his heart attack,' he told her. 'I don't know. I think I want to take over from him, though. At least he has a pretty competent manager to run things meanwhile, and, anyway, I'll have to wait till the war's over.'

'Won't they recall you to England?'

'I don't think so. I hope not.'

She smiled up at him. 'So do I.'

'Despite what we both know now?'

'It was a shock at first, learning about my mother and Wilhelm. But it's all right now.'

He laid his hand gently on her cheek. 'I love you, Illana Brannigan. That much hasn't changed. Has it for you?'

She was silent for a moment, then said, 'Have you ever seen one of the old boats in full sail as it rounds the cliff in a last, anxious rush for harbour?'

He did not reply at first, perturbed by her evasive response. 'I've seen them,' he whispered then. 'I visited here as a child, remember.'

'I'm not yet ready for harbour, Barry. Not now.'

'I wasn't proposing marriage.'

Her impish smile took him by surprise. 'I was – thinking it at least!'

'Then why— '

'Warn you off? Because I love you, too, because I'm scared

that if I ever put into harbour, I'll never want to leave. Am I making this sound complicated?'

He laughed but it was a short, sad sound. 'What else do you want to catch out there?' he asked gently. 'Is this to do with Vaughn?'

'Perhaps,' she replied and shrugged, then added more passionately, 'Oh, Barry, I blamed Wilhelm for his death – I still do – though I didn't want it to end like this for him. But there are others besides Wilhelm, others who are to blame for many wrongs. Perhaps you're right, perhaps I have some noble quest to expose them all, to stop them from causing any more pain.'

'I didn't mean it to sound that way.'

'It didn't. All I know is that I don't feel ready to finish my work yet, and the OB is my work. Vaughn's death makes me more determined, I suppose.'

Barry smiled. 'When I spoke about taking over my father's canning factory, I said it would have to be after the war. We'll both be in Johannesburg till then, Illana. Do we carry on seeing each other? Shall we try again?'

'It's what I want,' she replied without hesitation. 'Who knows,' she added more lightly, touching his cheek, 'when the time comes for you to change your role to that of parochial industrialist, I might be more than ready to rush after you.'

'At full sail?'

'If the wind's right,' she replied slowly, 'I'll head straight for harbour.'